PRAISE FOR M. K. LOBB

"A dark and delicious murder mystery. M. K. Lobb has created a fantastical and evocative world, blending the genres of fantasy, romance, and murder mystery into one epic story. With lush prose, gripping characters, and an intricate lore that will keep you turning the pages, *Seven Faceless Saints* is an absolute hit."
Adalyn Grace, *New York Times*-bestselling author of *Belladonna*

"*Seven Faceless Saints* is the rich taste of ceremonial wine, stolen kisses at midnight, a gallery lined by shrouded statues, and the flames of a corrupt system as it burns to the ground. M. K. Lobb has crafted an intricate world that is both dark and alluring; the perfect backdrop for the tempestuous romance of the two protagonists."
Lyndall Clipstone, author of *Lakesedge* and *Forestfall*

"With an impressive and balanced command of gorgeous prose and compelling pace, *Seven Faceless Saints* draws its readers into a mystery as intelligent as it is intriguing. I thoroughly enjoyed the richness of Ombrazia, which perfectly complements the fresh, compelling characters Lobb has so artfully woven into this story's every page. Truly, this is an exceptional debut, sure to find many, many fans."
Ayana Gray, *New York Times*-bestselling author of the Beasts of Prey trilogy

"Bleak, bloody, and beautifully drawn, *Seven Faceless Saints* is a book with teeth."
Nicki Pau Preto, author of the Crown of Feathers trilogy

"A dazzlingly sinister tale of magic, mayhem, and murder. Lobb's debut has truly got it all... Prepare for your next obsession."
Allison Saft, *New York Times* bestselling author of *A Far Wilder Magic*

"M.K. Lobb's debut is enthralling, taut, and utterly immersive... I devoured this book in one sitting."
Emily Lloyd-Jones, author of *The Bone Houses*

"A thrilling mystery that is as full of twists and turns as it is searing romantic tension, *Seven Faceless Saints* is a heart-stopping saga about a religious elite teeming with corruption and the rebellion that works to bring them down from within."
Kelly Andrew, author of *The Whispering Dark*

"Emotionally complex characters, rhythmic writing, and a cunningly crafted mystery distinguish Lobb's series launch, which balances action and romance with meditations on faith and fate."
Publishers Weekly

"The genre-bending high fantasy murde
narrative raises some interesting que
unquestion
School Libr

Also by M. K. Lobb and available from Titan Books

Seven Faceless Saints

DISCIPLES
OF
CHAOS

M. K. LOBB

TITAN BOOKS

Disciples of Chaos
Print edition ISBN: 9781803365442
E-book edition ISBN: 9781803365459

Published by Titan Books
A division of Titan Publishing Group Ltd
144 Southwark Street, London SE1 0UP
www.titanbooks.com

First edition: February 2024
10 9 8 7 6 5 4 3 2 1

A CIP catalogue record for this title is available from
the British Library.

Printed and bound by CPI Group (UK) Ltd, Croydon CR0 4YY.

For those who have mastered the art
of sharpening edges
but are still learning how to be soft

Prologue

MILOS

Night was falling, and the wind had teeth.

Milos fastened the top button of his jacket with unsteady fingers as he gave the house behind him a final glance. The details were scarcely visible beneath the impending dusk, but he knew the place as he did his own reflection—the simple rectangular windows, a wilting garden, and the cracked plaster walls revealing the dusty stone beneath.

He didn't know whether he would be coming back. For reasons he couldn't quite verbalize, he didn't care.

He readjusted the leather bag on his shoulder, his blood alive in his veins. All at once, he couldn't move fast enough. Something had changed these past few days. He felt it like an incurable itch just beneath the surface of his skin, and he only grew more certain of it as the hours passed. His body had felt the shift before the rest of him caught on, and until now he hadn't been able to identify the sensation that plagued him.

Now he knew.

It was the need to *flee*.

Or at least, something of the sort. His heart pounded within the cage of his chest as if he was being pursued, but Milos had the odd, inexplicable sensation that he was running *toward* something. It was pulling him close, and he had little choice in the matter.

Framed that way, it rang of madness even to himself. But he could feel the truth of it as he could feel his magic coiled around his bones. It was that, perhaps, which urged him onward and stoked the excitement burning within him. He swallowed hard, lifting his chin to the darkening skyline. His lips formed a prayer.

If he continued heading in the direction he was going, such prayers were bound to get him thrown in prison. For now, though, he pictured his patron saint at the edge of the sky, listening. Watching.

The dark countryside stretched out before him like fields of oblivion. Beyond it the sea lapped against the cliffs bordering the pass separating Brechaat from Ombrazia. If he strained to listen, Milos imagined he could hear the waves. An impossibility, of course. But the world felt so very small when he couldn't see more than a few yards ahead.

Was it his saint that pulled him south? Something divine dragging him forth by magical tethers?

Milos shivered, though not from cold. Discomfort was a foreign sensation smothered by focus. He set his gaze southward and continued on.

Led by Chaos, or else toward it.

1

DAMIAN

As a child, Damian Venturi had always longed to be more story than boy.

He'd cut his teeth on tales of the saints and the disciples blessed with their magic. He'd dreamed of glory in the northern war, gripping weapons in hands that didn't shake. He'd envisioned captaining ships across star-studded waters and standing at the edge of the world, shoulders squared in holy righteousness. He'd imagined falling in love.

He'd pictured it all with Strength at his side, certain that his father's patron saint would one day bless him, too.

The thought made Damian's lips twist as he knelt beside Battista Venturi's gravestone. The glistening slab of marble was longer than his father had been tall, opulent and unnecessary. A grand bit of rock for a man who'd thought himself quite grand indeed.

No matter how many times he came here, Damian couldn't shake the haze of bitterness. His frustration was an unforgiving thing. When his father had died, Damian had known despair. He'd watched crimson spread across the stark white of the Palazzo floor and felt the dull, inescapable thrum of that despair in his bones. It was as familiar to him as the sound of his own voice. Now, though, he was shedding layers of misery like ill-fitting clothes and replacing them with years' worth of repressed anger.

He tented his fingers in the lush grass, nails scraping the dirt. The saints, if they were out there somewhere, weren't in the business of liberation. Disciples died like any flesh-and-blood creature. Death made equals of them all.

Damian should know. He'd buried a bullet in a disciple himself. And perhaps that was the reason he kept coming here: to make himself suffer. To endure some sort of penance for the fact that he'd killed yet again, and this time had been the worst. Worse even than the swift deaths he'd carried out during his time on the northern front.

Because this time it had been so fucking *easy*.

"I bet you wish you'd seen that, don't you?" Damian murmured to the gravestone, gaze sweeping the familiar epitaph: BATTISTA VENTURI—ESTEEMED GENERAL, HONORED BY STRENGTH. His father would be remembered not as a loving husband or doting father, but by his role and status. Given the man he'd become by the end, Damian supposed it was apt.

He brushed off his hands and pushed himself to stand, swallowing the acrid taste in the back of his throat. As he shifted, sunlight glanced off the flat stone. It felt like a mockery.

"I wondered if I'd find you here."

Roz Lacertosa drew up beside him, mouth set in a hard line. She was as beautiful and unruffled as always: high-necked black shirt baring only a glimpse of her slender throat, long dark hair drawn into a tight ponytail. She stared at Battista's grave, her expression of vague distaste unwavering. Damian couldn't very well blame her.

"How long have you been out here?" Roz trailed her fingers up the small of Damian's back. Her touch made him shudder, and he shrugged.

"Not long."

It was a lie, and the weight of her cutting gaze told him she knew it. Her fingers found his chin, and she turned Damian's face to hers in a grip that demanded no argument.

"He doesn't deserve this... *vigil*. Besides, Enzo killed him—not you."

Damian gently removed her hand from his face and pulled her into his chest, inhaling the scent of her skin. He pressed his lips against the side of her neck.

"Damian, please," Roz said, gripping his bicep. The words, though, were tinged with humor. "Not in front of your father."

He snorted, pulling her away from the Palazzo's sparse graveyard. His spirits were already lifting. The summer wind was warm, a trailing caress through his hair, and he could hear the crashing waves of the sea in the near distance.

"Your hands are dirty," Roz observed, holding up their intertwined fingers. The revelation didn't appear to bother her, but Damian cringed, attempting to disentangle himself.

"Sorry."

She held fast. "What were you doing?"

He gave up, not wanting to let go of her regardless. "The chthonium Enzo had left on each of the victims' bodies? I buried it beside my father. I didn't want to have to look at it anymore." Truly, he didn't know why he'd kept it as long as he had. He would never forget the way it had been shoved into the empty eye sockets of those the disciple had murdered.

"You should have thrown it in the sea," Roz said, squeezing his hand tighter. "But good—I'm glad. Some things are better buried and forgotten."

Damian didn't bother telling her he could never forget what Enzo had wrought in their city. He changed the subject. "How did your meeting with the rebels go?"

She seemed to consider the question as she walked at his side, boots tapping against the cobblestones of the wide path leading up to the Palazzo.

"As well as could be expected, I suppose." She gave a haughty toss of her ponytail. "Some of them are still hesitant to trust me. They'll be at the meeting, though."

"You mean they're hesitant to trust *me*." Damian was, of course, referring to how Roz's friends hadn't been at all pleased to discover she'd been working alongside a security officer.

She blinked against the late afternoon sun, lashes casting long, delicate shadows on her cheeks. "They trust you enough to guarantee their safety at the meeting. Besides, they know you helped solve the murders, and that we're friends."

"I'm sorry," Damian said, thrusting an arm out to stop her in her tracks. "Did you say we were *friends*?"

Roz's blue eyes darkened in feral amusement. "We've always been friends, Venturi."

"I think you know that's not what I meant."

She made a low hum in the back of her throat, glancing skyward as she feigned consideration. "So we're *not* friends?"

"Rossana…," Damian growled. They'd reached the side of the Palazzo, and Roz shoved him over to the wall until his back was flush against the cool stone. He could have resisted, of course, but he didn't.

"Do you want them to know I can't stand to be away from you?" she murmured, hands exploring the planes of his chest. There was wickedness in the curve of her smile. "Do you want them to know I'm obsessed with the sound of your laugh and the feel of your skin?"

Damian meant to answer, but Roz claimed his mouth with hers. It might have been a chaste thing, had she not been in the process of slipping her fingers beneath the hem of his shirt. A single touch of her lips, and he was consumed by fire. He never tired of kissing Roz. The press of her body against his, the familiar sweet scent of her hair, the way their mouths fit together as if they'd been created solely for that singular contact...But she pulled away too soon, taking with her the gasp she'd drawn from somewhere in his chest.

Her eyes lifted to his again, and Damian knew they were battling the same unspoken thoughts. They had been for days, and yet something kept them from voicing the subject. It was easier that way. Easier for Damian to go about his work at the Palazzo, trying to force some semblance of order following the deaths of Battista and Chief Magistrate Forte. Easier for Roz to spend time with her mother in the apartment that used to be Piera's and focus on what came next for the rebellion.

"Just say it," Damian said hoarsely, arms dropping to his side. "I can tell you keep putting it off, so just say it, Roz."

She scanned his face, her own expression hard. Not suspicious, but searching. "I thought it might upset you."

"That you can see what's wrong with me?"

"There's nothing *wrong* with you."

"Roz, please." Damian dragged a hand down the side of his face, still warm from kissing her. He remembered her words from last week: *I see you. Even the dark parts.* "When I killed Enzo, I felt *good* about it. There's something...bad inside me."

She gave an obstinate lift of her chin. "You thought he'd just murdered me. I'd be pissed if you didn't feel at least a little satisfaction."

"I'm serious."

"So am I."

Damian waited, wondering if she would say more. If she would admit she'd noticed the flashes of wild fury that sliced through him when he wasn't expecting it. He'd felt it that night, and it had been happening more frequently in the days since. After nearly three years at the front, he was accustomed to flashbacks, but this was something else altogether. There were strange, terrifying moments during which he felt too big for his skin. As if he wanted to rip free of his own body the way Enzo had stepped out of the chief magistrate's form, letting the illusion of flesh fall to bloody pieces around him. Nothing about the feeling was right. When a disciple of Chaos was stalking Ombrazia's streets, Damian had thought he was losing his mind. Now that Enzo was dead, shouldn't that fear have died with him?

But it hadn't. If anything, it was worse than ever.

"We went through a lot," Roz said, interlacing their fingers and using her thumb to stroke the back of his. Although the action was intended to comfort, the words were not. They were simply a statement of fact. Roz rarely tried to soothe—she spoke what she perceived to be the truth. "You're spending too much time worrying about how you ought to be reacting, instead of just letting yourself work through it."

Damian wanted to believe her. But he'd known all manner of horrors in his life. Things that stayed with him, the guilt and misery forming a gradually tightening noose around his neck. This was different in a way he didn't know how to describe. He could feel himself unraveling, yet couldn't muster anything more than indifference when it counted. He felt *violent*. There was no other word for it. Unhinged and incognizant of consequences during those brief interludes where he was certain he'd lost hold of his sanity. He couldn't shake the sensation that something horrible clung to him like an invisible shroud.

"You're right," Damian told Roz, because he couldn't bear to continue the conversation. Perhaps sensing his dismay, she pulled him in the direction of the Palazzo.

"Come on. I want a good seat for the meeting."

Damian wasn't sure there *was* such a thing as a good seat for an event like this, but he didn't bother saying so. He followed Roz to the Palazzo's heavy front doors. The ancient stone building seemed to gather up the sea-tainted wind, compelling it to hush.

Above them, metal-tipped spires rose to pierce the gray sky, the tallest of them hazy within the press of clouds. Once, Damian had thought the Palazzo beautiful. A shining refuge from the mud-laden front where he'd lost his friends and his innocence. Now, though, the very look of it sent cold threading along his bones. Death had followed him here, and he could not shed her. She lingered in the echo of his boots across the marble floors and peered at him from the eyes of the statues lining the main entrance. Every time Damian crossed the threshold, he could see his father's body at the bottom of the stairs and smell the acrid scent of rust and gunpowder.

But he forced himself to nod at the officers on duty—Matteo and Noemi—before allowing the cool, quiet air of the marble entryway to envelop him.

The silence didn't last long.

Damian's surname rang through the foyer, a nasal bark of impatience that dragged a sigh out of him.

"Salvestro." Damian turned to face the disciple of Death, casting his name like a whip through the space between them. "What can I do for you?"

Despite being the newest Palazzo representative, Salvestro Agosti had taken to leadership as though he'd been bred for it. Perhaps he had—it wouldn't be unusual for a powerful disciple. Blessed by Death, he could glean the final moments of the recently deceased with a mere touch, but his air of superiority seemed to suggest he could read the living just as well.

Salvestro descended the staircase, his eyes on Roz. He looked impeccable as always: suit perfectly pressed, dark hair coiffed, obsidian rings glinting on his long fingers. His mouth stretched into a wide smile, though the rest of his face was set in icy composure. He walked as though balancing a crown atop his prematurely lined brow.

Damian had not known the man long, but he knew enough to hate him.

"Now, Venturi," Salvestro said with an air of false pleasantry, "you told me no one would be allowed in the building until the meeting commenced." The words were for Damian, but his gaze never wavered from Roz's face. It was impossible to tell what he was thinking, although not hard to guess.

Damian kept his spine straight, jaw tight. "Thank you, Signor Agosti. I'm well aware of the security plan. Signora Lacertosa is my personal guest."

"Is that so?" Salvestro proffered a hand. "Salvestro Agosti the third, disciple of Death."

Roz curled her fingers around his in a grip that looked painful. "Rossana Lacertosa the first. Disciple of Patience."

Salvestro's lips twitched. "An honor." His voice was clipped when he finally bothered to look Damian in the eye. "Speaking of security, I've decided you were right. Too much of an officer presence will make the unfavored ill at ease."

Damian frowned. They'd had a brief argument about this two days prior, when Salvestro had asked about his plan for the meeting's security detail. The disciple had said it wasn't nearly sufficient, ignoring Damian's assertion that too many officers might make the unfavored feel scrutinized. "Double the numbers," Salvestro had snapped. "That's an order."

Damian had bit his tongue to keep from pointing out the obvious: Salvestro was not chief magistrate, and therefore not in charge of him. But he'd complied nonetheless, knowing that doing so would put Salvestro in a better mood come the day of the meeting.

Now Damian was perplexed.

"That's not what you said the other day." He tried to keep his tone from venturing into accusatory. "What changed your mind?"

Salvestro waved an impatient hand. "I want this meeting to go smoothly. The fewer unfavored running their mouths, the better."

Damian knew Roz would speak up before she uttered a word.

"If you're hoping for this meeting to go *smoothly*," she said, voice dripping with false sweetness, "best to keep your own mouth shut as much as possible."

The look on Salvestro's face would have been priceless if it hadn't made Damian's stomach plummet. Whatever interest the disciple might have shown Roz moments before was now replaced by disbelief and derision.

"Soft for the unfavored, are we?" Salvestro's nostrils flared. "I'd say I expected better from a fellow disciple, but then again, you're already in bed with them." His cool eyes flicked to Damian, who ground his teeth until his jaw ached.

One of Roz's brows ticked upward, a barely perceptible movement. Her smile was scornful. "If you're jealous, Signore, you can say as much. Who could blame you?"

Damian wished vehemently for the earth to shudder open and swallow him whole. He wasn't sure whether Salvestro could fire him, and he wasn't keen on finding out. If the man was a shoo-in for chief magistrate, as many seemed to think, this could end very badly indeed.

"Forgive us, mio signore," he muttered, the apology sticking in his throat. Heat flared behind his cheeks. "We'll stick to the original number of security officers, then."

His attempt to bring the conversation back around was a miserable failure. Salvestro drew himself up in a single, fluid motion, smile broadening as his gaze met Damian's. "I bet it's nice for you, isn't it, Venturi? Wearing a fancy uniform, a disciple girlfriend on your arm... I bet it's almost too easy to forget you're unfavored. That you're *nothing*."

"Who the hell are *you* to—" Roz started, but Damian cut her off with a furious shake of his head.

It was too late. She'd taken the bait. Salvestro placed a hand over his heart, rings clinking. "Did you train her to speak up for you, or does she do it out of pity?" He *tsk*ed. "It's embarrassing, I imagine, being unable to fight your own battles. But it's your job to hold your tongue, isn't that right, Venturi? And we all know how important this job is to you."

Roz had frozen, finally catching on. Still Damian said nothing. Fury clouded his periphery and gathered at his center. It was a vicious thing, unfamiliar in its ferocity. He had the sense that it was scratching at his composure, clawing at his resolve, urging him to crack. His fingers longed to clamp around Salvestro's neck, his nails eager to sink into flesh and coax forth hot blood. He yearned to feel the ineffectual pulse of the man's throat as he fought for air.

"I *said*," Salvestro repeated slowly, as if speaking to an imbecile, "it is your *job* to hold your tongue. Correct?"

"Yes." Damian forced the lone syllable through gritted teeth. It tasted like bile.

Salvestro waited.

"*Yes*, mio signore."

With an air of infuriating smugness, the disciple clapped Damian on the arm. "Such a good soldier." He cut a glance to Roz, who was stone-faced. "I do so look forward to this meeting."

Salvestro's echoing steps were quickly swallowed up by the hallway, but the smoldering wrongness at Damian's core remained a living, visceral thing.

2

Roz

"I'm going to kill him," Roz declared as she and Damian made their way to the council chambers.

"I'd rather you didn't." Damian didn't look at her when he spoke. Was he angry, or was he still thinking about what Salvestro had said? Everything that had gone wrong was her fault, yet Salvestro had made them both pay for it by humiliating Damian in front of her. Saints, Roz hated that man. His smug smile was emblazoned in her mind, and she longed to see it slide from his face. Preferably through force.

"I'm sorry," she said. "I didn't think that he would—"

"Let's not talk about it." Damian's mouth was a rigid line as he wrenched open the wooden doors to the council chambers. He used more force than necessary, and the motion stirred the air. "You can wait inside. The unfavored are to sit on the far side of the room."

Of course he knew she wouldn't want to sit with the rest of the disciples. But Roz hesitated, brows drawing together. "You're not coming?"

"I'll be back once I make sure everything is in order. I need to brief the extra officers—let them know they're no longer needed."

Roz studied Damian closely. She felt she was seeing him for the first time that week. After everything, she would have expected him to look thinner, more strung out. Instead, the opposite appeared to be happening. His chest strained beneath the fabric of his navy uniform, and he somehow looked *bigger*, all muscles and broad shoulders. His jaw was hardened steel, set so aggressively that a tendon in his neck stood out. She was reminded of how he had looked in the vision Enzo showed her. Where she'd seen the disciple of Chaos carrying out every facet of his plan, right up to his own death—*before* it happened in reality.

She traced her disciple's ring with an impatient finger. Right before the illusion had ended, she'd been looking at Damian. He'd been shrouded by the oppressive darkness of the Shrine, pistola in hand. She could only watch as Damian's eyes turned to darkest obsidian, an unrecognizable smile ghosting his lips.

"All right," Roz said, because there wasn't much else to say.

Damian inclined his head. "Your friends are already here."

Then he was gone. Roz turned to see Nasim Kadera and Dev Villeneuve looking her way. She approached them, passing the security officers stationed at the perimeter of the enormous room. A table longer than the entirety of Bartolo's tavern dominated the center, though additional seating had been set up wherever there was extra space. The deep crimson walls were lined with colorful tapestries and portraits of people Roz assumed were previous Palazzo representatives, and an intricate chandelier hung from the vaulted ceiling, cut glass glittering like gems in the light.

Behind Nasim and Dev, Alix, Josef, and Arman sat huddled together in conversation. Farther back still were Rafaella and Jianyu, then Nicolina with Zemin and Basit. Alix smiled at Roz, their friendly face full of cautious optimism. Arman merely nodded, and Josef gave a half-hearted wave. Nobody was happy to be here, Roz knew. The unfavored—rebels in particular—didn't trust the Palazzo or its disciples. But they'd come because this was what they'd been fighting for: a place at the table.

A seat had been left open for her beside Nasim, who was sitting in the first row. Roz sank into the hard-backed chair as if it might assuage the turbulence inside her.

"What's wrong with you?" Nasim demanded. Her inky hair hung loose around her face today, freed from its usual braid. Dev leaned across to better hear Roz's reply, his shoulder pressing into Nasim's.

"Nothing's wrong with me. Salvestro Agosti, though, has a number of things wrong with him—the first being that he's a complete and utter bastard." Roz crossed her arms, glaring at the door as though the disciple of Death might appear there.

"You met him?" Dev's brows shot up.

"I wish I hadn't."

His mouth twisted in a wry grin. Dev had fallen into a deep, self-destructive grief after his sister's murder, but knowing Enzo was responsible seemed to have made things better. His face was still gaunt, his eyes dulled by weeks of sadness, but at least he'd pulled himself out of his ongoing drunken stupor. "I can imagine this is going to go well then."

"He's not the chief magistrate," Nasim pointed out.

Roz pursed her lips. "He seems to think he is, though. You should have heard how he spoke to Damian. But with any luck, there won't *be* a chief magistrate going forward." If they were going to make meaningful changes to Ombrazia's political system, it was time to wipe the slate clean and start over. A handful of disciples in charge of the entire city, led by a chief magistrate believed to divine the will of the saints, had historically not been kind to the unfavored. Given that they had no magic with which to contribute to the economy, their needs were rarely considered at all. Regular blacksmiths and masons would never be as efficient as disciples of Patience and Strength, respectively. Tailors and alchemists couldn't hope to compete with disciples of Grace or Cunning, and nonmagical healers were useless when one of Mercy's disciples was available. Ombrazia had long decided what skills were to be rewarded, and the unfavored possessed none of them.

Dev wrinkled his nose. "You think the current representatives will be willing to step down?"

"No. I think they'll have to be convinced. After everything, though, they're definitely scared. They've seen what the rebellion can do, and they won't want it to happen again."

"And you're certain Damian will have his officers under control?" Nasim asked for what must have been the fifth time this week. Roz knew Nasim wasn't the only one who'd entertained the prospect that this might be a trap. Inviting rebels to the Palazzo, where law enforcement darkened every hallway? If Roz hadn't known Damian and his friends the way she did, she might have doubted it herself. With both the general and the chief magistrate dead, however, the Palazzo was weak. Its best option was to make peace with dissenters before it splintered completely.

"*Yes*," Roz said. "You can trust Damian."

Nasim said nothing, but anxiety rolled off her in waves.

"It'll be fine." Roz squeezed Nasim's wrist. "If things start going sideways, I'll speak up on behalf of the unfavored. I'm a disciple— they're not going to do anything to me." Besides, if an argument started up, she wouldn't be able to sit quietly. She needed to be involved, or there was the distinct possibility her head would explode.

"Roz." Nasim's voice was firm. "Just because you no longer live in Patience's sector doesn't mean you can side publicly with the rebellion. What if the guild kicks you out? How are you going to make money?"

"I live above a functioning tavern," Roz reminded her, but her skin crawled. *Could* Patience's guild kick her out? She'd never heard of it happening to a disciple before, unless a crime had been committed. She tried to keep her true beliefs a secret from the rest of the disciples, but it was foolish to think she could do so forever. Now was as good a time as any to give up the charade.

Dev was focused on his fingernails. "The tavern does okay, but it doesn't make *that* much money. We can speak for ourselves, too, you know. We don't want you to sacrifice everything."

Nasim nodded, and Roz ground her teeth. *We*, Dev had said, making it painfully clear Roz wasn't one of them. She had been, though. She'd been unfavored most of her life. She knew what it was to suffer under this regime—her father had died at its hands. Now that she was a disciple, was that supposed to just...go away? Was she supposed to forget, and be thankful for the blessing? To embrace her new status and simply move on?

She couldn't.

They quieted then, as a number of people began to file into the council chambers. Disciples took their seats on the other side of the room, and Roz straightened as Vittoria entered alongside a group of friends. Her ex-girlfriend and the other disciples of Patience shot her curious looks when they saw where she was sitting. Roz offered a bland smile in return, as though nothing was unusual. She'd always felt separate from them, but now the proverbial line was a true one. Her days of creating metal weapons in Patience's temple were over.

Palazzo representatives and guild leaders began arranging themselves at the table. The representatives were clad conspicuously in red coats with embroidered gold stars, but Roz's gaze snagged on Salvestro. He sat at the place of honor, as comfortable there as if he'd already been put in charge. His hands were clasped before him, rings glinting in the light of the chandelier. The neck of his shirt dipped to reveal the pale hollow of his throat. He must have felt the weight of Roz's attention; his eyes met hers for a moment before he turned away, utterly dismissive.

The representatives scoured the room in vague surprise. Despite the open invitation to the rest of the city, they obviously hadn't expected so many to attend. The space was packed, and the differences between the two sides of the chamber were blatant. The disciples were well-dressed in clothing made by Grace-blessed tailors. There was no other explanation for the way their attire fit so seamlessly, flowing like silk regardless of fabric or texture. If any of them appeared ill at ease, it was only due to the proximity of the unfavored.

The unfavored themselves appeared tense. Though most had worn their best, evidence of poverty was obvious in frayed threads and worn shoes. There was a harshness about them that the disciples didn't possess. Most were likely veterans of war. Roz couldn't blame them for being uncomfortable in the presence of those who had sent them there.

On Salvestro's right, an elderly man in a gray suit cleared his throat.

"As I'm sure many of you know," he said, "I'm Mediator D'Alonzo. As an adviser to the representatives, I often head meetings in this very room. It is my honor to do so today, despite the circumstances being rather more grim than usual. I hope that, like myself, you have all been praying for the departed souls of those recently lost."

Damian sidled into the room as the mediator spoke. He wore what Roz called his officer face: expression impassive, jaw wired tight. He tilted his head slightly, gaze pinned on Salvestro's back. Dark fury still lingered about him like an unrelenting storm.

A moment later, Kiran and Siena slipped into the council chambers. Kiran shot Roz a small grin as they passed.

"Why are they late?" Nasim murmured.

Roz shrugged. Her focus returned to Salvestro, who kept glancing at the door as if he expected someone else to appear there. Unease thrummed beneath her skin, but she couldn't pinpoint why. Anyone in Ombrazia worth worrying about was probably already in this room.

D'Alonzo was still speaking, his hands folded on the polished table. "We have a number of things on the docket to discuss. The reality is, we need to need to establish how to move forward." His voice held a gravelly tremor. "Tragically, both our general and our chief magistrate have gone to be with the saints, but we can honor their memories by reestablishing order in the city they both cared about so greatly.

"Now, my colleagues and I have spent the last few days in close consultation with the Palazzo representatives." This he directed at the group of observers. "They will each retain their current roles, though naturally a new representative of Grace will need to be chosen. Chief Magistrate Forte's death means that role has been vacant for the past week." A curly-haired woman three seats down nodded—the leader of Grace's guild, Roz supposed. "Of course, that means the role of chief magistrate must also be filled. After much deliberation we have decided that Salvestro Agosti, disciple of Death, is perfect for the role."

Murmurs went up from the small crowd. Roz felt as though someone had thrown a brick at her. She widened her eyes at Nasim and Dev, who wore matching expressions of horror.

"He has to be joking," Nasim hissed. Dev only shook his head. Roz was numb as Salvestro rose to his feet, smiling a wide, close-lipped smile.

"Thank you," he said, although no one had clapped. Only a handful of people even looked pleased. The rest, Roz suspected, were put out that their own guild's representative hadn't been chosen. Salvestro scanned the room, managing to look even more self-important, and Roz tasted acid. What was it she'd thought about Salvestro that first day at the Basilica? He looked like a man who expected power. And now, just like that, it was going to be handed to him.

"Signor Agosti will be appointed chief magistrate in one week's time," D'Alonzo said. "A ceremony will be held at the Basilica after he has completed seven days of fasting and prayer. This will allow him to establish a relationship with the saints and prepare for his new role."

Roz clenched her fists in her lap. This wasn't how it was supposed to go. This was *not* the point of the meeting.

Across the room, the mask had begun to slip from Damian's face. Roz could see the minute narrowing of his dark eyes. Anyone who didn't know him well wouldn't have suspected a thing; he didn't move a muscle, his focus never wavering from Salvestro.

"Should the new chief magistrate not be another disciple of Grace?" asked the curly-haired woman. "No offense intended, Signore. It's just that Chief Magistrate Forte hardly served for a lengthy period."

"No one said it had to be a long time," the curvy disciple across from her retorted. Mariana—leader of Death's guild. Roz had met the woman while they were investigating Enzo's murders and hadn't much cared for her.

Displeasure settled in Salvestro's brow. Before he could speak, however, Roz saw her chance. If others were going to openly voice their opinions, why shouldn't she?

"I thought the whole intention of this meeting was to establish a new way forward. Possibly one without a chief magistrate at all," she said loudly, keeping her tone polite. "Evidently people weren't satisfied with the way things were, so how can you think it's a good idea to keep them the same?" This question she posed to the table, not just D'Alonzo. In her periphery, Nasim tensed. Damian took a step forward, dismay in his face. Surely he hadn't expected her to stay quiet?

D'Alonzo looked at Roz in bewilderment, as if he'd only just noticed that the other half of the room was occupied. "And you are?"

Salvestro waved a hand, silencing the mediator. "Allow me, Signore." He leaned forward, his next words directed at Roz. "Changes *are* happening, whether we like them or not. Changes in personnel and the way this place is run. The system, however, remains the same."

"I don't recall everyone agreeing on that," Roz argued. Her anger felt like something chemical that might bubble up and overflow.

Salvestro shrugged. As if it was *nothing*, and all of this was unimportant. "Decisions were made, then changed." He considered Roz again. Was it a sort of vile pleasure she saw in his face? Or had he judged her and found her lacking? "You were blessed by Patience, correct? You'd do well to exercise some of that."

"I've *been* patient. I thought we were here to discuss a new system of governance."

"There is no need to change a system that works just fine. Deaths happen, and leaders are replaced," Salvestro explained, as though she was an idiot. The rest of the watchful room might as well have evaporated. "That is the way of politics. Issues are identified and dealt with. Rebellions rise and are crushed."

Icy cold shot through Roz's veins. If she didn't know any better, she might have thought Salvestro *knew*. The way he spoke was almost too pointed.

"Would it not be preferable to have a system people don't want to rebel against in the first place?" she shot back.

"There will always be those who are dissatisfied."

"There's a difference between dissatisfaction and being desperate enough to launch a full-fledged attack."

"And yet the rebels are not even the reason we're forced to make these changes. That was the disciple of Chaos's doing." Salvestro planted his palms flat on the table, fixing Roz with a disdainful glare. "Keep your fool mouth shut, girl, and leave the politics to those of us who understand it."

Roz's brows shot up. She could feel Nasim practically vibrating at her side and saw Damian go rigid across the room.

"I think," Dev interjected, shifting beneath the stares that suddenly snapped to him, "the issue Signora Lacertosa refers to is that of the unfavored. Currently we have little say in the way Ombrazia is governed, and I understood today's meeting was open to us so that we might provide input." A number of the rebels murmured their agreement.

"And what do any of you know about running a city-state?" a broad-shouldered Palazzo representative piped up, making the woman beside him giggle. "Why should you need a say? You have nothing to offer Ombrazia."

"Because you don't *allow* us to offer anything," Alix snapped, their usually calm voice laced with ire. "Anything we can do, a disciple can do better. Faster. That's what you think, at least. We've all but had to establish an economy of our own, and it's not sustainable."

"You seem to be doing just fine," the representative said, his words dripping condescension.

"Are you joking?" This was from Josef—he was on his feet, and the sheer size of him had several officers inching forward. "If we're not struggling to make a living, it's only because we're being shipped off to fight in *your* pointless war."

Mediator D'Alonzo slammed his hand down on the table. "Enough!"

Neither his command nor the resounding noise had much effect. Nasim was standing now, too. "How many of us have to die fighting the Brechaans? How many of us have to wonder if our loved ones are still alive?"

"You are doing your *duty*!" Mariana shouted from the other end of the council table. Her cheeks were flushed. "Given what you lack, it is the least any of you can do."

From there, everything dissolved into pandemonium. Roz couldn't have said how many people were yelling over one another; it was impossible to tell. Normally she would have lent her voice to the fray, but she couldn't help noticing Salvestro had risen and backed away to where Damian stood guard by the door, as if he might make a run for it.

He wasn't making a run for it, though. He was saying something to Damian, and whatever it was drained Damian's face of color. Damian glanced over his shoulder to where a tall woman in military garb darkened the threshold. She had more medals pinned to her chest than anyone Roz had ever seen. Her expression was no-nonsense, and everything about her stance suggested utter confidence. Her graying brown hair was drawn back in a tight bun, and her flinty gaze was unyielding. Disgust rippled across her sharp features, and she barked an order that Roz couldn't hear.

She could make out the shape of the woman's lips, though, as a slew of officers appeared behind her and flooded the council chambers.

Arrest them, the woman had said.

3

DAMIAN

Damian's mind refused to process the scene before him.

"We have guests," Salvestro had said moments prior, looking far too pleased with himself. It had taken Damian a moment to understand what he meant. Of course they had guests—the council chambers were full of them. But he'd followed Salvestro's gaze, glancing into the corridor to see a veritable army of security officers.

None of them were his.

He'd seen the woman with a general's insignia on the shoulders of her uniform. Military green, not Palazzo blue. Had heard her harsh command and pressed himself against the wall as officers forced their way into the room.

There were dozens upon dozens of them. Certainly more than Damian had under his authority. They made a beeline for the side of the room where the unfavored sat, and that was when he realized what was happening. He bellowed a warning, but nobody heard him in the commotion. *Roz* didn't hear him. These were military officers—the type who stood guard at the perimeter of the Ombrazian camps up north. The type who chased down deserters. And the woman with them was a military general.

Damian didn't know her, but she was more decorated than his father had been. Being a military general was different from being a general who worked in the Palazzo. Battista's job had been largely administrative. This woman, though, was from the front lines. She would have spent years clawing her way up, gambling with lives in the process. Damian knew without a doubt that despite technically being the same rank, his father would have bowed to her.

She watched the scene play out with cool impassivity. All around them, officers were taking the unfavored into custody. Only a few of the civilians had weapons—rebels, Damian assumed—but even so, they didn't stand a chance. The officers moved with uncanny efficiency, snapping cuffs around wrists and fending off blows with ease. One of them had Nasim restrained, and although she bared her teeth at him, she didn't fight back. Damian's heart lurched as he mentally prepared for Roz to involve herself, but she had disappeared from sight. *Hell*, where was she?

He pushed off the wall, scouring the sea of bodies for her tall figure. All around him, disciples were ushered out of the room. Those who remained looked on with confusion. A number of Damian's security officers did the same, or else tried to catch his eye for some kind of signal. Kiran and Siena were in the latter group, their expressions panicked, but Damian could only shrug at them in horrified bewilderment. Other officers had leapt into the fray and were conducting arrests alongside the military officers. Damian had one hand on his gun, the other clenched in a fist. They were going to get a fucking earful from him later.

"Damian!"

He spun, searching wildly for the source of Roz's voice. He spotted her a beat later, an officer at her back, her knife on the ground by her feet. Her expression was sheer rage, but beneath it was disbelief. She was wondering if he'd known about this,

Damian understood with a jolt. He gave a frantic shake of his head as he forced his way through the crowd. The officer who had detained Roz was trying to guide her to the edge of the room, but she was standing her ground. At least until he yanked her sideways, causing her to stumble. Damian's anger flared white-hot. He didn't know how he made it to her, only that he did, and the next second his fist was slamming into the officer's temple. The man staggered, eyes unfocused. A hand wrenched Damian back, and he whirled to find himself nose-to-nose with Kiran.

"What are you *doing*?" his friend demanded, face devoid of its usual humor.

Damian heaved a breath. He knew hitting another officer was a mistake, but he couldn't bring himself to care. "They're arresting her. They—"

Kiran's hair was coming out of its knot, and he tucked a dark lock behind his ear as he spoke. "They're arresting everyone who seems to be unfavored. I take it you didn't know about this?"

"Of course I didn't."

The room was nearly empty. Only Damian's officers, the Palazzo representatives, and a handful of military officers remained. The disciples had all been made to leave, the unfavored dragged out in handcuffs. Damian wondered where they were being taken, but had the terrible sensation he knew. He sought out Roz again, but the place where she'd been standing was occupied by somebody else. Slate-gray eyes rooted him in place.

"Signor Venturi, I take it," said the general. "I've heard much about you."

Damian gave a shallow bow, forcing himself to swallow the putrid anger still stirring in his throat. Had she seen him punch that officer? "An honor, Signora."

She didn't smile, or even react. When she spoke, it was to the rest of the room, her voice devoid of emotion.

"I am General Caterina Falco. You will address me as 'General.' I've held my current rank for the past five years. Prior to that, I spent nine years as head commander at the front, though my first promotion was in the training bureau. I've spent nearly my entire life at war, and the only reason I'm stepping away now is to help get this place back on track. I'm sorry to hear about Battista Venturi's death—he was a great man. As long as I'm in this building, treat me the same way you did him, and we'll get along just fine."

There was a pause, but then everyone nodded. A few of Damian's officers shot him accusatory glances, likely suspecting he'd withheld news of Falco's arrival. At his place by the door, Salvestro was practically radiating delight, as if he could fathom nothing better than being around this brusque, unpleasant woman. With some effort, Damian managed to nod. That brief moment of uncontrollable violence had faded, and as logic returned, he formulated a plan. He would play nice with Falco. He would figure out where they had taken Roz, and he would get her pardoned. After all, they had no proof of any crimes committed.

"Now," Falco said, "a considerable number of you already know me from your time spent up north. I did bring some reinforcements of my own"—she gestured at the green-clad officers—"in order to help boost your numbers." Finally her gray eyes found Damian's again, but he couldn't identify the expression in them. Did she expect him to assist with this? Why hadn't anyone sent word ahead of time?

"With your cooperation," she went on, "I have no doubt we will be able to restore order to Ombrazia." She laced her fingers together, disciple's ring winking in the light. She had to be Strength, like Battista. If not that, perhaps Cunning. "I'd like to thank Signor Agosti for sending word about your circumstances. My letter replying to his request for help only arrived earlier today, but as you can see, we are happy to assist. We may be rather spread out at the moment, but our goals are shared ones nonetheless."

Cold unfurled in Damian's stomach. *Salvestro* had summoned General Falco to the Palazzo? He'd written to the front without telling anyone? No doubt that was the reason he had recanted his order to increase security at the meeting. With Falco coming, additional officers would only get in the way.

"Why weren't we told of this?" demanded Eoin, the muscular representative of Strength who had spoken up during the meeting. He was a square-jawed, auburn-haired man in his early twenties, possessing the unfortunate habit of saying exactly what was on his mind at all times.

"I planned to tell you once I knew the general was sending aid," Salvestro said, ignoring Eoin's glare. "I know her personally, you see, and sent news of recent events. How we appear to have lost the confidence of the populace. Or," he added, a sneer curling his lips, "some of them, at least. After last week, much of Ombrazia's power is concentrated in the north, not at the Palazzo. I think you'll agree that needs to change. Besides, General Falco will be able to take over Battista Venturi's duties in his absence." He said it as if Damian's father were on extended vacation somewhere, rather than dead in the ground.

Lekan, Mercy's representative, shifted closer to Eoin. "This still feels like something we ought to have been consulted on."

"I had an idea I thought would help this city. I used my connections to execute it. Surely we both want the same thing? Surely your top priority is the safety and order of Ombrazia?" Salvestro surveyed Lekan with a gaze to cut glass. It wasn't a question, but a challenge.

"Of course" was Lekan's smooth reply.

Salvestro really *had* established himself as the authority here, Damian realized. Even the other Palazzo representatives weren't willing to put up much of a fight. On Lekan's other side, the disciples of Cunning and Patience stood in unreadable silence. From what Damian could tell, none of the representatives knew quite what to make of the past week's events. These people were supposed to be leading the city, yet they hadn't a clue what to do without someone to guide them. In the absence of Chief Magistrate Forte, they seemed content to fall in line behind Salvestro.

"Enough," Falco said softly, and Damian got the immediate sense that she didn't need to raise her voice to incite fear. "Salvestro was right to get in touch. I knew his father well as a youth—we were both disciples of Death, you see." She assessed each representative in turn, her gaze passing over Damian entirely. "Now, you needn't worry about the arrests we conducted here tonight. My officers will take care of everything. The unfavored will be thoroughly questioned at the prison so that we might glean the names of the rebels responsible for last week's attack."

"And if they're innocent?" Siena dared to ask from where she stood with the other Palazzo security officers. "Will you let them go?"

Falco gave a curt shake of her head. "You bring me to the second reason I didn't arrive here alone. Now more than ever, it's imperative that we bolster our numbers in the north. You see, Brechaat's general recently died from illness. In Brechaat, positions are passed on by name as opposed to merit, so this means his son now commands the southern front. The boy is young and inexperienced, and we continue to control the main port of trade on the northern river. No matter what the heretics try to take from us, we will not allow them to be successful. If we can double the draft, or perhaps even triple it, we may be able to win this once and for all."

A few of the representatives nodded, pleased, but Damian felt sick. How many more unfavored were they going to sacrifice for this supposed victory? Had anyone thought of that? Did they care? People like Salvestro and Eoin had no real stake in this fight.

Their families weren't fighting and dying on the northern front. To them, the Second War of Saints was nothing but a faraway battle told through tales and news reports.

"So everyone you arrested here tonight will be sent to war?" Damian heard himself ask before he could think better of it. "Whether they're guilty of rebel activity or not?"

"Correct," Falco said, her uncompromising glare boring into him. "That is their duty to this city."

He thought of Roz and knew she would allow herself to be shipped north with her friends. If the rebels were going to suffer, she would suffer with them.

At the realization, Damian felt as if he'd been injected with something debilitating. His pulse skyrocketed, his vision blurring. When it passed, he was left with nothing but rage and that now-familiar sense of wrongness. It made sweat bead along his spine. "One of the people you arrested today wasn't unfavored. She's a disciple—she just happened to be sitting with them."

As a disciple, Roz had the choice to fight or not. Damian only needed to convince her it wasn't worth it.

Falco's thin lips turned up. "I'm aware of that."

"You—*what?*"

"I know who she is. What she's done."

The world froze, then bottomed out from under Damian's feet. Nobody knew Roz was the leader of the rebellion. Nobody except him and the rebels themselves. Kiran and Siena knew she was affiliated with it because Damian hadn't been able to keep the secret from them, but they'd begrudgingly understood and promised to keep quiet. There was no way for Falco to know about Roz when she'd only just arrived here, unless Salvestro had discovered something and told her in his letter.

"I know that girl came for you on the boat, Venturi. I'll admit, I had intended to do this in private, but your game is ended. A deserter, pretending to be an honorable leader?" Falco shook her head gravely. The weight of her stare was damning, and Damian's mouth went dry, his brain disconnecting from his body.

What the hell was going on? Nobody who would recognize Damian had seen him leave that northern-bound ship. But if one thing was certain, it was that she *knew*. Somehow, Falco knew he'd fled the ship to avoid returning to war. She'd thought him a coward, a traitor, before she'd so much as laid eyes on him.

His cheeks burned as blood rushed to his face. Though he felt the weight of stares, he saw nothing save the general's impassive expression. When she refused to break the silence— to spare him the misery of enduring it—Damian knew he had to speak.

"I don't know what you're talking about." It sounded like he was choking on the words. His eyes found Kiran and Siena. Neither appeared to be breathing.

The general followed his gaze. "Oh, yes, I know those two were involved as well. Did you all think you would get away with it? That you could simply return here and take up your old positions?"

Damian didn't bother trying to deny it a second time. There was no point. All around him the silence was full of shocked apprehension. A few of his officers shot him sidelong looks but said nothing. Salvestro, on the other hand, looked like a starving man who had just been offered a feast.

At the same time, a slow trickle of relief flowed through Damian. This had nothing to do with the rebellion. They didn't know about Roz or her role in what happened last week.

"Hand me your badge and weapons." Falco's tone left no room for argument.

Despite his horror and embarrassment, Damian nearly laughed. He pulled the badge from his chest and tossed it in one smooth motion. It clattered against the council table, suddenly appearing small and insignificant, and spun to a stop in front of Falco, who pocketed it.

"Weapons, Venturi."

With uncharacteristic clumsiness, Damian pulled the pistola from his belt and the archibugio from across his back. He ripped the blade from his pocket, and another from his boot. Those, too, he set on the table, arranged in a line from largest to smallest. Falco motioned for an officer—one of hers, not Damian's—to take them away.

"Is that it?" she asked, and he nodded. The silence in the council chambers was suffocating.

"Good," Falco said. "Calvano. Pesci. Deal with the other two— they can go to prison with the rest."

Two men stepped forward, and Damian followed suit. "*No.* They didn't do anything, I swear it. I told them to come after me, and they complied because I was their commanding officer."

Siena was already shaking her head at him. *Don't bother,* she seemed to be saying, but how could he not? How could he let their lives, their careers, be destroyed on his behalf?

His insides felt submerged in acid. Uncharacteristic violence flared through him like a lit flame. His hands burned with the desire to take Falco's neck in his grasp and squeeze until her cheeks reddened, eyes *bursting*—

He gave his head a shake and exhaled an uneven breath. Every part of his body was tense, ready to lunge despite his better judgment. Other than his own two feet, there was nothing tethering him to the earth. He was somewhere else entirely, watching Falco through a film of crimson-tinged unreality. Damian clenched his jaw hard enough that a twinge traveled down the side of his neck, and let Falco's men lead him out of the council chambers. The general followed close behind, and Damian couldn't help addressing her as the door slammed.

"Is this necessary?"

"Necessary?" she repeated, steel gaze trapping his as the men secured his wrists. The metal was icy cold, the cuffs painfully tight. Patience-made, so there was no use struggling. "Yes, Venturi, I believe it is."

"I'm not sure you have the grounds you think you do."

"Oh, but I *am* sure." Falco wasn't even looking at him anymore. Her focus was on the end of the hallway, where three more of her officers were rounding the corner. "And I think, very shortly, you'll see why that is."

As the trio drew closer, Damian understood. His stomach bottomed out as if he'd been dropped from a very great height.

Because one of those men was someone he recognized. He was tall and russet-haired, slighter than Damian, and unsmiling. He'd shaved the moustache he'd once worn, and it made him look younger. More innocent. Rather than the typical officer's badge, his uniform bore a golden crest right above the heart—a crest in the shape of an anchor.

Russo.

Last Damian had seen Michele's elder brother, Roz had fired a bullet just above the man's head.

They shouldn't have left him alive. Damian had known it even then, despite urging Roz to spare him. Russo was the only one who'd seen him escape the ship. In his eyes, Damian had already gotten off easy once. He'd been sent back to the Palazzo while Michele had been gunned down in the north.

The worst part was that Damian couldn't argue. He *had* gotten off easy. He should have died alongside his best friend. But he hadn't, and Russo would never forgive him for it.

He could get in line. Damian would never forgive himself, either.

"Venturi!" Russo crowed, coming to a halt. The officers flanking him stayed a few steps behind, stone-faced and unfamiliar. Russo looked healthier than when Damian had seen him last: cleaner, broader, cheeks less hollow. But it was clear his hatred for Damian hadn't faded with his hunger as he said, "I knew you'd get caught eventually. How stupid can you be, coming back here to take your old job?" A laugh scraped out of him. "You couldn't bear not being in a position of authority?"

Damian could almost feel the tilt of a ship under him, could almost taste salt on the air. The first time he'd been at Russo's mercy, he'd come away with a split lip and a bruised body. The memory had him bracing. "That's not why I came back. After everything that happened, the other officers wanted me here. And I saw no reason to let them down."

Rather than hit him, Russo spat on Damian's boots. "Ah. So it was your *honor* that got you into trouble, was it? Strange—you didn't seem to possess a shred of it when you leapt off my ship, running like a coward with your tail between your legs."

"That's enough, Capitano," Falco said smoothly, though Damian knew she'd given Russo the chance to face him on purpose. She wanted him to know why he'd been caught and to look the man who'd made it possible in the eye. "I didn't make you captain of the fleet so you could goad deserters when we tracked them down."

Russo saw the bewilderment on Damian's face and arched a brow. "That's right, Venturi. I'm in charge of the military fleet now. What's it like to see a man succeed without getting anything handed to him?"

"I'm glad for you," Damian rasped, surprised to find he meant it. If things had been different, if Michele had lived, he and Russo might have been friends. They might have crossed paths on the front lines and built the kind of solidarity only people facing the same danger could. "Your brother would be proud of you."

Now Russo *did* strike him. He wasn't a large man, but without the opportunity to block, Damian took the entire force of the blow. His head snapped hard to the right. Pain bloomed at his cheekbone, radiating outward.

Falco wrenched him back by the handcuffs, *tsk*ing as if he'd been the one to resort to violence. "Alexi, please. Take him to the prison as well, will you? I need to continue this meeting."

For a moment Damian couldn't figure out who she was talking to. It took him a moment to realize Alexi must be Russo's first name. "Why not put me in the cells here?" he asked, unable to hide his confusion.

Falco scoffed. "I know you still have allies here, Venturi. Besides, you're far too familiar with the Palazzo. Better to be overcautious, I always say." Her gaze slid back to Russo. "Keep the violence to a minimum, would you? I need him coherent."

Russo muttered something under his breath, but inclined his head in acknowledgment. Falco slipped back into the council chambers. When she was gone, Damian felt oddly more apprehensive. It wasn't that anything about Falco seemed particularly safe, but she at least appeared to play by the rules. When it came to Russo and his ilk, Damian wasn't so sure.

"You know what, Venturi?" Russo said, clapping him on the back hard enough that Damian coughed. "I owe you for this. I was starting to worry people didn't get what they deserved."

Damian kept silent as the officers led him down the hallway and out of the Palazzo. What was there to say? He had no defense. No reason to fight. After all, he *had* deserted, hadn't he? He'd known it was wrong at the time, and he'd done it anyway. He moved as if in a dream, his stomach hollow, as if his insides had been scooped out. When they reached the prison, he let himself be transferred to the custody of the guards and ushered into a cell on the second floor.

"Alexi," Damian said as Russo turned to leave. Their gazes locked.

"Venturi." Russo said his name as if the syllables left a bitter taste in his mouth, but his expression didn't change. He looked tired. He looked like Michele. "Don't you dare call me that."

"Do you know why I loved Michele?"

Russo reared back, anger glinting in his eyes. "Don't speak my brother's name."

Damian continued anyway. "He was a disciple, but he dreamed of better things. That was why he fought, and what he fought for. He made that dream seem so real, I would have followed him into hell to achieve it. Some days I still wish I could." He lowered his voice. "I know you hate me for continuing to live when he died, but that's nothing compared to the hatred I feel for myself. Michele should have lived. He was better than both of us."

Russo said nothing—only pressed his lips together.

"You've become everything he would have hated, you know. You've decided ruining my life will be your revenge. And honestly, I don't blame you. I know it's easier that way. I know it's easier to direct all your fury at me than at something far more powerful than both of us."

"You have *no idea*." Russo forced the words out past gritted teeth. "You don't know what I endured to get to where I am."

Damian stared at him. "But I do understand. I know you grew up unfavored, which surely meant Michele was the golden child. I can only imagine how it felt to love and hate him in equal measure."

"Shut your mouth, Venturi. Or I swear on the saints I'll kill you, Falco's orders be damned."

"Then do it." Damian pressed his chest to the bars of the cell. He didn't know *what* he was doing, exactly, but he didn't care. An almost manic energy flowed through him. "You have a gun. Shoot me right here and now."

Russo paled in the shadows. "What?"

"You heard me. I'm a deserter. A criminal. A traitor. Show me you believe my death is what Michele would have wanted. Show me you truly believe it will make you feel better."

Hesitation was written in the lines of Russo's body, in the premature wrinkles around his mouth. Even clean-shaven, he looked older than Damian knew he was. He held his gun gingerly, as if he thought it might somehow backfire. "What kind of game are you playing, Venturi?"

"It's no game. You've wanted to kill me all this time, haven't you? So do it. Pull the trigger."

The pistola wavered as Russo's hand shook. Whether from rage or something else entirely, it was impossible to tell.

"Kill the boy who would have died for your brother in a heartbeat," Damian whispered. His heart slammed against his ribs, a warning and an encouragement.

Russo's nostrils flared, his chest heaving. For a moment Damian wondered if he'd made a grave mistake. If Michele's brother really would shoot him and prove once and for all that his hatred was more than just a cover for grief.

Then Russo holstered his gun and was gone.

4

DAMIAN

Damian could scarcely remember ever feeling so hopeless, and that was saying something.

He lay half-slumped over on the cot in his cell. His mind was still somewhere in the Palazzo council chambers. His body felt heavy. For a breath of a moment, he'd truly thought things might change in Ombrazia. And now here he was, just another unfavored boy in a city of shadows. A traitor and a deserter. Only yesterday he'd had dozens of security officers at his back, and now he was alone. Powerless. Terrified.

Because there was no way this ended well. He knew what happened to people who deserted. He'd seen it happen to Jacopo Lacertosa. Draft dodgers were imprisoned, but deserters were killed. What would happen to Roz? To Siena and Kiran? The punishment for helping someone else desert was nearly as bad.

Saints, Damian had failed all three of them.

"Hello?"

A rasping voice sounded from the other side of the wall, making him go tense. From what he'd seen as he was led past the other cells, there were no other prisoners in this wing. The other unfavored must have been locked up elsewhere. "Who's there?"

There was a pause before the other person responded, as if they were second-guessing their decision to speak to him. Then: "I saw them bring you in. You're a security officer from the Palazzo, aren't you, boy?"

Damian stood, pressing his hands against the stone wall. It was an older person, he thought. Much older than he was, at least.

"I was." He neglected to say he'd been the head of security. "Who are you?"

The person coughed before answering. It was a woman; he was sure of that now.

"I'm nobody important," she said, amusement lacing the words. How she was able to find humor in this place at all, Damian didn't know. "They'll arrest anyone for heresy, though. Even an old unfavored woman."

"You're unfavored?"

She hummed a confirmation.

"What did you do to get thrown in here?"

A gravelly laugh. "You tell me first, figlio."

Damian rested his forehead against the cold wall, shuttering his eyes. There were no windows in this section of the prison. The dark was enough to drive people mad if they were in here long enough. "I'm a deserter."

What use was there in lying about it? The whole city would know soon enough. He might as well tell an old woman he couldn't see.

To his surprise, though, she heaved a sigh. "I don't blame you, figlio. The front is no place for anyone, let alone a young boy."

"I'm not a young boy," Damian protested.

"Are you yet twenty?" When he was silent, she said, "Then you're a child. And no child should be sent to war."

He wanted to argue that anything childlike about him had died alongside Michele, but he suspected it wouldn't do any good. "I told you why I'm here. Now it's your turn."

"I told you. Heresy."

"You were caught worshipping Chaos?"

"No. Worse."

"What's worse than that?" Damian couldn't help saying, thinking of Enzo. His jar of eyeballs, and the murders he'd committed in the name of raising his patron saint.

"Everyone knows what happened last week. How a disciple of Chaos terrorized this city with his sacrifices, and how it culminated in his death."

Damian frowned in the dark. "What about it?"

The woman was quiet another moment. "I was born in Brechaat, you know. When I was a wee girl, we had stories about things like that."

"Things like what?"

"*Seven saints, seven sacrifices*," she recited. "There's an old tale that claims sacrifices are required to raise a saint. Some believe that's how the reincarnations of Strength and Chaos came about prior to the first war. But my mother was a scholar, you see, and she determined the old texts had been mistranslated. *Seven for Chaos, seven for Patience, seven for Grace*...you get the idea. It was never about raising the saints themselves, though. A saint *is* their magic, and thus any sacrifices only strengthen the magic associated with a particular saint. Seven kills in Chaos's name, and all his disciples would grow more powerful."

Damian shook his head, trying to parse out his thoughts. "It doesn't matter. Enzo—I mean, the disciple—wasn't successful. He only killed six people, so there were only six sacrifices in the end."

"That's where you're wrong, figlio."

"I'm not," Damian said hotly. "I was there. He tried to make me his final sacrifice. And I didn't die."

"I wasn't saying you're wrong about the disciple only having killed six people. I'm saying you're wrong about there having been only six sacrifices."

Damian couldn't figure out what she was trying to get at. It simply didn't make sense. How could there be more sacrifices than there were deaths? The woman stayed silent, letting him unravel things on his own, but Damian didn't know what she was waiting for him to understand.

Finally she clucked her tongue. "A seventh person died in the Shrine that night, did they not?"

No, Damian thought. He had lived, and so had Roz. Her death had been nothing but an illusion. Enzo had wanted to—

Then his thoughts came to an abrupt halt.

Enzo.

Enzo had died in the Shrine that night.

"Saints," Damian breathed. It was so painfully obvious, yet he'd never stopped to consider it. "*Saints*, Enzo was the seventh sacrifice, wasn't he?"

The woman hummed that same somber sound of acknowledgment.

Now that the first realization had washed over him, they kept coming. "He would have had chthonium on him, which lets Chaos know a sacrifice is for him. Seven people were sacrificed to the same saint." Damian dragged a hand down the side of his face. Was that what he had felt, the moment he'd killed Enzo in the Shrine? Had that rush of *something* been his first time experiencing close proximity to old, powerful magic? And if it had, did it mean every living disciple of Chaos had grown stronger as a result?

Then a more terrifying thought: Was that why Damian had felt so strange lately? Was he subject to another disciple's influence? Or had Enzo's hold never really left him?

Too many questions whirled through his head, stinging him like infuriated bees. He knew it was foolish to jump to conclusions when he hadn't any proof, but the woman's assertions aligned so *well* with what he was experiencing. With his own incessant fears.

"Are you saying Chaos's disciples are stronger now?" Damian said, heart hammering in his ears. "And when you tried to tell someone, they arrested you for it?"

"Like I told you," the woman croaked. "Heresy."

"But what if you're right?"

Her laugh was like nails on stone. "What does that matter? They don't want to hear it."

Damian blew out a breath between clenched teeth. Only a few weeks ago he might have thought the woman mad. Spouting Brechaat's tales of magic was a surefire way to get locked up. Now, though, he wasn't so quick to dismiss her.

"Have you ever crossed paths with a disciple of Chaos?" he asked, his voice barely a whisper.

She was quiet for a long moment. Damian had begun to think she wasn't going to respond at all when she finally said: "My father was one. I didn't inherit the magic. Wasn't blessed."

"Why did you come to Ombrazia, then? Surely your father was safer in Brechaat."

"He didn't come with me, figlio. I left to get away from him and to make a better life for myself. Do you not know how my homeland struggles?"

Right. Disciples were far less common in Brechaat, and their economy suffered for it. "Before you left, did your father ever... influence you?"

"Rarely. His power wasn't strong. It's a myth that all disciples of Chaos are able to control people the way that boy in the Palazzo did. Most can only show you brief flickers of things that aren't true. The stories make them seem far more frightening than they are."

Damian paused to digest that. It had never occurred to him that Chaos's disciples varied in terms of their power. He didn't know why. It made sense, given the variation in how other disciples inherited magic. Battista had been able to shape stone with a touch, but his father before him had struggled to do more than dent it.

"And being controlled?" Damian said, though he already knew. "What does it feel like?"

There was the echoing noise of the woman shuffling on the bed, and when she spoke again, her voice sounded much closer. Damian tilted his ear to the stone.

"It feels like insanity," she said softly. "Like losing your mind but being cognizant of it all the while. It feels like losing yourself, forgetting who you are, until you're released and it all comes rushing back. It's like reality, but *wrong* somehow. The longer you're exposed to their magic, the worse it becomes."

He didn't ask how she'd learned that at the hands of her father. He didn't think he wanted to know. "What happens to those who *are* exposed to a disciple of Chaos's magic? Do they just return to normal afterward?"

"Of course," the woman said, then corrected herself. "In most cases, anyway. There are legends, you know, that say the magic can linger, eventually driving one to madness. They say some people simply aren't able to purge themselves of it."

Before Damian could digest that, a door slammed somewhere, making him jump. There was another shuffling sound as the woman moved, followed by her slow, even breaths. Was she pretending to be asleep? Should he do the same?

He didn't get the chance to decide. A light flickered into existence, growing brighter as footsteps reverberated through the hall. They stopped outside Damian's cell, and he squinted into the impassive face of General Falco.

"Venturi," she said. "Get up."

"Where are my friends? They shouldn't be punished for what I did. I forced them to—"

"I said get *up*."

She had already decided not to believe his version of events, clearly. As Damian's eyes adjusted, he saw Falco had two of her officers standing by. It made him wonder if his officers had refused to follow her or if she merely didn't trust them.

Then he remembered it didn't matter. They thought him a traitor now.

He stood, allowing himself to be reshackled and ushered out. As they passed the adjacent cell, he chanced a peek into the shadows but couldn't see the old woman. There was only the outline of what appeared to be a pile of blankets on her cot.

Falco strode a few steps ahead, quickly and with purpose. Damian swallowed, his throat constricting. He hadn't a clue where she was leading him, but he wasn't about to give her the satisfaction of asking. The men flanking him were equally silent, staring straight ahead. He wondered what they were thinking. Damian had been like that once. A good soldier, content to do what he was told without asking questions. Never wondering whether the people he escorted were in the right or wrong.

They went down a flight of stairs, then another, then a third. Although the rooms were no more claustrophobic than his cell, Damian could sense they were deep underground. That, more than anything, made him uneasy. He knew what people did down here, where the stone walls were thick enough to muffle sound. A chill that had nothing to do with cold climbed the back of his neck.

"In here," Falco instructed his escorts, and the men led Damian into what he recognized as an interrogation room. He'd been in one many times before, though not on the side where the officers pushed him to sit, locking his cuffed hands to the table. Falco sat down opposite him. Even after the men exited the room, she continued to stare at Damian as if she expected him to speak first.

"Just ask what you came here to ask me," he snapped eventually, unable to bear the silence.

Falco's smile was grim, nowhere near reaching her eyes. "Let's start with the question you avoided earlier. Did you really think you would be able to desert without any consequences?"

"No." It was the truth. Damian *hadn't* thought he would get away with it. It was why he'd nearly changed his mind. But Roz had convinced him, just as he'd always known she would. Roz could have convinced him to do anything.

"So you knew you would be caught, yet decided to do it nonetheless?"

"No," he said again, frustration pulsing through him. "Yes. I mean, I knew it was a possibility. My father was the general, after all."

"Right." Falco's mouth tilted. "I can't imagine the guilt you must feel, dishonoring him like that. He must rest uneasy in his grave."

"I don't care." Damian hadn't meant to say it, but now that the words had escaped, there was no taking them back. "My father acted as though everything I did was intended to dishonor him. If your intention is to make me feel bad, it's not going to work."

Falco's eyes flashed, and she tented her fingers on the table between them. Damian could see the tendons straining in the back of her hands. "Fine. Then tell me, what do you know about the night your father died?"

He chose his words carefully. "I know Enzo, the disciple of Chaos, tried to kill me. I know I killed him instead."

"I'm not interested in that portion of the evening. I'm interested in what happened prior to that, when the Mercato burned. When this very prison was broken into."

"I don't know anything about that." Damian had never been much of a liar, but this one sprang easily to his tongue. This *wasn't* just about him deserting, then. He was being questioned about the rebellion. Did she suspect something?

Falco's brows pulled together, the sole outward sign of her displeasure. "You know what, Venturi? I don't think you're being honest with me. I think you know quite a bit more about that night than you're letting on. I came to Ombrazia to see this city return to order, and that won't happen until I find those responsible for its unrest. Do we understand each other?"

"Yes. But unfortunately, I can't help you."

Falco stood and circled the table. Damian felt the hairs on the back of his neck rise with her proximity. As she approached his other side, hands clasped behind her back, she sighed. "You know, both Salvestro and Alexi warned me this might be difficult. But I, in my naivete, hoped you might still possess some loyalty to your government. It pains me to see I was wrong."

The general didn't sound as though it pained her, Damian thought. She was practically vibrating with anticipation to do whatever it was she planned to do to him. He shifted on the frigid chair. "You can torture me all you like, but I have nothing to tell you." That, at least, wasn't entirely a lie. He *didn't* have anything to tell her. Because no matter what Falco did, he would never betray Roz and her friends like that.

"Torture you? Please, Venturi. You were the Palazzo's man, at least for a time. That ought to count for something, no?"

He had no reply. Falco studied him for an excruciatingly long moment. Finally, when his mouth had reached bone-dry, she spoke again.

"That disciple of Patience wasn't sitting with the unfavored in a onetime show of solidarity, was she?"

Damian shrugged, though his body strained against the restraints. It was all he could do not to leap out of his seat.

"She either supports them, or she's one of them. And I intend to find out which."

Damian's voice ripped out of him in a snarl. "Don't you *dare* touch Roz."

Falco sat back down, watching his aggravation with interest. "Tell me what you know about the rebels. Give me names."

"I can't," he rasped, fully aware of how true that assertion was. If he gave anything up, he hurt Roz. If he didn't, he *still* hurt Roz. How the fuck could he win this?

The answer was painfully clear: He couldn't, and Falco knew it.

Damian couldn't meet her gaze. She tapped a finger on the edge of the table. Her voice was lower now, dangerous and sinister. "It's best not to care for anyone, you know. It makes them all too easy to use against you. The girl is here, and she will suffer if you don't give me what I want. You'll be able to hear it. That way, you'll learn soon enough that I always keep my word."

"You're sick," Damian spat.

She shrugged. "I'll do whatever it takes for Ombrazia."

He took a shuddering breath. This woman truly believed everything she'd done was for the good of her country, no matter how deranged. He didn't doubt for a moment that Falco really did have Roz here, with someone poised nearby to hurt her.

His pulse ricocheted higher, heart settling in the back of his throat. He felt disconnected from his body. Falco watched him with the stoic confidence of one who held all the cards and was certain of victory. Damian didn't think he'd ever hated anyone as much as he hated the general in that moment. He longed to see her frightened. To see that impassive mask crack and reveal something human.

As he had the thought, gunfire hurtled through the air around them.

The noise jolted something within Damian, and he automatically ducked, heat searing through his veins. Falco did the same, shielding her face and uttering a string of curses. When nothing happened, Damian lifted his head, glancing around wildly. The darkness in the room had grown thicker, colder, like a dense mist. He stretched out an arm and watched, perplexed, as tendrils snaked around his wrist, dissipating when he moved. Gooseflesh rose along his skin. It behaved like smoke, but the ease with which he could breathe meant it had to be something else. Perhaps he ought to have been disturbed, but he wasn't.

"What the *hell* was that?" Falco growled, her voice tinged with panic as she bent down and unshackled him from the table. "*Get up. But don't think for a moment that I've finished with you, Venturi.*"

She escorted him bodily from the room, barking the names of officers who didn't appear to be nearby. As Damian stumbled forward, struggling to see through the dark haze, he was seized by the unholy desire to *fight*. Only a moment ago, the logical part of him had known fighting would only make things worse, but that part had fled. He couldn't get it back. He felt filled to the brim with something wicked and wholly violent. His vision swam, the muscles of his stomach tightening. Rage pulsed in him like a living thing. Before he could think about what he was doing, he yanked his cuffed hands from Falco's tight grip, lunging forward to encircle them around her neck.

Falco bellowed something Damian didn't hear. The darkness seemed to grow even thicker, coagulating in his lungs as she thrashed against him. He refused to let go. He pulled harder on the cuffs, jamming the metal against her throat. Her hands were on his arm, nails digging into his skin, but he didn't feel the pain. All he wanted to feel just now was the life draining from this woman's body.

But then, from the far end of the hallway, someone cried out. Someone whose voice Damian knew like his own heartbeat. He jerked his hands back, freeing Falco's head and tossing her aside.

Roz. She was here, and not far away.

Damian snatched the general's pistola from her prone form and ran like hell.

5

ROZ

If Roz died here, she was going to be pissed.

Whatever the reason for the gunshots that had echoed through the city prison, she was sure it couldn't be good. The noise had reverberated off the stone walls with a ferocity that made her ears ring, spurring the officer outside her cell to leap to his feet. He'd stared down the corridor, hand on his holster, as if he couldn't decide whether it was worth investigating. Roz had silently willed him to go, but after pacing the area for a moment, he'd sat back down.

Until the darkness came, that was.

It swept through the space faster than Roz could fathom, thickening the air and drowning out all traces of light. She'd suspected it must be connected to whatever commotion had resulted in the gunfire and ran to the door of her cell, heart hammering against her ribs. If the officer fled and *left her here*—

"Hey!" she yelled, unable to see him, banging her fist against the stone. It did nothing but cause her hand to ache; if the officer was still close enough to hear, he ignored her. Roz let out a final infuriated growl. The prison had been built to contain each type of disciple, and since metal bars obviously wouldn't have kept her in, she'd been placed in a cinder block cell with a small opening to look through. The unfavored, as far as she could tell, must have been lodged on the main floor. She'd been able to hear them as she was led past the stairwell. Down here in the basement, she was by all appearances alone.

The next moment, however, the darkness began to lift slightly. Roz could make out a sliver of the officer's face in the dim, contorted in dismay as he watched whoever, or *whatever*, was coming toward him. Was someone coming to break her out, just as the rebels had done last week? Or were she and the officer both about to die?

Saints, she wished she still had her knife. She tensed as the officer pulled his pistola, then winced as he fired a shot. If she lived past today, her ears were never going to recover. She strained her neck, trying to see farther down the corridor. The bullet evidently hadn't found its target. Or if it had, it wasn't enough to stop whatever had the man suddenly stumbling back.

"How the hell—?" he spat, but never completed the question. A large figure hurled itself toward the officer, slamming him into the hard concrete floor. The sound of his body making contact was one Roz was fairly certain no human body should make.

The darkness blanketing the hall dissipated further, and Roz started. *"Damian?"*

He straightened, chest heaving. The front of his hair was damp with sweat, his eyes wild. He looked like a man who'd torn his way out of hell.

"Roz." Her name was a relief-laced exhale. Damian turned the unconscious guard over, and Roz saw that his hands were cuffed together. Why in the world had *he* been arrested?

"The cell key is in the front pocket of his trousers," she told him, knowing what he was looking for. A moment later Damian was brandishing a Patience-made master key, by the looks of it. It likely opened every cell in the prison. He inserted it into the lock, and relief shot through Roz when she heard the telltale click. He pushed the heavy door open with a grunt, and Roz nearly leapt into his arms, but something in his expression stopped her. There was an unfamiliar stoniness about him, a visceral danger he didn't normally possess. The line of his mouth was knife-straight in the dim light, his cheeks skeletal.

"Thank the saints," Damian said, and suddenly Roz knew him again. He shuttered his eyes. "Are you okay? I heard you scream."

"Oh." Roz frowned, trying to remember. "The gunshots—I thought the officer was going to take off and leave me here, so I yelled at him. What the hell happened? Why are you handcuffed?" Without waiting for him to answer, she grabbed him by the arm, lifting his hands so she could examine the cuffs. The heat she usually fought to ignore flared beneath her skin.

"They're Falco's," Damian told her. "They'll be enchanted."

Logically, Roz knew it was true. A disciple of Patience would have used magic to bind them to Falco, and you couldn't undo another disciple's work like that. But she couldn't help feeling that she *could* manipulate them, if only she tried. So although she recoiled from the sensation of her magic in her veins, she gritted her teeth and pressed her blazing hands to the shackles. She needed to free Damian—just as when she'd destroyed the porthole on the military ship, that need was more important than anything else.

A heartbeat later, the handcuffs fell away.

Damian stared. "How did you do that?"

"I guess they weren't bound to Falco after all," Roz said, but something uncomfortable churned within her. She gave an evasive shrug. "Why are you here? Not that I'm unhappy to see you."

Damian raked a hand through his hair, seemingly incognizant of the blood circling his wrists. "Falco knew I'd deserted. Russo told her."

"Russo?" It took Roz a moment to place the name. "Michele's brother. The man I nearly killed on the ship."

"Yes. He's at the Palazzo, too. I think Falco made him commander of the fleet for selling me out."

She thought of shattered glass and gunfire echoing through a too-small room. The sharp tang of antiseptic and sea salt. "You should have let me kill him."

"Maybe," Damian agreed soberly. "Anyway, I think I was brought here shortly after you were. Siena and Kiran should be here as well. Falco knew they were involved in my escape and had them arrested, too. She plans to question all the rebels, and was in the middle of questioning *me* when the shots went off. In the confusion, I got the jump on her."

"Where is she now?"

"Probably right where I left her. Maybe she's dead."

He didn't sound at all perturbed by the idea, and Roz arched a brow. Perhaps it was simply the effect of too much adrenaline, but something was off about Damian. Regardless of how many people he'd killed, Roz knew he hated unnecessary violence. Even Enzo's death had been hard on him.

"I *hope* Falco's dead" was the reply she settled on.

Damian toed the officer on the ground. "Yeah, well, this guy definitely isn't. We need to get out of here. If we go back the way I came, I think you'll be able to escape through one of the back doors. I'll meet you at the tavern once I've freed Siena and Kiran, okay?" He passed Roz the fallen officer's pistola. It was still warm, and being armed made her feel better instantaneously.

"Forget escaping. We need to get the rest of the unfavored out."

"No time."

She positioned herself in front of him. "Dev and Nasim are here somewhere. They don't deserve to be, and neither does anyone else. I'm not leaving without them."

Damian's jaw was set, expression uncompromising. "And I'm not letting you get locked up again. Do you know how it felt, watching you be manhandled like that when I couldn't do a damned thing?"

"Then *help* me!"

Roz waited, resenting every second that ticked past. She knew Damian was doing the mental math, trying to figure out how they could possibly free two officers and dozens of unfavored before being recaptured. She wasn't quite sure, either. But she did know there was no way in hell she would abandon her friends here.

Damian brought his teeth together so hard it was audible. "Fine. At least this cursed fog will provide cover." He jutted his chin toward the man on the ground. "Take his uniform. Since I'm already wearing one, nobody will question us unless they get too close. If it looks like we're going to get caught, you *run*. Understood?"

"Fine," she lied.

Damian stood guard at the end of the corridor while Roz slipped into the uniform—luckily the man had another shirt underneath, though there was nothing to be done for his lower half. The next moment they were racing up the stairwell, guns out, squinting through the fog. She barely noticed where they were going as Damian led her around one corner, then another. His steps were impressively quiet for someone of his stature, and it took Roz a moment to realize he'd come to a halt. She pulled up just short of slamming into his broad back. "What is it?" she hissed.

No sooner had she asked the question than did she see the guard pacing the far end of the corridor. It was evident that they would be discovered as soon as he reached the wall and turned around to restart his loop.

They exchanged a look. When Damian tilted his head to the right, Roz knew they were thinking the same thing. He slipped silently into the cell—this one had bars, its gate wide open—and she followed suit. The guard's footsteps grew louder, and Damian gathered Roz into his chest, his arms firm around her waist. He smelled like ash and something vaguely metallic. Roz was reminded of how they'd huddled behind a statue in the Shrine only a couple of short weeks ago, trying to avoid detection by the chief magistrate. How she'd stiffened at the sensation of his body against hers, and yearned to put his knife into his gut.

Now she felt Damian's lips at her ear, his breath in her hair, his heartbeat thudding against her spine, and didn't hate a single minute of it.

She could have done without the imminent threat of death, however.

Roz stopped breathing as the guard passed, and she felt Damian's heart rate pick up. The officer's hand was on his holster, but his eyes were focused straight ahead; clearly he didn't expect anyone to be here. Roz raised her pistola just in case he turned around, but Damian shoved it down with an impatient hand. When she peered questioningly at him over her shoulder, he shook his head.

I know him, he mouthed.

Roz fought the urge to remind Damian that the last time he'd decided to spare a man's life, it had gotten them both arrested. She poked her head out of the cell, squinting through the darkness, and motioned for Damian to run. She could hear the dull murmur of voices from the end of the hall, and her heart lifted. *Down here*, she indicated, and he nodded, following her.

Through the fog she could make out the faces of the rebels behind the cell doors. Damian got to work with the key while Roz manipulated the locks to open, sweat beading at her brow.

"Roz." Alix was the first one she freed, panic in the set of their mouth. "Did you hear the shots? There was some kind of skirmish when officers came to get the first group. I don't know what happened. Nasim and most of the others are already gone."

Roz had already moved on to the next cell, hands numb despite the heat of her power. She didn't need to look at what she was doing. Her attention was on Alix. Night had fallen, and moonlight trickled in through the small window at the end of the cell block, illuminating their pale face. "What are you talking about?"

"A bunch of the general's men came by a couple hours ago. They were escorting prisoners to the docks."

Dread lanced through Roz. The cell door nearly hit her as Josef swung it open, and he reached out to steady her. "They can't have. Damian said they were going to question everyone first."

Alix lifted a shoulder. "I was never questioned. Maybe they planned to do it once we were on the ship."

Once there's no escape, and no point fighting. Roz's ears roared. "Nasim is gone?"

Josef and Alix both nodded. "Saw them guide her past my cell," Josef said.

"What about Dev?"

"Here." His voice came from behind her. Shaky with relief, Roz pivoted to see Dev approaching with a stone-faced Damian. Siena followed a few paces behind. Dev grabbed Roz's arm, his grasp firm. "Nasim was sent away. Most of them were."

"I heard," Roz said, frustration making her want to scream. She'd been trapped here only a handful of hours, and she was already too late. There were so many people she hadn't been able to save. Was that what this had really been about all along? Forced conscription?

"Kiran is gone, too," Siena put in. Her voice was carefully controlled, but a muscle flexed in her neck. "I think we were the last row to be shipped out."

"The shots," Roz breathed. The memory of the sound now seemed far more alarming. "Was anyone hurt? Do you know?"

"*We* might be if we don't get the hell out of here," Damian said. He indicated the stairwell with his free hand. "There's no time to stand around. We got everyone we could—now go. Down the hall and out the door to the north."

Their companions obliged, and Roz followed, leaving Damian to bring up the rear. Her muscles were so tense that she was surprised she could run at all. Though she knew everyone was doing their best to be quiet, it was impossible to hurry down a narrow hallway as a group without the excruciating echo of footsteps. No doubt the guards would overhear, and yet for a brief, shining moment, Roz thought they were going to make it out.

Then a bellow filled the corridor behind them.

"*Venturi!*"

"Shit," Damian spat. "That's Falco."

"I take it she isn't dead then," Roz gasped, clutching the stitch in her side. Up ahead, Siena had faltered, turning to see whether they were in trouble. Roz shook her head, waving at her to keep going. Judging by the clamor, Falco wasn't the only one on their heels. She had to be accompanied by at least two other officers, maybe more. The slap of boots against stone echoed throughout the hall, amplified tenfold so that Roz could almost believe they were being pursued by an entire army. She picked up the pace as they reached the northern wing, relieved when she recognized this part of the prison. It was where she'd found herself face-to-face with Damian last week, caught in the act of helping the draft dodgers escape. It was where he'd discovered she was a rebel.

The footsteps behind them grew more agitated. "Duck," Damian ordered, and he fired a shot behind them. It didn't make contact, but Falco's curse echoed in the ringing stillness that followed.

That strange mist was growing thicker again, and Roz squinted in an attempt to make out the others. She caught sight of Dev's pale head near the exit. Siena was directly behind him, and she hoped to hell the remaining rebels were somewhere up ahead.

As she drew closer, Roz saw the fuzzy outline of a female guard at the other end of the hall, heading straight for Dev. The woman's gun appeared to be out, but she must not have been apprised on the escaped prisoners yet, because she didn't shoot.

"*Dev!*" Roz screamed. "Nine o'clock!"

He understood at once, pivoting to barrel through the exit. Roz didn't hesitate. She fired a barrage of bullets, narrowly but pointedly missing the guard. The woman leapt for cover, fumbling to return fire, clearly struggling to distinguish enemy from ally through the fog. Thanking hell for her stolen uniform, Roz sprinted past the guard to the exit, Damian at her side.

Warm, clean air filtered through her heaving lungs. A handful of stars winked through the clouds overhead. They had made it— they were out.

"Don't stop now," Damian grunted, his words nearly lost in the gunfire that punctuated the air around them. "We need to take cover."

Each inhalation sent a sharp ache shuddering through Roz's chest. "Dev and the others will have headed to Bartolo's. I bet Siena is with them." She turned to glance at Damian. "Palazzo security—they don't know about the tavern, do they?"

"You mean do they know it's a rebel hangout? Of course not. Do you really think I would tell them?"

"I think you'd tell Siena and Kiran."

"You can trust them."

Roz hoped it was true, brushing the sweat from her brow as they continued toward Chaos's abandoned sector. The sound of gunshots faded, but she could hardly think straight.

"They'll find out eventually, you know," Damian said quietly as they turned down another alley. "Falco and her people, I mean."

"I know," Roz told him, and it was the truth.

What she didn't say was that she planned to be long gone from Ombrazia by the time that happened.

6

Roz

The door to Bartolo's was locked, the windows dark behind cracked shutters.

"Now what?" Damian demanded, gaze darting back and forth down the otherwise abandoned street. He looked as tense as a bow strung too tight.

"Relax," Roz told him. "They're here." Rather than try the door again, she knocked, an uneven rhythm that reverberated through the ancient wood. A moment later it opened, Dev's shadowed face appearing in the crack.

"Oh, thank the saints," he breathed, and stood back to allow them to enter.

"The saints had nothing to do with it," Roz said. She pulled her stolen uniform off, discarding it in a corner. "Be thankful we can run fast."

The familiar tavern swam into view as her eyes adjusted, and she saw that two of the tables were occupied. Josef and Arman sat at one. Alix and Siena sat at the other, with a third chair Roz assumed had belonged to Dev. It was difficult to say who looked more uncomfortable. Alix's back was ramrod straight, their chair angled away from the officer. Siena was equally stiff, her hands clenched in her lap, but her expression of obvious distaste faded when she caught sight of Damian. She leapt to her feet in a fluid motion, crossing the space between them.

"You're okay." It was both a question and a statement.

Damian nodded. "So are you."

Siena inclined her head. "Villeneuve said I could hide here"— she glanced over a shoulder, lowering her voice—"despite some protestations."

Roz could only imagine how that might have played out. Josef, especially, would be loath to let a Palazzo security officer into Bartolo's. Even Damian wasn't exactly welcome here. The other duo was deep in quiet conversation, though Roz saw them shoot furtive looks across the room every so often.

"It's Dev," said Dev. "And there's no need to thank me."

"I didn't," Siena pointed out sharply, then softened. "Though I probably should have."

Dev's only response was a grim smile. "Come sit," he said to Roz and Damian, gesturing at the table where Alix sat alone, watching them. Roz shook her head. Normally the familiar smell of liquor and oak calmed her, but tonight it only reinforced the fact that she needed to get away from this place.

"Falco will find us here. Maybe not tonight, but I doubt she'll give up until she does. We're fugitives now—all of us. Josef, Dev, and Arman might be safe," she amended, "if only because Falco's officers couldn't have gotten a good look at everyone amid the commotion, but I wouldn't take any chances. Damian and I, though, are too dangerous to associate with. Siena, they'd likely recognize you as well. As far as I know, you and Kiran were the only other officers taken into custody."

"That's true," Siena confirmed. "I'd never planned to stay here, though. I suppose…" She dragged a hand over her hair. "I suppose

I'll have to go and stay with my family."

There was no mistaking the pain in her voice. It was reflected, Roz saw, in Damian's face. No matter how much Roz hated the Palazzo, she couldn't exactly blame them. In the span of less than a day, they had lost the place that was their job and their home. The city they'd pledged their lives to protect was no longer safe for them.

"What about Kiran, though?" Siena continued, giving Roz the segue she'd been hoping for. "Surely they wouldn't send him back to the front as well. He's done his time."

"People are often called to do more than one tour," Damian reminded her dully, and Roz knew he was thinking of their fathers. She cut in.

"We can rescue Kiran when we go get Nasim."

All eyes landed on her. Dev's head snapped up, cautious hope shining in his face. "We're going after her?"

"It's not like we can stay here. And I'm not letting my best friend be taken away." Roz thought of Nasim's parents, who had already lost their son. The ache they must still feel, not knowing whether he was dead or alive. Roz knew that ache. She'd endured it for three years while Damian was at the northern front. She couldn't do it again.

Perhaps it was horribly selfish to think that way, but it was only because she cared for Nasim so much that she knew she couldn't bear the uncertainty. Roz knew Dev wouldn't be able to bear it, either. He'd already lost his sister, and although neither he nor Nasim had ever admitted it, it was clear they had a connection quite beyond their friendship.

"I'm coming, then," Siena said decisively. "Kiran would do it for me."

"*No*," Damian interrupted. "This is madness. You don't understand what the front is like, Roz. You can't just march up to a battlefield and grab the friends you want to bring home. It doesn't work like that."

Roz's temper flared. "You think I don't know that? I know it'll be dangerous—maybe impossible—but I have to try. It's not like there's anything left for me here."

"Your mother is here. Are you really going to leave her on her own?"

He said the words quietly, but they tore through Roz like a blade, striking the softest parts of her. "That's not fair."

"It's just a fact."

She shoved her guilt and all thoughts of her mother aside. She knew Damian, and understood what he was doing. He was trying to protect her. Giving her reasons to stay because he was terrified of what awaited her in the north. The idea of her in the very place that had broken him, Roz supposed, was the stuff of his nightmares.

But this wasn't about Damian. This was about Nasim, and the rest of the unfavored who had gone to that meeting to create pressure with their presence. Roz had been the one to bring news of the meeting to the rebels, and she knew attending hadn't been easy for them. It had been a risk, and now they might pay the ultimate price. What was she supposed to do? Stay in Ombrazia, a wanted fugitive in her own city, and hope that at least a couple of them made it back whole?

If her life was forfeit regardless, she might as well do something with it.

"Roz," Alix began in a halting tone, very clearly trying to avoid looking at Damian, "if you *do* go, I'll make sure Caprice is taken care of. She likes me well enough."

It was true. Caprice didn't like meeting new people, but she endured Alix's presence, a fact that had surprised Roz ever since the two first met.

"That won't be necessary," Damian growled before Roz could say anything. "If this is what you want, Siena and I will go. We'll find Kiran *and* Nasim."

Roz bristled. "You're worried about me, but not Siena?"

"She's an officer and a former soldier. She's been there before."

"So? The same risks apply."

Siena crossed her arms. One sleeve of her uniform was torn, the stitches splitting further with the motion. "Stop talking about me like I'm not here. Roz, you may be a rebel, but you have no idea what real war is like. If we get caught up in that, we're dead. And Brechaat's new general adds another element of unpredictability."

"I'm going," Roz snapped. "We can all go together, or Dev and I will go separately, which would be rather silly. It's up to you."

Damian's face was a mask of cold fury. It made his features more severe, and Roz was reminded once more of the way he'd looked in the illusion. Not just a boy with the power to rip the world apart, but a man who would do it happily. "Don't do this, Roz."

Alix cleared their throat. "If you'll excuse me, I need to be... elsewhere." Their chair screeched against the wood floor, and they made their way to the bar, dragging Josef and Arman along with them.

"We're in this situation because of me," Damian said. "Because Russo blames me for Michele's death. I should go north alone—this is my fault."

"I'm the one who forced you to desert," Roz reminded him sharply. "Or have you forgotten?"

Because she hadn't. She could still see his fractured expression as his honor battled with his desire to live. He'd always been too good for Ombrazia and that saints-cursed war.

"I would have come with you in the end, anyway."

"Liar."

Damian trapped her gaze. All at once, he looked impossibly vulnerable. The ghost of his younger self was still there, Roz realized, behind the cut of his cheekbones and his shadowed jaw. Pieces of him had been hollowed out, but the Damian Venturi of her childhood still lingered beneath the surface.

"I'm not lying," he said, and though Dev and Siena were well within earshot, the quiet confession was only for her. "I've never been able to deny you anything. You know that."

Roz swallowed. She did know. She'd taken advantage of it more than once, and not only as children. Damian's devotion was absolute, something she didn't quite know how to navigate. But so was hers.

"Then you know there's no use arguing with me. If you're going north, then I'm coming." She spoke fiercely, leaving no room for interjection. "I spent three years wondering if you were alive. Don't you dare make me spend another day not knowing."

She knew she had him then. She had won, and saw the breath rush out of him, and nothing had ever felt less like victory.

"I don't know if I can save you up there," he said, but with an air of obvious capitulation. "I don't know if I can save any of you."

Siena rolled her eyes. "You and your hero complex need to stop. It's not up to you keep everyone alive, you know."

Damian was silent, but Roz knew what he was thinking. How he could never free himself from the belief that it *was* up to him. Ridiculous, really, when keeping himself alive had proved complicated enough on its own.

"How are we going to get there?" Roz asked. "We need a plan."

Dev worried his lower lip. "We'll have to go by boat, right? Anything else would take far too long."

Damian nodded. "That's the only way to get to the front, regardless."

"Just a minute." Siena sat back down, pulling a folded piece of paper from the inner pocket of her jacket. As she laid it out on the table, Roz saw it was a map bearing a compass rose shaped like the Palazzo crest. Tiny ink marks dotted what Roz recognized as the heart of Ombrazia.

"It's for security patrols," Siena explained. "Every officer has one."

Damian was dubious. "Didn't they search you?"

"Not well. Anyway, once they took my weapons, they weren't worried about much else." Siena rotated the map, pointing at a narrow waterway in the north. "Unless things have changed, this is Ombrazia's main base, and this Brechaat's. Right?"

Roz and Dev peered over her shoulder as Damian nodded.

"Okay. So Ombrazia currently controls most of *this*," Siena continued, indicating with a finger. "But Brechaat still controls this end of the river, given that it's their main port of trade. Now, they're pushing us back at this border *here*. If we want to make it to the base, we'll have to travel up and around." She traced a path along the edge of the map.

"Why wouldn't we just cut right through there?" Roz said, pointing at what might have been an inlet. It was a straight shot from its shore to where the Ombrazian base supposedly was, assuming they could get across the river somehow.

Siena looked at Roz as if she were mad. "Because that's Brechaan territory."

"We have to go that way. We're already hours behind the military ships; Nasim and the others could be sent anywhere when they arrive, and then we might never find them. Hell, they could already be *dead*."

"We can't go through Brechaat," Damian argued. "They'll kill us on sight."

"How would they even know we're Ombrazian?"

"There's almost certainly a checkpoint at the border."

"So we'll find a way past it."

"If it was that easy, Roz, we wouldn't still be at war."

Roz glowered. It was Dev who spoke next. "How much time would we save by cutting through Brechaat?"

Siena exchanged a glance with Damian, then shrugged. "I don't know. A day, perhaps. Maybe less."

"Okay. That gives us enough time to catch up *and* get ahead. We could be at the Ombrazian base when the ships arrive." When nobody answered, Dev grew more pleading. "We should at least try. If we can't cross and end up having to go around, fine. But I need to get to Nasim." His voice cracked as he reddened. "*We* need to get to her."

Damian raked a hand through his hair. "Saints, you two are unbearable. Fine. We'll try to cross, and when it doesn't work, we'll go around."

"*If* it doesn't work," Dev corrected him.

"I said what I meant."

"We'll make it work," Roz said, partially to assure Dev, but mostly to assure herself. If they couldn't catch up to the boat carrying their friends by the time it docked, it would be nearly impossible to find them. Roz wasn't ignorant. She knew the war stretched along the entire northern border. There were dozens of places where new soldiers might be stationed. To get to Nasim, Roz would search them all if she had to, but chances of success would be far slimmer.

"And after?" Siena asked soberly. "Like you said, we can't come back here, whether we're successful or not."

"I return for my mother, then head for the Eastern Isles." Roz had already begun forming a mental plan. The isles were a trade partner of both Brechaat and Ombrazia—to this day, they hadn't taken a side. "You can do whatever you like."

She and Caprice could rebuild their lives. After all, they'd already done it once. Would Damian come along, though? Would any of her friends?

"I go where you go," Damian said at once, and Roz relaxed slightly. "But we need to leave as soon as possible. Where are we going to get a boat?"

"We could borrow one from a fisherman," Dev suggested, but Roz shook her head. Fishing was one of the few reliable means of income for unfavored citizens, and she wasn't about to take that from them, borrowed or otherwise.

"A fishing boat wouldn't get us through northern waters," Siena said. "We need one that's disciple made."

She was probably right. Sails made by disciples of Grace could adjust themselves to the strength and direction of the wind, and as far as Roz knew, none of them were particularly skilled at sailing. Kiran had been good at it, but of course he wasn't here.

"We'll have to take one from the Palazzo docks," Damian said. The prospect didn't appear to enthuse him. "They're Grace-made and equipped to deal with rough waters. They're also fast. It's our only real chance at catching up to the military ship."

"So we have to go back to the Palazzo." The corners of Siena's mouth turned down, but Roz could tell she knew Damian was right.

"If you think about it," Roz said, "it might be the perfect place to go. Nobody will expect us to return there. Not when we're supposed to be on the run."

Damian nodded, though he didn't look convinced. Roz, on the other hand, was practically vibrating with anticipation. Her sense of danger seemed to have evaporated the way it always did when she was angry enough. And saints, she was angry. They'd been tricked. Promised discussions of peace only for the attending unfavored to be captured and detained, the majority of them sent away.

Roz had been a fool to hope. A fool for each stolen moment of optimism, however fleeting. Council meetings and personnel changes weren't enough, and she'd been naive to think they might be. Institutions like the Palazzo never changed—not if they could help it. You had to burn them down and start over.

When she returned, rebels in tow, Roz wouldn't make the same mistake twice. Until then, there was nothing for her here—with one exception.

"Before we go," she said, "I need to see my mother."

7

DAMIAN

"You don't have to say goodbye," Damian whispered to Roz outside the door to her mother's apartment. "You can still stay here."

Her withering glance made his heart stutter. "Is this why you wanted to come with me? We've already had this argument. I'm not having it again."

That wasn't why he'd asked to accompany her upstairs. Telling Caprice she was leaving would be difficult, and he wanted to be there for her, just in case she needed him. Not that she ever really needed anyone. In fact, she would hate it if he said such a thing aloud, so he didn't. Instead he muttered, "You're a disciple. You never should have been arrested in the first place. If I hadn't hesitated on the ship, we would have been gone by the time Russo arrived, and he never would have seen either of us."

Roz's throat shifted as she swallowed. When she spoke again, her voice was harsh. "Stop trying to blame everything on yourself. I made you desert, even though I didn't have the right to make that decision for you, and we both know it. I just couldn't bear losing you a second time. But if I could go back—if I could do it all over—I wouldn't choose differently. So I'm sorry,

Damian, for being a huge fucking hypocrite. I'm selfish when it comes to you."

He didn't quite know what to say to that. "Roz—" he began, pained, but she cut him off.

"Later," she said, then entered the small apartment. He would have waited outside, but she beckoned him in, the motion stiff.

The room was dated and sparsely decorated, smelling brightly of cleaning solution. It was also far too warm, a fire burning in one corner despite the mild night. As he glanced around, Damian saw nothing of Roz here. It was too tidy. Too... sterile. Nothing like the disaster of her childhood bedroom. This was obviously a place meant for Roz's mother, not Roz herself. The realization made him sad somehow.

And there, on the green velvet sofa pushed up against the wall, was Caprice Lacertosa.

After seeing her through the window of Roz's old apartment nearly three weeks ago, Damian had thought he was prepared for this. He wasn't, though. Nothing could have prepared him to see the woman he'd once thought of as a second mother like... *this.* Her bony frame was folded into itself, hands clasped tightly in her lap. Her eyes, a shade darker than Roz's, were fixed on nothing in particular.

Damian tensed. Last time, Caprice had screamed upon catching sight of him. He was braced for it to happen again.

But Roz's mother didn't scream. She turned, her expression shifting into a smile. A bright, heart-shattering smile.

"Damian," she breathed, sounding so like her old self that he faltered.

"Hello, Signora." He didn't know how else to respond. At his side, Roz was aghast, something tortured veiling her features. They both watched as Caprice stood and crossed the room toward Damian. When she reached him, taking him into her frail arms, Damian froze like a man held at gunpoint. Something in his chest tightened to the point of pain, and he was abruptly reminded of how his mother used to hug him before she fell ill.

"You made it back," Caprice said, taking Damian's face in her cold hands. Her eyes were shining. For a moment it was as if no time had passed and nothing had changed.

"Yeah," he said gruffly. "Yeah, I did."

Roz's expression was even more pained now. She took her mother by the hand and guided her back to the couch, spine very straight. "Mamma," she said, "Damian and I have to go away for a while."

Confusion crowded Caprice's joy. "Why?"

It was a simple question, but Roz stumbled over it, looking to Damian in wide-eyed distress. Clearly she hadn't come up with a lie ahead of time, which was unlike her. "It's—well, uh. We're going to—"

"Visit my family," Damian put in. "In northern Ombrazia." If Caprice was still living in the past, she likely thought his mother and father were still alive. Perhaps even recalled them moving north for his father's promotion. Caprice may have been a bit confused, but she was perceptive, and Damian had no doubt she would grow suspicious if Roz took too long to come up with a story.

"Oh." Caprice blinked up at Damian, the corners of her eyes crinkling. "I do miss your mother. I hope she's well."

"Very well, thank you," he replied without missing a beat. "She'll be glad to know you were asking after her."

The look Roz gave him was equal parts somber and grateful. She squeezed her mother's shoulder. "Do you remember Alix? They've brought you food a few times. I'm going to ask them to continue doing that while I'm away. Is that all right?"

Caprice's brows drew together, and for a moment Damian feared she would decline. But she said simply, "Okay."

"Good." Roz relaxed.

"Why doesn't Piera visit?"

Damian blanched. Had Roz not told her mother Piera was dead?

Roz swallowed, the column of her slender neck shifting. "Piera's gone, Mamma. Remember? We talked about this."

He hadn't expected Roz to go with the truth this time. He watched, awkward and miserable, as Caprice's eyes filled with tears. She leaned her head against Roz's shoulder, and for a moment they only clasped hands, silence stretching to fill the room.

"I miss her," Caprice said, and Roz nodded.

"So do I."

A shuddering exhale. "How long will you be gone?"

Roz glanced to Damian before responding. "Perhaps a week. Not long." She squeezed her mother's fingers. "I just don't want you to worry about us."

"I always worry about you, tesoro. This city can be dangerous for two unfavored traveling alone."

Damian fought to keep his face from betraying his shock. It took a considerable amount of effort, and he must not have done a decent job because Caprice's attention shifted back to him. She frowned. "You look unwell."

Roz shot Damian a look that suggested she might murder him in his sleep.

"I'm fine" was his husky reply.

Roz moved to block him from her mother's view. "You don't need to worry about us, Mamma. Have you seen the size of Damian?" She laughed uneasily. "Now, let me help you into bed. It's late."

Damian sank onto the couch in their absence, staring blankly at the uneven floorboards. Roz's mother didn't know she was a disciple. How was that possible? Was she truly so secluded from the rest of the world that Roz had managed to keep it from her?

And now they were planning to leave Caprice alone in this apartment, without full-time care, so that they could flee the country. Nothing about this felt right. On top of that, nothing about *Damian* felt right. If he hadn't already abandoned his trust in the saints, he suspected this would have been the moment that convinced him he was going to hell.

"Okay," Roz said as she reappeared, sitting beside him with a sigh. "Sorry. I didn't realize she was going to—"

"Why did you keep it from her?" Damian said, unable to stop himself from interrupting. "That you're a disciple, I mean."

Her expression turned defensive. "I don't see what that has to do with you."

"I'm only asking."

"Why do you *think* I kept it from her?" All at once Roz sounded impossibly tired. "My father returned from his first northern tour hating everything about disciples. And could you really blame him?" She examined a few strands of her hair. "My mother hated them just as much, and eventually, so did I. You saw how confused she is already. How was I supposed to tell her I had become a disciple of Patience? It would only have made everything worse."

"But you go to Patience's temple all the time," Damian said, trying to wrap his head around what Roz was saying. "Or at least, you did."

"She didn't know that. She scarcely speaks to anyone but me. Do you know how hard it was to move her from our old apartment into this one? Being outside frightens her."

"Oh."

"Yeah." The edge to Roz's voice lingered. She studied Damian's face as if daring him to tell her she was wrong. As if expecting him to say she wasn't doing a good job of caring for her mother. He wouldn't, though. Of course he wouldn't.

"Roz, about the north…," Damian said, pivoting to face her. Her eyes were blue fire, hair framing her face in a dark spill. The words slipped out before he could reel them back in. "Once I return there…I don't know that I can be the man I want you to see."

"Stop it," Roz said fiercely. "I don't care what versions of you I see, Damian. I want to know all of them."

Did she, though? Did she want to know the version of Damian that feared he was still plagued by the vestiges of Enzo's control? The one that felt he was being corrupted from the inside? He wanted to tell her what he'd learned from the old woman in the prison, whether or not it was the truth, but he'd lost track of the number of times he'd complained to Roz about feeling wrong. She'd attempted to comfort him, of course, but Damian could tell she didn't think there *was* anything wrong with him. And though Damian loved her for believing it, he couldn't shake the feeling it wouldn't make a difference.

I see you, Damian, she'd told him the night he'd killed Enzo. *Even the dark parts.*

But he didn't want her to see those parts. Why would he?

"Roz—" he began hoarsely.

"Shut up," she said, grasping his shoulders. "Shut *up*." Her hands slid up his neck, fingers intertwining behind his head. She shifted onto her knees, which made them more or less the same height, and Damian tilted her chin up with a finger. She was beautiful in a way that was simply unfair. In a way that made all thoughts drain from his mind, and all arguments flee from his tongue. If her beauty was a weapon, he didn't care. He would let it strike him through the heart.

"I almost killed her today," he said to Roz, a soft confession. "Falco, I mean. I think I would have, if I hadn't heard you scream."

Roz stilled, scanning his face. "And?"

"I don't . . . I mean, that's not *me*. I hate killing." He tried to pull away from her, cheeks burning, but she wouldn't let him.

"It's okay," she insisted. "Sometimes people have to die. Sometimes they even deserve it."

"I felt out of control. Like I didn't know what I was going to do next."

She arched a brow, her finger tracing circles at the base of his neck. "That's called rage, Damian. It's okay to feel it." Before he could reply, she leaned forward, pressing her lips to the hollow of his throat. "You can only go so long without letting it consume you."

Chills danced along Damian's skin, and he shuttered his eyes. "I feel like—like I'm forgetting how to be *good*."

That gave her pause. She straightened, then pulled him to stand. "That's how you know you haven't forgotten. Because you still care. As long as you're worried about being a good person, you probably are one."

"And you?"

Roz tilted her head, a flash of mischief in her eyes. "What about me?"

"Do you worry about that?"

"No. Not often. But I don't care about being good. I care about making the rest of the world better. And if I have to be bad in order for that to happen, then so be it."

Damian skimmed a hand down the side of her torso. Her black shirt still clung to her ribs, sweaty from the run here, but he didn't care. She was perfect, and she smelled like cinnamon and rain and the night.

When she kissed him, though, Damian couldn't help but think it tasted like finality. Not because she drew back almost at once, breathing "We need to go," but because something deep inside him seemed to snap to awareness.

Something that frightened him far more than the prospect of returning to the north.

8

Milos

Milos could remember the night they came for him.

His family had told him to hide the moment they heard the thud of boots outside the front door. He remembered wondering what he'd done wrong. Why his parents feared only for him, and why none of his siblings were told to hide as well. He remembered how his mother's eyes were too large in her face, and how his father's voice became an unfamiliar, edged thing. Nobody knew they were coming. Nobody ever knew when they would come— only that eventually, they always did.

Bitter fear had coated his tongue, a tang that reminded him of blood. He'd sat in his parents' closet, surrounded by the scent of his mother's perfume, one ear pressed to the keyhole. It was difficult to make out the words, but he could hear the voices. The loud, authoritative tones that undoubtedly belonged to important men, and the anxious lilt of his mother's response. They had almost certainly come from the Palazzo. Milos had seen their kind patrolling the streets many a time, marveling at their smart navy uniforms and the weapons strapped across their backs. Once, he had told his mother with no small amount of pride that he would be like those men someday.

His mother had smiled at him, but it hadn't reached her eyes. Milos remembered wondering if it was because his family was unfavored and she thought his goals too lofty. For them, the glittering Palazzo with its disciples was an unreachable thing.

Milos heard the men talking to his siblings then, and shoved his way out of the closet. He was still out of sight, he reasoned, as long as he didn't leave the bedroom. Silent as a mouse, he crept to the door, straining to listen once more. From there he could see flashes of the men through the gap by the hinges. One was dark haired, the other light. He heard the questions they asked his brother and sister, and his siblings' quiet denials. Milos could tell by the men's reactions that they were disappointed. His frustration had mounted. *He* would have answered yes to those questions. He'd experienced precisely the things they were asking about, and they would have been pleased. His parents ought to have known that. He'd told them all about the strange things he could do. Didn't they want to make these men happy? They were forever talking in hushed tones about the way the Palazzo seemed to ignore their kind—the ones not blessed with magic.

Milos hadn't been able to help himself. He hadn't known better, at the time.

He could still see the expressions of sheer horror on his parents' faces as he shoved the door open. How his father's gaze had shuttered, and he'd exhaled through his nose in what could only be dismay. The way his mother's eyes had flown wide, fear overtaking her as she went perfectly still.

She'd screamed when they took him away. Screamed and screamed while Milos sobbed at the sound. It would ring in his ears for the rest of his life—the single most significant memory of the woman who had raised him.

He hadn't come back.

He had known even then that he never would.

9

Roz

Their route to the Palazzo docks was as convoluted as possible. It took more than twice the usual time, but Roz barely noticed. Her head was full of the goodbyes she'd given her mother, Josef, Alix, and the others who remained. Would they be safe at Bartolo's? They knew to hide if any officers came knocking, but what if that wasn't enough? What if Roz returned to find them all recaptured? What if she returned without Nasim by her side?

What if she never returned at all?

Normally the thought wasn't one she would entertain. If Roz was good at anything, it was carrying out a task without dwelling on the possible consequences. But the prospect of leaving her mother without a single family member was almost too horrible to bear. *Almost.* She would bear it, however, if it meant saving Nasim.

Was this to be her life? Constantly being forced to choose between terrible options?

Damian motioned for everyone to stop. His uniform was gone; he and Siena now wore clothes provided by Josef and Roz, respectively. A practiced hand clutched his pistola, and his stance was rigid. "We'll make a run for it here," he said, indicating the stretch of grass that separated the road from the Palazzo docks. "The next security rotation should be in about—"

"—four minutes," Siena finished, glancing down at a tiny clock on a chain. She shoved it into her pocket. "We shouldn't run, though. It'll only draw attention if anyone notices us. Which they hopefully won't, given the dark."

Dev arched a brow. "*Hopefully* is doing some heavy lifting there."

"You're right," Damian told Siena, ignoring Dev. "We'll aim to take that boat, docked right where the harbor narrows." He pointed. "The smallest of the three. No use taking an armored one when there aren't enough of us to properly man it."

Roz knew the types of weapons Ombrazian warships boasted, given that disciples of Patience made many of them. She didn't relish the idea of being unarmed in the event they were pursued by military vessels, but a smaller boat *would* be faster. "What if we're caught, and there's a fight? Are you two going to be mad if I shoot?"

Damian's mouth thinned. "Don't unless you absolutely have to."

"No offense," Dev said, "but I'm not particularly worried about the lives of Palazzo security just now." There was fire in his eyes—the kind Roz hadn't seen there for quite some time. "If they come for us, I'll shoot to kill. Consider it penance for choosing the wrong side."

"Not everyone got to *choose* their side, you bastard," Siena snapped back, her usually calm demeanor evaporating. "Officers are mostly unfavored, too, you know. We were soldiers first. If you were offered a job that allowed you to leave the front—and provide for your family—are you telling me you wouldn't take it?"

"I would never work for the Palazzo."

"Well, some of us aren't interested in suffering for foolish ideals. Some of us just want to live. You haven't even *been* to war," Siena continued, cutting Dev off as he opened his mouth again. "So don't act like you know a damn thing about what you would or wouldn't do to get away from it."

"Don't condescend to him," Roz said furiously. "Dev lost both his parents to the war. Enzo murdered his little sister. Do you really think he doesn't understand suffering?"

"*Stop it.*" This was Damian, who looked as if his head was about to explode. Even Roz shut up. "Since we're going to be traveling together—whether I like it or not, apparently—we're going to have to get along. That means no bickering, because frankly, I don't want to hear it. Do I make myself clear?"

Siena nodded, and Dev looked chastised. It occurred to Roz that she had never seen Damian in his element like this: impatiently flinging orders, expecting them to be followed. Was this how he was at the Palazzo? Did the other officers follow him not merely out of respect, but also because they feared him a little?

His nostrils flared as he massaged the back of his neck. "Good. I don't know if you've noticed, but the four of us aren't exactly inconspicuous, and I'd like to be on our way before we lose the cover of night. So let's go before I regret this."

As they slipped out from the cover of the buildings, a voice sounded from the dark, making Roz's stomach flip over.

"I think you'll find you already do, Venturi."

Roz turned, already knowing who she would see. She'd heard that voice only a handful of times, but something about Salvestro Agosti's low drawl was difficult to forget.

He stood with his hands in the pockets of his long black coat, looking for all the world as if he was taking a pleasant night's stroll. Roz might have believed it, if not for the half dozen heavily armed officers at his back. If any of them knew Damian or Siena, they didn't let on.

"Drop your weapons," Salvestro ordered.

Dev caught Roz's eye, and she understood his silent question: Should they fight, taking out as many officers as they could before they were inevitably killed? Or were they going to let themselves be detained again?

For a moment, Roz wasn't sure herself. But then she heard Damian and Siena's weapons fall and knew there was no point. Her hand felt numb as she let her own pistola slip to the ground. Dev copied her, his displeasure palpable.

Salvestro grinned, stepping into the moonlight. "What a pity. You were so close to escaping. And *you*." He leveled his gaze at Siena. "You could have redeemed yourself, you know. A few more years at the front, and then you might have been allowed to return to the Palazzo, assuming you survived. You were a good officer. But loyalty can be a flaw, especially when it's to someone like this. This *disgrace* of a leader." He spat at Damian's feet, narrowly missing his boots.

Damian didn't react except to say, "You were planning this, weren't you? That's why you let me pull back on security for the meeting. You knew General Falco was going to show up because you invited her. You knew what would happen because you two planned it together."

Salvestro gave an exaggerated clap. "Oh, very good." One of the officers behind him snorted, and he shot the woman a small smile. "If it makes you feel better, Venturi, I was never going to let you stay on as head of security, even before I knew you were a deserter. An unfavored boy, occupying a position like that? It's frankly embarrassing."

"Shut *up*," Roz said, taking a step closer to Salvestro. Damian might be willing to endure that kind of abuse, but she certainly wasn't. She tilted her chin up at the disciple of Death, trying to ignore the firearms pointed her way. "I thought you were supposed to be at the Shrine preparing for your new role. Rather unprofessional of you to shirk your prayers. Is this the kind of guidance you're getting from the saints? Did they want you to prance around after dark, collecting fugitives?"

Salvestro's teeth gleamed. He was really rather handsome, with his onyx hair and aristocratic features. That was how Roz knew the stories about the saints couldn't be true: No benevolent deity would bless Salvestro Agosti. Not unless they had reprehensible taste.

"You'll have to do better than that if you want to distract me, girl. My relationship with the saints is none of your business."

Before she could form a retort, Damian pushed her out of the way. "Take me back into custody and let the others go. My crimes are my own."

"*No*," Roz snarled, but Salvestro wasn't having it regardless. His face contorted in false confusion.

"Except your companions are here now, when they ought to still be in prison. Seems you're not the only criminal present, Venturi. Speaking of which, did you know you injured our new general? Not terribly, thank goodness, but she certainly isn't happy. That was a mistake. I suppose all the confusion was your fault, too?" Suddenly he was serious again. "Tell me how you did it."

"I didn't," Damian said tonelessly. "I've no idea what happened at the prison—I simply took advantage."

"Should I pretend to believe you?"

"It's the truth. I swear it on the saints."

"Those words mean nothing in your mouth," Salvestro spat. "Since your life is forfeit, I'd quite like to kill you myself here and now. Unfortunately, the general thinks you should stand trial. An example to the rest of Ombrazia, if you will."

Roz knew what that meant. *A public execution*. Ombrazia didn't do public executions anymore—hadn't for decades. Were these the types of changes Salvestro and Falco were going to implement if they were allowed to remain in power?

"Fine," Damian said, and he didn't sound like himself. He sounded like a man who'd fought the world and lost. A man who'd realized he couldn't run, couldn't hide, and was prepared to face his fate. "But let the rest of them go. Please."

Salvestro laughed. It was higher than his usual voice, that laugh, and sent chills along Roz's skin. Against the soft crashing of the nearby waves, it seemed to echo for miles. "I don't think so. It's very sweet that you care, though. Sacrificing yourself for your friends?" He clucked his tongue. "So bold. So honorable. If it's any consolation, I'll take you first."

He motioned for one of the officers to approach. This was it, Roz thought. They had failed before even managing to leave Ombrazia's shores. They had failed, and the unfavored would continue to suffer, and the war would rage on. She dug her nails into her palms as Damian held up his hands.

Then she saw the moment his face changed.

The hopelessness and frustration disappeared from his eyes, replaced by something unfamiliar. Something cold.

Dev's breathing was harsh behind her, but Roz barely noticed. She saw Damian relax his shoulders as an officer approached from one side, Salvestro watching self-righteously from the other. Siena's face was screwed up, but even she appeared resigned. If they tried to fight, they would undoubtedly be shot. They were out of options, and they all knew it.

That was when Damian struck.

He moved faster than Roz would have thought possible. In a single motion he pivoted to avoid the officer and fastened one arm around Salvestro's neck. His free hand, impossibly, was holding a knife. Roz hadn't a clue where it had come from. Damian pressed the blade into Salvestro's pale skin, a gentle caress, and they all watched in bewildered silence—the officers included—as a line of crimson welled against his throat.

Salvestro let out a sharp breath, fingernails scrabbling against Damian's arm.

"Tell me," Damian murmured, barely loud enough for Roz to hear. "Would you like to live to see tomorrow?"

Salvestro was silent.

"Answer me."

"*Yes.*" The word was somewhere between a snarl and a croak.

Damian waited, and horror dawned on Salvestro's face as he realized what for.

"I do not bestow honorifics upon *scum*."

The knife pressed in deeper. The part of Roz that wasn't frozen in bewilderment yearned to watch the disciple die, but the other part of her knew his death would only make things worse. Besides, this was Damian. He didn't kill—not even men like Salvestro.

"Damian," she said urgently, and her voice seemed to trigger something in him.

He lifted his head, a kind of animal focus in his gaze as he dragged it to rest on the officers. "Let us go, or your next chief magistrate dies."

For another long moment it appeared the officers were too flummoxed to respond. Roz couldn't blame them. She felt as if making a single wrong move would—what? Snap Damian out of whatever the hell this was?

At her right, Siena and Dev were equally immobile. Their eyes were enormous as they watched Salvestro panic, though Roz thought she saw a hint of mirth at the edges of Dev's lips.

Finally, though, one of the officers had the gall to say, "You won't kill him."

Damian pressed the blade in deeper still, making Salvestro give a strangled gasp. *Watch me*, the action said. Blood trickled down the disciple's neck onto his white collar, a red stain spreading across the fabric. Roz knew she should be horrified, but something inside her tightened with glee. Fear, she decided, looked good on Salvestro Agosti.

"Come on," Damian said, looking from Roz to Siena. Still holding Salvestro by the neck, he began walking backward, dragging the disciple along with him. Salvestro tried and failed to stand, his heels skimming the grass in a way that shouldn't have been as amusing as it was.

"You fire at any of us," Damian told the officers, still backing away, "and you'll find out exactly how fast I can slit a man's throat."

Roz knew none of them would shoot. Not at Damian, at least. There was a high likelihood of hitting Salvestro if they did.

One by one, she, Siena, and Dev reached the ship Damian had indicated earlier. It swayed atop the water beside them, Palazzo flag thrashing in the wind. Roz's eyes were locked on Damian, who had dragged Salvestro to the end of the dock. With his arm around the other man, the two of them silhouetted by the moonlight, they could have been lovers. Apprehension lanced through her. The officers continued to advance, archibugi raised, but not a single one loosed a bullet. Roz gripped Dev's arm, finding it tense.

"Drop the guns," Damian bellowed over the roar of the sea. "Once you do, I'll let him go. You already know we can't shoot you." Indeed, their own weapons sat in the grass a few yards away. Roz could see the glint of metal against the dark.

There was a moment of hesitation before the officers complied.

"Excellent," Damian said.

Then he shoved Salvestro into the water.

10

DAMIAN

Damian watched the docks shrink as Dev steered the ship into the wide expanse of black. In the glow that emanated from shore, he could still see the water rippling where he'd dropped Salvestro, though the disciple had since been retrieved by a couple of the officers. The rest had loosed a barrage of bullets upon the ship, the projectiles going wide as the men fumbled with their guns. A few had made contact with the side of the vessel, but the damage was minimal.

"They'll be after us at any moment," Roz was saying. "Dev, can't we go faster?"

Dev's reply was all but lost in the wind. "It only goes as fast as it goes."

Damian turned away from the bow, becoming aware of Roz and Siena staring at him. "What's wrong?"

He already knew the answer. Threatening Salvestro had been a risky move. It was something he normally wouldn't have dared. In that moment, though, he'd known he could fight. More than that—he'd been desperate to. He'd felt a fiery need to press his knife against Salvestro's slender throat. He knew it was mad, but couldn't bring himself to care. The part of him that *should* have cared scraped insistently beneath his skin, yet he found it far too easy to ignore.

It was Roz who finally shattered the silence. "What the hell was that, Damian?"

Saints she was lovely, with her sea-damp hair and stormy eyes. Damian remembered how she'd said his name when he'd had Salvestro by the neck. It had almost made him let go. Had almost reminded him that he was a boy who avoided violence, not one who reveled in it. But in that moment he'd hated Salvestro more than he wanted to be good.

"What do you mean?" he said. "That was Salvestro Agosti trying to ruin us like the bastard he is."

Roz kept staring at him. There was concern in the lines of her face. "What you did...It could have gone so very badly."

"I thought you liked taking risks."

"*I* do. You don't."

Damian shrugged. "I guess I knew it would work."

"How?" Siena demanded. "Salvestro had six officers with him. If even one had been a more confident shot, you could have died."

"Well, I didn't die," Damian said, irritation bubbling within him. "None of us did. Am I missing something? Are you angry I didn't let us all get dragged back to prison?"

"Of course we're not angry," Roz snapped, undoubtedly angry. "I know this wasn't exactly the plan, but don't jump down our throats for caring. If I didn't know any better, I'd say you're coming unhinged."

The only thing unhinged about him, Damian thought, was how badly he wanted to pull her belowdecks and kiss her until he couldn't remember his own name. At the same time, though, her words struck something in him. Hadn't he feared the same thing? That he was losing his mind?

The realization felt like sinking into frigid water, and Damian's thoughts cleared. Anger drained out of him like water running downhill.

"Sorry." He massaged the bridge of his nose, trying to alleviate the headache that had just come on. "I don't know what came over me."

"For what it's worth," Dev said over his shoulder, "I don't care what you do, as long as it gets us to the front lines." He rotated the ship's wheel. They were well away from the shore by now, even the tiniest pinpricks of light swallowed by fog and distance.

Siena tipped her chin to the dark sky. "Well, the stars are gone, so that's not exactly a good start."

"Don't tell me you believe that drivel about the stars being the saints' eyes," Roz said, rolling hers. "If anything goes wrong, it's because the entire Palazzo knows we're on the run. I guarantee we're already being pursued—probably by Russo." She scowled, peering into the dark as if it might lift to reveal the captain. "Personally, I hope he catches us. This time I won't make the mistake of leaving him alive."

Damian followed her line of sight, lungs tightening. He knew he ought to hate Alexi Russo. At the same time, though, he couldn't look at the man without thinking of his younger brother. Couldn't imagine killing him without seeing Michele's face in his mind. Michele had saved Damian's life with his solidarity, his goodness. If Damian let anything happen to Russo, what kind of friend did that make him? He'd let Michele down in life. He couldn't do the same in death.

"Ah," Roz said, scrutinizing Damian in the way that meant she knew what he was thinking. "Regular Damian has returned."

"I didn't go anywhere," he told her. "And you know why I didn't want to hurt Russo. That remains in effect."

"You've got to be kidding me. He got us thrown in *jail*."

"He was doing what he thought was right." Damian couldn't say he wouldn't have done the same once.

Bright spots that had nothing to do with the harsh wind appeared on Roz's cheeks. "You're unbelievable. But fine, I'll kill him so you don't have to."

"You will not. He's Michele's—"

"I *know* he's Michele's fucking brother, and I know you cared about Michele. But that doesn't make you liable for his family." Roz's face was stony. "I cared about *you*, and it wasn't going to stop me from shooting your father."

"It did stop you, though," Damian pointed out. "The fact that you cared about me, I mean. You didn't shoot him because I asked you not to."

He didn't know what to make of her resulting silence. It seemed to span a hundred breaths.

Eventually she said, "I didn't shoot Russo when you asked me not to, either. Honestly, I'm beginning to wonder about your judgment when it comes to deciding who should be spared."

Damian felt as if he had been punched. He was almost relieved when Dev cleared his throat. "Not to interrupt, but we might have a problem."

He glanced up, about to ask Dev what he meant, but the question died in his throat, a different one slipping out. "What the *hell*?"

A light fog had hung in the air since they'd departed the docks, but now it had thickened, darkened, spreading smokelike across the surface of the water toward them. The sight was eerie enough that Damian couldn't help feeling something bad would happen when it reached the ship. This was *not* normal fog. And yet it was vaguely familiar to him; he remembered the mist that had spilled through the prison corridors in the wake of the gunfire.

Everything inside him seemed to tighten. A chill slunk across his skin that had nothing to do with the mist. Both times this had happened, he'd been trying to escape: first the prison, now the city. Was this someone's—or *something*'s—way of attempting to stop him?

"That's no normal weather," Siena said, echoing what Damian had been thinking. Her face was grim. "Should we get into the cabin?"

The great sails rippled as the wind picked up. Siena's braids whipped around her, and Damian shivered against the sudden onslaught of cold.

"If it's not normal weather," Dev yelled over the gusts, "then what the hell is it?"

Nobody answered him. Damian cast his gaze around for Roz. She wasn't standing where she'd been moments before, and his heart gave an uneven stutter before he spotted her walking slowly to the bow of the ship. She was peering into the distance, her expression inscrutable. Damian went to join her, intending to pull her away, but Roz held up a hand before he could touch her. Something like consternation crossed her features. If she was still angry, she didn't show it. She didn't look at him at all.

"It feels like magic," Roz murmured to herself. Then, more loudly: "It's magic. I can feel it."

She didn't appear concerned, though, Damian noted as he studied her face.

"What is it?" he asked.

Her eyes looked more gray than blue, that usually impeccable dark liner smudged around them. "It doesn't feel *bad*. In fact, it's familiar, in a way."

"Is it the same fog that was in the prison?" Siena asked, voicing Damian's earlier thoughts. She had followed them to the bow and was watching the dark clouds roll in with cautious interest.

"It must be. I just didn't realize it then. I was too focused on trying to escape. Besides, the city center is so full of magic it's hard to differentiate anything at all."

"Maybe it's trying to stop us from escaping," Damian said.

Siena nodded thoughtfully. "Obviously Salvestro and his men saw us escape. Who knows what lengths they've gone to in order to try and catch us." A heavy spray of seawater breached the side of the boat, spattering the deck, and she spat out a mouthful.

"Or maybe it's trying to help us," Roz suggested. "After all, we couldn't have escaped the prison without it."

Damian shook his head. "Even if it is magic, it's not *trying* to do anything. Magic doesn't function without someone to command it."

"Then who's commanding this?" Siena asked. "The disciples in the Palazzo are powerful, but their magic is specialized. Nothing can manipulate nature."

A horrible suspicion took root in Damian. There was only one type of magic they didn't understand.

"At the prison," he began haltingly, "the woman in the cell beside me had been arrested for heresy. She was born in Brechaat and told me a story they have there. A story that says if someone makes seven sacrifices to a saint, then that saint's magic grows stronger."

Both girls turned to look at him.

"You think this is Chaos's magic?" Siena said. Her voice was soft, as if she feared the saint himself might overhear.

"That's a *story*," Roz emphasized. "You said as much yourself. Besides, even if it's true, it wouldn't matter. Enzo never managed a seventh sacrifice. Neither of us was killed."

Damian massaged his dominant hand, remembering how it had felt to pull the pistola trigger. "*He* was, though."

Everyone was silent as the implication of that statement sank in.

"Is that even possible?" Roz said finally. "Would Enzo even *count* as a sacrifice?"

"I don't know, but think about it. He died in the Shrine, and he almost definitely had chthonium on him. If the rest of his sacrifices were carried out properly, he met the same criteria."

"Enzo thought he was going to raise Chaos, though. He never said anything about magic."

"What if that was by design?"

"Hold on." Siena lifted a hand. By now the fog was so thick that her face rippled in and out of clarity. "Is it possible to strengthen a saint's magic?"

Damian gave an uneasy shrug. "That's what the old woman told me. She was arrested for trying to warn people. Why would she risk that, if she didn't truly believe it could happen?"

Siena was ashen. "*If* that's possible, Ombrazia is in serious trouble. Because even if we don't have any disciples of Chaos— that we know of, at least—Brechaat does. We could lose the war."

Not only that, Damian thought. They could lose everything. Disciples of Chaos, if they were powerful enough, could do anything. Make you *see* anything. The wind roaring in his ears seemed abruptly louder, and he felt unsteady in a way that had nothing to do with the sway of the ship. Were they being targeted by someone they couldn't see? Someone as powerful as Enzo had been, or perhaps more so?

His greatest fear, though, was this: that the magic was following *him* because he hadn't been able to shake Enzo's influence.

Seven kills in Chaos's name, and all his disciples would grow more powerful.

That wasn't the only thing the woman had said, though. When Damian had asked what being controlled by magic felt like, she'd said, *It feels like insanity. Like losing your mind but being cognizant of it all the while.*

He suspected he knew exactly what she meant by that.

Attacking Falco, then Salvestro…Roz had been right. That behavior wasn't like him. He hadn't wanted to hear it because that meant acknowledging something was very wrong with him. But there *was* something wrong with him, wasn't there?

Everyone could see it. Even now, Damian could feel the others watching him more closely, wondering if he was going to crack. Could a disciple of Chaos's magic still control you if they were dead?

"Damian." Roz was at his ear, at his side, in his space. He felt her, smelled her, and tried to take comfort in it. "Are you okay?"

He hadn't realized he was bent half-over, hands pressed to his thighs as if he was going to be sick. Another spray of seawater lashed against the side of the boat, and the deck shifted beneath his feet. His breaths were too short, his chest too tight.

"I'm fine," he told Roz, the words too hoarse for her to hear. He repeated them. They sounded false even to his own ears. He flexed his hands and stood up straight. Darkness still bore down on them, and nothing was visible in any direction except gray mist and bottomless dark water. Damian could see Roz, though, silhouetted by the fog, tendrils of her hair sticking to the side of her neck. Flashes of white appeared in his periphery as the sails adjusted to the wind.

Roz's lips parted, and there was a wariness about the way she watched him. "No, you're not."

Damian had the sudden urge to leap into the saints-forsaken sea and let it wash him away. Instead he pulled Roz into him, holding her body tight against his own. He didn't know why. He just knew that he needed to touch her. She went perfectly still, then relaxed and held him back, one small hand sliding around his neck. Her skin was damp but warm. Grounding. He could almost believe her presence made the madness slither further away.

Siena cleared her throat. She looked ashen in the moonlight and mist. "Not to interrupt," she said, "but if Chaos's magic *has* grown more powerful, I think we need to talk about what that means."

"It means Brechaat will be even less safe than we thought," Damian said hoarsely.

"It means every Ombrazian soldier might as well be a sacrifice," Roz added, detaching herself from Damian to straighten. The fire had returned to her eyes. "The only reason Chaos didn't win the First War of Saints is because his numbers were small, and he was battling a patron saint of Strength."

Damian thought of Kiran. Of all the others who had been forcibly drafted, potentially about to encounter a threat they couldn't fathom.

"We're working with hypotheticals," Siena said, shaking her head in frustration. "We need to find out if such a thing is even possible. I'm not going into Brechaat unprepared."

Roz pursed her lips. "Except that we don't have a way to find out."

"We do, actually. And it's on the way."

"*What's* on the way?" Damian asked.

Siena's attention lingered on the fog that enveloped their ship, dragging them into clouded obscurity. "The Atheneum."

11

ROZ

Roz knew about the Atheneum.

It was supposed to be Ombrazia's oldest building, nestled into the stone along the coast of the westernmost cliffs. Possible but difficult to access, since the only ones who visited it regularly were the disciples of Death charged with protecting the information it held.

Because the Atheneum held *everything*. Or at least, that was the rumor. It was a place of knowledge, of answers, of secrets. Roz had heard of people who'd traveled to the Atheneum to ask it a question, only to return knowing more than they'd ever wanted to. Others said it was merely a library containing everything mankind had ever written down. Last the Atheneum had crossed Roz's mind, she'd been trying to find a cure for her mother's state. At the time, though, she hadn't a way to get there and was half-convinced it wasn't a real place.

"Going to the Atheneum would be a waste of time," Roz decided a short while later. Dawn was upon them, and they'd since migrated to the stern of the boat where Dev still manned the wheel. "If we're trying to catch up to the military fleet, we don't have time for a detour."

"Especially when no one knows exactly where the Atheneum is," Dev said. Roz had relayed the important elements of their earlier discussion to him, and he'd been quick to take her side. "That's the whole point. In order to protect the Atheneum's information, its location is known by as few people as possible. Hardly anyone has even been there."

"*I've* been there," Siena said impatiently, surprising them all. "Ages ago, with my grandmother. You ask the Atheneum a question, and if it contains the answer, it'll give it to you. It's up on the cliffs, just like everyone says, but accessible only by boat."

"You're just bringing this up now?" Roz frowned.

"Frankly, I didn't think it was any of your business. But it's on our way—I can get us there."

"I never said you couldn't. I just don't think it's worth it."

Dev tore his attention from the horizon. The air around them was clear again, as if the strange oppressive fog had never existed. "I'll admit, it sounds like a lot of work just to have a few questions answered."

Siena glared at them both. "By all means, if you want to go tromping into Brechaat unprepared, be my guest. But *I* would rather know if Chaos's magic is going to be a concern or not. Did you know that some people believe the Chaos disciples Ombrazia sent to their deaths were actually rescued by Brechaat? For all we know, enemy territory could be crawling with them. And if what Enzo did has made them more powerful—"

"Siena's right," Damian said tersely, speaking for the first time in quite a while. His complexion was better, Roz noticed, but there was still an unnatural tension about him as he leaned against the side of the ship, arms crossed over his chest. The early sunlight gilded his dark hair as he shifted his weight.

Roz gaped at him. "Are you really willing to lose Kiran in the name of making an unnecessary stop?"

"It's not unnecessary. If we're going to save anyone from the front, we need to know what we're up against. There's no point in trying to save them at all if we don't take the time to properly plan."

Dev said, "Why don't we just operate under the assumption that Chaos's magic *is* more powerful? We'll take the necessary precautions either way."

"And what *are* those necessary precautions?" Damian pushed off the side of the boat. His nostrils flared, a desperation about him. "Stick to the shadows and hope everything is okay? We know next to nothing about Brechaat. Everything about it was wiped from Ombrazian records ages ago. If disciples of Chaos are a true threat, we need to know how to deal with that. How to—how to free ourselves from their influence."

He tripped over the last sentence, and Roz thought she knew why. She'd felt the same helplessness during their encounter with Enzo when he'd trapped them in his illusions. The worry was understandable, she supposed, but she wasn't about to capitulate to it. "If there was a way to do that, we'd already know. Dev is right—we'll just be careful. We don't need the Atheneum."

"I said we're *going*, Rossana!" Damian's voice sliced through the air with the precision of a blade. He drew himself up to full height, lips curling back to reveal clenched teeth. His face was contorted in a fury Roz had never seen before. And there, beneath it, was something like...fear?

She knew where she'd seen this version of Damian before.

This was the way he'd looked in the illusion Enzo had shown her.

At the very least, this was the way she'd felt while looking at that false version of him. Awed and a little frightened. Not because she thought he would harm her—never that—but because she hadn't known *what* he would do. That was how she felt right now. As if she were looking at someone unfamiliar, unpredictable, with the knowledge that she could no longer trust him to protect himself.

Because she couldn't, could she? Whatever inner turmoil Damian was dealing with, it turned him into a creature guided by impulse.

"Damian," Siena said firmly, "enough. I know we're all exhausted, but we can't start yelling at one another."

Damian ignored her. He was still glaring at Roz, consternation knitting his brow, as if he could make her agree through sheer force of will. His face was inches from hers, and she stubbornly lifted a hand to shove him away.

Damian grabbed her wrist, lightning quick. His grip was warm despite the relentless mist of icy seawater. Roz didn't try to pull away.

"This isn't the Palazzo," she reminded him, narrowing her eyes. His fury had ignited her own. "You don't get to make all the decisions here."

The tilt of his mouth was unnerving. "It's a Palazzo boat, and I'm the saints-damned captain." He let her go and, with an impatient flick of his wrist, signaled Dev away from the wheel. Dev hesitated, but relinquished his position. Siena moved to Damian's side, compass at the ready, though not before directing a displeased shake of her head at Roz. As if all of this had been *her* fault.

"Come on," Roz muttered to Dev, pulling him across the ship and into the cabin. It wasn't much—a couple of cots, a desk, and a living space—but it was private and far less wet.

The second the door shut behind them, Dev turned, brows shooting up. His blond hair was dampened to a dark gold, and he clawed it back from his face. "What the hell was that?"

Roz craned her neck to peer out the tiny cabin window. As she did, the sails adjusted themselves, shivering in the wind. They were changing course in order to reach the Atheneum, no doubt. "Something's wrong with Damian."

Dev eyed her quizzically. "Besides the fact that he's an asshole, you mean?"

"He's not usually," she grumbled, collapsing into a moth-eaten chair. After being awake all night, Roz felt it might as well have been a feather bed. "Listen—when we were in the Shrine, Enzo showed me something. An illusion. In it, Damian was killing him. I saw that *before* it happened in real life." She chewed on the inside of her cheek. "I can't forget the look on Daman's face. It was as if he'd gone mad. And maybe I'm imagining things, but he looks the same way now."

"So you think he's actually losing his mind?"

"I have no idea what's going on with him. But I can't shake the feeling that Enzo was trying to...warn me, somehow." The moment she said it aloud, guilt swelled within her. Enzo had tried to kill both of them. It didn't make sense that he would try to warn Roz about anything, especially Damian. At the same time, though, he was an illusionist. He could have shown her anything at all and had chosen to show her *that*. Why?

"What would he have warned you about Damian?" Dev asked dubiously.

"Hell if I know. Maybe it wasn't a warning, then, but a threat? Maybe he *did* this to Damian."

"How?"

Roz tipped her head back, blowing out a long breath through her nose. "No idea."

"Maybe the Atheneum isn't such a bad idea after all. No—hear me out," Dev warned, because Roz had already opened her mouth to argue. "You know I want to get to Nasim as badly as you do. But a place like that might be the only way to find out exactly what disciples of Chaos are capable of. If Enzo *did* do something to Damian, we ought to know. Otherwise how can we trust him?" Dev's tone was serious. "The way he's behaving, he could ruin our chances of getting to Brechaat altogether."

"He won't."

"How can you be sure?"

She couldn't. Roz knew as much, yet couldn't bring herself to admit it.

Dev sat down beside her, suddenly looking very tired. "How the hell did we get here, Roz?"

It was a good question. A mere week ago she had been full of cautious positivity. With Forte and Battista dead, it had seemed things could only improve. So how had everything gotten *worse*?

Roz knew the answer: Falco. If you gave one person—the wrong person—too much power, the results could be devastating. In a single day, the new general had managed to turn everything upside down. She had just enough people behind her that it had simply been allowed to happen. Part of Roz wished Damian *had* killed Falco back at the prison. Without her, Salvestro would flounder. He was a man who'd never known true suffering. A coward at heart.

Roz wanted them both dead.

She clenched her fists so tightly that her nails left an ache in her palms. Did it never stop? The pressing, tightening sensation that came only from losing people you could never get back, and the soul-shredding desire to expunge it through violence?

"I don't know," she told Dev. "I don't know."

The day and night that followed were relatively uneventful. In a strange, unspoken agreement, they slept in shifts—Roz and Dev steering the ship while Damian and Siena stayed in the cabin, or vice versa. In terms of navigation, they had little to go off save Siena's compass and accompanying instruction. When Roz wasn't dozing, she hovered beside Dev in silence while he manned the wheel, her thoughts circling. Though she'd come around to the idea of stopping at the Atheneum, she was still frustrated with Damian. She yearned to speak with him, but somehow it never felt like the right time. Here they were, trapped together in the middle of the sea, and yet they might as well have been a thousand miles apart.

By the afternoon of the second day, the skies had begun to threaten rain, but Roz could still make out a rocky cliff face in the distance. The waters had become more aggressive with the proximity of land, and she nearly lost her footing as she made her way to the stern of the ship.

"Where are we?" she asked Damian and Siena, who were taking their turn at the wheel. Siena pointed in response.

At the top of the cliffs, where the earth leveled out, a thick copse of trees partially concealed an enormous building. From what Roz could see, the elaborate stone formed a semicircle where it faced the sea, wide pillars set at intervals rising above the treetops. Farther back, spires shot skyward, gray against gray, as though they were melting into the clouds.

"Is that the Atheneum?" Dev came to stand beside Roz, suppressing a yawn.

"Yes," Siena said.

Roz tilted her head to get a better look. "It looks…"

"Threatening?" Dev suggested.

Now that he said it, Roz couldn't think of a more appropriate descriptor. It reminded her a bit of the Basilica, if someone carved away all the beauty and replaced it with cold, harsh lines.

"It looks like a prison," Damian muttered.

He looked exhausted, the strain in his face growing even more pronounced as Roz drew up beside him. She wondered if he'd been sleeping at all. Noticing her proximity, Damian unfurled his fingers, holding one hand out in a silent plea. An apology?

Roz took it. His skin was too hot.

"I needed to come here," he muttered for her alone. "I need…" He trailed off, shaking his head. "Never mind."

"Tell me," she said, but Siena's voice interrupted.

"This place is exactly as I remember it."

At the intrusion, Roz wrenched her hand away from Damian's. His lips parted, and she realized too late that the abruptness of the action had hurt him.

Dev scowled up at the Atheneum, then at Siena. "Creepy as hell, you mean?"

"More or less."

Roz wiped her face, suddenly aware that the skin beneath her eyes must be stained black. "You're the one who wanted to come here."

"I was," Siena agreed. "We have questions that require answers. It doesn't mean I *like* it."

"Isn't it essentially just a huge library?" Dev asked as the ship approached what Roz could describe only as a makeshift dock. It didn't look very secure, as though any reasonably large vessel might well float away with it, but Damian didn't seem concerned. He drew up beside the wooden structure, already busy with a length of rope.

"It *is* a library," Siena told Dev. "Of sorts, anyway. You'll see what I mean."

They dismounted the ship one by one. The shore was nothing more than eroded rock, and it took Roz a moment to find purchase.

Damian leapt down beside her. "How the hell are we supposed to get up there?" he asked, tilting his head sharply to peer up the steep cliff face.

"There are stairs somewhere," Siena said, her voice grave. She pivoted, scanning their surroundings, then pointed. "Ah."

A short distance away, Roz saw, was what appeared to be the start of a treacherous staircase.

Dev groaned. "We have to *climb* up?"

"How did you think we were going to get there?" Siena's shoulders were stooped as she navigated the uneven earth. "Fly?"

It was the closest thing to a joke Roz had heard from Siena, but she couldn't bring herself to laugh. Her gaze was miles away, fixed on the horizon. As of now, there wasn't another vessel in sight, but everything in the distance was a near-invisible haze. Somewhere out there, she knew, someone was following them. It was only a matter of time before they caught up.

"How long will this take?" she asked, turning to scan the stairs where they disappeared around the cliffside. "Our boat isn't exactly inconspicuous."

"We'll be quick," Damian said. "Just as I promised."

Siena nodded, starting up the first few steps. "We'll split into pairs once we're inside. It'll be faster that way."

"We should all separate," Roz insisted. If the rumors were correct, the Atheneum was far larger than it appeared from the exterior, and she wanted to spend as little time there as possible.

"No." Siena's tone implied she would hear no argument. "The Atheneum is amazingly useful, yes, and once you're inside it'll almost always give you the answers you seek."

"But?" Roz prodded.

"*But*," Siena said, "it doesn't always like to let people back out."

12

DAMIAN

As they neared the top of the cliff, even Damian was out of breath.
It had begun to rain, and water slithered down the back of his neck,
turning his clothes heavy and uncomfortable. They hadn't spoken
throughout the climb, focused as they were on maintaining their
footing. The stairs seemed to grow more slippery with each passing
minute, and though he knew she was more than capable, Damian
hadn't been able to help watching Roz as she navigated the turns of
the staircase before him. If she fell, he would catch her. It was why
he'd opted to bring up the rear, though Roz would hate it if she knew.

He kept his eyes glued to her back, watching the sway of her
hips. The rain had turned her ponytail to a dark, whiplike thing,
and it snaked around her shoulders whenever she deigned to
glance back at him, which wasn't often.

Damian knew he'd fucked up. The way he'd spoken to her
on the boat... Well, he didn't know where that had come from.
Normally he'd never dare address Roz in such a way. She wasn't
one of his officers. Was that why she'd pulled away from his touch?

He hadn't known what else to do, though. He *needed* to
come here. If the Atheneum held all the answers, he needed to

ask how to free himself from the madness eating away at his mind. He needed to know if it was possible Enzo's influence still plagued him. Was this his penance for murdering the disciple in cold blood? Had he made a sacrifice of his own—one he hadn't intended to make?

Damian released a shuddering breath as they reached the top step, muscles screaming. Before them the Atheneum seemed to take up the entirety of their surroundings. The building felt ancient. Unfathomable. Its looming presence somehow changed the feel of the wind. Quieted it.

"Now what?" Dev's voice was too loud. He was standing directly beside Damian, their shoulders all but touching. Damian shifted away.

"Now," Siena repeated, sounding less sure than Damian was accustomed to, "we knock. Well, Roz does. The archivists prefer fellow disciples."

Without needing to be convinced, Roz broke away from their group, striding up the wide front steps to the Atheneum's towering door. Given the masterfully carved stone, Damian couldn't help wondering if it had been crafted by a disciple of Strength. Roz rapped her knuckles against the door three times, then stepped back as it opened—no—as it *slid apart*. A crack appeared directly down the middle of the colossal stone slab where there hadn't been one before, confirming Damian's suspicions. It was accompanied by a thunderous scrape that echoed from somewhere in the belly of the Atheneum, raising the hairs on his neck.

No wonder Siena spoke about the place as though it had a mind of its own. Although Damian couldn't sense it the way Roz likely could, he knew instinctively that this building was full of magic.

Damian took the steps three at a time. He didn't know *what* the hell was going to answer, and he didn't want Roz standing there alone. But as the stone parted farther, what appeared from the darkness beyond was…a woman. She held a lantern and wore a long, strange robe that was almost the exact shade as her light skin. Her hair was long, mahogany, and unbound, and her frame was terribly slim. She couldn't have been much older than Damian's mother when she'd died, but her face was sunken in a way that made her look weathered.

If Damian hadn't known better, he would have thought her more a specter than a living person. Given the dim light, he couldn't glimpse much of the room beyond, but the air that drifted out was cold and heavy, smelling vaguely of parchment and decay. It reminded him of the crypt beneath the Palazzo. Of ice at his fingertips and Death at his back.

The woman smiled, and Damian saw with a jolt that she had no teeth. How had she managed to lose them *all*? If she was an archivist, then she was a disciple of Death, and disciples would never be forced to suffer medical issues. Not while Mercy's magic existed. He'd once seen a disciple mend a broken limb with a series of careful touches.

The archivist licked her lips, tongue flicking past the fleshy pink of her gums as she assessed their group. Damian tried not to react, but he wanted nothing more than to back away from this door, flee down the cliff face, and never return.

"Good afternoon," Roz said simply. "We're looking to gain entry. We have some important questions to ask."

The archivist bobbed her head, nonplussed. If Damian hadn't known better, he might have thought their presence expected here. The woman twisted her knobby fingers together. "A disciple of Patience, yes?" Her voice was somewhere between a whine and a whisper, the least pleasant bits of each.

"Yes." As always, Roz didn't look happy to be admitting it.

"Tell me, are you hungry?"

Damian froze. It was a different voice that emanated from the archivist's mouth this time: deep and masculine, with a light rasp. The shift was far more unnerving than the odd question, but if it affected Roz as well, she didn't show it.

"Er—we're on a rather tight timeline."

"She means hungry for information," Siena muttered.

Roz's nose wrinkled. "Oh. Then yes, I suppose?"

The archivist's gummy smile widened, the skin of her cheeks stretching taut. Her flesh looked too thin over the bones of her face, as if it might rip to reveal the cartilage beneath. Unease suffused Damian's blood. There was something about this woman he didn't trust.

She stepped aside, gesturing that they should enter. "Please, do come in. Take all the time you need." When she laughed, it was a high-pitched sound that skittered off the walls. "Stay forever, if you like."

"I said we were in a rush," Roz grumbled. What Damian could see of her mouth was a tight line, but she crossed the threshold regardless.

As Dev made to follow, an arm shot out to stop him. He glared at it, then lifted his gaze to meet the archivist's. "What the hell?"

The woman shook her head, still smiling that horrible smile. Her eyes were enormous in her face. "This is not a place for the unfavored."

Damian was about five seconds from grabbing the archivist's arm and snapping it. He stepped to Dev's side. "She's not going in there alone."

Roz turned. Already it looked as though her body was being enfolded into the shadows of the Atheneum. "They're with me," she told the archivist, then addressed Siena. "I thought you'd been here before."

Siena grimaced. Clearly she hadn't anticipated this. "I have. My grandmother was a disciple of Cunning, though, and I was only a child. Neither blessed nor unfavored yet."

The archivist used her outstretched arm to push Dev aside, beckoning Damian with her free hand. "You may enter alongside your friend."

He didn't pause to ask why, lunging inside before she could change her mind. If he and Roz had to do this themselves, so be it.

Roz, though, was not content to go without Dev and Siena. "What can we give you to let them pass?" she asked the archivist.

There was a slither of light fabric on stone as the archivist stepped back, making to close the door. "There is nothing you have that I could want. I care only for knowledge."

"Perhaps we have information you don't. Something you could add to your collection."

"That is impossible." Her voice was an old man's, gravelly and weak. "And it is not *my* collection. We guard it on behalf of the saints themselves."

Damian couldn't see Roz very well, but there was a shuffle as she drew something out of her pocket. "I assume you heard about the murders committed in the heart of Ombrazia by a disciple of Chaos?"

The archivist paused. "Of course."

"How would you like the coroner's reports for the earliest victims?"

The woman's eyes narrowed, her irises black in the dark. "How do you come to have such a thing in your possession?"

The question, Damian thought, was why Roz *still* had the reports in her possession.

"Do you want them, or not?"

"Let me ensure they are genuine first."

Roz held the documents out for her to inspect, but did not let go. There was no mistaking the gleam of want in the archivist's eyes as she took in the cramped script and blacked-out sections. "What happened here?"

"The coroner was told to redact the name of the poison that killed the victims."

"And what was it?"

Roz shrugged. "Let our friends in and I'll tell you."

There was a pause, a silent collision of wills, before the archivist's mouth twisted. She stepped aside, pulling the enormous door wide with more ease than her sticklike arms ought to have allowed. "Agreed."

The moment Dev and Siena were inside, the stone slabs slammed back together, sealing them in the entryway. There was no light save for the flickering candle in the archivist's lantern, and it sent trembling orange beams up the seemingly endless walls.

"Now," the archivist said. "You must answer."

Roz thrust the coroner's reports at the woman. "It was vellenium."

"Intriguing."

The next moment, both the archivist and her light had floated away, Siena and Roz on her heels. Damian hurried to follow. He could hear Dev breathing somewhere behind him and was fighting to control his own harsh breaths when the other boy spoke.

"Scared of the dark, Venturi?"

"No," Damian said shortly. "I'm scared of being stuck in here forever. You should be, too."

Dev gave a soft snort. "I think the archivist was joking when she said that."

The archivist didn't strike Damian as the joking type. But he said nothing more as they caught up to the others, footsteps echoing on the stone floor. How was this a library at all? Where were the *books*? He tipped his head back, unable to make out the ceiling. He knew it had to be there—after all, they'd seen the roof from outside—but from within there was nothing but infinite darkness.

"Do not look up." The archivist's soft voice sounded from just beside his left ear, and Damian started, backing away from her. How had she moved so quickly? "You need not be concerned with what is up. What you desire is *down*." The archivist pointed at another, smaller doorway. She was grinning once again, and Damian found himself wishing she wouldn't.

There were a number of lanterns lining the wall beside the door, and the archivist stooped to light two more. One she handed to Roz, the other to Siena. When she straightened, robe rippling like wrinkled skin around her ankles, she said, "When you are ready, you may open the door. Please do not disturb the dead."

Damian tilted his head to the side, blinking as he tried to digest her words.

"I'm sorry," Roz said. "Did you say 'the dead'?"

The archivist nodded. "May you find the information you came for." Her voice was that of a child now—the most horribly unsettling variation Damian had heard so far. And then she was gone, brushing past them into the dark, her lantern flickering into nothingness.

Damian gaped at her back until it disappeared, then turned to Siena. "Are there a few things you forgot to tell us about this place?"

Her smile was mirthless. "I warned you, the Atheneum doesn't always like to let people out. They get sucked in by the promise of unending answers and never want to leave. They stop caring about everything else, and time passes without them noticing. They forget things like exhaustion or hunger. Eventually, they can waste away and die. That's why I said we ought to go in pairs."

"If people are dying in there," Roz said slowly, "what happens to their bodies?"

Siena grasped the ancient iron handle of the door, giving it a shove. It swung open, sending a blast of frigid air in their direction. "It's cold in the heart of the Atheneum, and kept perfectly dry so as not to harm any of the parchment. I've heard Mercy's magic might be involved as well, since the bodies simply mummify."

This was a disturbing thought. Disciples of Mercy tended to be healers above all, but perhaps their power was capable of more unsavory things as well. Then again, maybe the rules of magic as Damian understood them didn't apply in the Atheneum.

Dev mimed gagging. "You don't think that was pertinent to share beforehand?"

"What difference would it have made?"

"I would have been more emotionally prepared."

"You'll be fine," Roz told him, though she didn't look thrilled at the prospect of walking through a dark, freezing library where one could potentially encounter mummified dead people. "We'll go in, ask our questions, then come right back out."

Siena nodded, using her lantern to illuminate yet another stairwell. "Damian, you and I will stay together. Roz and Dev, don't lose sight of each other. The stacks are organized by topic, so you need to walk among them until you come across a subject that might be useful. Once you do, write your question down, then burn the parchment. If the Atheneum has the answer, the book containing it will fall from the shelves. Assuming it is, in fact, a book. Information here exists in a number of formats. So," she added, an afterthought, "watch your heads."

Dev gave Siena a look that suggested he thought she'd lost her mind. Damian, however, was focused on the fact that he would not be partnered with Roz. He wanted to argue, but had to admit this way made the most sense. It wouldn't be fair to have Siena and Dev together, given that they scarcely knew each other.

"I can see you worrying," Roz murmured beside his ear. The warmth of her body was a sobering juxtaposition to the cold air emanating from the doorway.

"I'm not worried. I just don't like that this place has magic we don't understand."

"We're here *because* of magic we don't understand," she reminded him. "In fact, you made sure of it."

Damian said nothing. She wasn't wrong, but how could he tell her the real reason he'd been so desperate to come?

Together they walked into the mouth of the stairwell. It was a great marble thing that spiraled down into the earth; it was very much like walking into a giant silo. Books, manuscripts, scrolls, and old newspapers lined the walls of their descent—more books than Damian had ever seen in his life. It was difficult to pay attention to them, however, given the cold that slunk into his bones. It was cold in a way he'd never experienced before, and each time he exhaled, the cloud of his breath dissipated so fast it might have been snatched from his very lungs. Goose bumps skittered along his skin, and he heartily regretted his exposed arms.

Roz lifted her lantern as they descended, illuminating shelves upon shelves that seemed to have no end. Faded plaques were visible at intervals: The one closest to them read HISTORY OF THE OMBRAZIAN MILITARY, 1052–1053.

"How far down does this go?" Damian asked, his voice reverberating back to him.

"Far." Siena trailed her fingers over the spines running alongside the stairs. They came away dusty, and she wiped them on her trousers. "I told you—the Atheneum contains a copy of every work of nonfiction ever published in or about this area. The archivists have been maintaining it for centuries. Millennia, maybe. I wouldn't be surprised if it goes past sea level, and you saw how long it took us to get to the top of the cliff."

They came to a fork in the staircase, which split off into two and continued on in opposite directions. Damian's stomach tightened. Roz's face was gilded by the amber light, her pupils enormous. She was excited, Damian realized, and somehow it made him more loath to let her go on without him.

"All right," Siena said. "Damian and I will go left. Roz, you and Dev take the right. Remember, look at the plaques to see if you've entered a section that might be useful. We'll meet back here in an hour."

Roz nodded, the set of her mouth determined.

"Are there likely to be more archivists down here?" Dev asked. "I just want to know if we should be concerned, should we come across someone *not* dead."

"Why would you be concerned?" Roz answered before Siena could. "They won't bite." She snickered at her own joke.

Siena did not laugh. "The archivists remove their own teeth to symbolize the fact that they consume only knowledge."

Damian cringed, and he saw Roz's amusement fade. "Saints."

"*If* you come across anyone else, ignore them. Especially if it's someone who's been wandering the stacks for a while. They're beyond help at this point." Siena caught Damian's eye. "Ready?"

He nodded, turning to say something to Roz before they separated—what, he didn't quite know—but she was already gone. Emptiness spread through his veins.

"Yeah. I'm ready."

13

DAMIAN

The stairway leveled out to reveal a long hallway enclosed by impossibly tall shelves. The flame from Siena's lantern pulsed valiantly against the dim, but it did little to reveal what lay beyond. Everything smelled like old leather and smoke, and the air was cold in Damian's nostrils. He saw Siena shivering with each step and knew he wasn't alone in his suffering, but neither of them said a word.

FAUNA OF SOUTHERN OMBRAZIA, the plaque on the shelf to his left read. Beyond it, SPECIES ENDANGERED BETWEEN 350 AND 1000.

"This isn't right," Damian muttered, eyes scanning EDIBLE CREATURES AND THEIR MANY USES. "We should be looking for something about magic, or maybe history."

Siena furrowed her brow. "Everything is grouped by subject. Apart from that, I don't think there's any order to it. I guess we just keep walking until we find what we need. And," she added, "maybe we never will. Roz and Dev might find it first."

"How come you know so much about this place?" Damian wondered. "I thought you said you'd only been here once."

-Damian fought to swallow past the ache in his chest. "I didn't know that."

Siena shrugged, a wistful smile on her lips. "My grandmother had lived with us all my life. When they started drafting younger soldiers, she was terrified I'd be sent up north. She was desperate to know if I had any chance of being a disciple. Since my mother didn't know which saint my father was descended from, or how close a descendant he might have been, we had no idea what my chances were. The waiting tortured my grandmother. Eventually, she brought me here. Took me into the heart of the Atheneum and found the section that delineated the history of every Ombrazian family. Then she asked about my father."

"And?" Damian said softly, dreading the answer for reasons he couldn't put into words.

Siena shrugged. "Nothing of interest. Supposedly he was very, *very* distantly related to a disciple of Grace, which meant I wasn't likely to be blessed. And honestly, I think my grandmother's disappointment that day was worse than if we'd just waited to find out. She was desperate for good news, you know? Her side of the family had been steadily losing magic for generations. She wanted something more for me. And though it wasn't my fault, I felt like I'd let her down."

Damian shook his head, though he understood the sentiment perfectly. "But you didn't. It sounds like she cared about you enough that she wanted your life to be easier than your mother's was. Free from any suffering."

"Oh, yes," Siena agreed. "My grandmother loved harder than anyone I've ever known. I was a kid, though, and I couldn't help feeling like I'd wasted her time. We'd come all the way here only to get the answer neither of us wanted." She heaved a sigh, but it carried a note of acceptance.

Damian huffed a laugh. It seemed to get stuck in the back of his throat, and he let the conversation lapse into silence for a breath. "I'm sorry."

"Why?"

"I know what it's like to feel you've let someone down."

"Ah." Siena worried her lower lip. "Yes, I suppose you do. But my grandmother did her best to show me it wasn't my fault, and eventually I began to believe it."

Damian's father had never done such a thing. Never went out of his way to make Damian feel better about being born unfavored. As if it were somehow *his* fault he hadn't been blessed, and not a matter of chance. As if he'd somehow proven himself unworthy in the womb. "I'm glad."

They continued walking through the tall, narrow tunnels of the Atheneum, turning every so often when the topics didn't become more useful. Damian hadn't a clue how much time was passing, but given the way Siena continued resolutely onward, he felt confident their hour wasn't yet up. He wondered how Roz and Dev were doing. If they'd come across anything helpful.

He wondered why Roz hadn't said a word to him before allowing the dark to swallow her up.

"Oh, *shit*." Siena abruptly halted, dragging Damian from his thoughts. The orange light was a wavering glow against her brown skin, and her eyes were large as she stared straight ahead.

"What?" Damian followed her gaze, any other questions dying in his throat.

The archivist hadn't been lying about the bodies.

It wasn't that he thought she was, but part of him hadn't truly been expecting to come across one. Surely any dead were removed by the archivists as soon as they were discovered?

Apparently that was not the case.

In the corridor up ahead, a body lay propped up against the nearest bookcase. It was slightly hunched over, as if the person had slid down the books' spines to collapse in a final resting place. A chin rested against a hollowed chest, and spindly fingers caressed the stone floor, one of the hands having been thrust out as if to break a fall. The second hand rested on the dead woman's stomach.

Because it *was* a woman, Damian saw as they grew nearer. Her skin was sallow, jaundiced, and waxy. Her clothes were quite nice, and her hair was still mostly intact, though it looked as though it would pull away from the scalp with a gentle touch. The sweet, nauseating stink of the dead didn't accompany her. It was like she'd been mummified, just as Siena had said.

He crouched beside the woman, noting the ridges of bone beneath the stretch of yellowish skin. Her eyes were closed, her jaw slightly open where it rested against her chest.

"Dehydration," Siena said from behind him. "She would have wandered down here for days."

Damian straightened. "How come neither of us feels the desire to stay here? I mean, I don't know about you, but I can't wait to leave. How do people simply stop caring about their own lives?"

"We only came to ask one question. But the more you ask, and the more answers you receive, the more you want to know. You become frenzied, more desperate in your search for the right shelves, the right subject. For some people, it consumes them."

"And if it consumes us?"

"It won't. Like I said—one question." Siena directed her light away from the corpse. "It's sort of like gambling. If you make one bet, it's not that difficult to walk away. It's when you're in too deep, when you're certain the next round will be the one, that you should start worrying. Besides, we're together. It's hard to get sucked in when you're not alone."

Damian hoped to hell she was right. He let his gaze follow the line of the dead woman's slumped form, all the way over to the plaque beside which she lay. His heart gave a jolt. "Wait."

Siena, who had already taken a couple of steps, turned. "What is it?"

He pointed at the plaque, which read simply: SAINTS AND THEIR MAGIC.

"Oh." Siena blinked, then frowned. "What a place to collapse. Good eye, though." She traced the spines of a few books, blowing on her finger when it came away dusty. "All right. Let's start with something broad."

"Was Enzo truly the seventh sacrifice?" Damian suggested.

"I said *broad*, Damian. How is the Atheneum supposed to know who Enzo was? How about: What happens if you make sacrifices to a specific saint?"

Now it was Damian's turn to consider. "That's *too* broad. There could be hundreds of answers. Ask if sacrifices make a saint's magic more powerful."

"That's a good idea, actually," Siena yanked a book free from the corner of the nearest shelf.

"What are you doing?"

She didn't respond right away. The book was very like a journal, and there was a pen tucked into its spine. Damian watched as Siena plucked the pen loose, then blanched when she ripped one of the pages free. It made a horrible tearing noise, far too loud in the silence.

"What are you doing?" he hissed. It wasn't like her to vandalize, especially in a place like this.

Siena shot him an impatient look. "I told you, the question needs to be written down. There's a notebook above every plaque. Here—hold this." She thrust the lantern at Damian, who saw no option but to take it. Siena tore a corner off the page she'd removed from the notebook and scrawled their question down in small, cramped writing. When she finished, she gestured for him to give the lantern back. Perplexed, Damian did so.

"I don't see why we're—"

Before he could finish his statement, Siena removed the top of the lantern and dropped the piece of parchment into the flame. Damian sucked in a breath, watching it blacken and curl, sending tendrils of smoke slithering upward.

"And this works how, exactly?"

"You'll see." Siena tipped her head back.

Damian copied her. The smoke kept rising, he saw, rather than dissipating as it should have. In fact, it seemed to grow oddly brighter as it went up, up toward the unfathomable dark of the ceiling.

Then it was gone.

A moment later, there was a trembling. Barely enough movement to notice, but loud enough that Damian leapt back, narrowly avoiding the dead woman. His numb skin prickled, though this time he didn't think it was from the cold.

"Watch out," Siena advised, and not a moment too soon.

Damian heard the book wriggle loose from somewhere up above them. It dropped through the air and landed with a reverberating *thud* on the hard stone, exactly where he'd been standing only a moment prior. The sound was deafening as a gunshot. Damian jumped, and even Siena winced, though she must have been expecting it.

She knelt beside the book, which was titled *Saints and Sacrifice: The Unredacted Publications.*

Damian loosed a breath as she opened it. He knew the book well, of course—it was the title of the tome from which all his knowledge of the saints derived. It was the book his father had read him every night before bed, the book he'd been forced to pray over, and the book that lined the pews in the Basilica.

Except it *wasn't* that book, was it? Not exactly, anyway.

"There's an unredacted version?" he said to Siena, who looked equally as shocked. She flipped through the pages, shaking her head.

"I suppose there has to be, doesn't there? The one you and I grew up with says hardly anything about Chaos. It has the origin story, of course, and the tale about him and Patience, but that can't be all there ever was." She glanced over her shoulder, as if she'd heard something Damian hadn't. "We're running low on time. If anything about sacrifices was removed from this book, where do you think it would've been?"

Damian gave an involuntary shiver. His lips were beginning to lose feeling. "Go to the part where humanity learned about war. I don't think there were any killings prior to that."

Siena nodded, turning to the section with confidence. She, too, had grown up with the stories. One finger traced the faded lettering as she scanned the pages. Damian peered over her shoulder.

"There," he said. "That's where Chaos comes in, followed by Death and Mercy."

She turned the page, then gasped.

Damian drew back at the image that awaited them. He hadn't known there *were* images in *Saints and Sacrifice*. Certainly there weren't any in the copies he'd read. This version, though, showed a disturbing black-and-white rendering of one man disemboweling another. Even without shades of red, the accuracy of the image was such that Damian had no difficulty identifying what were clearly organs. There was a shadow in the background, and although it was nothing more than an outline, the lines of the shrouded head meant it had to be one of the saints. Watching.

Watching a *sacrifice*.

That wasn't the part that made Damian's skin crawl, though. The worst bit about the sketch was the expression on the first man's face. He was committing a murder, his arms coated from fingers to elbow in the second man's blood, not a weapon in sight. As though he were clawing his companion apart with his bare hands. All the while, his mouth was frozen in an eternal scream, his eyes wide in unfocused horror. Something dark ran down his chin, blackening his teeth.

"What," Siena said, her voice hushed, "is *this*?"

Damian had thought it quite obvious. It was someone possessed by an unholy force, tearing apart his fellow man before his patron saint.

"Read," he croaked as something deep inside him detached.

Siena did, first in her head, then aloud in what Damian assumed was a summary. He scarcely paid attention. His head was full of the drawing. Of the sheer terror on the man's face, and how he thought—just maybe—he knew the feeling.

"Damian." Siena's voice came again. "Are you listening to me? It says it right here, in the original source. People sacrificed one another before their patron saints in an attempt to make their magic grow stronger. Seven sacrifices, and each offering must be laid to rest with a symbol of their chosen saint."

"Chthonium," Damian murmured, thinking of the black orbs Enzo had used to replace his victims' eyes.

"Yes, I suppose you could use that for Chaos. Do you know what this means? It says right here: *If the ritual was successful, all the saint's children would feel it and be imbued with that saint's power.*" Siena's fingers were shaking as she flipped the page yet again, mercifully covering the drawing. "We were right. That woman you spoke to in the prison was right. Disciples of Chaos might be more powerful than ever before." She slammed the book shut, shoulders tense. "The only question is, why wasn't anyone doing this long before Enzo? Who wouldn't want power like that?"

Damian took the book from her, turning it over in his hands. He didn't have an answer. He wanted to say *Saints and Sacrifice* was full of nothing but stories. The saints had ruled his life for too long, and he had only just begun to let them go. But what if there were kernels of truth in every myth? What if the stories about the origins of the world lay alongside something very, very real?

Something like magic?

He could feel himself coming undone again. *Not here*, he thought to himself, panic racing through his blood as his heart sped up. *Not now*.

His body, though, wouldn't listen. Or was it his mind that refused his pleas? Damian didn't know. He needed to find out what was happening to him. He'd hoped to find a more subtle way to go about it—whispering questions where Siena couldn't hear, perhaps—but there was no time. No way to hide from her, nor anyone else.

He thought of the face in the drawing and wondered what his own looked like.

Shoving the book under his arm, he grabbed the lantern and ran like hell.

14

Roz

Roz was grumpy, starving, and colder than she'd ever been in her life. She and Dev hadn't found anything useful. The Atheneum was a maze of endless, dark corridors. Her nose was full of dust. She'd stuffed her hands under her armpits in an effort to regain some feeling in her fingers, but so far it was proving futile.

"I hate this place," she grumbled for what must have been the twentieth time, squinting at the plaques. How could it be that the topics were becoming even *less* relevant?

"You don't say." Dev gave a long-suffering sigh, and Roz cut him a look.

"You know how the archivist said there were corpses down here? How would *you* like to be one of them?"

"I would not," he said, unperturbed. Roz had passed the lantern to him some time ago, and his fingers were white-tipped on the handle. The cold pebbled the skin of his bare arms, which looked paler than ever in the dim light. "Don't you think it's time to turn around?"

Roz made a noise in the back of her throat. She didn't like the idea of leaving before they'd accomplished anything, but they needed to regroup. Hopefully Damian and Siena had found the right section of the Atheneum. Why didn't the archivists provide a map of this accursed place?

"Yeah," Roz said. "We don't want them to think we got lost."

Dev nodded, turning to go back the way they'd come. He was even less interested in the tomes than Roz, who found it difficult to be interested in anything when she was so cold.

"Do you think Nasim is okay?" he said as they retraced their path.

Roz shrugged, scowling at a plaque that said BLOODLETTING, and beside that, METHODS OF CENTRIFUGE. Who the hell had organized these shelves? "She'd better be. I'm trying not to think about it."

"I can't *not* think about it."

"Nasim can take care of herself. At least until that ship reaches the front."

Dev made a noncommittal sound.

Roz shot him a sideways glance. "When are you two finally going to admit you're obsessed with each other?"

"What?" he sputtered, reddening. "Obsessed? I'm not—we're not—"

"Do you take me for a fool, Dev Villeneuve?"

Dev groaned, tugging at the ends of his hair, which had finally dried to its regular golden shade. "It's complicated, okay?"

"Because you're afraid we won't get her back? We *will*."

He went silent for a moment, avoiding Roz's eyes. Her heart lurched.

"What is it?"

When Dev finally met her gaze, his was strangely emotionless. "I'm not ready to care about someone only to lose them again."

The words seemed to skewer Roz, and for a moment she didn't know what to say in response. "You already care about Nasim, though."

"Yeah. But either of us could die. Hell, *all* of us could."

"So?"

"So, I feel like if I don't say anything...maybe it won't hurt so much."

It wasn't that Roz hadn't considered these possibilities, only that she didn't want to dwell on them. What good would it do to worry when it was too late to change course? When she didn't *want* to change course?

She knew why Dev felt that way, though. It had only been a couple of months since he'd found Amélie dead. And saints, she couldn't blame him for being afraid to care about people. Look at what had happened to her father. To Piera. Even to her mother. Roz had loved them—loved her mother still, of course—but most of that love had turned to grief. When you loved someone, then lost them, love could sour and turn poisonous. It could sit in your veins like a toxic sludge and make you want to claw your heart out. Would loving someone quietly, though, not have much the same effect?

"I get it," she told Dev, because it was the truth. She couldn't begrudge him that when she was so tired of hurting, too.

If he had anything more to say, he kept it to himself.

They were nearly back to where they'd separated from Siena and Damian, the wide mouth of the stairway stretching out ahead of them like a gaping maw. Roz adjusted her shirt, trying to cover more of her exposed skin, then froze when she heard someone call her name.

"*Rossana.*"

She turned, peering down one of the corridors she and Dev hadn't searched, and was bewildered to see Damian stumble into the light.

He was breathing as though he'd just ran a marathon, eyes wild. Roz opened her mouth and shut it again, taking in the panicked heave of his chest, his burnt-out lantern, and the way he clawed at the books nearest to him. It didn't make sense that he was here. And why was he alone?

"Give me that." She snatched the lantern from Dev, inclining her head toward the stairwell. "Head back to our meeting point, just in case Siena shows up."

Dev was watching Damian with something that might have been fear. He began a slow retreat, like someone trying to circumvent a sleeping beast. "Are you going to be okay with him?"

"Of course. *Go.*"

The moment Dev disappeared into the stairwell, Roz stepped closer to Damian. He was holding the edge of the bookshelf, white-knuckled, as though it were the only thing keeping him upright. His face was wan, pale in a way she hadn't seen since they were children and he'd contracted the stomach flu.

"Roz." He said her name again, and it came out a pant. "I was right."

She didn't know what that was supposed to mean. Carefully she set down the lantern, bending to look him in the eye. "Are you okay? Where's Siena?"

No response.

"What were you right about?"

Damian clenched his teeth together, drawing himself back up to full height. It was only then that Roz noticed he was carrying a book under his other arm.

"What did you find?"

"*Saints and Sacrifice: The Unredacted Publications,*" he hissed, and indeed the gold lettering on the spine spelled out just that. "I need you to listen to me, Roz. Can you listen to me?"

She plucked the book from beneath his elbow. It was old and handwritten, the binding peeling away from the pages. Damian made to grab for it, but Roz held it out of reach. "Talk. I'm listening."

He huffed in frustration, the muscles of his arm flexing as he unclenched his fists, stretching his fingers. "We were right about Chaos's magic growing stronger. This version of *Saints and*

Sacrifice confirms it, assuming you believe the stories in there. Enzo did everything right. He was the final sacrifice."

"Okay," Roz said, vaguely disturbed but not altogether shocked. They'd assumed as much—it was merely a matter of having the Atheneum confirm it. "Okay, we'll just have to be extra careful once we've crossed the border. Make sure we encounter as few people as possible."

"That wasn't the only thing the woman in the prison said." Damian abruptly switched topics, scrubbing a hand through his hair as if he wanted to rip it out. "I asked her about Enzo. About what disciples of Chaos can do, and what they can do to *us*."

Roz didn't need him to explain further. It was becoming clear she and Damian had been asking themselves the same questions. "You think Enzo's magic is still inside you somehow."

He exhaled, the flex of his jaw creating a sharp angle. His expression was pure, undiluted distress. "You knew? I—"

"I didn't know anything," she said. It wasn't a lie, either. As for whether such a thing was even possible...well, Roz didn't know. She wanted to hear what Damian had found inside that book.

His face contorted as if in pain. "That woman told me Chaos's magic can linger. And that book"—he gestured at it with disgust—"confirms as much. It can happen. It *is* happening. I'm all wrong inside. I can feel it, and it's getting worse. But the worse it gets, the less I care." Damian took a step closer to her, mouth a daggered line. The pain had shifted to something darker, vaguely threatening, and Roz believed him. She believed the wrongness, and that it had nothing to do with trauma. For the first time in her life, she felt a thrill of fear in Damian's presence.

"Enzo's dead," she told him needlessly.

"Yes." Damian tilted his head. His squeezed his eyes shut, brow creasing. "I murdered him. Saints, it felt so fucking good."

Roz slapped him hard across the face.

She hadn't meant to. Or at least, she hadn't planned on it. It was just such a not-Damian thing to say that she felt the sudden, panicked need to try and wrench it out of him.

"*Damn it*, Roz." He put a hand to his cheek. Pink was already blooming beneath the surface of his skin. "You think I don't know that's messed up?"

"You hated killing Enzo," she told him fiercely. "I tried telling you you'd done the right thing, but you didn't want to hear it."

"I hated it after, yes. At the time, though, it felt right." Damian flinched beneath Roz's gaze. "That was when I first knew something was wrong. I just didn't want to pay attention to it. I couldn't, with everything else going on. Thinking you were—" He shook his head, lip curling over his teeth. "I don't understand. How I can still be affected like this, with Enzo gone. I couldn't find anything in that stupid book about what happens if the disciple who controlled you dies. What if this never goes away?"

Roz turned the book over in her hands, flipping it open. The spine gave easily, worn from years of use. It opened to a story she knew well:

They say it rained the day Chaos fell from grace.

It didn't end there, though. Where the story she knew was short and concise, this one continued past the line about Patience knowing precisely when to strike. The script was smaller in the subsequent section, as though intended to be a footnote.

When Patience saw the damage Chaos had wrought on earth, and how the extent of his power had altered him, she realized he needed to be contained. She had watched far too many of their children fall. And thus she took up her blade and slew her lover herself.

The rivers spilled over with her tears, and Death, her loyal friend, made her an offer: If Patience was willing to give up her humanity, Death would use it to retrieve Chaos from the beyond and bestow upon him a mortal life.

Patience accepted Death's offer, and so was Chaos revived. But the moment breath returned to his lungs, Patience became untethered from the mortal plane, the connection between the lovers severed. They were no longer two halves of a whole. They no longer balanced each other in power, for what use is a man to a saint?

And so was Chaos struck from the pantheon, condemned to walk the earth a harmless mortal, while Patience became the first to ascend to the next realm. The other saints eventually followed, their own humanity lost to time and magic.

Never again did the lovers' paths cross.

"Patience is the true reason Chaos fell?" Roz said, gaping. "Why was that removed from circulated copies?"

Damian shrugged, but the question had been rhetorical. She already knew the answer.

"Because it doesn't fit the narrative." Roz stared at the words without really seeing them. Had Patience *died* for her lover in the end, then? Was that what the story meant when it said she'd ascended to the next realm? "Surely the Palazzo wouldn't want anyone to know Patience gave up anything for *Chaos*. And having the original Chaos die as a mortal man makes him seem far less dangerous than he's supposed to be."

"I suppose," Damian said, though she could tell he wasn't overly worried about it. "There's more. Go to page one hundred thirty-eight—that's the story I'm worried about."

Roz did. The script on the page in question was cramped, flowery, and difficult to decipher. She skimmed until she found the part Damian had surely been referring to. Her stomach churned, and she lifted her head.

"You said it yourself, Damian—these are all just *stories*, like the kind you read to a child. They're meant to make people feel as if they understand the world. It's not a book of information."

"So?"

"*So*, just because it's in the book doesn't mean it's happening to you." The page Damian wanted her to see told the tale of a man who escaped a disciple of Chaos, only to find that the disciple still controlled him. She slammed the book shut. "These are fearmongering tales for Ombrazian children. This kind of stuff was probably passed around even before the disciples of Chaos were banished."

"That doesn't mean it's not true," Damian argued. "Siena and I asked a question, and this book is what we received in answer. That must mean something."

"Is that why you left Siena? To read this on your own?"

He drew a hand down his face, pausing when it covered his mouth so that his reply came out muffled. "Yes. I don't know what I was thinking. I didn't want her to ask why I was interested, so I just…left her." He swore again, this time with more feeling. "Saints, what was I *thinking*?"

"We'd better go make sure she found her way back," Roz said. The last thing she wanted to do was spend more time in this place searching for a lost member of their party. "I'll bring the book. We can take a closer look at it on the ship, and try to figure out what to do." If what Damian had said about the sacrifices was true, Enzo's magic might be the least of their worries. How many living disciples of Chaos were out there, potentially finding themselves with newfound power?

"I really doubt we're allowed to take anything with us," he said, dubious.

"Oh, so *now* you're concerned with morality?" Roz clutched the book to her chest, teeth chattering. If they didn't get out of here soon, she was going to turn into a human icicle. "Come on."

♦ ♦ ♦

As it turned out, Siena had found her way back to the stairwell, and she was furious. Roz didn't intervene as she yelled at Damian for abandoning her.

"What the hell *was* that?" Siena fumed, angrier than Roz had ever heard her. Her expression as she stared at Damian, though, was nothing short of utter bewilderment. "And after I had *just* explained why it was important to navigate the Atheneum in pairs? You're lucky I had a packet of matches on me. What if I'd never found my way out?" Siena shook her head in disgust. "If I didn't still consider you my commander, Damian, I'd hit you. I swear on the saints I would."

"I already did," Roz advised, not blaming Siena one bit for her rage. Had Damian left *her* in the dark of the Atheneum, alone and unable to see a thing, she would have wanted to do far worse.

"Siena, I am so sorry." Damian shook his head as if to clear it. "I don't know what came over me."

She was not appeased. "What were you *doing*? Why did you take off?"

His lips parted, but no sound came out. Roz stilled, waiting to hear if he would speak the truth. If he planned to tell the others about his fears and what they'd learned.

"I thought I saw...something," Damian said lamely.

"But you didn't bother to warn her?" This was Dev, suspicion written in the creases around his eyes.

Saints. This was never going to work—not if their group was rife with tension and distrust.

"Tell them the truth," Roz said, and Damian whirled, wide-eyed, like he couldn't believe her betrayal. She understood his panic: He was accustomed to being a leader. To presenting a front of confidence and capability. But they couldn't go on like this.

Damian dug his nails into the side of his face, eyes shuttering as Siena and Dev watched him with guarded expressions. He sighed. Then he told them what he'd told Roz, albeit more calmly than he had before. Siena softened, the frustrated set of her mouth shifting into concern.

"Is that even possible?" she asked, referring to what Damian had suggested about the remnants of Enzo's magic. "Why would it still be affecting you, and not the rest of us?"

He offered an odd twitch that nearly passed for a shrug. "I've no idea. Why it would only affect me, I mean. It *is* possible, at least according to the book I found." Damian inclined his head at the tome Roz still held in the crook of her arm. "It's a collection of stories, but at the very least it proves this isn't a new concept."

Siena started, seeming to really look at Roz for the first time since they'd returned to the stairwell. "Why do you have that?" She glanced back to Damian. "Why does she have that? Books can't be removed from the Atheneum. Nothing can."

"We can't just leave it here," Roz insisted. "And we don't have time to read it right now. What if it can tell us more?"

Siena didn't answer. Instead she snatched the book from Roz's grasp so fast that Roz didn't have the chance to fend her off. "Do you have any idea what would happen if we tried to leave with this?"

Nobody said a word.

"Nothing. *Nothing* would happen," Siena continued, "because the Atheneum wouldn't allow us to leave at all." She chucked the book down the stairs where it landed with a deafening thud, pages splayed open on the stone floor. "We'll have to figure this out on our own. At the very least, we found what we came for."

Roz bit down hard on the inside of her cheek. She knew Siena was right, but it felt like a mistake, leaving that book behind in the dark. Damian must have felt the same—everything about his posture was resigned as they followed Siena out of the stairwell.

To Roz's distinct horror, the archivist was waiting for them. She melted out of the shadows like a specter, her toothless mouth set in a disconcerting smile.

"Did you find what you came for?" she asked in a singsong voice, and something about the way she framed the question suggested she knew exactly what they'd been looking for.

"Yes," Siena said. "Thank you."

That smile didn't falter. "It's polite to put things back where you found them, you know."

Roz frowned. The archivist couldn't be talking about the book on Chaos's magic—could she? She had no way of knowing where they'd left it.

"We do know," Siena advised the woman, sidestepping her to get to the main entrance.

Dev gave a polite dip of his head. "Please accept our apologies if anything is out of place."

The archivist only watched him go with an impassive gaze.

Roz was the last to follow, and as she did, the woman's hand shot out to grab her wrist. Her grasp was tight, almost viselike, and far too cold to be natural. Roz whirled, grabbing the archivist's bony forearm, prepared to fight.

The archivist's face, though, held no vitriol. Her eyes were huge and serious as they trapped Roz's.

"Remember the story," she said, quietly enough that none of the others could hear. "Remember how it ends."

Roz's frown deepened. "What?"

The archivist released her, smile returning so fast it was alarming.

And then she was gone, engulfed by the shadows of the Atheneum once more.

15

MILOS

When Milos reached the river pass that separated Ombrazia from Brechaat, someone was waiting for him.

It was a young man he didn't recognize, though something about him was oddly familiar. His hair was reddish-brown, his face tired but good-natured. He stood at the edge of the water, staring out into the dark, as if he could see something there that Milos couldn't.

"You feel it, too, don't you?" the man said, his voice nearly lost in the wind. "You're not the first one to show up here."

Milos didn't know what the man meant. Or at least, he was certain they couldn't be thinking of the same thing.

"Forgive me," he said. "I'm in rather a hurry. I need passage on a boat headed—"

"South," the man finished for him. "Right?"

Milos halted. The young man turned, and abruptly Milos realized where he had seen him before. He dropped to a knee. "Forgive me," he said. "I did not recognize you."

The man motioned for him to rise. The gesture was impatient, but lightly amused. "I've been looking for you, Milos Petrescu. You went farther than the rest."

✦ ✦ ✦

There was a place few people knew about in the mountains of northeastern Ombrazia, close to the border with Brechaat. That was where Milos had been brought following the fateful day he'd been taken from his family.

He'd been blindfolded at the time, but he'd seen what the place looked like on the day he left. The exterior was set in the mountainside, dark and imposing, though smaller than he would have anticipated. It looked as if it had been built in a rush, for there was little of note about the wide stone slabs and formless entryway. It was nothing like the carved opulence of the Ombrazian temples. Milos had known why: This was a place in which to be forgotten.

By the time he arrived there he had stopped crying, too exhausted from hours of panicking to muster a reaction. Even at thirteen, he'd already accepted the inevitable.

Milos had heard the scrape of the great stone doors against the rock floor. A putrid smell rushed from behind them, and he immediately retched. There was nothing in his stomach to bring up, or he surely would have choked on more than bile. For a boy who had not yet encountered death, he knew inherently that he had just inhaled the scent of it.

Strong hands prodded him forward, and the ground began to slope. His teeth chattered in fear and trepidation. The sound of his footsteps echoed close by, and Milos knew the space around him had narrowed as they descended deeper into the earth. The smell grew worse, but he could do nothing save bear it. He didn't know how long he walked, shuffling along that uneven stone ground, but it felt like an eternity. There was a noise like rusty hinges squealing open. He resumed sobbing quietly as he stepped forward, anticipating that he would enter some kind of cell, but then the floor dropped out from under him.

He fell with a cry, though the drop wasn't far. His limbs crumpled on the hard stone beneath him. Pain radiated along the length of his body.

The hinges screeched again, and this time the sound came from above. A clang followed.

Alone, Milos had removed the blindfold and looked up into darkness.

Footsteps retreated.

He knew they would not return.

"You were there," Milos told the young man. "The day they got me out. You and your father."

The man waved his words away, but he was smiling. Last Milos had seen him, he'd been only a boy. His face had been rounder, though equally serious. He'd been shorter, too, and less muscled than he was now. There was no doubt, however, that this was one of the people who had rescued him from the oubliettes in the Forgotten Keep.

Or at least, that was what the Brechaans called it. Milos doubted the Ombrazians bothered to speak of it at all. Certainly he had never heard his parents mention such a place.

Now, of course, he knew it was where the Palazzo sent disciples of Chaos. They rooted them out as children, taking them north and locking them up underground, where they were left to die. The Brechaans knew of the place, Milos soon learned, and always came to rescue the Ombrazian youth. They had pulled him out of the darkness, tossing the body of one of their own dead in his place. It didn't matter what the deceased looked like, they told him—by the time anyone bothered to check the oubliettes, the body wouldn't be recognizable anyway.

"I know you want to leave," the man said. "I can feel the pull, too. So can every other disciple of Chaos. I don't know what it is or why it makes us more powerful, but I'm not sure it can be trusted."

Milos *did* feel the pull, and wanted nothing more than to seek out its source. But if there was anyone in Brechaat to whom he ought to listen, it was the man before him now. How many disciples had he and his father rescued from the keep over the years? How much had they done for Brechaat as a whole? It was an honor to be before him. It was a blessing to be alive.

"You said you'd been seeking me out," Milos said. "What is it I can do for you?"

The man inclined his head at the hill that rose up behind him. The medallions on his jacket flashed in the moonlight. "Why don't you follow me?"

16

ROZ

The hours that followed were relatively uneventful, and that, more than anything else, made Roz nervous.

They'd returned to find the ship exactly as they'd left it, which should have been a relief but felt more like an improbable twist of luck. The inlet where they'd docked was well enough away from the expanse of sea that it was possible they simply hadn't been spotted, but as another night passed, Roz couldn't shake the thought that any pursuers ought to have caught up by now. She wasn't the only one glancing over a shoulder almost constantly; Siena and Dev were doing the same. Only Damian didn't seem bothered.

He should have been, though. Instead, his gaze was fixed unblinkingly in the direction they were going. Roz couldn't understand him. At times he seemed normal; at others he seemed viscerally afraid.

And then there was the Damian who seemed not to know fear at all. The Damian that was a warped version of the boy she knew. Was this the man he might have become, had he been more like Battista and less like his mother? Was magic doing this to him?

The following day was calm, but the evening brought with it the promise of more rain. The air was thick, a smattering of pale stars winking into existence behind the layer of clouds. Roz pulled her hair into a tighter ponytail, taming the strands that whipped against her face.

"We should head into the cabin," Siena called as the first few raindrops began to fall. "We're about to get soaked, and there's enough of a gale that the sails will keep us on our course."

Damian gave a curt nod, locking the wheel in place, and the four of them made their way inside. The moment they were free of the impending storm, Dev fell into the nearest chair, fixing an empty look on the garish crimson rug that covered a small section of the wooden floor. "We'll be at the border soon. What's the plan?"

They'd already discussed their findings from the Atheneum: how it apparently *was* possible—likely, even—that Enzo's sacrifices had strengthened Chaos's magic, and what that meant for the remainder of their journey. Roz was loath to go over it all again, but she had the sense Dev was simply looking for reassurance. So with a confidence she didn't feel, Roz said, "We stop at the last Ombrazian port before the border and, hopefully, swap our ship out for one that's a little less...conspicuous. A Brechaan-made ship, preferably."

"Then we can cross into Brechaat at the pass where they conduct most of their trade," Siena continued. "We'll try to draw as little attention as possible. Once we're across, we go the rest of the way on foot."

"And hope we don't encounter any disciples of Chaos," Dev muttered.

"The chances are slim," Siena reminded him in a matter-of-fact tone. "Disciples aren't common in Brechaat. The people are mostly descended from the unfavored that fled there after the first war, remember? And the remaining disciples of Chaos probably diluted their bloodlines enough that there won't be many of them left. If there were," she added, "Brechaat would have used them in the war effort by now."

That was a good point, Roz thought. In a battle being fought mostly by unfavored, the presence of *any* disciples of Chaos would have been a huge asset.

"Even if there aren't many disciples of Chaos in Brechaat," she said, "we don't know how powerful Enzo's sacrifices might have made them. The things he could do…what if that's the norm, now?" Roz thought of the security officers in the Palazzo, frozen in their respective illusions. "Enzo controlled dozens of people at once. If they *all* have that kind of power—"

"Then Brechaat might be able to win the war," Damian said, speaking for the first time since entering the cabin. His eyes were glassy, his brow lowered. He didn't seem to be fully present, though he added, "Ombrazia doesn't have any disciples with which to fight back. Not enough to make a difference, anyway. That's what happens when you don't force them to enlist."

There was a beat of silence. No one argued—how could they? Damian was right. For years Ombrazia had relied on the fact that Brechaat would always be weak. A land of the unfavored. If that ever changed, they weren't prepared to reckon with it.

"Then we *all* have to leave," Roz said. The declaration was harsh, decisive. "We rescue Nasim and Kiran, return for my mother and the other rebels, then head to the Eastern Isles."

"You're probably right," Siena sighed. "Best-case scenario, we get caught up in a war where both sides want us dead." She dragged a sleeve across her brow, fingers tangled in the cuff. "It's just that my family's there, you know? And Noemi." Her teeth clamped down on her lower lip. "I doubt I'll be able to convince them to leave."

Roz glanced at Damian. He was still fixated on nothing in particular. A statue of a man she only somewhat recognized. Evidently he wasn't going to be much help in this conversation.

"I'm sorry," Roz told Siena. She gripped the other girl's shoulder in what she hoped was bracing reassurance. "All you can do is try."

Siena gave a wry smile. "You don't have to comfort me."

"I know. But I get it—I'm the only other one who left family behind."

She regretted the words the moment they left her mouth. Dev averted his gaze, suddenly far too interested in the edge of the carpet. Roz started toward him.

"Dev, I didn't—"

"No. You're right," he said, shrugging. "My family's gone. Everyone I *care* about is gone. Apart from you, of course. And if we don't get Nasim back—"

"We *will*. Besides, that's not true. The other rebels care about you."

He fixed her with a look that was almost pitying. "They care about me in the way people care about their colleagues. This is all that's left for me, Roz. You, Nasim. This mission. And that's fine. For some reason, it just hadn't occurred to me that there's no point in returning. I lived in that damn city my whole life, and now there's nothing there for me." He let his head fall back against the chair, then inclined his chin at Siena. "Who's Noemi?"

A pause. "Just a girl I know."

"Is that all?"

Siena's laugh was half-hearted. "It shouldn't have been."

Dev gave a knowing nod. He looked as though he might say more, then seemed to think better of it.

It wasn't an uncomfortable silence, Roz realized. It was the kind of lull that could as easily have filled the air at Bartolo's, punctuated only by the thunk of glasses on tables. Quiet companionship. When had that happened?

But then her gaze slid over to Damian, and she wished abruptly that she *were* at Bartolo's. She could use a drink of something stronger than water.

"If magic can become more powerful," Roz said slowly, "shouldn't it follow that it can be weakened, too?"

"Logic would suggest as much," Siena agreed, and a shadow crossed her face. "I might know something about that."

Dev sat up in his chair, and Roz tilted her head, suspicion threading through her. "What do you mean?"

With a grimace, Siena reached into the pocket of her trousers and withdrew a folded piece of parchment. For a moment Roz thought it was the map she'd shown them back at the tavern, but when Siena unfurled it, she saw only a block of text. One edge of the parchment was jagged, as though it'd been ripped in half.

Siena's guilt suddenly came into context. The sheet hadn't been ripped in half—it had been ripped out of a *book*.

Dev understood at the same moment Roz did. He guffawed, pointing a finger at Siena in equal parts shock and glee. "You stole that from the Atheneum! And after telling us to follow the rules of the place?"

Damian's entire demeanor shifted, his attention snapping to Siena as if he'd been roused abruptly from slumber.

She held both hands up. "I thought it might be important, okay? I found it just after Damian abandoned me." Cutting him a pointed look, she smoothed the parchment out on her lap. "Most of the page isn't useful, but it does prove there's a way to undo what Enzo did."

Siena pointed at a line near the bottom of the page, and Roz leaned over her shoulder to read it.

To commence the process of undoing, you must offer what was given.

"What does that mean?" she asked, though a horrible part of her suspected she already knew.

Dev wiped a hand across his mouth. "Don't tell me it's saying the only way to weaken Chaos's magic is to do exactly what Enzo did. He killed six people. He *murdered* my little sister."

"I didn't say we should do it," Siena snapped. "You asked the question, and I happened to have the answer. We can't even be certain the disciples of Chaos are an actual threat."

But it wasn't only about the disciples of Chaos, was it? Roz kept staring at the words, hoping she might somehow divine a different meaning from them. "If we're right, and Damian really *is* being affected by Enzo's magic, that's another thing that needs undoing."

"No." Damian's arms were crossed, the planes of his face cold. His defiance came so swiftly that it took a Roz a moment to process it.

"What do you mean, *no*?" She mirrored his stance, tilting her chin up to meet his gaze. "Do you want to be stuck like this forever? You said yourself you think you're going mad."

"I'm fine."

"You're kidding." She flung a hand out at him. "This isn't you, and you know it. You were *terrified* of it."

His mouth twisted cruelly, the expression alien on him. "Are you trying to *fix* me, Roz?"

"Damian." Siena was on her feet, his name harsh on her tongue. "She's right. You're not yourself. We're hours from crossing into Brechaat's territory, and we can't afford any rash decisions from you."

Damian took a step forward, his brows lifting. "*Rash decisions?* I don't make rash decisions. I am your *commander*." He hurled the last word like a threat. "Nothing about me needs to be undone. I don't need to be fixed."

Before any of them could respond, he turned on his heel and wrenched the cabin door open, disappearing into the storm. A slew of raindrops pelted Roz's face before the door slammed in his wake.

"What the hell was that?" Dev muttered, one hand gripping the arm of the chair he still occupied.

Roz didn't have an answer. She turned to Siena. "Does that page say anything else of use?"

Siena gave a helpless shake of her head. "Only what you read. '*Offer what was given.*' Preferably in a holy place."

"No place is holy once Roz turns up there," Dev muttered, and Roz shot him a withering glance.

"You two try to get some rest. I'm going to go talk to Damian."

For a second she thought Dev might argue, but then he nodded. "Be careful. Don't get blown into the sea."

She knew it wasn't the sea he was most worried about.

As it happened, Roz did not get blown into the sea, but the downpour was heavy enough that she didn't see what difference it would have made.

Her clothing was soaked through in seconds, cold and uncomfortable where the fabric clung to her skin. It was impossible to tell what was rain and what was seawater; the waves were a veritable roar in her ears, drowning out everything but the periodic cracks of thunder in the distance. They crashed against the side of the boat in a foamy white spray that breached the railing and spilled across the deck. It was a struggle to keep her footing, but she managed, squinting through the deluge to Damian's familiar figure at the bow. She screamed his name, but he didn't turn, a lifelike figurehead staring into the inky collision of sky and sea.

Roz swallowed an ache in her throat as she drew up behind him. The first time Damian had told her he felt *wrong*, it was into the curve of her neck as he held her at the edge of the lake, the day after the rebellion made their move. Roz had grabbed his chin, forcing him to look into her eyes, and saw something strange there. Something she suspected was borne from the moment he shot Enzo dead in the Shrine. She didn't know what had shifted in Damian that night—only knew it was a change even three years of war had not wrought. Never had she thought it would come to this: that she would look at him and see someone she didn't know.

"Damian!" She said his name again, hating that she sounded tentative.

Finally he turned. His eyes looked black, his pupils blown wide. The ship lurched, forced closer to shore by the vicious waves, and Roz went with it. She slammed into the nearest railing as equilibrium evaded her, a curse slipping off her tongue. Damian was at her side in a heartbeat, grabbing her by the arms and yanking her around so that he stood between her and the sea. "Try not to get tossed overboard, would you?"

It should have been a joke, but the words held nothing of his usual lightness. Roz's anger reared. "What do you care?"

Damian stared at her through the sheets of rain. His hands still gripped her shoulders, but neither of them moved. "What do you *mean*?"

"I don't know what changed, but it seems to me like you don't care about anything anymore." The rain beat down harder, soaking her hair through to the scalp. She shivered. "You were terrified of what you were feeling. Terrified! And now you're angry because you think I want to *fix* you? Damn it, Damian, we're all just trying to help you."

"Rossana." He said her name roughly. "There are more important things to worry about—"

"You think that now. What happens in an hour, when you change your mind? When you break down because you think Enzo's magic is still controlling you?"

"I wasn't done." His voice was terse, bringing Roz up short.

"What?"

"I. Was. Not. *Done*." Damian enunciated the words, freeing one of her arms to lay a hand on her damp cheek. The ship gave another violent lurch, but he kept them both steady, water streaming down his temple, his cheeks, like a barrage of tears. His gaze was furious, and Roz wasn't prepared for the words that accompanied it. "Don't say I don't care anymore. There is no version of me that doesn't care about you, Roz. There is no version of me that you do not own."

Her lips parted, but no words came. She wanted to tell him she wasn't trying to own him. That the version of him she loved most was the one with softness, perhaps because she possessed precious little of it herself. She wanted to say that his pain and fear were a part of him, just as much as the color of his hair or the shape of his mouth. But Damian didn't seem to need a response.

"When you touch me," he said quietly, nails scraping the skin of her cheek, "I remember how to be calm."

Roz didn't know what to say to that. Lightning flared overhead, the sudden brightness leaving an imprint across her vision. She inhaled sharply, tasting the rain along with the briny tang of the sea. Then she reached up and placed a hand over Damian's, pulling his fingers away from her face. The loss of warmth made her feel oddly bereft.

"I'm going to find a way to undo it," she told him. "What Enzo did, I mean. Whether you like it or not."

"No." The word was a crack of a whip as he stepped away from her. "Don't you see, Roz? I'm *happy*."

"You weren't," she reminded him, a chill working its way across her skin. "You only say that now because it's easier."

He shook his head. "You don't get it. It hurts so much less."

"Pain is part of life."

"Well, I don't *want it*!" Damian's voice rose to a roar rivaling that of the waves. He stared at her with wild, angry eyes, chest heaving. The softness she'd seen in him only moments before had melted away so completely, Roz wondered if she had imagined it.

And that was when she understood.

Whatever was happening to Damian, he had stopped fighting it quite so hard. That was why things were different. Why he was fluctuating between madness and despair with less frequency. He was starting to give up, and perhaps had stopped feeling despair at all. A jolt of horror shot through her at the realization.

"Damian," she said urgently. "I need you to listen to me." She grabbed the soaked fabric of his shirt and wrapped a hand around his wrist, remembering what he'd said about her touch calming him. "Don't give in. I know part of you still wants to fight this—this madness, or whatever you want to call it—and I need you to keep trying. Okay? For me."

He looked at her for a long moment, expression inscrutable. It felt like trying to read a book in a language she had yet to learn. What would happen if he said no?

Before he could respond, though, there was a crash that had nothing to do with the ferocious storm. It was the a door slamming, Roz realized belatedly, and she whirled to see Siena hurtling across the deck toward them, a finger thrust at the rock face in the near distance.

"We missed the final port!" she yelled over the tempest, face screwed up in panic. "We've come too far!"

Damian pulled free of Roz's grip, which she'd unconsciously let slacken. He braced his hands against the railing, ignoring the water that crested over the side of the ship, drenching him from head to toe. His focus was on the same landmass Siena had indicated.

"We were traveling with the wind," he bellowed over his shoulder. "Between that and the Grace-made sails, I didn't think to factor in how much faster we'd be going!"

It took Roz a moment to catch up, but once she did, she felt her entire body brace in horror.

They'd missed the last Ombrazian port—the one where they'd been planning to trade ships. They were coming up on a distinct narrowing of the sea, penned in on both sides by rocky cliffs.

It was the pass Siena had referred to earlier. The one that signified the crossing of the border.

They were headed directly into Brechaan territory.

17

DAMIAN

Damian's hands were slick on the wheel of the ship as he tried to steer it back out to sea. No matter how he strained, each rotation was ineffectual. The storm was too aggressive, the waves too powerful. They pressed against the side of the ship with an unfathomable weight, pushing it closer and closer to the pass.

At some point Dev must have heard the commotion and burst from the cabin as well, for he now stood at the other side of the deck, rain-drenched and fighting with the sails, trying valiantly to set a different course. Damian knew it wasn't going to matter. The way things were going, they were either going to be forced to navigate the pass or they would find themselves slammed into the rocks. The shore was too close. They could try to fight nature all they liked, but she would not be bested.

"It's no use!" Damian hollered at Roz and Siena, both of whom were watching him with enormous, frightened eyes. He didn't feel the fear himself—he knew where it *should* be, coiled in his chest with enough pressure to crack something vital, but it simply wasn't there. Instead he was clearheaded, filled to the brim with staunch determination. "We're going to have to go through the pass!"

"We *can't*," Siena barked back. "This is a Palazzo ship! We're flying the damn crest!"

Behind her, Dev must have overheard. He let the sail go and tilted his head back, gaze snapping up to the flag. "I'll get it down!"

Damian barely made out the words, and it was another beat before he understood. By that time Dev was already scaling the mast, jacket billowing in the wind as rain buffeted his slim figure. Roz was beneath her friend in an instant. Her wet hair had come loose from its ponytail, sticking to her arms and neck. "Dev, *no*! The lightning!"

Dev ignored her, and Damian couldn't pretend he wasn't glad for it. Their vessel was obviously Ombrazian, but removing the flag would at least remove any visible connection to the Palazzo.

"Leave him be!" he told Roz as he gave another almighty heave of the wheel, squinting in the rain as he prepared to navigate the ship through the pass. He felt like a single point of control in a world of madness. Every few seconds he adjusted his stance as the ship lurched and the deck shifted beneath his feet. Normally, Damian would have resented the ankle-deep water that soaked through his boots, but the rest of his body was soaked enough that it didn't make much of a difference. He heard splashing behind him, and chanced a quick look over his shoulder just in time to see Siena approach.

"Give me the wheel," she told him, breaths coming rapidly. Her face was streaked with rain. "If Dev falls, you're the only one who might be able to catch him."

Damian thought it unlikely *anyone* would be able to catch Dev if he fell—the boy had a better chance of plunging right into the sea. But he also knew Roz would tear this whole ship apart if anything happened to him, so Damian relinquished the wheel.

Dev had nearly reached the top of the mast. It was swaying precariously in the gale, and he was clinging on for dear life. Roz was getting a face full of rain, her head tilted back to the sky.

"He's almost there," Damian told Roz loudly, as if she hadn't already figured that out. "He'll be fine."

"I know," she snapped.

At that moment the ship crested a particularly large wave, and Dev's legs slipped free from around the mast. Roz let out a gasp Damian couldn't hear, her lips parted in a silent scream. He braced himself as Dev's feet scrabbled for purchase on the damp wood. The boy slipped down the mast ever so slightly. A crash of thunder rent the air. As if unconsciously, Roz grabbed Damian's hand, her wet fingers twining with his so tightly that he winced.

But Dev didn't fall. He managed to wrap his legs around the mast once more, resuming his climb.

The sea was narrowing. Rocky cliffs were closing in on them from both sides, the waves shattering into sprays of foam. The pass itself was the length of three large ships set end to end, and although Damian couldn't see them yet, he knew Brechaan sentinels stood guard along the rock face. He wondered if they were watching. Could they make out the Palazzo flag through the sheets of rain?

Roz's grip tightened, and Damian glanced up to see Dev clinging to the mast with one hand, the other brandishing a blade. The Palazzo flag flapped so wildly in the wind that at first it seemed he would never be able to hold it long enough to cut through the strings. He managed, though, even as he was beginning to slip again. The flag whipped and thrashed as if alive, but the next moment Dev had shoved it down the front of his jacket and begun his descent.

He relinquished his grip a little less than halfway down the mast, letting himself fall to the deck in a spray of water. The ship careened, and he rolled across the wood before finally coming to a halt inches away from Damian's boots.

Roz helped Dev to his feet, then swatted his arm hard enough that it must have hurt. "You're fucking mad."

Dev grinned weakly, waving the corner of the flag at her. His complexion was deathly pale save for two spots of pink on his cheeks. "I never claimed to be anything else."

"Well, keep that hidden," Roz advised, and Dev shoved the flag farther down the front of his coat. "It'll still be a miracle if we get through this." To Damian she said, "Will they question us?"

Privately, Damian thought it would be a miracle if they made it *that* far. But he said, "Yes. They'll probably search the ship, too. I know we didn't bring much, but if you have anything with you that might draw suspicion, throw it overboard. Now."

"I'll make a sweep of the cabin," Roz said.

Once she was gone, Dev tilted his head at Damian. Studying him. "You were going to try and catch me, weren't you? If I fell."

Damian frowned. "You had a better chance of being flung into the sea."

"That's not what I asked."

"I'd do anything for Roz." Damian stared right back, realizing for the first time that Dev must be the shortest of the four of them. He was by no means a large man, but he held himself like one. "She would have wanted me to catch you, so I would have done it. If she'd wanted me to throw you overboard, I would have done that, too."

Dev's laugh was wry. "Fair enough."

As Damian squinted through the rain, he saw that the ship was about to enter the pass. Siena was navigating the ship past the cliffs, her frame visibly tense even from where Damian was standing. At first he thought it was because she wasn't accustomed to manning a vessel, but then she beckoned them over, her expression communicating what her words did not: *Be silent*.

"What is it?" Damian hissed.

Roz had just exited the ship's cabin, and Siena waited for her to join them before she replied, "Look."

It took Damian a moment to understand what he was supposed to be looking at. Then he saw them: Brechaan soldiers, their outlines hazy against the cliff face. They looked tiny from here, like little toy sentinels.

"Soldiers," Roz said needlessly. "So what? I thought we expected this."

"That's not the point. They're not *moving*."

"They're not supposed to. They're sentinels."

Siena exhaled impatiently. "They should definitely have seen us by now, and they still haven't shifted an inch. That's odd, especially given that we're sailing an Ombrazian ship. None of them have even raised a gun."

"Are they statues?" Dev suggested. "I mean, maybe the real sentinels are elsewhere, and the ones we can see are a decoy of sorts."

Now that they were closer, Damian realized Siena was right. It *was* odd. He'd stood watch countless times before, and every good soldier knew to regroup at the sign of a potential threat. At a place like this, there should've been Brechaan boats coming out to meet them or cut off their path. But nothing happened, and none of the figures so much as took a step.

"No, Villeneuve, they are not statues," Siena said. Damian could tell she was nervous, because the words lacked any condescension.

The tension in the air was as thick as the scent of salt. Even Damian had a vague sense of foreboding, though it didn't affect him the way he might have expected it to. It gave him more energy, somehow, and he felt ready to fight.

Siena was still scanning the cliffs with intensity, and Roz's lips parted as they passed directly by the nearest sentinel. He wore what Damian knew to be the typical long-sleeved uniform of Brechaat's army—dark green with black buttons—but the man didn't so much as follow the progress of their ship with his gaze. He didn't even lift his archibugio.

"Is this some kind of trick?" Siena hissed, but Damian barely heard her. His insides had turned to ice.

He knew *exactly* where he had seen this before.

Memories came to him in fragments: running through the Palazzo, trying to track down Enzo after he'd disappeared with Roz. A dark hallway blocked by security officers who hadn't moved at Damian's approach. It was only later that he'd realized they were trapped in an illusion.

"It's not a trick," Damian said, having no idea why he was keeping his voice low. It wasn't as if the soldiers could hear them. "We've seen this before. They're being controlled by a disciple of Chaos."

Beside him, Roz stiffened. A muscle twitched in the side of her neck, and he knew she was remembering the same things he was.

Dev gaped. "Why would you think that?"

"Look at them." Damian jutted his chin toward the nearest sentinel. "Their eyes are open, but vacant. As if they're looking at something else entirely. That's because they are. Enzo did the exact same thing to a few of the Palazzo security officers the night he finally revealed himself."

Dev let out a low whistle. "Wasn't Enzo unusually powerful, though? It can't be easy to control this many people at once."

"It's not," Roz put in darkly. "Or at least, it shouldn't be. But who knows what the average disciple of Chaos can do now."

"So one has been here. Recently."

"They might still be here," Siena said, and the four of them were quiet after that.

They were almost at the narrowest section of the pass now, where a small building had been constructed on the flattest part of the cliff. The checkpoint, presumably. Soldiers were clustered around it, each and every one of them immobile. Damian was braced for someone, *anyone*, to leap forth and attempt to bar their passage, but nobody did. He didn't like it. His tense energy had nowhere to go, and his body was desperate to expel it.

"Why would a disciple of Chaos do this, though?" Roz growled. "Surely no one from Brechaat would influence their own soldiers. I mean…" She gestured with a hand at the open waters ahead. "We're essentially being allowed to enter without any issues."

Which meant that somewhere nearby, a disciple of Chaos had grown strong enough to let them cross the border without being intercepted by a single soldier.

The rain had let up slightly, though the storm still roared around them, turning the pass into a wind tunnel. For a long moment, none of them spoke. It was only when Roz finally broke the silence that Damian realized they must all have been thinking the same thing.

"Someone wants us here," she said. "For some reason, someone actually *wants* us in Brechaat. And they've made it so that we can't be turned away."

18

ROZ

They docked the ship around a bend just past the checkpoint. This side of the pass was better insulated from the storm, but it quickly became apparent to Roz that they would not be returning the way they'd come.

"It's going to have to stay here," Siena muttered, eyeing the ship over her shoulder as they ascended the slippery cliff path. "It's too much to hope that whoever wants us here is going to let us back out again."

They'd left nothing incriminating on board, but it would be immediately obvious to any Brechaan who set foot on the vessel that it was Ombrazian. They might have taken down the flag, but that hadn't been the sole indication of Palazzo ownership.

Dev was looking back, too, but not at the ship. He was focused on the checkpoint, as if fearful the soldiers might suddenly snap out of whatever illusion they'd been placed under. Roz couldn't blame him—if pursued, their group would be easy enough to catch. They had scarcely slept, and their food supplies had been meager at best. She could feel the pull of exhaustion in her muscles, and it was a struggle to focus her vision.

She wondered how Damian remained upright. He undoubtedly looked the worst of them; he said little, and his shoulders were tense as he navigated the steep incline of the path leading away from the water. Roz wanted to comfort him, but something in his expression held her back. His gaze was unfocused, as if all his attention was directed at moving forward. If she touched him, Roz feared he might snap. He hadn't wanted her here. And although so many other things about Damian had changed, that hadn't. She watched as water trickled down his neck from his hair, already growing out from its short military cut.

The difference in Brechaat's climate wasn't obvious, but what Roz could see of the dark landscape was certainly unfamiliar. The trees scattering the cliffs grew squat and spiky—nothing like the lush, rounded green she was accustomed to. In a way, though, it was beautiful. The jagged terrain blocked any sign of civilization, making their surroundings feel wild and unknowable. The site of a storybook adventure, with no promise of a happy ending.

Maybe it was because of the tales her father had told her as a child. Tales of the curious north, unblemished by his own experiences there. He spoke of enormous cats that prowled the mountainside, and tiny waterfalls secreted away in the forests. He told her how the sun looked paler against the gray skies, how it slunk away earlier in the eve, and how, if you looked hard enough on a clear day, you might glimpse snow atop the very tallest peaks.

You could get lost here, Roz thought. You could run and run and never look back.

They had nearly reached the top of the cliffs now, and there wasn't much to be seen up ahead save a dense copse of those same prickly trees. Siena directed them toward it, insisting they needed to get out of the rain so she could look at her map. Roz knew as well as anyone that you were supposed to avoid trees in the event of lightning, but it wasn't like they had any alternative forms of shelter.

"We need to move away from the coast, then loop back," Siena said once they were protected from the worst of the rain. She pointed at the northern section of her map, which was largely blank. "Then we should be able to access Ombrazia's main base while avoiding the front lines."

Roz ground her teeth, mentally attempting to calculate the distance. "We won't be able to get there tonight, will we?"

Siena shook her head. "We could camp out here."

"We need dry clothes," Dev pointed out. "We should try to get to a city. Or at the very least, some kind of village."

"That's not safe." Siena put the map safely back into her jacket, beginning to wring moisture out of her braids.

"It's not like anyone here will recognize us," Dev argued.

"That's the problem. They'll wonder who the hell we are, and that can be just as dangerous."

Roz honestly wasn't sure which was the better course of action. She was desperate to be clean and dry, but the thought of getting into trouble and wasting yet more time made her hesitate.

Damian crossed his arms over his broad chest. Unlike the rest of them, he wasn't quite out of the rain, and it spattered his shoulders as he worked his jaw. "There will be a village nearby. I doubt they'd set up a checkpoint too far away from civilization."

"And we should sleep," Roz decided. "Even if just for a few hours."

"Then let's go." Damian stepped away from the trees entirely, his face shadowed. "We ought to wait out the storm anyway."

Before they could take another step, however, he held up a hand, eyes tightening. His entire stance changed, like that of an animal scenting danger. Without uttering a word, Siena mirrored him, drawing a small blade she'd found aboard the ship. Roz already had her own knife in hand.

"What is it?" Dev whispered.

"Don't you hear that?" Damian said, low and urgent. "Someone's yelling. They must have discovered our ship."

"So what? We're not on it."

"So, it means—*look out!*"

Roz whirled. She'd grown accustomed to the sound of gunfire, but not when it was coming from directly behind them. The unmistakable sound of an archibugio punctured the air just as Dev spun behind the nearest tree. Roz did the same, though not before catching a glimpse of a dark figure as it sprinted up the cliffs toward them, silhouetted by what little moonlight reflected off the thrashing sea. A Brechaan sentinel.

"We need to run," Roz said through her teeth, trying desperately to make out the others amid the dark trees. She was comforted only by the thought that if she couldn't see them, the sentinel probably couldn't, either. "We don't stand a chance, even with the four of us. Not when he has a gun."

Siena's voice came from somewhere to her left. "He may not be alone, either."

Roz could see Damian now—he was only a short distance away from her, and she suspected he'd put himself there purposefully. He shook his head. "If there were others, he would have waited for them. Somehow he's broken free of his illusion."

Or maybe he'd never been trapped in the first place, Roz thought. Who knew how many soldiers patrolled the area surrounding the pass?

"Then what do we do?" Dev's voice asked. He sounded unsteady, and Roz knew he was thinking of Nasim. Of what would happen to her if they died here tonight.

"Run," Damian said. "*Now.* I'm right behind you."

Another shot went off. Roz cringed, ducking her head to follow Dev and Siena deeper into the trees. She heard their rapid steps crunching through the undergrowth and had only taken a dozen of her own when she realized she couldn't hear Damian following. Her damp ponytail whipped her face as she halted. *"Damian!"*

She couldn't see him, and he didn't answer. She sprinted back the way she'd come, thankful the patter of rain mostly covered the sound. Her heart slammed against the back of her throat. What was Damian *doing*? He couldn't be trusted to make good decisions—not the way he was currently.

He was standing where she'd left him, peering out from behind the tree. The Brechaan sentinel was close—far too close. The next shot he fired was thunderous, the cover of the forest amplifying it tenfold. Damian tensed as the sentinel approached his hiding place. She held her breath, frozen in panic and indecision. Why hadn't Damian run? Why was he *still not running*?

She saw something flash in his hand, and she understood.

Damian leapt out of the trees. In the same instant, Roz hurled herself toward the sentinel, her thoughts blanking at the crack of a final gunshot. She was sure it had only narrowly missed her, but she felt nothing more than a fleeting sense of vague relief as she let her own knife fly.

Her grip was hot—*so hot*—but it evaporated the moment the blade left her hands, as if the metal had taken the heat with it. She'd always had decent aim, but the darkness combined with the sentinel's unpredictable movements meant her knife had little to no chance of striking him.

Except that it did, just as she'd somehow known it would.

Roz could still feel the remnants of her magic in her bones. It had flared there as she held the sentinel in her mind. And then, for the first time in her life, she'd successfully channeled that connection into the metal.

That wasn't how it was supposed to go. A disciple of Patience wasn't supposed to be able to enchant a weapon to find its mark.

And yet the blade lodged itself perfectly in the sentinel's throat.

All the breath shuddered out of her. Killing, Roz learned then, was as easy as she'd always imagined. The knife caught the man unaware, and he had no way to defend himself. The archibugio he carried was too long and unwieldy to turn it on them with any degree of effectiveness. It should have been horrible, seeing the knife lodged in his skin, but the adrenaline pumping through Roz's veins had left her devoid of all rational feeling.

Killing was easy. It was the dying that was traumatic.

She was unconsciously approaching the sentinel when she found herself wrenched away. The hand at her collar was rough, the grip too strong to break. She knew instinctively that it was Damian—who else?—but she couldn't bring herself to look at him. Her gaze was locked on the sentinel as he dropped his archibugio, hands scrabbling at his throat as though he might be able to hold the blood in. He choked and sputtered as blood sluiced down the front of his neck, ink-dark beneath the cover of night. The sight and sound of him struggling to breathe was a horrible thing, and Roz could only watch as he slipped to his knees, hands slick with his own life. His eyes snapped up to Roz's, and she braced herself for the hate in them, but there was only sheer panic.

He knew he was dying, and he was terrified.

It was you or us, she wanted to tell him, but surely he already knew as much. What did the explanation matter, anyway?

She might have stood there forever if Damian hadn't forcibly turned her to face him. His expression was thunderous—Roz didn't think she'd ever seen him so angry. She felt her horror slink away, defiance replacing it.

"What the *fuck*," Damian snarled, "did you do that for?"

Roz lifted her chin to return his glare, but the words she needed to say wouldn't come. How could she tell him the truth? That she'd seen the glint of light off his blade, and understood what he was about to do. That she couldn't let him do it because this wasn't *him*, and once the Damian she knew was back, he wouldn't be able to bear having done such a thing.

Roz, though—she could bear it. It was wretched, and sickening, but it would not destroy her. She would think of the panic in the sentinel's eyes before she went to sleep at night, but it would not keep her from slumber. Maybe there was something wrong with her, for she'd always known she was capable of killing long before she'd done it. She would find comfort in the fact that she had been the one to survive.

She couldn't be honest with this version of Damian, though. How could she explain that she only wanted to save him from grief, from guilt, when the boy before her now seemingly experienced neither?

I killed him because I can live with it. You can't, and besides, you've already killed enough.

Roz didn't say that, though. She tried to block out the sentinel's dying, gagging breaths as she said, "I thought it was about time I saved our lives."

It was partially true. After all, Damian had been the one to kill Enzo. The anger didn't leave his face, but Roz thought something in him softened. "You should have kept running. I had it under control."

She shrugged. "I could barely see you. I just knew he was getting far too close."

Damian ran a hand through his damp hair. He looked a little fevered, a flush to his otherwise pale cheeks as he tilted his head to study her more keenly. "Don't lie to me. You didn't think I could handle it, did you?"

A jolt shot through Roz. Even now, he read her too well. "No, that's not—"

"I said *don't lie*. You wanted to spare me the trauma of killing him. You still want me to be the weak, passive boy you're accustomed to."

Roz swallowed hard. Damian's face was a study in angles, the flare of moonlight that parted the clouds casting one of his cheeks into stark relief.

"You were never weak or passive," she whispered, forcing the words through a mouth that was suddenly dry. "You were—*are*—one of the strongest people I know. And...I miss you."

She hadn't meant to sound so raw. But now, seeing Damian like this, she was abruptly flooded with misery. What if she couldn't figure out how to get him back? What if this was who he was from this point forward? She hated it—the way she could be so close to him yet feel he was miles away.

Pain glazed his eyes, though they remained inscrutable black. He crossed the small distance between them, the ground crunching beneath his boots, and cupped her cheeks in his hands. "You don't have to miss me," he murmured. "I'm right here."

He wasn't, though. And yet the feel of him was so familiar that for a moment Roz nearly let herself believe it.

"*Roz!*"

Her name sounded from behind them, and the moment shattered. She drew in a breath as Dev appeared between the trees, Siena at his side. His eyes were wide with terror.

"We're fine," Roz told them.

Dev scanned her from head to toe. "We heard gunshots."

"I see you dealt with that, though," Siena added, nodding at the sentinel crumpled on the forest floor. He'd finally succumbed to his injuries—Roz hadn't even noticed the moment he'd gone silent.

Damian grabbed the man roughly by the legs, dragging him farther into the cover of the trees. "He acted alone. There's nothing to worry about." He retrieved the archibugio with familiar ease. "Someone will find his body eventually. Let's get the hell out of here."

With that, Damian led them deeper into the forest, but not before thrusting Roz's knife into her hands. It was still covered in blood; he must have plucked it from the sentinel's throat. She stooped to wipe it on the ground with numb fingers.

When she straightened, she saw that Dev was watching her.

Why? His lips formed the silent question. Why had she killed the man like that?

Roz only shook her head. The better question, though, was *how*.

19

ROZ

Their path through the forest was a dark, brief one. Roz remembered little of it, her feet moving of their own accord, hands groping the air in front of her to push any rogue branches aside. She thought more of Damian than she did the dead sentinel, and that made her feel even worse. She'd *killed* a man. Taken his life and wiped his soul from the earth. Yet the sadness in her heart lingered for another reason entirely.

To commence the process of undoing, you must offer what was given.

They needed to undo what Enzo had done. After what they'd seen at the pass, Roz knew that if they encountered a disciple of Chaos, they didn't stand a chance. The Ombrazian army didn't stand a chance. More than that, though, she wanted Damian back.

Offer what was given.

What had Enzo given, other than the murders of six people? Chthonium, she remembered, was to signify that the sacrifices were for Chaos. Enzo had offered that. Then, of course, there was his horrible jar of eyes. Roz didn't have either of those things. She didn't know how she could ever get them. She wondered if she should have taken the sentinel's eyes, then immediately recoiled from the prospect. What would she even have done with them? Started a jar of her own? The mere idea was repulsive. Killing one person had been brutal enough—surely there had to be another way.

The thoughts circled in her head as they walked, the earth growing spongy beneath her feet. They maintained a rapid pace, and Roz wondered if she was so tired that she had stopped noticing the exhaustion. Nobody spoke other than to gauge their progress, and she knew the others must feel the same. When the trees finally parted, she saw Damian had been right; there was a village on the other side of the trees.

It was only then that Roz got her first true impression of Brechaat.

It was a small settlement, not dissimilar to those on the outskirts of central Ombrazia, but everything about it was noticeably…downtrodden. The buildings were crumbling, some roofs beginning to cave in. Others had collapsed entirely. The roads were overgrown and lined with disposed-of items. The few residents Roz saw hovering outside looked sallow, unhealthy, their faces drawn and their bodies too thin. They were either ignoring the rain or didn't have anywhere to go. It reminded Roz of unfavored territory, only worse. No matter how the Palazzo treated them, the unfavored in the heart of Ombrazia rarely went hungry. There were exceptions—children whose parents had been drafted, or those without family who couldn't find work—but this was different. Here, everyone appeared equally miserable.

Though it was too dark to see across the water, she knew they were drawing closer to the front. Every so often gunfire went off in the distance, causing Damian and Siena to flinch. The Brechaan citizens must have been accustomed to the sound; no one reacted. In fact, they didn't seem to react to much at all, given how unconcerned they were with the arrival of four strangers. It gave Roz enough confidence to approach a group of young men outside a tavern, hoping in their drunkenness they wouldn't notice how much of a mess she looked.

"*Rossana,*" Dev hissed, but she ignored him.

"Buona sera," she told the men, although the evening was far from nice. "Sorry to bother you. Is there an inn nearby?"

Normally a group of intoxicated strangers would be more than happy to talk to her, but these men only looked at her dully, as if they couldn't quite comprehend her question. Finally one of them pointed to the building next door. It seemed to be connected to the tavern, though the rooms beyond were dark.

"The only inn is right here, Signora. Doesn't get much business, but Eduardo owns both these places." The man gestured at the tavern entrance. "He's inside. Large fellow, gray hair, serving drinks. You can't miss him."

Roz was braced for further questions, but they didn't come. The men simply seemed…disillusioned. As if Roz could have been anyone at all, and they wouldn't have cared. Of course, they had no reason to assume she wasn't from Brechaat—after all, it should have been harder to get here.

She didn't like that it hadn't been.

"Thank you," she told the man, then returned to the others. "That's the inn just next door. The owner is in the tavern."

Dev nodded, and so did Siena, though she looked grim. Damian didn't react at all. He was merely watching Roz, the lines around his mouth tight. When she stepped toward the tavern's entrance, he moved to hold the door open, releasing a rush of sound that made her head spin. Everything smelled like liquor and unwashed bodies. Roz shoved her way through the crowd, realizing only when she made to push a short woman out of the way that her hands were bloody. She felt a sense of irritated detachment, attempting to wipe them on her shirt before slamming them down on the bar top. "I take it you're Eduardo?"

The man outside had been right—you couldn't miss the owner. He was easily the tallest person Roz had ever seen, even with his shoulders hunched. His gray hair was nearly as long as hers, tied back in a leather thong, and his face had the same gaunt quality as the rest of village's citizens. Eduardo turned, setting down the empty glass he'd been drying. He even towered over Damian, though Roz suspected Damian could have snapped him in half.

"Can I help you?" Eduardo's voice was higher than she'd anticipated, but oddly gravelly.

"We'd like some rooms." Roz raised her own voice to be heard over the clamor. "I understand you're the owner of the inn."

He jerked his chin in assent. "It's not very well maintained at the moment, I'm afraid. We don't get many visitors."

"That's fine."

"Where are you four from?" Eduardo eyed Roz's face closely, and she couldn't tell whether it was with interest or suspicion.

"A little farther north."

His face twisted, and now she *knew* he was suspicious. Damian took a step closer to Roz's side, bristling, but Eduardo's next words surprised them both.

"Escaping the front lines then, are you?"

Roz relaxed infinitesimally. He didn't suspect they were from an enemy state—he assumed her caginess meant they were Brechaan soldiers trying to escape the war. What did that mean, though? She had no idea if deserters were treated in Brechaat the way they were in Ombrazia. "And if we did come from the front lines?"

Eduardo lifted one frail shoulder. "None of my business. Just keep your mouths shut about it." He lowered his voice, so Roz had to lean forward to better hear him. His breath smelled like whiskey. "Ombrazia's destroyed enough of us already. But for the first time, with everything that's changed recently, I think we might have a chance." He grabbed a large key off the wall behind the bar, barking an order at another man to come take his place. "Follow me."

They complied, Roz beckoning Siena and Dev to follow. Eduardo led them to the back of the tavern, a damp scent replacing that of alcohol. The walls and floors were matching wood, and a single step led up to a door that Eduardo unlocked and shouldered open. They all emerged into a dimly lit room not dissimilar to the tavern's main space.

"How many rooms?" Eduardo asked, rounding a chest-high counter and rummaging around behind it.

"Four," Roz said firmly. This place could clearly use the income, and they could all use a decent sleep. Siena shot her a look of consternation—undoubtedly, she considered separate rooms an unnecessary luxury—but Roz was already placing money on the counter. "How much?"

Ombrazia and Brechaat used the same currency, but it was worth far more here. Eduardo's eyes widened as he mentally calculated the payment Roz offered. "That will do nicely." He handed over four keys. "Second floor. Two on the left, two on the right. Forgive the dust."

Roz took the keys, handing one to each of her companions. Dust was the least of her worries. "What did you mean by what you said earlier? That with everything that's changed, we might have a chance against Ombrazia?"

Dev and Siena, who hadn't heard the original conversation, shot her confused glances. Damian's gaze, though, snapped to Eduardo with almost feral interest. "Yes. What *did* you mean?"

Eduardo rested his elbows on the counter. He was forced to stoop in order to do so. "I think Calder Bryhn will change everything. He's not like his father, saints rest the man's soul. He's clever. Plays the game of war differently. People are saying he has a plan that will turn the tide of this accursed conflict."

"What kind of plan?" Damian asked too quickly. Roz elbowed him hard in the ribs.

Eduardo shrugged. "How should I know? My time at the front is over—the only good thing about being my age—but it's said Calder isn't afraid to take risks. He'll do whatever it takes." The older man's expression tightened. "I need to have hope, you understand. You've seen what the war is like."

"We have," Siena murmured.

"It's crushing us." Eduardo's gaze unfocused, and there was a beat of quiet before he gave himself a shake. "Well. I don't need to tell you that. You'd best head upstairs—it's late. Tavern's about to close down, but I'll be next door if you need anything."

Dev cleared his throat. "I don't want to put you out, but do you by chance have any clothes we could buy? Ours are…well." He indicated his drenched outfit.

Eduardo considered, brow wrinkling. "I'm sure I can find you something. Wait here."

A moment later he was back, a pile of clothing under one arm. He left it on the counter, accepted their payment, then departed after wishing them a pleasant remainder of the night. Dev removed his jacket without ceremony, draping it over one of the chairs so that it could dry. Roz did the same, relieved to be free of the damp fabric.

"Well," Siena said, glancing down at her timepiece. "We've still got a few hours before dawn. I, for one, intend to take advantage of it." She looked at them each in turn. Her expression cleared. "I'm glad we all made it here."

Dev snorted a laugh, and even Roz couldn't help a smile. "So am I."

Damian, on the other hand, was clearly not interested in any kind of celebration. He was stern as he said, "Tomorrow we'll continue on to the front lines. It shouldn't be more than a couple of hours from here."

With that, they made their way upstairs. The clamor was still audible from next door, but the walls muted it slightly. As promised, everything was covered in a thin layer of dust. The floor was carpeted in a maroon-and-cream pattern that had seen its fair share of stains, and the green wallpaper was beginning to peel.

Roz meant to say goodnight to Damian, but when she turned around, he was already gone. The ache in her chest deepened.

Her bedroom was small, but not dissimilar from the one she was accustomed to staying in at Bartolo's. There was a bathing room attached, and she stripped off her wet clothes and cleaned herself as quickly as she could, shivering in the frigid water. The clothes Eduardo had brought her were too large, but at least they were dry. She slipped them on, pulled her hair into a ponytail, and sank onto the bed, listening to the screech of the tap as Damian turned on the water next door. It was all too reminiscent of the night they'd spent together nearly two weeks ago. Roz felt as if their story was playing over again, an unending loop that never quite managed to end in happiness.

Maybe there was no happy ending for the two of them. Each time it seemed there might be, something went wrong. Even though they'd found their way back to each other, she could feel Damian slipping away again.

It felt so much worse when he was standing right in front of her.

Roz heard the water shut off, and then there was silence. Her heart thudded against her ribs. Despite her exhaustion, she knew she wouldn't be able to sleep.

Unable to help herself, she slipped into the hallway. She hesitated outside the door to Damian's room, but pushed the apprehension aside and rapped her knuckles against the wood.

There was no response. Not a sound emanated from inside. Roz knocked again, and when she was still met with no response, cold slid into her veins.

She tried the door. It was unlocked, so she shoved it open.

Damian was there, standing in front of the mirror by the bed. His arms were braced on either side of the dresser. He was dressed, but his hair was wet, black against his skull. Roz could see the striations of his triceps, the faint pattern of veins along the back of his hand as his grip tightened. He hadn't reacted to the sound of the door opening. His eyes were wild, focused on his reflection as though he expected to see someone else staring back at him.

Her stomach turned. "What are you doing?"

Damian whirled, slamming his hip into the edge of the dresser. He cursed once, low and sharp. "Don't you *knock*?"

"I did." She lifted a brow as Damian's gaze cut through the shadows to meet hers. His pupils were blown wide, irises ringed in black. The way he studied her through his lowered lashes was too calm.

He didn't answer the question. "I'm not in the mood tonight, Rossana."

Roz crossed her arms over her chest, watching the way Damian's lip curled over his teeth. If magic *was* changing him, then she only needed to free him from it. Even Chaos's control didn't overtake entirely. It simply shoved reality to the side.

"Not in the mood for what?" Roz kept her voice even, a little goading. If there was one thing she knew about Damian, it was that he rarely shared his feelings until he could no longer contain them.

"This. Arguing with you." He waved a dismissive hand in her direction, no longer meeting her eyes. His shoulders flexed as he gripped the edge of the dresser once more, knuckles white and head bowed. "Leave. *Please*."

That was when Roz understood. It wasn't that Damian didn't want her here; it was that he didn't trust himself around her. His problem, she realized, was control. The way he'd attacked Falco and Salvestro and then tried to go after the sentinel made that clear enough. Whatever was happening, strong emotions made him lose himself further. Was that why he'd been avoiding her earlier?

"You need to relax," she said. The tension in his stance made her own body feel tired. "I'm sorry I killed the sentinel, but—"

His gaze snapped up, dark and accusatory. "This is precisely why I didn't want you to come here. The north ruins people."

"Is that what you think happened to you? That you were ruined?"

"I *know* it's what happened. But I'm rebuilding myself now."

"Damian, the only reason I had to kill that man in the first place is because you refused to run. If you had, we would have gotten away. This never would have happened."

He reared back as if she'd slapped him. "How can you blame *me*? I had everything under control. You weren't supposed to come back. He had to die, because he'd seen us. He knew we were associated with the ship and saw what direction we were headed. Even if we had managed to lose him, he would have been able to tell the other Brechaan soldiers exactly where to find us."

"You think they won't find us anyway? When they do look for us, do you think they won't come here? This must be the closest village to the pass. All his death did was buy us a few hours of time." Roz drew herself up tall, fists clenched at her side. "You were right, you know. I killed that sentinel because I knew you wouldn't be able to handle it. That if you ever broke free of—whatever *this* is"—she waved a hand at him—"then you'd look back at the choices you made tonight and know they were foolish. You're being irrational and reckless, and that's saying something, coming from me."

Damian pushed off the dresser, closing the distance between them. His eyes were wild. "Foolish? Irrational? *Reckless?*"

Roz took an automatic step back. Her heartbeats were tiny, individual explosions in the cage of her chest.

"What if you can't fix me, Rossana?" Damian lowered his voice, the words a grating rasp. "What if this is just the way I am now? Maybe Enzo did something to me, and maybe he didn't. Either way, don't you want me to accept it?"

"You don't need to accept it. We'll find a way to—"

"How do you think I feel, seeing the way you look at me? I can tell you don't trust me, and I don't know how to fix that. I don't know which of my emotions are *real*. Which ones come from the part of me you're willing to accept and which ones don't." He shuddered, a muscle leaping in his clenched jaw. When he spoke again, it was barely a whisper. "I can't tell the difference. But one thing hasn't changed, and it's that you—you make me insane."

Roz took another step back, colliding with the closed door. She barely felt it as Damian braced a hand against the wall just above her head. She could hear his breathing, fast and uneven. Could smell the clean scent of him.

This really *wasn't* Damian, she realized distantly. Damian was gentle, careful, inexperienced. Whatever was happening now… this wasn't the way things were between them. And yet her blood had flared to life in her veins, traitorous poison that it was.

"Listen," she murmured. "I—"

But she didn't get to finish. Damian shoved her hard into the wall, his mouth meeting hers hungrily. Viciously. Roz's pulse skyrocketed. She relinquished control, breathing him in as his teeth scraped her lower lip. He growled her name.

Roz, this time. Not *Rossana*.

He pressed his body firmly into hers, and the hand not bracing the wall slipped down to her hip bone. Her insides were liquid fire. The more furiously Damian kissed her, the more aggressively she responded, until they were all hot breath and bruising touch. This was not the man Roz knew, but just now she didn't particularly care what version of Damian she got.

She wanted them all.

Roz knew it was wrong, and still she couldn't help herself. She felt his mouth dip to her neck, felt his teeth against her jugular. Her fingers curled in the hem of his shirt, shifting the fabric up, and Damian let out a snarl of a laugh. His lips moved to her ear.

"Patience," he breathed, and she stiffened at the invocation of her patron saint.

"That's not one of my many virtues."

He exhaled against her, bringing goose bumps to the surface of her skin. Roz heard his nails scrape the wall. Rather than reply, he bent his head so that it rested against her shoulder. When she dragged her fingers down his spine, she found it tense.

"You're the only thing I know to be real," he whispered.

Roz traced the lines of his abdomen. "I told you, I'll find a way to fix this."

"No," Damian said on a laugh, his voice abruptly unfamiliar. "No, you won't."

Ice slithered through Roz's blood. She shoved him away, and he blinked at her through eyes clouded by something indiscernible. "Why would you say that?"

He didn't appear to have an answer. Instead, he finally slipped his shirt off, revealing the lightly tanned planes of his chest and stomach. He approached her once more, bracing his hands on either side of her head, breathing hard. She didn't know if she wanted to run or kiss him until she was insensible of everything else. Doing the latter felt strangely like taking advantage of someone intoxicated.

She would undo what Enzo had done, with or without Damian's compliance.

She reached for him, thumb brushing the hollow where his collarbones met, and dug her fingers into his skin. Damian brought his chin up in a motion that was part daring, part deference, his unblinking gaze locked with hers. Roz used her grip to push him gently downward, watching as his body responded. His hands dropped to his sides as his knees hit the floor.

"Don't you trust me?" she asked him quietly.

Damian's jaw was taut, his voice solemn. Reverent. "Only with my life."

He meant it, Roz realized. She didn't know why it felt like a blow. "Good."

And that was how she left him, slipping out the door and back down the hall to her room.

20

DAMIAN

When Damian woke the next day, he wished Roz was beside him.

After she'd left him last night, he'd felt bereft. His need for her had always been there, but now it was an overwhelming thing, filling his chest like a too-deep breath. It felt like obsession. He remembered the way he'd knelt before her, gaze lifted like a man worshipping at the shrine of his patron saint. Somehow, Roz tethered him to her in a way he was powerless to resist.

He realized his hands were fisted in the bedsheet, and he relaxed them, frowning up at the ceiling. Light emanated from behind the worn curtains, trickling into the room in a thin beam. Suddenly he sat up. His breath was a tangled thing in his chest. For a moment he couldn't place the sensation of disquiet, and then he heard the thundering of boots in the stairwell.

It was the clamor on the first floor that had woken him in the first place. The voices must have been absurdly loud because he'd been sleeping like the dead.

He leapt to his feet just as the door flew open.

Brechaan soldiers spilled into the room, the deep green of their uniforms recognizable in a way that had Damian feeling more awake than ever before. His knife was in his hand—he'd slept with it under his pillow—but he wasn't fool enough to think he could do anything with a half dozen guns pointed in his direction. The soldiers seemed to fill the whole room, but there must have been more still, because Damian could hear footsteps and shouting in the hall. His heart squeezed in his chest. *Roz.*

"Drop the knife," a thin man who was clearly in charge barked. Damian let his gaze dart around the room, seeking escape where there was none. He wasn't close enough to grab any of them the way he had Salvestro at the docks. Besides, Salvestro hadn't been armed. The Brechaans were.

Lips forming a snarl, Damian let the knife fall.

Two men surged forward, yanking his arms behind his back and shackling his hands together. They weren't the Patience-made cuffs Damian was accustomed to, but a rough metal that was far too tight. A third soldier—a woman—pointed her archibugio at his head. He could feel the barrel of the weapon as it brushed his hair. They could clearly tell he wanted to fight back and refused to give him the room. Damian didn't know how their group had been found—couldn't think of anything other than the ship that indicated they were Ombrazian—but saints, they should have known better. Here they'd been, like fowl waiting to be picked off by a hunter.

The man in charge was all cold suspicion as he took in Damian's Brechaan clothing. He looked like a typical soldier—his hair was little more than bristles, and he was clean-shaven—but his features were too large for his thin face, and Damian couldn't help but think he looked very like a boy. Just another child, handed a uniform and forced to grow up too quickly. He had to be fairly young, perhaps in his midtwenties, though the five or so soldiers at his back ranged from teenaged to fully gray. Their army uniforms hung off their lean frames, as if they'd been made for larger people.

"Now," the man said once Damian had been secured. "Tell me, what is a group of Ombrazians doing on this side of the river?"

His voice was soft but harsh, lacking the lilt of one who'd grown up speaking the northern dialect. He wore nothing that indicated he was of higher rank, and Damian couldn't remember if Brechaans worried about such things.

"We don't want any trouble," Damian growled, because he knew it was what he ought to say. Next door, he supposed, Roz was likely saying something similar. She would have been believable, though, tone confident and gaze steady. Damian had never been able to manipulate. It was why Roz always claimed he was easy to read.

The man gave an incredulous laugh. "You don't want any trouble?" He leaned closer, and the woman with the archibugio shifted away. "Ombrazians, you say, who don't want any *trouble*?"

Damian didn't know what the hell that was supposed to mean, but he lifted his chin. "We were merely passing through. Besides, you've no proof we're Ombrazian."

"I don't know how you made it through the pass, but did you think we wouldn't recognize the make of your ship?" The words were derisive. "Do you think we haven't seen disciple-made sails?"

How could Damian explain they'd managed to cross the pass only because someone had *let* them? Did this man not know about Chaos's magic? Did he not realize there were disciples of Chaos in their midst, stronger now than ever before? Trying to explain any of that, though, was undoubtedly a horrible idea.

"I don't know what ship you're talking about," Damian said stubbornly. The man would know he was lying, but if Brechaat had anything akin to due process, he wasn't about to admit his crimes. "The pass is used to facilitate trade, is it not? Countless ships must travel through it weekly."

The man exchanged a look with one of the other soldiers, who arched a disdainful brow. To Damian he said, "Do not act like you don't know your armies have blocked the river on the other side of the pass. We've not been able to participate meaningfully in trade for years. Why do you think our people are *suffering*?"

Damian shook his head, anger roiling within him, but he kept his mouth shut. He knew as well as anyone that it was Brechaat who was encroaching on the once-shared river, not Ombrazia. That was why the Second War of Saints had started in the first place— because the enemy state was desperate to gain control of key trade routes, and take its revenge for all it had lost in the first war.

It required physical effort to stay silent. Damian focused on the pain in his wrists, the scrape of the rudimentary handcuffs. When it became apparent he would not respond, the woman with the archibugio gave a meaningful tilt of her head. "*Milos.*"

The man in charge straightened at what was presumably his name, giving a single curt nod. "We'll be going now." The other soldiers parted as Milos made for the door, turning to snap over his shoulder, "Bring him!"

Someone shoved Damian forward, and he stumbled into the hallway, dizzy with a combination of fury and frustration. This had all happened too quickly, and he couldn't wrap his mind around it. What would the Brechaans do to them? Worse, what would happen to Kiran, to Nasim, if they stayed at the front?

It was the first Damian had really, truly allowed himself to think of his friend since the day of the meeting. Kiran was the best of them all. Unfailingly positive and loyal, despite everything he had suffered. Damian had already lost one best friend to the war. If he lost another, it didn't matter how many soldiers held him at gunpoint: He would show this whole cursed state what it was to know terror.

He was guided down the stairs, surrounded on all sides. It was like being in a living cage. When they reached the main floor of the inn, the first thing Damian saw was Roz. She, Siena, and Dev stood in the midst of yet more soldiers, though Damian had evidently been deemed the main threat. Dev wore an expression that could be interpreted only as morose, as if he'd already accepted their fate. Siena was watchful as always, but her shoulders visibly relaxed when she saw Damian descend the steps. Roz, surprisingly, looked the most distressed. Her gaze kept flicking to the counter where Eduardo had handed them the keys last night. At first Damian thought she was watching Eduardo himself, currently engaged in conversation with a soldier, but then he saw what had been laid out across the countertop.

It was a flag bearing the Palazzo crest. The very flag Dev had cut down and shoved into his jacket. The jacket he'd removed last night, which was still strewn over one of the chairs only inches from where Damian stood.

Suddenly the look on Dev's face made more sense.

"Oh, you fucking *moron*," Damian snapped, elbowing the nearest soldiers in an attempt to reach Dev. The other boy refused to meet his eye. *That* was how they'd been discovered. Of course it was. Eduardo had found the flag in Dev's jacket, indubitably tying them to the Ombrazian ship. He'd summoned the Brechaan soldiers, and now their whole mission was doomed.

Whoever had gotten them this far needed to step in again before they got killed.

Milos came around to Damian's side, wrenching him back. There was no mistaking the bitter satisfaction in the man's dark eyes. "That's right. You can lie all you want, but your own accomplice gave you away." Milos clicked his tongue. "I don't know what your plan was, but doubtless your commander won't be very happy with you."

"We're not with the Ombrazian army," Damian snapped, and Milos scoffed.

"You must take me for a fool."

"It's true," Roz put in, overhearing. One of the other soldiers moved in front of her, trying to block her view of Damian, and she strained to see around him. "We're just trying to—" Her explanation cut off as she was shoved toward the door. There was a sigh somewhere to Damian's right, and he saw that Eduardo had rounded the counter, consternation written in the lines of his tired face.

"I ought to be surprised you deceived me *and* took advantage of my hospitality, but I suppose I can't expect any better from Ombrazians." He shook his head in disgust. "Please remove them."

Damian barely heard Roz's second attempt at an explanation. He was alight with rage, his insides fire.

And yet when it mattered most he could no longer remember how to burn.

Damian didn't know where they were being taken, but nearly an hour after being led out of the village and along a narrow dirt path, they arrived at what looked like a military command post. It wasn't far from the village, and wasn't in much better shape, either. It was gated, set back from the road amid an uneven copse of trees, and far wider than it was tall. Nothing about it was particularly notable. It was, Damian supposed, typical of military buildings—designed for efficiency rather than aesthetic. Facing into the distant north, it appeared the sole sign of civilization against a mountainous backdrop.

The soldiers hadn't spoken the whole way here, with the exception of Milos and one of his inferiors arguing quietly at the front of the procession. Damian had walked with his eyes on his boots, forcing his mind to go blank. Every so often he'd attempted to glimpse Roz or Siena, but they were behind him somewhere, and he'd been jabbed in the back with the butt of an archibugio every time he turned his head. He felt like a wild animal being ushered to slaughter, and now the moment of reckoning had arrived.

Milos ascended the steep stairs to the entrance, two more soldiers hurrying forward to yank the great wooden doors open. Beyond it the walls were the same cool gray stone as the exterior. Damian shrugged off a chill as they were led down a long hallway, footsteps echoing in an uneven cadence. At the end of the corridor another door led into a large room with a window overlooking the hills and river below. The rest of the space was far less intriguing; a long table was the sole piece of furniture, and no effort had been made to maintain the crumbling stone walls. Water dripped from one corner of the ceiling in an uneven, relentless patter.

"Araina, fetch him, would you?" Milos said, and the woman who'd pointed her gun at Damian's head back at the inn nodded, golden braid swinging as she ducked out of the room.

"What is this place?" Roz demanded once Araina had disappeared. "Who is she getting?"

None of the Brechaans answered. Roz's gaze slid to Damian's, and something about it was cutting. The memory of the words she'd thrown at him last night seemed to settle heavily on his shoulders.

You'd look back at the choices you made tonight and know they were foolish.

He didn't know how to make Roz see that he was better this way. The things weighing him down before now felt like vaguely irritating memories. He felt stronger, no longer tethered down by his fears. The only time he doubted himself was when Roz got too close. When she made him think about the things he was trying to ignore.

If this was to be the end for them, then he was glad to have changed. The older version of Damian wouldn't have fought nearly as hard as he was prepared to.

"We weren't lying to you," Roz appealed to Milos again. "We're from Ombrazia, yes, but we're not with the army."

At first Damian thought the young man was going to ignore her, but he turned around, his expression thunderous. "*I'm* from

Ombrazia. I know what it's like there. They tore me away from my family, condemned me to death. I was a *child*."

Roz gave a sharp intake of breath. "You're a disciple of Chaos."

The tilt of Milos's mouth was bitter. "And yet I am just a man."

Be that as it may, Damian was immediately on edge. He wondered briefly if it could be Milos who had let them cross the Brechaan border, but dismissed the thought—it was obvious he didn't want them here. If he was controlling any of them, would they know?

"Relax," Milos growled, noting their apprehension. "I've no need of illusions when I have my fellow soldiers."

"We don't agree with what Ombrazia does to disciples of Chaos," Roz said staunchly. "We don't agree with most of what happens at the Palazzo. I'm glad you escaped."

Milos stared at her for a long moment. Emotion flickered across his features, though Damian couldn't say what it was. Distrust? Regret? He wished Roz would stop *talking* to the people who were supposed to be their captors.

Araina returned before Milos could reply, but she wasn't alone. She stood aside, holding the door open for a young man dressed in an identical green uniform. Shrewd hazel eyes narrowed beneath dark brows as he surveyed their group. He was handsome, though perhaps a bit too pale, and definitely too thin. His hair was a deep copper, too long for military regulations. When he smiled, Damian knew at once he was not someone to be tested. That much was evident in the way the other Brechaans straightened in his presence. But there was also an unmistakable air of tiredness about him—one Damian recognized as stemming from being forced to endure too much in too short a time.

"General Bryhn," Milos said, dipping his head.

Calder Bryhn. A jolt went through Damian, followed by a flare of animosity. This was the man who had taken control of Brechaat's military. He was, at this moment, Ombrazia's primary enemy.

Calder was young, though Damian had expected that. The previous general, his father, would have been only in his forties. Unlike the other soldiers, he'd rolled up the sleeves of his uniform shirt, and medals of tarnished gold decorated the breast pocket. *His own?* Damian wondered. *Or his father's?*

"Well." Calder clasped his slender hands together. His voice, oddly pleasant, was a smooth tenor. "Ombrazian soldiers, come to chat."

"We're not soldiers," Roz began crossly, but Milos had already stepped forward.

"They were discovered by an innkeeper after attempting to take refuge in the nearby village. Somehow they managed to navigate the pass without being stopped. Rest assured, the sentinels are being questioned about the incident. Strange thing is, nobody remembers seeing the ship go by, which made me wonder if—"

Calder made a cutting gesture, and Milos lapsed into silence. Damian wondered what the man had been about to say.

"Tell me," Calder said, tilting his head. "Who sent you?"

"Nobody sent us," Dev grunted, shifting his weight. There was an apathetic dullness in his eyes. If he thought they might forget it was his fault they were here, he was sorely mistaken.

Calder snorted. "Don't bother lying. You Ombrazians have brought nothing but trouble since you started this war."

"*You* started this war," Damian couldn't help interjecting. "Brechaat started this fight because you wanted what we had. Everyone knows that."

The general pivoted to stare at him in unbridled disgust. "Is that the bullshit they teach you down there?"

"Bullshit?" Damian repeated, baring his teeth. "What are you—"

Calder gave a harsh laugh. "Oh, this is too good. Do you mean to tell me you don't know *your* people started this battle? After the First War of Saints, once our states had separated, your chief magistrate decided he wanted all this northern land back." The general gestured in an arc, indicating their surroundings. "He thought we would be easy enough to conquer. After all, disciples had always congregated around the Palazzo, so there were scarcely any up north. Brechaat became a land of the unfavored. Well," he amended, "excepting Chaos's disciples, though precious few of them survived the first war. We've never had much, but at least we haven't let an entire group of people suffer for what they can't control. Any suffering has been at *your* hands."

Siena gaped, and Damian gave a vicious shake of his head. "You're a liar."

"No," Calder said mildly. "You're brainwashed."

"Or maybe you are."

"Brechaat still promotes heresy," Siena pointed out, discomfort written in the lines of her face. As if she wasn't sure she spoke the truth, but felt compelled to say it nonetheless.

Calder raised a brow. "Because Ombrazia struck a saint from the pantheon, *we* are the heretics? Our beliefs never changed. It was yours that did. How, then, are we the ones in the wrong?"

"Because you lost," Roz said, surprising everyone. She lifted her chin to address Calder directly. "You lost the first war, so therefore you're wrong. It's that simple, isn't it? The victor gets to decide what is right and true."

Her words didn't immediately register with Damian. At first he thought she was arguing with the general, but in the silence that followed, he wasn't so sure. Was she saying Calder was right, and Ombrazia had lied simply because they'd been able to?

Calder stared at Roz for a long moment. Then he beckoned to his soldiers. "Bring them to the window. Let us see if they know truth when it sits before them."

21

Roz

At first Roz wasn't sure what she was supposed to be looking at.

The Brechaan landscape stretched into the distance, mountains rising to pierce the fog behind it. She saw stretches of forest, a crumbling building nestled in the hills, and the winding river she knew led to the sea. On the other side of the river, across a wide bridge, she could see what must be the northern front lines.

"I didn't realize we were so close to the front," Siena said under her breath, turning somber. "It looks worse than I remember."

Canvas tents were nestled amid a section of land devoid of foliage, and dark figures flitted back and forth between them. So close to the river, the ground must have been pure mud. It was easy to see why they had set up there, however: Farther down, a number of ships bobbed atop the waves. They took up enough of the waterway that it would have been impossible for another vessel to pass by.

If Damian felt the same discomfort, he didn't show it. His face was blank as he stared across the water, and it was impossible to tell whether he felt anything at all.

"The front wasn't always this close," Calder said coldly. "You know that well, I suppose."

Siena shook her head, never tearing her attention from the window. "Last I was at war, your camps were much farther down the river."

Calder's mouth thinned. He inclined his head at the vessels blocking the waterway. "Take a closer look. These aren't our camps."

Roz dragged her gaze back to the river, watching the boats' masts sway in the wind. She'd thought them part of Brechaat's fleet—this was their territory, after all—but then a flag unfurled long enough for her to recognize the symbol on it. She straightened as understanding dawned. "Those are Ombrazian ships."

"Well spotted. This isn't the only location they've claimed, either. Your military maintains control of the river all the way to the other side of the continent. They have for some time." Calder faced Roz, pinning her with a cold look. "You saw the village—the circumstances there are not unique. We haven't been able to engage in proper trade for years. People can't get what they need. They can't make a living. Do you truly believe *we* started this war?"

Roz didn't know what to say. Even Damian was silent, the muscles of his jaw working furiously. The makeshift shelters were Ombrazian, yet they were well across Brechaat's border. Hadn't they always been told it was Brechaat who was pushing into Ombrazia's territory, and not the other way around?

Dev gave a soft intake of breath, and Roz wondered if he was coming to the same realization. The rebels had always suspected they were being lied to. They just hadn't known the extent of it.

"None of us were near this place," Siena said, her angled brows drawing together in confusion. "We were all stationed farther south. That's where the bulk of the fighting happened. How could so much have changed within the last year?"

Roz studied the ships for another moment, then thought back to the village. Of the deterioration, and the hunched, thin shoulders of the people in the streets. Understanding flooded her like she'd been doused in frigid water.

This wasn't two states at war.

"This is a *siege*," she said. "Isn't it?"

Calder's lips pulled into a grimace. He was by no means a large man, and he might have been new to his role, but in that moment Roz got the sense he could be dangerous. "So you do see."

Now that she knew this much, the revelations kept coming. Each one stung like an individual pinprick, and bile rose in the back of her throat. There was, however, an odd satisfaction in knowing she'd been right. Their leaders were as corrupt as she'd always thought. All those warnings about Brechaat taking control of the river, and potentially impacting trade—none of it was true.

"We're trying to starve you out," Dev muttered, shaking his head in disbelief.

The proclamation was met with more silence. Roz could tell by Siena's face that she was grasping for a different explanation where there was none. Damian, on the other hand, looked like a man carved from stone.

It was Siena who eventually spoke. "Why would they lie to us about this?"

Milos snorted from behind her, and he was the one to answer. "Fearmongering. Propaganda. If Ombrazians unquestionably believe Brechaans are evil, aren't they more likely to support the war effort? If you believe you're fighting against villains, does it not make being drafted easier to stomach?" Despite his sharp tone, there was a bleakness to the words. "Does it not give you a sense of righteousness?"

Beside Roz, Damian continued to work his jaw. He didn't want to believe it, and Roz knew why: Battista Venturi would have known this. Would have played a part in it. It was yet another thing his father had lied to him about. If Roz hadn't been so disgusted, she might have been sympathetic.

Calder nodded at Milos, then continued, "What you know about the First War of Saints, I assume, is mainly fact: The reincarnations of Strength and Chaos went to battle, and Chaos lost. If you believe the stories written in *Saints and Sacrifice*, you will know that Chaos always falls. The original patron saint created war against the wishes of his six counterparts. As such, he cannot win his own. The patron saint of Death made sure of that. She ferries him to the beyond as soon as she can."

"We only just found out our version of *Saints and Sacrifice* may not include all the original stories," Roz muttered, thinking of the book from the Atheneum. "But yes, we're familiar with what happened during the first war."

"And then?" Siena urged. Anxiety laced the question, and Roz could understand why. It never felt good to have your closely held beliefs called into question.

"Then," Calder went on, "the second war began. Brechaat and Ombrazia had separated following the first one, of course, and as a result we suffered greatly. It was mainly the unfavored who sided with Chaos, and those people were sequestered in the north. This meant that Ombrazia became the land of disciples and that Brechaat now belonged primarily to those who were not blessed. At first it seemed like the ideal solution: separate the two groups who couldn't get along. But nobody stopped to consider what this meant for Brechaat. Without disciples gifted in craft, we couldn't participate in the economy the same way. Anything we *did* produce was done with far less efficiency. And so began our hardship."

His knuckles whitened as he intertwined his fingers. "But even victory was not enough for your people. With the ascension of a new chief magistrate, Ombrazia decided it wished to be whole again. It wished to reclaim the land it had lost when we separated. Mind you, Brechaat didn't have much. But we had a number of access points to the east river that the chief magistrate coveted, and recapturing them would streamline trade. So Ombrazia attacked."

"Brechaat never launched an attack because it wanted our resources, then," Roz said, icy rage unfurling inside her. "That was a lie."

Calder shook his head. "Why would *we* attack? We had no hope of winning. The only reason we weren't immediately crushed is because we had a competent leader, and because Ombrazia didn't send disciples to fight. The general at the time used the landscape to our advantage, and we were able to hold out for years. But as you can see, your troops managed to take control of the river eventually. *You* are conquering *us*." Calder put a hand to the pistola at his belt, and for a heartbeat Roz wondered if he would use it. "You've taken control of our resources. You're making our people suffer."

"How do we know things aren't different elsewhere?" Damian said finally, but there was little conviction in his voice. "Maybe Ombrazia has taken control of this particular area, but—"

"Oh *please*, Damian." Roz cut him off. He might not be the same person he'd been a couple of weeks ago, but his beliefs were too deeply held to change overnight. Even when his whole personality was altered, he wanted to believe the people he'd served were the good guys.

What reason did the Brechaans have to lie? They had gained nothing in the first war, and even less in the second. They had nothing to hide, except perhaps their weakness. On the other hand, it made perfect sense that Ombrazia would provide a distorted version of events to its citizens.

Calder appeared vaguely surprised at Roz's outburst. He clasped his hands behind his back, executing a semicircle around the room before coming to stand at her side. Despite the gaunt lines of him, he was tall. Easily as tall as Damian. He smelled like clean air and the sea. Between his fingers he held a knife, and he spun it around a few times, grip deft and agile. Roz went perfectly still, keeping her expression neutral. This was a man practiced with a blade.

"Why do you pretend to pity us?" Calder mused, trapping her with his gaze.

"Get away from her," Damian snarled, lunging forward, but Calder didn't afford him a glance. Two of the soldiers yanked him violently back, and Roz heard Siena's sharp inhalation. Damian's muscles strained as he fought against them, veins standing out beneath his skin. He thought Calder was going to hurt her—that much was clear. But despite the way Calder twirled his knife, Roz had the sense the general didn't intend to use it.

She widened her eyes and pressed her lips together, trying to tell Damian without words to back down. He didn't seem to notice, and she watched with dismay as he was forced to his knees. When he stared up at her, she was reminded far too forcefully of the previous night. He'd been full of reverence then. This, if she wasn't mistaken, was the first true fear he'd shown in days. She saw his pulse leap in his throat as he glared at Calder through slitted eyes.

"I'm not pretending to pity you," Roz told the general coolly. "I'm happy to tell you the truth, but for someone who claims to be so concerned with such things, I get the sense you don't want to hear it."

He furrowed his brow. "I would like nothing more than for you to be honest. I wish Ombrazians were capable of that." The pause he left, though, was a clear opening to continue.

"We may be Ombrazian, but our loyalty does not lie there." Roz kept her tone clipped. "In fact, we can never return. We're no longer welcome anywhere near the Palazzo. But do you truly believe Brechaans are the only ones harmed by the war? Our unfavored are *suffering*. They're sent to battle whether they like it or not. Half the time their families aren't notified of their deaths because no one's bothering to keep track. If they desert, they're executed on sight, their names disgraced." She was speaking quickly now, her entire body tense with the force of her fury. "Ombrazia may have more than Brechaat, but if you're not a disciple, none of it is yours. You are *nothing*. Tell me you don't know how that feels."

Calder arched a brow. Perhaps he was displeased she spoke so openly, but Roz no longer cared.

She took an unsteady breath. "Our entire lives, we were taught that Brechaat started this war. That you were the danger, the heretics, and we had to keep you in check for the good of our nation. But if you say that's not true, then I believe you. My father died because of this war—because Ombrazia deemed his life unworthy. And you may think me a liar, but the only reason we're here in the first place is because we want to save our friends from the same fate." Roz thrust a finger toward the window. It shook, and she hoped it wasn't obvious enough that Calder noticed. "They were taken from us, and we don't want them to die for a country that never cared about their lives in the first place."

From the corner of her eye, she saw Dev nodding emphatically. But she kept her attention on Calder, never flinching beneath his scrutiny.

"The war killed my father, too, you know," he said after what felt like a full minute. "Not directly. It was the stress. The constant pain of feeling as if he was letting his people down. Of watching them die, over and over again, when he had no choice but to send them into battle. His heart couldn't take it anymore, and it failed him." Calder's own pain lingered in the twist of his mouth. "Personally, though, I think he was relieved. I think he would have died far earlier, had duty not kept him here. Duty to Brechaat. Duty to me."

Roz knew what Calder was insinuating, and it made her stomach churn. She knew he wasn't sharing this to comfort her or to empathize. Calder wanted her to understand that he, too, was furious. That he had known pain, and grief, and let it forge him into someone who would not rest until he got justice.

So Roz did not apologize. It didn't matter if she was sorry for his loss. Instead she nodded, rolling her shoulders back, and said, "I understand."

"Do you?"

"Yes. Your father left you with an impossible task. An impossible war. And you won't show mercy because mercy was not shown to you." She leveled Calder with a look, ignoring everything else. Even Damian's harsh breathing faded into the background. "You have a plan, don't you?"

He gave a tight, sardonic smile, a dimple popping in his cheek. "Why do you ask?"

"Do you play cards much, General?"

Calder exchanged a bemused glance with Milos. "Every so often, I suppose."

"Are you any good at it?"

"I like to think so."

"Then you know the look of a man who has just drawn an excellent hand. You've seen the way he suddenly tries not to call attention to himself and how it only makes him more conspicuous." Roz dipped her chin, leaning forward slightly. "You, General, have the demeanor of a man who has found himself holding a particularly good set of cards. And I'd wager I know why that is."

Calder dragged a hand along his jaw. It was difficult to tell what he was thinking. "Is that so?"

"Roz," Damian warned, but she was done dancing around the point. They had come here to rescue their friends, and if they were going to fail at that, she wanted to at least know what they would be up against.

"I think your disciples of Chaos have grown more powerful," she told Calder. The way he stilled, his expression too pleasant, Roz knew she had him. "I think you've noticed it happening, and you're trying to find a way to use them to your benefit. You remember the First War of Saints and think that this time could be different. This time, there are no saints. But a few disciples of Chaos, no matter how powerful, won't be enough. The people they murder will be innocent." She thought of Nasim facing one of Chaos's disciples on the front lines, and fought back a shudder. "You can try to build an army, but you still won't win. You'll only create more bloodshed."

She hadn't expected to convince the general of anything, but she also hadn't expected Calder to look as if he were trying not to laugh. Behind him, Araina had already failed at hiding her scorn: She gave an audible exhale through her nose, a muscle in her cheek twitching.

"A *few* disciples of Chaos?" Calder crossed his arms. "I'd ask how you know this, coming from a country that hates the seventh saint, but I'm more interested in why you think I wouldn't have enough."

Roz didn't answer, perplexed by the question. The answer seemed so obvious.

"They were almost wiped out in the first war," Siena said impatiently. "And those from Chaos's original bloodline—diluted though it may be—were likely to have remained in Ombrazia, since disciples often partnered with other disciples."

"And when their descendants showed an affinity for Chaos's magic, *you* tried to have them killed," Araina put in, her cheeks flushed. Whether due to anger or because she had spoken out of turn, Roz couldn't tell.

"We didn't try," she said heavily, remembering Enzo's fury. "We *did* have them killed. Or at least, the Palazzo did."

Calder shook his head. "It's easy to believe that, isn't it? After all, they disappear as children, never to be seen again. But no: Ombrazia did not kill *all* their disciples of Chaos. In fact, I would hazard to guess they didn't kill most of them. You see, it's difficult to destroy a group of people who can distort reality."

Roz had the terrible sense she knew where this was going. "What are you saying?"

"I'm saying Chaos's disciples were never gone. They always found their way out. And if they didn't, someone else made sure of it." He cut a look at Milos, who dipped his head. "The disciples that were banished over the last fifty years? Milos is not the only one who ended up here. Nearly all of them have. I'm not *trying* to build an army, girl." Now he did laugh, the sound biting. "I've already got one."

Her heart gave a stuttering beat. "What? But the Ombrazian ships—"

"Are not my main concern just now. I'm content to let your armies get comfortable. You're correct: Attacking those camps would only lead to more bloodshed. Which is why I have no intention of attacking the camps." Calder drew a finger along the flat edge of his blade, expression thoughtful. "Outside these walls, on the other side of the river where the cliffs block the bend, I have ships of my own. Two dozen disciples to a vessel, all newly powerful. At first I wasn't quite sure where I would send them. But then I began to realize: Why waste time crushing Ombrazia's armies in the north, when the Palazzo will only send more bodies? Who knows how many unfavored they would sacrifice before capitulating? So instead, I'm going directly to the source—the Palazzo itself."

"You're taking your armies south," Siena said, face a mask of horror. "You're planning to march right into the city and win the war that way."

Calder shrugged. "Ombrazia may be full of disciples, but mine are more powerful. They won't see us coming."

"And why would you tell us this?" Roz demanded. She ought to have been as alarmed as Siena, as silently furious as Damian, but a large part of her relished the idea of the Palazzo being overrun with Chaos's disciples. What she *didn't* relish was the prospect of innocent lives being lost. How many unfavored would fall if the heart of Ombrazia was besieged?

"Ah. Yes." Calder tapped his chin. "I believe it when you say you hate the war, but unfortunately, you're now prisoners of it. You have information I require. You're my bargaining chip, should violence alone not suffice."

At that, Damian was the one to laugh. It was a sudden, rough sound, with a wild edge. He jerked his head up to meet Calder's gaze. "What makes you think anyone in the Palazzo would care about *us*? You're better off killing us now, for all the good we'll do you. They might even send you a letter of thanks."

Dev made a noise in his throat that suggested he had little interest in being killed. Part of Roz was still frustrated that his carelessness had gotten them here in the first place, but if Calder planned to kill *any* of her companions, he'd have to step over her dead body.

"Your leaders may not care for your lives," Calder admitted, "but I suspect they will care very much about what you could tell us. I may not have been general for long, but I'm no fool. I have no intention of simply marching onto Ombrazian shores. Far too much time has passed since the First War of Saints, when my people were forced up into the north. As much as I hate to admit it, I have no knowledge of your lands, nor do any of my soldiers. We don't know where the Palazzo lies, or how best to approach it. Most of all, we don't know the patterns of your security officers."

A small jolt of surprise shot through Roz, though she didn't know why. As evidenced by the Atheneum, Ombrazia had retained nearly all information when it separated from Brechaat. Maps, books, and the like were a luxury Brechaat didn't have access to. And even if knowledge had been passed down verbally over the many years since the first war, too much had changed in each city-state. There was a reason Siena's map was partially blank in the north.

"There's nothing we can tell you" came Damian's curt reply. "None of us are of any importance, as far as the Palazzo is concerned."

Calder chuckled. "I don't think that's true." He leaned down to address Damian properly. "I've been at war my entire adult life— did you really believe I wouldn't recognize the son of General Battista Venturi?" He tilted his head. "I must say, you look just like him."

Before Roz could fully process that, the room went dark.

22

DAMIAN

Damian blinked furiously through the onslaught of the dark mist, trying to get a clearer view of the general. To make sure he wasn't anywhere near Roz with that knife still in hand. At the same time, Damian's thoughts whirled. It was *him*—it had to be. Calder Bryhn was the powerful disciple of Chaos who had led them here. He was the reason they'd been allowed through the pass, and the reason they'd been captured. He knew Damian was related to Battista Venturi. Likely thought him important and had been planning this all along—

Before Damian could voice his realization, though, he felt the jarring pain of a knee in his back, shoving him facedown against the floor. At the same time, his shackled wrists were wrenched back with enough force that he felt his shoulder dislocate. A grunt of agony escaped him, and though he tried to fight against the weight of the soldiers pressing him down, it was futile. Their voices were a meaningless cacophony. He thought he heard Roz call out his name, but she was lost in the fog and confusion.

Damian's cheek was pressed to the cold stone floor. He could only watch the slow approach of Calder's feet as the general came to crouch beside him.

And then, right before his very eyes, Calder waved a hand and the fog disappeared. The world cleared, the light returning.

"*You*," Damian croaked.

But Calder only frowned as if Damian had spoken a language he didn't understand. The amusement was gone from his features. "Well. This *is* a surprise."

Damian didn't know what that was supposed to mean. Didn't care. His heart thudded frantically against the ground as if trying to break loose of his skin. He could make out Calder's hazel eyes, narrowed and intrigued, before they disappeared as the man stood up.

"Please don't hurt him," Damian heard Roz say, her voice more vulnerable than he was accustomed to. "He doesn't know what he's doing, he's been acting strangely since—"

Calder cut her off. "You don't even know, do you?" To someone else he commanded, "Help him up."

Hands pulled Damian back to a kneeling position, his breaths lost to the pain in his shoulder. He wasn't sure how he managed to move at all, but a moment later he was looking into Calder's thin-lipped grimace, Roz's wild face, and Siena's wan one. Dev wasn't visible at all, hidden as he was behind the general.

Calder stepped forward, taking Damian by the chin in a way that was oddly gentle. Damian immediately tried to wrench away, but the other man's thumb drove into the joint beneath his ear. "I confess myself rather pleasantly amused," Calder murmured, "to learn that Battista Venturi's son is a disciple of Chaos."

A moment of absolute silence followed his proclamation. The greatest silence, though, seemed to exist within Damian himself.

"You're mad," he finally snarled, and Calder's fingers trailed along his neck before he released him.

"You don't understand." Roz tried to step forward, but the soldiers flanking her pulled her back. She gave a twitch of irritation.

"Damian's not a disciple of Chaos. Something happened to him when Chaos's magic grew stronger." Haltingly, she gave a brief explanation of how Enzo had carried out his sacrifices in Ombrazia, the events of which had culminated at the Shrine.

"Oh, something happened to him, all right." Calder circled Damian, considering him the way a collector might an unusual piece of art. "If I had to guess, I'd say that you, Signor Venturi, were so opposed to the mere idea of being a disciple of Chaos that you managed to repress it for years. Once Chaos's power grew, however, it became impossible to ignore any longer." He stopped pacing. "It hit you in a way you weren't prepared for. The magic forces its way out whether you like it or not."

"I am *not* a disciple of Chaos." Damian felt his body quaking; he could barely keep himself upright. He couldn't be. It didn't make any sense. "My father was a disciple of Strength, as was his father before him."

"And your mother?"

"Her lineage goes back to Cunning."

Calder's lips twitched. "I'm sure it does."

Anger spooled hotly at Damian's core. "You don't know a *thing* about me or my family."

"Tell me, how were you able to enter Brechaat? The pass is not easy to navigate, especially for outsiders."

"Someone obviously wanted us here. You're the one who intends to use us to bargain with the Palazzo—why don't you tell me."

"*Think*," Calder snarled. "Think, and you will realize I speak the truth."

Without intending to, Damian remembered the fog in the prison. The way he'd managed to escape Falco, and how he'd yearned to end her life. He thought of hurling Salvestro into the water, the mist that had shrouded them as they'd sailed away, and the desperation that had possessed him at the Brechaan border.

Sweat beaded on his brow. He was more confident now, that was all. He'd overcome his aversion to killing, and he no longer feared the way he once had. That didn't make him a disciple. There were other explanations for the magic that had plagued them the whole way here.

"You know I'm right," Calder murmured. "I can see it in your face, even if you haven't fully accepted it. You will, though. Like any other saint, Chaos will not be ignored."

Damian couldn't seem to process what Calder was saying. He had always longed to be something more. Something better. But although he didn't detest disciples of Chaos the way most of Ombrazia did, he had always known to fear them. Certainly he didn't want to *be* one.

Did he?

His gaze slid to Roz—the way she had frozen, slack-jawed in bewilderment—and he wondered what she was thinking. If she was remembering the same moments from their journey.

"That can't be," Siena cut in, her denial a sharp thing. "We would have known before now if Damian was a disciple."

Calder was nonplussed. "Not necessarily. Some people don't show signs for years, either because they're late developers or because they've repressed their magic." He tilted his head at Damian. "What changed, apart from the obvious?"

Damian bared his teeth but didn't respond. The ache in his shoulder throbbed dully. Nothing had changed. *Everything* had changed. He'd reunited with Roz, and pulled away from the saints. He'd lost his rank not once, but twice, and his father had died.

Battista had died.

It had broken Damian, yet afterward he'd never felt so free. Was that the difference? Had he been holding this part of himself back, afraid of what his father would say or do?

But if Calder was right—if Damian truly was a disciple of Chaos—then why didn't magic come when he called for it? Why had he only ever used it without knowing? Why couldn't he trap everyone in this room in an illusion and trick them into freeing him? He had so many questions, and Calder Bryhn was the last person he wanted to ask.

The general lowered his gaze, clearly done awaiting a response. "Then again," he said, "perhaps it was not a personal event. Perhaps you felt the shift in power, just like the rest of us."

There was a pause, and Dev made an apprehensive sound in the back of his throat. Roz, however, appeared intrigued. "You're a disciple of Chaos, too?"

"Not a powerful one, even now." Calder pursed his lips. "But yes."

"Then you can help Damian."

"Help him with what? He has nothing to fear in Brechaat. At least," he amended, "not because of his association with Chaos. His relation to Battista Venturi, however, is another story."

"I don't need *help*," Damian snapped, but Roz shot him a look that was part frustration, part pleading, before turning back to Calder.

"This isn't about whether or not he's a disciple of Chaos. I'm telling you, it's more than that. His whole personality has changed. The disciple that terrorized Ombrazia...we thought it was his lingering influence, maybe."

"I know nothing of that," Calder said, ignoring Damian's muttered denials. "And nor do I care. You're here to help us get to your Palazzo—nothing more. If the information you give me proves correct, you'll be freed once the war is won. If you lie, I promise you will regret it." He smiled grimly, and though Damian detested him in that moment, the general didn't particularly seem to relish the threat.

"You don't have to threaten us." Roz attempted to shrug away from her guards, her eyes sparking. "How about this? You help us get our friends back from the Ombrazian front, and we'll guide you to the Palazzo without any trouble."

Damian frowned, his yearning to see Kiran again colliding with his distrust of the Brechaans. Calder may have presented himself as just, even reasonable, but he was still the man who had them in shackles.

"You'll help us anyway," the general objected.

Roz didn't miss a beat. "Yes, we all heard your vague threats. But if you do this, I'll help you *willingly*. You see, I want you to win the war."

Damian's head snapped up, and he couldn't help the harsh words that tore from his throat. "Roz, *no*. I won't let you."

In his periphery he could see that Siena's jaw had dropped, and even Dev appeared perplexed. Roz, though, merely arched a brow.

"Do not presume to think you *let* me do anything, Damian."

The window behind Calder rattled as a breeze barreled past the building. The general's eyes glinted with distrust. "Why on earth would you want Brechaat to win?"

Roz threw up her hands. "I just want the war to be over. All it's done is ruin lives. It certainly ruined mine, and I haven't even played any part in it. Those who have power in Ombrazia aren't good people, so by all means come and destroy them, but the citizens aren't to be touched." She furrowed her brow, conducting some mental calculation. "If we can get there three evenings from now, we'll arrive the night Salvestro Agosti officially becomes the next chief magistrate. Everyone will be at the ceremony—it should make the Palazzo easier to surround."

Calder's lips curled up. "Intriguing."

"Roz, we have *no* assurance the rest of the city will be left alone!" Siena said, panic-stricken. "Who do you think will be forced to contend with this? The security officers. They'll have to protect Falco and Salvestro."

Damian knew without looking at Roz that it was a sacrifice she was willing to make.

Meanwhile, Araina scowled at Siena. "Disciples of Chaos don't need violence to get things done. Surely you know as much."

A soldier attempted to pull Siena back, and she quieted, but not before returning Araina's glare.

Calder resumed his pacing, eyeing Roz with skepticism. "Why should I believe this is what you really want?"

At first it appeared she had no answer. But then Damian saw she was fidgeting with something behind her back, shifting her shoulders with a *clink*. The next moment she was holding her handcuffs out to Calder. They dangled from her fingers, the metal twisted and strange in her grasp. "I could have gotten out of these ages ago, but I didn't. Because I care about my friends more than anything, and I wasn't going anywhere without them. I believe you when you say you're not the bad guys. Or at least, I believe you don't want to be."

How did she do that? Manage to look so calm and confident, addressing Brechaat's general as if she were the one doing *him* a favor?

Calder snatched the handcuffs from her. "A disciple of Patience. Interesting." He appraised her as if her magic might manifest in the angles of her face. "I'll admit you have my attention. How powerful are you?"

Roz hesitated, then said, "Powerful enough."

"In that case, you do something for me *and* guide us into the heart of Ombrazia without necessitating force on my part. In return, I will retrieve your companions from the front and ensure my army takes the Palazzo without taking lives."

"What do you want me to do?" Roz massaged the skin around her wrists, shooting a furtive look at Damian. He wondered if she could see how badly he wanted her to refuse.

"We'll discuss it momentarily," Calder said. "Do we have a deal?"

"That depends. Do you have a way into the Ombrazian camps? How do you plan to rescue our friends?"

"Give me a thorough description of them, and I'll have one of my spies pass a message along. If your friends manage to steal away, they'll be allowed to cross into Brechaat without difficulty. If they don't make it, it's not my problem. You still owe me what you promised. Do I make myself clear?"

"*Roz*," Damian said, a last-ditch attempt, then grunted as he was yanked back by his injured shoulder. Through the haze of pain he saw Roz swallow.

"Fine," she said. "We have an agreement."

Calder nodded. "Then follow me."

The words turned out to be only for Roz—Damian, Siena, and Dev were quickly herded in the opposite direction, down a long hallway into a stone room without a single window.

"Just until Calder directs otherwise," Araina explained before shutting the door, the lock clicking behind her. Damian couldn't help but think she sounded a little too pleased.

There was no handle on this side of the door, so he didn't bother pushing against it. Instead, he searched himself for the magic Calder had assured him he possessed. The very action of doing such a thing was absurd, but if there was ever a time when power would be useful, it was now. The idea of leaving Roz alone with the Brechaans made Damian want to crawl out of his skin.

But no matter how he searched, he found nothing save his own futile desperation.

23

Roz

Roz hoped she looked more confident than she felt. Every aspect of her bargain with Calder was dangerous, but if she had something the general wanted, she would use it to her benefit.

She wanted to believe his spy would be able to find Kiran and Nasim, but she knew better than to hope. Worst-case scenario, no one would be able to find them. Or the Brechaans might lie about having tried. The best-case scenario was that her and Damian's friends left the north as deserters. She regretted not asking the general to save all the rebels—regretted it in a way that made her ache right down to her core—but she knew it would have been impossible. Besides, if Calder's disciples really *could* end the war, the Ombrazian soldiers would make their way home regardless. Right?

She knew it was a childishly optimistic view to take. The reality was this: They were at Calder's mercy. Luckily, Roz suspected he had more than he let on.

She thought of the way Damian had looked as he was led away. How his eyes had met hers across the room, full of naked vulnerability beneath the rage. She'd given a small shake of her head, trying to communicate that she was fine. He'd relented and gone with the soldiers, but Roz could tell he was precariously hanging on to self-control.

"You need to help Damian," she told the general now. "He's hurt."

"Signor Venturi will be helped once he calms down. I won't put my soldiers in any danger."

"He isn't dangerous."

Calder frowned at her. "Yes," he said, almost pityingly. "He is."

He didn't appear to relish the thought of Damian in pain, so that was something. To distract herself, Roz asked, "What makes you so sure he *is* a disciple, and not being controlled by someone else's magic?"

"I could sense it," Calder said. "Couldn't you?"

Milos was holding the door open, and the general made his way over to it, beckoning Roz along with him. Araina had returned as well, now gluing herself to Roz's side. Damian and the others couldn't be far, then. The woman's gun was still drawn, and she never looked at Roz directly. If circumstances had been different, Roz might have been struck by how lovely she was. Tall and muscled, with golden hair and nearly black irises, Araina was striking. The kind of woman she would have flirted with, once upon a time.

"Like I said, I'm far from a powerful disciple," Calder continued as they walked down the corridor, "but I'm particularly skilled in pinpointing magic's source. How do you think I was able to build an army of disciples?"

"I haven't seen any proof of this army." Roz lengthened her stride to keep up.

"You will. Some have been with me for years, but others I intercepted as they were drawn south, following the pull of Chaos's power. That's how Milos came to be here." Calder nodded at the other man.

"I am in your debt once more," Milos said softly.

Roz frowned, slowing a little. "What do you mean, once more?"

Milos's eyes were on the general's back as he answered. "Calder and his father freed me from the Forgotten Keep—the place Ombrazia brings disciples of Chaos as children and leaves them to die."

She recoiled. "I've never heard of such a place."

"Of course you haven't." Milos's smile was bitter, a little sardonic. "It's forgotten, after all."

Calder stopped, obviously overhearing. "You owe me nothing," he told Milos. Then to Roz: "Ombrazia considers itself a land of the devout, but it has many terrible secrets. We saved as many of your disciples as we could, but not all of them." A pause. "Not enough."

After what Enzo had said, Roz had assumed young disciples of Chaos were killed, but somehow knowing the method was worse. They didn't deserve death at all, of course, but leaving them to suffer in dark isolation? That was crueler than making it quick.

"When it comes to Damian Venturi," Calder continued, "he's lucky he managed to repress his power as long as he did. I suspect his father would have killed him personally. And to answer your earlier question more completely, I'm certain Venturi's a disciple because the one who controlled you both that night is dead. His power would have faded by now."

"I thought a disciple of Chaos's influence could linger."

"Yes—for hours, perhaps, but rarely longer than that."

They were outside now, though they'd exited through a different door. Roz had a clear view of the scene she'd glimpsed through the window: They were mere yards from the river, the Ombrazian camps rising in the distance. The rickety bridge glinted in the midday light.

"But it can be undone, right?" Roz couldn't help asking, remembering what they'd learned in the Atheneum. *Offer what was given*. "I mean, Chaos's magic was strengthened through sacrifice, so it can also be weakened again. Then Damian would go back to normal."

No matter how many times Calder confirmed it, she couldn't fathom the reality of Damian being a disciple—especially not a disciple of Chaos. So much of his life, he'd been plagued by the fear that being unfavored meant he wasn't good enough. Being blessed by Chaos, though...to those in Ombrazia, that was worse than being unfavored. Roz couldn't shake the feeling she ought to have noticed somehow. She'd known Damian almost her whole life. How could she not have realized? How had he never shown a single indication of possessing magic?

"That's what they say," Calder agreed, an edge to his voice. "When it comes to Venturi, however, becoming a disciple does not change you. I don't know him as you do, but I can tell you that much."

"He's different," Roz insisted. "The real Damian is levelheaded. He avoids violence as much as he can." To her horror, she felt pressure building behind her eyes. "He cares about people even when he shouldn't."

"I don't know what to tell you. Perhaps his father's teachings are more deep-seated than you realized, and his struggle is borne from self-loathing."

"He rejected Battista's 'teachings' long ago. This is something more."

Calder shrugged. "Then maybe there are things at play that I do not understand. I'll admit, I've never tried to sacrifice innocent lives in the name of making my patron saint more powerful."

"So you think Enzo was wrong to do what he did."

The general looked askance at her. "Of course he was wrong. Do you think me a monster?"

"But it's benefiting you now," Roz pointed out.

"And? It happened, so I've taken advantage of it. That doesn't mean I believe it was right. You may think me mad, but I pity him. To grow up in Ombrazia, always trying to avoid detection…that must have been a miserable existence. I confess I'm not surprised he became what he did." At Roz's grimace, he gave a crooked grin. "I am not a bad man, Signora—ah. Your surname?"

"Lacertosa," she told him, because there didn't seem to be any reason not to. "Roz Lacertosa."

Calder inclined his head. "Signora Lacertosa. You may think me cruel, but I simply do what I must, even if the choices are difficult."

"I don't think you're cruel." She was surprised to find it was the truth.

"No?"

"I've known cruel men."

He inclined his head. "Then perhaps you'll understand why I don't wish to undo what has been done. Not yet, at least."

They stood at the edge of the river now, and Roz shoved her hands into her pockets, ignoring the way Araina's scrutiny intensified. Ensuring she wasn't reaching for a hidden weapon, probably. "Because then your army wouldn't be strong enough to take the Palazzo."

"Right." Calder stared out across the water, something wistful in his gaze. Perhaps Roz should have been frightened, but she saw only a young man sharpened by loss and a crushing sense of duty. Calder Bryhn reminded her of Damian, she realized suddenly. Or at least, the way Damian had been.

The wind buffeted Roz's face, and she slitted her eyes against it. "Why am I here?"

Calder's face hardened as if suddenly remembering they were not friends. He pointed at the bridge Roz had noticed earlier. "The Ombrazian army built that bridge," he said. "See how it stretches from the far side of the shore to the isle in the middle of the river? It's a large part of the reason we've been unable to participate in trade. It's not merely a bridge—it's a barrier. Somehow it lifts for any Ombrazian ships that need to pass, but Brechaans can't get by." Calder indicated the closer side of the isle. "Obviously, taking this route isn't an option. It's too shallow, and only the smallest ships can pass through. Our major trading partners know this, and they stopped coming here years ago."

Roz could already see why she had been brought here. "The bridge is reinforced with Patience-made steel. It recognizes the Ombrazian vessels, but doesn't let anyone else through."

"Precisely." Calder appeared startled she'd been able to surmise that so easily. "It detaches from itself, lifting in the middle."

"And you want me to undo the magic that keeps the Brechaan fleet from being able to pass through."

"Yes."

It was a tall order. Roz wasn't sure she *could* undo it. For one, it all depended on whether or not she was stronger than the disciple who'd put it in place initially. On top of that, undoing another disciple of Patience's work was a blatant show of utmost disrespect. People had been removed from the guild for daring to do such a thing. It wasn't that she *cared* about the guild's rules—it was that she'd been careful to follow them for so long now, knowing a slipup could mean an end to the stipend she received by virtue of being a member. The stipend that kept her and her mother afloat.

"If I do that," she asked Calder, "you'll hold up your end of the deal?"

He dipped his chin, eyes hard. "I always keep my promises. I already have someone passing a message to your friends at the front. If you can do this for me, I'll know you mean it when you say you don't support the Palazzo."

"Agreeing to help you infiltrate it wasn't proof enough?"

"I can't be sure you're serious until the time comes. If I'm going to work with you, I need to be certain you won't lead me astray. Of course, the alternative is that I hold your friends' lives in the balance to *ensure* you won't betray me."

What a frustrating man. The worst part, though, was that Roz understood him. She would have done the same had their roles been reversed. Allowing someone to guide her into the heart of enemy territory without any proof they wouldn't betray her? It was unthinkable.

"Fine," she said heavily. "I'll try. I can't promise it will work, though."

Damian would lose his mind if he knew she was agreeing to this. It wasn't that she thought it would be overly dangerous, but being the first to carry out one's side of a bargain was never exactly *safe*. She had no proof Calder had actually delivered a message to Nasim and Kiran. But what other choice did she have?

"How am I supposed to get out there?" she asked, realizing there wasn't a boat in sight.

"Swim, I suppose" was Calder's simple reply. "The isle isn't far, and you seem physically fit enough. I'll create a simple illusion to shield you, but a boat would be far too conspicuous."

She gritted her teeth. He was undoubtedly doing this on purpose. But he was right—the center of the bridge wasn't *that* far. She stripped off her jacket, shirt, and boots, handing them to Araina. The other woman held the items away from herself as if they might have some kind of disease. Roz scowled, standing unashamedly before them in only her tank top and trousers.

"Good luck," Calder told her, and he sounded like he meant it.

This was an outrageous request. Roz knew that even as she waded into the river, breath catching at the cold. It wasn't so frigid as to be unsafe, but she knew she would have to move quickly to keep her blood pumping. With a last resentful glance at the general, she dove into the water.

It was even colder once her whole body was submerged. She gasped, heart going wild in her chest. This was a test—nothing more. If it appeared she was going to drown, or freeze, Calder would likely send someone out to assist her. He wasn't the type to stand by and watch someone die.

She hoped.

But he'd been right about one thing—Roz was fit. She was a decent swimmer, too, from years spent frolicking with Damian in the river near their childhood homes. She swam as quickly as she could, thankful the waves weren't against her. The return trip would be the difficult one. Her entire body was shuddering with the cold, but it only spurred her to move faster. She refused to feel the panic tightening her chest. She couldn't think about what kinds of creatures might live in the northern sea or the fact that the water wasn't clear enough for her to see anything past the sweep of her own arms.

As she swam, she remembered a day very like this one, the sky heavy with the promise of rain and a large military boat bobbing in the waves. She could remember scrabbling up the side of it, the frame of its metal porthole coming apart in her hands. That was what her magic did—it destroyed. And that day, determined as she was to save Damian, was the first time she'd ever let it. Could she do it again? Freeing herself from handcuffs was one thing, but undoing another disciple's magic was another entirely.

When she was only a few meters from the isle, she extended one of her legs, testing the depth of the river. Her toes met stone. Roz relaxed, finding she could stand without much difficulty. The water here came up only to her chest, and although the stones on the riverbed were slippery, she managed to get to shore, waterlogged trousers chafing the skin of her legs. Curse Calder and his miserable requests.

The isle was tiny, a small plot of land she could have crossed in minutes. The nearest bridge pier was only a few steps away, and she strode over to it, teeth chattering all the while. She might have to swim farther if she wanted to find the exact part the disciple had manipulated to allow Ombrazian ships through, but she wanted to try something first. She tilted her head back, examining the bearings that connected the bridge piers to the deck. They were metal, of course, but far too high to reach. Roz coughed, spitting salty water onto the rocks. She didn't know how to do this. She couldn't even remember what she'd done on the military ship to break open the porthole. It had simply happened when she'd focused her attention, and with far more dramatic results than intended.

She could see Calder and Araina unmoving on the shore, Milos a short distance behind them. Through the light cover of mist that must have been Calder's doing, it was impossible to see their faces, but Roz could tell they were watching her. She took a deep breath—or at least tried to, given her perpetual shuddering—and placed her hands on the nearest bridge pier. It was cold, and slick from algae, but nothing happened.

This was pointless. Reinforced with metal or not, if she couldn't reach the bearings, she wasn't going to be able to do anything.

She thought of Damian, Siena, and Dev, trapped somewhere in the compound. Thought of Nasim and Kiran arriving on the front lines. Roz wasn't easily convinced of most things, but she couldn't shake the thought that Calder was inherently *good*, at least compared to the other military leaders she was familiar with. If she could do this for him, she believed he would help her in return. She wanted him to reach the Palazzo. She wanted to watch it fall.

Her hands had grown numb, but as she pressed them more firmly into the bridge, she felt warmth spread along her arms and into her fingers, pooling there. The sensation was familiar enough by now that it wasn't exactly uncomfortable. Her next exhale caught in her chest, and she reached out with her magic, probing for something she couldn't see. To her surprise, she could *sense* the manipulations that some other disciple had made to the bridge. She shouldn't have been able to, given that she wasn't even touching the metal, but she could. It was like something alive, pulsing beneath her fingertips. Somehow, she had reached it indirectly.

But she didn't know what to do next. She'd never undone someone else's magic. Her body ached as she tried to hold on to the feeling, but at least the effort was warming her icy skin.

"Come *on*," she huffed. She'd spent her entire life holding back. She knew she could be powerful when necessary.

There was a sound like a thunderclap, and at first Roz thought that was exactly what it had been. The world seemed to blur at the edges, and the sound came again. This time, though, she recognized it for what it was. Something in the very foundation of the bridge was cracking.

She wasn't undoing anything. She was destroying it.

Distantly Roz understood this, but she couldn't make herself move. She felt like an addict, unable to shift away once her magic realized it could flow freely. And saints, it felt *good*. She swore she could feel the earth quiver beneath her feet and heard an indecipherable shout on the wind, but still she didn't budge.

There was a horrible cracking sound, followed by a groan, and then the bridge began to collapse.

The deck separated in a number of places, great slabs of it plummeting into the water. The power of it sent waves crashing toward the sky. Only then did Roz wrench herself free. Her heart was alive in her chest, her feet soaked once more by the lapping water. She had to *move*, before she was either crushed or washed out to sea.

She turned and ran to the far edge of the isle. Adrenaline pulsed through her veins, and the part of her that lacked self-preservation felt something akin to glee. She'd done this. Her power wasn't only strong—it was magnificent.

She let out a sound somewhere between a laugh and a whoop as what was left of the bridge collapsed into the sea.

Then she leapt into the water, fighting the waves back to shore.

24

ROZ

Calder hadn't said much when Roz returned. She'd been able to see his triumph, but it was mixed with a bit of fear, too. The nod he gave her was wary, and then he'd allowed Araina to escort her back into the building, remaining outside to speak with Milos. Araina had wordlessly presented her with some dry clothes and a threadbare towel, indicating she was to spend the night in the room they had entered. The general, Araina said, had declared they would leave for Ombrazia the next day. Then she had slipped out, the unmistakable sound of a lock clicking in her wake.

After what Roz had just done, it seemed especially foolish to try and contain her in a room with a regular metal lock, but she made no attempt to escape. She wouldn't have been surprised to learn this was another of Calder's tests. It wasn't exactly a show of good faith to detain her, but at least she wasn't in some kind of cell. She didn't *trust* Calder, but she did want to be able to work together. Young and good-humored as he was, it was difficult to remember he was Brechaat's general. Perhaps that was another reason Roz had found it so easy to believe Ombrazia was the cause of all the turmoil associated with the second war. Nothing about Calder suggested he wanted anything other than an end to the conflict.

The room was empty save for a small cot, a desk—no chair, nothing in the drawers—and a carpet that partially covered the stone floor. A map had been pinned on one of the walls, and Roz studied it for a moment, intrigued by all the parts of Brechaat she'd never seen illustrated on any of the maps back in Ombrazia. Then she changed out of her wet clothes, lay down on the carpet, and stared up at the ceiling. She wondered where the others were. If they were still in the building, or if they'd been taken elsewhere. She wondered if they were angry at her for the deal she'd made with Calder. Surely they realized this was what the rebels had always been working toward—a way to tear down the Palazzo. Roz had few qualms about partnering with the enemy to finally ensure it happened.

She thought, as her gaze tracked the shadows on the ceiling, that Piera would have done the same.

Day turned into night, the hours slipping by. Roz avoided the cot—partially because she felt guilty knowing Damian, Dev, and Siena were in far less comfortable accommodations, but mostly because she didn't want to let her guard down. She must have fallen asleep at some point, however, because she jolted back to consciousness at the sound of the door opening. *Saints.* To let herself be vulnerable like that, even for a short while, was utterly foolish. She managed to pull herself into a seated position just as Calder appeared on the threshold.

"Were you sleeping on the floor?" he said, brows drawn together.

"No," she snapped.

Calder gave her a withering look that suggested he knew she was lying. "We'll leave at dusk to avoid being spotted by the Ombrazian army. My spy should have gotten the message to your friends at the front by now, though I haven't seen any sign of them."

Roz's heart sank. "We can't go without them."

"You don't get to decide what we can or cannot do." At her livid stare, he rolled his eyes. "If they show up on our shores after we've departed, they will be met with kindness. You have my word. But my enemies on the other side of the river will certainly have seen the bridge fall, and I won't be surprised if they send for reinforcements—perhaps even disciples of Patience—to rebuild it. We need to reach Ombrazian shores before they reach ours."

They had come all this way to save their friends, and no part of Roz wanted to leave before they had done just that. At the same time, though, she couldn't imagine trying to tell Nasim there'd been a plan in place to end the war and that she'd refused to see it through. Nasim would never allow Roz to put her life above so many others, no matter how much Roz might want to. It was why Nasim had always been a better choice to lead the rebels; she would sacrifice anything. Roz was no longer sure she could say the same. She would sacrifice herself, but she was too selfish to sacrifice those she cared for the most. Damian. Nasim. Dev. Even Siena and Kiran.

Calder had given her the space to think, and finally Roz looked into his expectant face. "Can your word be trusted?"

"Can *yours*?" he shot back.

She glanced pointedly at yesterday's clothes. "I swam through a freezing river for you. I betrayed Ombrazia when I destroyed that bridge."

"I am well aware. You have my thanks."

He was missing the point. "Do you seriously still not believe I'm on your side?"

"I believe it," Calder sighed, pulling at the ends of his hair. "According to a couple of my spies, the Ombrazian commanders are distressed. They can't fathom how we managed to bring down the bridge. In return, I said I would try to help your friends, and

I've done all I can." He tilted his head. "You truly wish to see the Palazzo fall?"

"I don't just want to see it fall. I want to burn it to the ground." Roz was surprised by the vehement truth of the statement. "I want to see the war won, not fought until there's no one left."

Calder's gaze was steady, assessing, but no longer suspicious. "Then the only thing left is for you to convince Signor Venturi to reveal the patterns of Ombrazia's security."

"I can do that," Roz said, hoping it was true.

"And you're certain the ceremony will take place two nights from now?"

The one where Salvestro would become chief magistrate, he meant. It would be, Roz hoped, the shortest reign to date. "Yes. It needs to happen then."

The general nodded, extending a calloused hand.

Without hesitation, she took it.

Several hours of uneventful captivity later, Roz stepped into the dusk, Araina dutifully at her side. The impending light of the moon glazed the distant sea silver. A ship bobbed in the waves, a familiar, shadowy silhouette. She couldn't see its flag from where she stood, but she knew it boasted Brechaat's ensign. Her heart lurched as the echoing tremor of a foghorn pierced the air.

Calder walked a short distance ahead, speaking fervently with Milos and a curly haired man named Feodor. She shifted her weight, impatient.

"Relax," Araina grunted. "They're right there."

Roz turned to see Damian, Siena, and Dev emerge from the building with a half dozen soldiers. Damian was moving rather gingerly, though he looked much better than he had. Calder had granted her request, then.

"Shoulder was dislocated," Damian grunted the moment he was close enough to be within earshot, noticing her assessment. "Medic put it back. What the hell did he want from you?"

Roz didn't have to ask who he meant. "I'll explain later."

Something in her tone must have unnerved him, because he said, "What did you *do*?"

"Let it go, Damian," she said, well aware that Araina was watching them closely.

Dev came up beside her, gaze roving her features. "Roz. You're okay?" He was no longer handcuffed, she realized. None of them were.

"Of course."

Siena was the only one who seemed to notice Roz wasn't wearing the same clothes—she scanned her from collar to boots, arching a brow, but said nothing.

"Get moving," Araina interrupted, indicating the ship. Roz made to follow the soldier, but Dev didn't budge.

"What about Nasim?" he said.

Roz shook her head, sickness in the pit of her stomach. "They haven't showed." Both Dev and Siena wilted. "If they arrive once we're gone, though, Calder says they'll be welcomed by Brechaat."

"And you *believe* that?" Siena said under her breath.

"I do," Roz said defensively. It wasn't as if they had another choice. She had to believe their friends would be okay. "The war is the reason they're in danger, and we have a chance to stop it."

"And you trust Calder?"

"I trust him enough for this. He knows we're not his enemies, and he's not ours. We want the same things." Her gaze slid from Siena to Damian, then back again. "You need to tell him how to avoid Ombrazian security patrols once we cross the border, and once we enter the city. Please."

Damian was stock-still. Siena, however, said, "That's the worst kind of betrayal. We can't just—"

"Do you *want* to risk your previous colleagues running into an army of Chaos disciples?"

Siena's shoulders drooped. "You have a point." She turned to Damian. "Are you okay with this? You know the rotations better than I do."

His laugh was humorless. "Does it matter if I'm okay with it? You're clearly already on board, and no matter what I say, Roz is going to do what she thinks is best."

"Do you have a better plan you'd like to share, Damian?" Roz snapped, but his words stung. What was wrong with doing what she thought was best? She didn't want to live in a world like this anymore. A world where her father was dead and her friends were in danger. A world where she should have *stayed* unfavored, instead of becoming something her father would have resented. If she could only help to fix things, wouldn't that make up for the parts of herself she hated?

"Calder is a good man," Araina put in curtly from behind them, making no effort to pretend she hadn't been listening. "His inclination is to trust, though he fights against it in order to be a good general. Despite what he may have said, he does not see every Ombrazian as the enemy. Our people were the same once." To Roz alone she said, "It is clear you have earned his trust. Do not make him regret giving it."

Then she stomped toward the sea, leaving them no choice but to follow. Roz hadn't known Araina was capable of stringing so many words together, but it was the same impression she herself had gotten from Calder, so she felt vindicated in the knowledge.

Her foot snagged on a little plant near the edge of the path, and Roz glanced down, chest tightening as she recognized the dark flower. *Vellenium.* The plant used to make the poison Enzo had killed his victims with. She wrenched it from the soil and pocketed it. When she straightened again, she felt Damian's good arm brush hers. Frustration radiated from his body. Even though he was physically beside her, Roz still missed him with a visceral ache. Once, she might have thought this version of Damian perfect for her. After all, surely they were more alike now than they had been before.

But the real Damian was soft in the places Roz was hard. He was careful where she was impulsive, and regretful where she was unrepentant. He was complicated where she was woefully simplistic—her focus was singular, his multifaceted. Roz, though, had focused on one thing for so long that she wasn't sure how to broaden it. She wanted revenge. She wanted justice. She wanted change. How could she not? She'd always been willing to die in pursuit of those goals, so how could she think beyond them?

If you were angry, driven, relentless, then you couldn't possibly crumble beneath the weight of all that the world had inflicted on you. Roz had abided by that principle far too long to stop now.

Damian made her want to change, though.

Or at least, he had.

As they reached the shore, Roz was able to see past the towering cliff face for the first time. She realized with a jolt that the ship she'd noticed earlier was far from the only one. There were four more waiting a short distance away, obviously arranged so as to be hidden from anyone who might be looking from Ombrazia's side of the river. The ships were moderate in size—nothing like Ombrazia's largest military vessels—but Roz could see dozens of figures milling about on the decks, the low hum of their voices growing audible as she neared. Up ahead, Calder glanced over his shoulder as if to gauge her reaction, a sly grin lifting one side of his mouth.

"I told you I had an army," he called back to her.

There were approximately two dozen disciples aboard each ship, Araina reminded them as they boarded the nearest one. The rest of the crew were merely regular soldiers who wouldn't be setting foot on Ombrazian land. Someone had to stay with the boats once they arrived, she declared, or Palazzo security officers would make quick work of them. Between Roz and Siena, they would discern the best place to anchor the ships, then row to shore with the disciples. Siena begrudgingly agreed that she could tell them the best routes to avoid any officers, while Roz, of course, knew the least-traveled roads of the city's underbelly.

Their presence aboard the ship was met with distrustful gazes. A sense of unease crept up Roz's spine at the sight of so many disciples of Chaos. They were easily identifiable—where the regular Brechaan soldiers ran about adjusting the sails or moving crates as they prepared to depart, the disciples stood clustered together, barely speaking. From what Roz could tell, they were citizens of all genders, and they ranged in age and skin tone, though she doubted any were younger than sixteen or older than fifty.

She wondered if they were worried. If they expected their attack on the Palazzo to be easily accomplished, given their strengthened power, or if they were preparing to lose some of their number.

"Keep to this side of the ship," Calder directed Araina, having sidled over to their group. His face was serious. "I haven't briefed everyone yet, so many will be wondering why we have Ombrazians aboard." To Roz he added, "There's a bunk area down those steps. You four stay in the room directly on the right. It's small, but separate from my army. They won't bother you."

She nodded. Above them, Brechaat's flag lashed in the wind. It bore a crescent moon with an arrow through it, misshapen thanks to the rippling fabric. This was it. They were going back to Ombrazia, and one way or another, things were going to get messy.

"Wait," Dev said softly, his gaze fixed on something over Calder's left shoulder. His breath caught. "Is that—?"

Roz looked in the direction he indicated. Three dark-haired figures had just crested the hill leading down to the water, the moon illuminating them enough that two were immediately recognizable: a very tall boy with narrow shoulders, his hair pulled back in a knot, and a much smaller girl with a long plait. The third figure looked to be another boy, though Roz couldn't tell if it was someone she knew.

"Nasim," she said, at the same time that Siena whispered, "Kiran."

25

DAMIAN

From what Damian could gather, Nasim and Kiran's escape from the front lines was indeed thanks to Calder. The messenger he'd sent had tracked down an Ombrazian soldier who had long been in the Bryhn family's pocket—it was the man's fourth tour at this point, and he resented the Palazzo even more than Roz—and from there the message had been passed on to their friends. Thankfully Kiran and Nasim hadn't been moved from the camps by the river yet, and once they'd ascertained the entire thing wasn't a trap, they stole away to the border where another of Calder's men had guided them to the Brechaan military base. Damian was surprised that even the most loyal soldier would be willing to escort two Ombrazians into their territory, but then again, Calder held an uncanny amount of sway over his army. They trusted him in a way that went beyond regular duty.

Damian didn't know what to think about the general. He hadn't thought about much at all since Calder told him he was a disciple of Chaos—he simply couldn't make sense of it. And he'd had hours to try and do just that, trapped in a tiny, windowless room with Siena and Dev. Their solitude was interrupted only by an apprehensive-looking soldier who'd come to deliver a meal and reset Damian's shoulder. Damian had refused at first—things like that ought to be dealt with by a disciple of Mercy—but with Siena's coaxing, he'd allowed it to be done. Every other moment he'd spent trying to summon magic, convinced that if he possessed the power Calder thought he did, he should have been able to do *something*. After all, he'd apparently been using magic since that first conversation with Falco back in the prison. So why wasn't it working? It grated against his insides. He knew he shouldn't want that power, but he couldn't seem to help it.

On the other hand, Calder had brought him Kiran, and for that Damian could only be glad. He hadn't realized how tightly wound he was—how heavily concern for his friend's safety weighed on him— until he'd seen Kiran's outline descending the path toward him. Perhaps he did still feel fear, then, if he could notice the absence of it.

Both Kiran and Nasim looked exhausted, their clothes dirty and hair unkempt, but obvious relief emanated from them when they saw Damian, Roz, Siena, and Dev. Siena had embraced Kiran with a cry of joy, and when Kiran moved to hug Damian in return, he let it happen. Roz had barreled into Nasim, her voice thick with barely suppressed tears, though she quickly regained control of herself to let Dev come forward.

Damian had only been half paying attention, but he'd seen the way Dev hesitated before pulling Nasim toward him. He saw the way they clung to each other as if the saints themselves couldn't wrench them apart. And though he tried very hard not to, he saw the way Dev's eyes moved to Nasim's mouth, his face full of a wanting so unmistakable and bittersweet that Damian wished the reunion had taken place somewhere else.

But then Nasim had disentangled herself, beckoning the third member of their group forward: a serious-looking older boy with her exact coloring.

"This is my brother, Zain," she'd said, eliciting a gasp from Roz and Dev.

"I never thought I'd be so happy to be in Brechaat," Kiran said to Damian now, having concluded the tale of their escape across the border. "Hell, I never thought I'd see you again."

"You and me both," Damian managed gruffly. "I missed you."

"*We* missed you," Siena said.

Kiran's mouth tilted in that good-natured way of his. "The Ombrazian camps are falling apart, you know. It's nothing like the last time I was here. There isn't much battle—we're just holding the land at this point, I think, because Brechaat has stopped sending soldiers to fight for it. And I can't exactly blame them, seeing as we're taking their dead."

Siena made a choking sound. "We're *what*?"

"They collect Brechaat's dead soldiers," Kiran repeated, expression turning grave. "I don't know why. Just to be horrible, I suppose. Apparently this is where Falco was based before she came to the Palazzo, and everything is a mess. There are hardly any high-ranking officers around, though I can't imagine where else they're being sent. People are deserting left and right, despite the fact that there's nowhere for them to go."

Damian grimaced. Falco was even worse than he'd realized, if she was giving orders for Ombrazia to take Brechaat's deceased. It was an unspoken rule of war that you didn't tamper with the other side's dead. They were always to be returned to their land, their families, assuming it was possible. "Falco did bring quite a few officers with her," he pointed out. "Why she'd do that to the detriment of the front lines, though, I've no idea."

Kiran shrugged. "I'm telling you, something weird is going on. It's like prisoners are being sent up here just to get rid of them. Even as we were arriving, another full ship was leaving, and I have no idea where it was taking those soldiers."

Damian cracked his knuckles, thinking. "Falco expects something big from Calder. It sounds like she's taking the best fighters elsewhere in anticipation of an attack. Or maybe she plans to launch one."

"But where?" Siena said.

They all went silent. What did Falco know that they didn't?

Before they could continue the conversation, Roz suggested they go belowdecks, away from the curious, watchful gazes of Calder's army. They obliged, filing down the narrow wooden stairwell. Damian had to duck his head to fit, and their musty-smelling room was only just tall enough for him to stand up straight. It contained a number of small bunks, and while Kiran and Siena clambered onto a bottom one, he didn't bother trying to fit. He remained by the door, shutting it once everyone had entered.

It felt oddly like a collision of worlds: him with his closest friends and Roz with hers. Although Dev and Siena were getting along now, the awkwardness was still palpable. After the night of Enzo's death, Nasim had treated Damian with civility, but he knew she didn't care for security officers.

It turned out Nasim's brother had been at the front for quite some time. He said little, his watchful gaze tracking the conversation, though it lingered on Damian every so often. Did he recognize him? Their time in the north would have overlapped, although Zain was a year or so older. Damian couldn't say he recalled ever seeing the boy before. Perhaps Zain knew him in the same way that Calder had. Perhaps he had looked at Damian and seen Battista Venturi in his face.

Nasim, on the other hand, never looked at Damian at all. She held her brother's hand tightly, as if he were a child she was afraid to lose. Everyone listened with rapt attention as Roz shared an abridged version of what had happened since the meeting at the Palazzo, ending with the plan Calder had concocted. Hearing it again, Damian shifted in discomfort. The part of him that remembered growing up under Battista's tutelage recoiled from the prospect of helping Brechaat do anything, let alone win the war.

But there was another part of Damian—a part that seemed to grow stronger the more he considered it—that longed for violence and destruction. The mere idea of Falco and Salvestro strutting around the Palazzo made him yearn to burn it to the ground.

"Saints, this sounds so risky," Kiran said. "And you're telling me this ship is full of Chaos disciples as we speak?"

Roz nodded, and Damian felt a wave of discomfort pass over him. Was he among that number? Having Kiran back lent a sense of normalcy, and Damian felt as if he had slipped into a set of familiar clothes without realizing.

"Better they attack the Palazzo than the Ombrazian camps," Nasim said, jutting her chin as if daring anyone to argue. "The people there don't stand a chance. The most seasoned soldiers and officers are being sent elsewhere, so Falco must suspect Brechaat is planning something. Whether or not she knows about the disciples, though…"

"She couldn't possibly," Dev cut in. "Right?"

Damian shrugged. Nasim had noticed the same thing as Kiran. Who knew what information Falco had uncovered or what her plan was? "Even if she does, she won't expect them to show up in Ombrazia. The fighting has been concentrated at the northern front for years. She'll expect Calder to launch an attack there."

"She definitely suspects something," Roz agreed. "It's almost strange no Ombrazian ships ever caught up to us. It makes you wonder if Falco sent any at all."

Kiran freed his hair from its knot, running his fingers through the dirty strands before retying it. He definitely looked the worse for wear, but his good nature hadn't faded. "Forgive me, but isn't this Bryhn fellow essentially Brechaat's version of Falco? What makes you so sure we can trust him?"

"Well, he told us he would get you away from the front, and he did," Siena pointed out. "I was skeptical, too, at first, but he's not like any general we've known before."

Roz tilted her face to the low wooden ceiling. The air down here was damp, and Damian felt it grow even heavier with whatever she was about to tell them. He wasn't the only one to notice—the rest of the group quieted, looking at her expectantly.

"I brought down the bridge for Calder," she said finally. "The one Ombrazia had built to block Brechaan ships."

Damian snapped his head around to stare at her. "You did *what*? How?"

Roz seemed a bit uncomfortable. "I don't know, honestly. Once Calder found out I was a disciple of Patience, he wanted me to prove I was trustworthy. And it wasn't like I could blame him— we're Ombrazian. Besides, that bridge was Patience-made, and its magic would only let Ombrazian ships through. That's part of why Brechaat is having such a hard time with trade."

Dev waved an impatient hand as if Brechaat's economy was of little interest to him. "Calder wanted you to prove yourself by bringing down an entire bridge?"

"Not exactly. He wanted me to undo the magic that made it into a blockade."

"Isn't that nearly impossible to do?" Siena asked, and Roz gave a noncommittal shrug.

"I didn't think it would work at first. But then it did, and the entire bridge just...broke apart. I didn't only undo the magic— I destroyed it. I don't know how. Ombrazia's military higher-ups are aware, obviously, and they're not happy. It's part of the reason Calder wants to strike now, before they can attack Brechaat in retaliation."

Damian eyed the curve of Roz's neck, the crease at the corner of her lip as she pursed them. Of course she was powerful. Everything about her suggested that she should be. And yet she held herself with an odd sort of trepidation, as if she expected them to be angry.

No, he realized as her gaze slid to his—she expected *him* to be angry.

"How are *you* doing, by the way?" Kiran asked Damian before he could say anything. "You seem a bit—"

"I'm fine," Damian said shortly, clenching his fists in his lap. "Calder thinks I'm a disciple of Chaos." He didn't know what made him lay it out quite like that, but at least it was done.

"What?" Kiran blinked. "But you're...I mean, *how*?"

"Your guess is as good as mine. Turns out my father might not have been the only liar in the family."

This he said mildly, but Roz's frown deepened. Zain, who had begun to inch back as if he thought Damian might be contagious, winced as Nasim delivered a gentle cuff to the head.

"Don't start worrying about Chaos disciples now," she advised her brother. "We're already on a ship full of them."

"So back in Ombrazia, when you were...struggling," Kiran said slowly, "was this the cause all along? Why didn't you tell us?"

Damian snapped his teeth together. "I didn't know. I still don't. I can't seem to do magic, for one thing." *And I want to. I didn't realize how badly until it became a true possibility.*

He didn't say the last part. He trapped the thought deep inside himself, a wild thing that railed against the enclosure of his ribs. How much longer could he keep it leashed?

"We thought Enzo's lingering influence was affecting Damian," Roz explained. "We asked the Atheneum about that, too. There are stories of it happening, but Calder doesn't think that's what's going on." She cut Damian a furtive look. "Once his disciples take the Palazzo—if they do—I still think we should try and undo what Enzo did. *Something* happened to you that night, Damian, I know it did. I saw it."

Damian leapt to his feet, his earlier calm evaporating. His blood raced, the room around him seeming to sharpen. He scarcely heard the words that left his own mouth. "What do you mean, you 'saw it'? Saw what, exactly?" Before Roz could answer he added, "I don't know how many times I have to tell you—I'm *happy* now. There's no reason to weaken Chaos's magic again."

Roz stood as well. "Even Calder agrees Enzo shouldn't have done what he did. It throws everything out of balance."

"I don't care what *Calder* thinks." Damian made the general's name a twisted thing. "Who is he to lead an army? Who is *Calder Bryhn* to win a war?"

Silence spanned between them like something infinite. Fury blurred his vision at the edges. He felt as if he was trying to steer someone else's body and speaking with someone else's tongue. They weren't his, these words, and yet no sentiment had ever belonged to him so fully.

The strange thing was, he didn't know what exactly Roz was trying to take from him. He knew only that undoing the result of Enzo's ritual was something he very much did not want. Knew it as intimately as if it had seeped into the marrow of his bones. The way his friends watched him, though, was unnerving. They looked at him as if he was a stranger. There was worry in their faces. Disbelief. And maybe, if he wasn't mistaken, a little bit of fear.

All at once the room felt far too small. Damian couldn't bear it. He couldn't bear any of this.

In a daze, he turned and walked out the door.

26

ROZ

This journey was faster than the first. Calder pushed his crew to continue through the night, and from what Roz could tell, the disciples were sleeping in shifts. She saw little of the general himself, other than when she and Siena supplied him with directions, and knew he must be busy making sure things were in order. She tried to tell herself everything was going according to plan, but all the while her heart was slowly fracturing. Damian—or at least the creature wearing his face— had slipped back in among them shortly after his outburst, muttering a vague apology and banishing himself to a top bunk. It was where he'd remained ever since, facing the wall in an unmoving stupor.

Perhaps Roz should have tried to talk to him, but she didn't. She was reaching her breaking point, and feared one more conversation with Damian would tip her over the edge. She attempted to distract herself by going over everything they'd learned about Enzo's sacrifices. Roz *knew* whatever had wrought this change in Damian had happened that night. But what exactly had happened? And how could she fix it?

The ship lurched, causing her to sink her nails into the damp wood of the railing. The waves had turned wild, crashing against the side of the vessel in crests of frothy white, as their second day at sea came to a close, the promise of darkness stealing its way across the orange-washed horizon. At her side Nasim and Zain were deep in conversation, though Roz hadn't heard a single word.

Zain Kadera, Roz had thought upon first seeing him, looked very like his sister. He had the same thick brows and dark hair, though his was cropped very short. They had the same eye color, and the shape of their mouths was similar, but the planes of Zain's face were harsh while Nasim's were more rounded. He said little, but kept his gaze on Nasim as if he couldn't quite believe she was real. It was clear he was not nearly as outspoken as his sister—he was quiet and unfailingly serious, though seemed easy enough to get along with.

As Nasim watched her brother with shining eyes, Roz slipped away to where Dev sat on a crate, hands folded in his lap. As she approached, she noted something strained about the smile lingering at the corners of his mouth. It was the type of smile people made because they felt they should be happy, not because they genuinely were. Roz couldn't understand it. She'd seen him with Nasim: how every so often their shoulders would brush, or their fingers would touch, only for one of them to pull back with color deepening their cheeks.

"Are you okay?" she asked.

Dev inclined his head. "Yeah. Are you?"

Roz forced a nod, following his somber gaze back to Nasim and Zain. "I know we're used to having her to ourselves," she said, trying for a joking tone, "but—"

He interrupted before she could finish, turning to her with bewilderment. "Do you seriously think I'm *jealous* of Zain? Because he has Nasim's attention? That's her *brother*."

Roz opened her mouth and closed it again. "I don't know. I mean, of course I know you're happy for her, but you can't help how you feel. It's normal to—"

Dev squeezed his eyes shut, leaning his head back with a groan. When he spoke, his voice was quiet. "I'm not jealous. Not like that, anyway."

She waited.

"It's just…after Amélie was killed, we…bonded. Over our grief, I mean, since we had both lost siblings." He indicated Nasim and her brother with a hand. "You know how resigned she was to Zain being dead. And don't get me wrong—I'm so relieved he isn't. I'm truly happy for her, and for their whole family. But now…" Dev swallowed, turning his face away. "Well, I suppose it's just hard to watch."

Roz heard the words he didn't say and understood at once. How had she been so oblivious? Nasim had something Dev never could—a happiness he would never know again. They were no longer grieving their siblings together. Now, he was grieving alone.

"I'm sorry," she whispered, rocking to press her shoulder into his. "I know it's not the same, but you're not alone. You're my brother. You know that, right?"

His mouth tightened, and Roz kept her gaze on the sea ahead, pretending not to see the sheen in his eyes.

"I've made a mess of everything, Roz. I'm the reason we got captured by the Brechaans."

"You're the reason we have a plan to end the war," she corrected him. "You're the reason we have Nasim back. We almost definitely would have failed without Calder. I mean, the flag thing was a pretty bad move, but it might have been a lucky one, too." She nudged him in the ribs.

Dev snorted. "Sleep deprivation will do that to you, I guess."

"You don't have to tell me. I'm pretty sure I fell asleep with my boots on that night."

He cracked a single wry, melancholy grin, then blinked in surprise. Nasim was making her way over to them, worry in the shape of her brows. Zain wasn't with her—he was talking to Kiran and Siena now, Roz saw, his hesitant laugh drifting over.

"Can I sit?" Nasim asked, pointing at the crate. Although there was room for all three of them, Roz leapt up.

"Be my guest. I was just leaving."

Nasim grabbed her arm. "What are we going to do about Damian?"

"We?"

"Yes, we." She scooted beside Dev, sitting far closer to him than Roz had. "You're miserable, Roz."

Trust Nasim to put it so bluntly. "*We* are going to try and make it through the night, and we'll worry about Damian tomorrow."

"We'll make it. I mean, we've made it this far. If one of us was meant to die, surely it would have happened by now."

Dev scoffed. "If you're going to tempt fate like that, don't do it so close to me."

Roz felt a pang at the sight of her friends bickering. It was so... normal. It made her feel, for a moment, as though everything really would be okay. She missed this—the three of them together, adrenaline high, about to do something inadvisable.

She wanted to tell them both how much she needed them. How every time they laughed together, she yearned to imprint it in her mind so she wouldn't forget the sound. When she was old, these were the things she wanted to remember about her life.

But such things were too serious to say aloud, and besides, Roz had never done serious well. So she merely slipped away, leaving them there together.

A heartbeat later, Calder's holler split the air. "Gather around—we're close!"

Roz spun to see that he was right. The Palazzo's spires were visible in the distance. The building was a beacon beneath the setting sun, all frigid stone and unnecessary gilt. She gave herself a shake. It was so *familiar*, and yet she hadn't been sure she would ever see it again. The general himself stood on a low crate by the nearest bulwark, arms crossed over his chest. Milos was at his side, thin face tight.

"Okay," Calder said, his voice carrying across the deck even with the howl of the wind. "It's nearly dark, which means we've timed this perfectly. We'll be guided to the best place to drop anchor, and then we'll go ashore in groups." He nodded at Roz over the heads of the small crowd. They'd run through the plan a couple of times already, but only in brief. Thus far, Siena and Kiran had filled in the gaps as far as knowledge of Ombrazian security went, but once they were ashore they would need Damian's help. In fact, Roz's role in the plan required him.

"There you are," a voice said in her ear. Roz whirled to see Damian behind her, as if he'd been summoned by her thoughts.

"Here I am," she said, frowning. He looked perfectly normal, unruffled, as if he hadn't just spent the last two days motionless belowdecks. She didn't know what to say, so she reverted to sarcasm. "Have you decided to be a person again?"

"I thought you needed me to tell Calder the security rotations."

Roz kept her gaze focused straight ahead on the man in question. "I do, but you didn't seem overly keen to help him."

"*You* asked it of me, though. Not Calder."

"And?"

In one swift motion he was in front of her, taking her gently by the jaw. His gaze bore into hers, sincere and unending. The head of his body radiated.

"I would do anything for you," he murmured. "If you demanded it, I would wrench the saints from the heavens one by one."

Roz swallowed with some difficulty. Damian's lips were at her ear, his fingers slipping to caress the slope of her neck, utterly heedless of the people around them. Her skin prickled. A lump building in her throat, she managed to shove him away. This wasn't *him*.

"Noted," she said hoarsely, feeling strangely off-balance. With a struggle, she refocused her attention on Calder.

"Milos, you'll lead one group," the general was saying. "Araina, you'll lead another, and I'll lead the third. Each of your groups will be accompanied by either Kiran Prakash or Siena Schiavone, since they'll know the rotation of the guards." Siena and Kiran looked at Damian; it would be Damian's job to tell them anything they didn't already know. "I've got Siena's map," Calder continued, "so that will have to be enough for my group. She's marked the locations to avoid. Our target is the Palazzo— leave the rest of the citizens alone. We're going to surround the building, then go in together on my signal." He tapped the pistola at his waist. "Three shots in quick succession. That should draw the attention of at least a few Palazzo security officers, and once they move toward the sound, I'll incapacitate them. That'll leave us with fewer to contend with once we get into the Palazzo itself. I know most of you can only hold an illusion for so long, and struggle to influence more than a couple of people at once, so you'll have to be smart about it.

"But I believe there are enough of us that we'll still be able to take control of the building. The Palazzo representatives and most of the city's disciples should be at the Basilica tonight, attending the ceremony to select the new chief magistrate. That means security will be concentrated there as well. Now, what we *don't* want is to back ourselves into a corner, so here's what's going to happen: Roz and Damian will be at the ceremony, since Damian should still have access to the Basilica's side doors. They'll watch it play out from the mezzanine, and when it's over, they'll head up to the bell tower and ring it once. From that bell we have just under twenty minutes to prepare for General Falco's return to the Palazzo. It sounds like she's the one who truly calls the shots in Ombrazia, so it's important we surround her and take her quickly. Our more powerful disciples, such as Milos and Laine"—Calder nodded at Milos and a pale blond woman Roz didn't recognize— "will manipulate whoever she happens to be with. We need her capitulation by whatever means necessary."

"And the chief magistrate?" Laine asked.

"From what I've heard, he's merely a figurehead, and not a very bright one. Dispose of him if you get the chance."

It was the only reasonable thing to be done, Roz figured, though she was surprised Calder had said it nonetheless.

Kiran took a step forward, clearing his throat. "Forgive me if this is a foolish question, but you have dozens of disciples here. Why can't you just put the whole city under an illusion?"

"It's not cumulative," Calder said patiently. "Our magic—and how powerful it may be—is specific to us, just like any other disciple's."

"And what if General Falco refuses to concede?" Damian's tone was sharp. He was so very close to Roz now, a hand on the back of her neck, fingers curving against her skin. "What then?"

Calder surveyed the small crowd, and something in his face tightened. He cared about these people, Roz realized. He worried for them. He was not an inherently violent man, but he would do whatever it took.

"Let's hope it does not come to that," he said. "But if it does, we may find ourselves using far more violence than we anticipated."

27

DAMIAN

The air tasted like ash and salt as night rolled in off the water. Damian and Roz were among the first to leave the ship; they folded themselves into a rowboat with Milos and a number of other disciples, none of whom spoke as they cut their way through the dark toward the shore. The ship had been anchored off the coast of Chaos's abandoned sector, as both light and security were virtually nonexistent in that area. Each disciple had changed from their Brechaan uniform into nondescript clothing Damian supposed would allow them to pass as unfavored citizens. As such, they carried only pistolas—not the long firearms a soldier would normally strap across their back.

Milos, Damian knew, would go back and forth from the ship until every disciple had been delivered to the coast of Ombrazia. From there they would head to the Palazzo. Meanwhile, Nasim, Dev, and Zain would stay on the ship with the crew. None of them had been thrilled about this, but Roz had pointed out that since they weren't playing a role in the plan, their presence was only likely to cause issues.

"We could get the rebels involved," Nasim had suggested before they'd left. "You know they don't hate Brechaat or Chaos the way the rest of the city does."

Roz had shaken her head. "The time for rebellion is past," she'd said, turning her attention to the spires of the Basilica jutting up in the distance, burnt copper beneath the setting sun. "It's time for a conquest."

She was quiet now, her face pinched, jaw set. Her discontent had been growing more obvious, and Damian knew it was because of him.

I'm better this way, he wanted to tell her. Or more important, *I can protect you better this way*. He didn't want to go back to the boy he was—the boy whose knees buckled beneath misery and guilt. The man Damian was now could love Roz better than that boy could have ever hoped to. He wished he could take all her anger and pain and gather it into himself now that he was better equipped to bear it.

Navigating the surface of the black water, Damian felt far too exposed. He was glad when they arrived at shore, and offered Roz his hand, but she clambered out of the rowboat without any trouble. She paused in the center of the narrow dock, her back to the shrouded streets.

"We'll head to the Basilica right away," she told Milos and the other disciples. "Listen for the bell."

"You're sure we'll be able to hear it from the Palazzo?" Milos said.

Roz nodded. "It can be heard throughout the entire city."

"Then go," he said, still crouched in the rowboat. Exhaustion already lingered in the lines of his face, but there was determination there, too. "May the saints guide us both."

Damian automatically glanced at Roz, but for the first time in recent memory, he didn't see her cringe at the mention of the saints. Instead she nodded, the shape of her mouth solemn. Then she turned to go, leaving it to Damian to follow her.

He did, of course. He always followed her.

The walk to the Basilica should have been nerve-racking, but Damian was full of inexplicable energy, as if something inside him was gearing up to explode. He and Roz kept to the shadows as much as possible, never speaking, their eyes and ears peeled for any indication of security officers patrolling the streets. The ceremony at the Basilica, however, meant that everything was quiet, especially once they moved out of unfavored territory. The familiar orange glow of the streetlights lit up the cobblestones at each intersection, and for the first time in Damian's life, they felt cold and unfamiliar. He'd loved this city once, hadn't he? Now he felt nothing save a putrid sort of anger in his stomach as they traversed it.

He wondered vaguely if this was how Roz always felt. Did each of these roads remind her of her father, and the way he might have walked them if he'd lived? Did the houses of every sector fill her with self-loathing because she'd become the very thing Jacopo Lacertosa had always resented?

The moment he thought the words, a realization washed over him. *He* had become the very thing *his* father had resented, hadn't he?

Before he knew it, he was following Roz down the alley that would lead them to the Basilica. The prominent building sat in the very center of a dusk-shrouded piazza, as bleakly grand as always. Roz came to a halt. Damian tore his gaze from the moon-gilded curve of her throat, the visible shiver of her rapid pulse. The piazza was empty, which had to mean the ceremony was already in session. A couple of security officers were positioned at the front doors of the Basilica, but they'd anticipated that. Damian recognized them: It was Matteo, one of his formerly trusted officers, and a boy named Petyr, whom he knew but not well.

"We'll wait until they're facing the other way," Roz hissed, crouching close to the nearest building. She'd gathered her hair into its usual long ponytail, one hand on the pistola at her belt. Her unflinching gaze was a weapon of its own. "Then we're going to have to make a run for it." She inclined her head at the Basilica's rearmost door. There was a wide expanse of cobblestone between it and where they waited. A number of the Basilica's stained-glass windows faced them, but it was impossible to tell whether anyone was watching.

"You go first," Damian told Roz.

For a moment her arm twitched as if she might reach for him, but she clenched her hand into a fist, letting it fall back to her side. Her eyes darted from one side of the street to the other. "Okay."

She ran, boots whisper-light across the cobblestones. Damian's heart gave an uneven thump as she disappeared around the side of the Basilica, but then her figure reappeared, motionless and expectant.

He mimicked what she had done a moment before, scanning his surroundings and listening hard for any sounds. When there was nothing, he crossed the piazza in a dozen long strides, averting his face from the stained-glass windows as best he could.

Roz pulled him over to the door. It wasn't one Damian had ever used before, given that he'd had no reason not to use the Basilica's main entrance. Even this rear door was opulent. In the lamplight he could see small carvings of the faceless saints climbing the stone around it, robed figures that stood out in relief amid intricate renderings of flora. The handle was a bronze knob worn by centuries of use. A lock was set into the door above it.

For a few brief seconds, Damian's confidence wavered. As head of Palazzo security, his touch had once given him access to every public building, but what if the lock had already been replaced or altered by a disciple of Patience? There was only one way to find out. He wrapped his fingers around the handle.

It didn't respond immediately, and everything in Damian tightened. Sure enough, however, the lock clicked a moment later. He shouldered the door open, cool air rushing forth to greet them. They were standing in a short hallway shrouded by darkness. He inhaled the familiar scent of varnished wood and stale air, waiting for his eyes to adjust. Once they did, he saw they were only a few steps from the staircase that led to the Basilica crypt. Next to it, another spiraled up into oblivion.

"Will that take us right to the mezzanine?" Roz asked. She spoke in a barely audible whisper, though no one else was around. In fact, the silence was almost unnerving, as if the cold stone had sucked all the noise out of the place.

Damian tilted his head back, trying to picture the Basilica's floor plan. "Yes," he decided. "We'll have to walk around the perimeter of the top floor, but it will get us there."

"Okay." Roz set her jaw, withdrawing her pistola and holding it in front of her as she began to climb.

Something unsaid rose between them as they were swallowed up by the stairwell, pursued by the light echoes of their footsteps. Damian could taste it alongside the lingering ash from sconces that must have been blown out some time before they arrived.

"Roz," he said, and when she didn't halt, he grabbed her gently by the waist.

She went still, leaning against his chest as he spread his fingers across her rib cage. Her breaths came in harsh bursts Damian doubted had anything to do with the exertion of the climb.

"No, no." He spoke into her ear, resting his chin in the crook of her neck. With her on the step above him, she was very slightly taller. "Don't be upset."

"I'm not," she ground out, but her voice broke.

"Tell me what you're thinking."

"What I'm thinking?" Roz tried to face him, but couldn't get her body twisted around. It was dark enough that Damian could scarcely see her regardless. "I'm thinking that even if we pull this off, it won't fix everything. I'm thinking that…" She trailed off, and he heard her swallow. "I'm thinking it's possible you'll be stuck like this forever. As someone I don't recognize, when what I need is my best friend. The boy who remembers how it feels to break apart on the inside."

He stiffened, releasing his grip on her waist. "I do remember."

"You could have fooled me." She hurled the words like a deadly weapon. They seemed to hang suspended between them, holding the seconds captive.

Damian pressed his lips together, trying to think of a way to make her understand. She *had* to understand, because he had no intention of becoming that boy again. "I remember everything—it just doesn't weigh me down anymore. It doesn't plague my every waking moment. Shouldn't you want that for me? Shouldn't you want it for yourself?"

Roz sniffed and kept climbing, her disembodied voice drifting back to him. "Had you asked me a week ago, I would've said yes without question. Now, I don't know. You're not *you* anymore…." She trailed off, the sound as insubstantial as the cool air around them.

Damian felt like someone had punched him in the stomach. He only wanted to help her. To take away her pain. He wanted to imagine he was doing that, but Roz made it sound as though he might as well not be here at all.

The mezzanine was deserted. It formed a semicircle around the second story of the Basilica, looking down upon the sanctuary. People didn't come up here to watch the sermons or ceremonies. They didn't come up here at all, in fact. As far as Damian knew, it hadn't been used in decades. There were a mere four rows of pews, the benches swathed in pale sheets. Cobwebs stretched between the spaces in the carved railing. With its empty seats and air thick with the scent of dust, something about the mezzanine was...somber.

It was, Damian thought, a place for forgetting.

He walked between the benches, the sheets fluttering in his wake. Each step kicked up dust. When he reached the first row, he pulled back the faded white linen and sat, gazing over the railing at the scene below.

But there was no one there.

"Roz." His voice echoed through the space, sharp edged. "Shouldn't the ceremony have started by now?"

Roz joined him at the balcony, her face a mixture of wariness and confusion as she stared down at the empty pews and deserted pulpit. "Yes. Would they have moved it elsewhere?"

"I doubt it. Every ceremony happens here." Even as he spoke, apprehension slithered through Damian's veins like a sixth sense. He scanned the perimeter of the sanctuary, biting down hard on his lower lip. Something wasn't adding up.

"What is it?" Roz whispered, alarm flickering across her face.

Damian wasn't quite sure how to reply, but Roz's words from one of their conversations on the ship echoed in his mind.

It's almost strange no Ombrazian ships ever caught up to us. It makes you wonder if Falco sent any at all.

All at once, Damian was certain she hadn't.

It was delusional to imagine they'd been able to escape a fleet of Ombrazian ships. If Falco had truly wanted to catch them, she would have done so. But from the very start, there had never been a single indication anyone was pursuing them.

"What's the one reason Falco might not have sent anyone after us?" Damian hissed through clenched teeth.

Roz blinked, gaze impenetrable. "How can you be sure she didn't?"

"Humor me."

"Maybe she didn't think we were important enough to pursue."

"I attacked her. Humiliated her," Damian reminded Roz. "Falco's not the type to let that go."

She turned, and he saw his own horror reflected in her eyes. "She needed her officers for something else."

"Remember how Kiran and Nasim said the best soldiers were being diverted away from the front?"

"She knew," Roz whispered. "Falco knew we were coming." She backed into the shadows. "Saints, Damian, we need to get to the bell tower *now*. If we ring it multiple times, maybe Calder will know something is wrong—"

Steps sounded in the stairwell. Automatically Damian glanced over the balcony again, this time finding the sanctuary swarming with military officers. Roz gasped his name, a sound of true panic. Roz *never* panicked. Her hands were on his arm, nails in skin, tugging, urging, but Damian didn't budge. He barely heard her. Instead, he was watching the mist now blanketing the mezzanine like an ominous shroud. It condensed and tipped over the balcony in dark spirals, moving like a tangible thing. Because it *was* tangible, wasn't it? Manipulatable, at the very least. Damian knew without attempting it that he could bend this mist to his will, should he so choose. It was part of him, and he was not frightened of it. Or if he was, the fear was nothing in the face of his desire for destruction. Ombrazia would not win tonight. It was Damian who would be victorious.

He hoped General Falco knew it as she appeared before him, flint-gray eyes finding his through the haze.

"Venturi," she growled. "I figured I'd find you here. But as a disciple of Chaos?" Disgust curled her lip as she raised her gun. The officers on either side of her did the same. "I ought to have known you were cursed in more ways than one. Your father should have put you down as an infant."

Despite her words, her face was tinged red, tendrils of hair coming loose from her tight bun. There was a wildness about her, and distantly Damian knew she was desperate to kill him. She'd been desperate to see him dead since arriving in Ombrazia, hadn't she?

Standing before him with that badge on her chest, Falco looked so very like Battista Venturi. Just another leader in a long line of leaders that had run Ombrazia into the ground, drenching it in blood and betrayal. They had never been the good guys. Battista had not been blessed by Strength. He'd been a coward of a man, feeding Damian too-pretty lies from the moment he took his first breath.

Beside him, Roz's lips formed a curse. She leveled her pistola at Falco, but Damian didn't reach for his weapon. This was merely an obstacle. A waste of time.

"You won't win," Roz snapped. "Whatever you think Calder has coming, your soldiers won't be able to stand against them. In fact, I feel sorry for all of you."

"*Calder?*" Falco's brows shot up, amusement twisting her mouth further. "You speak of him as though he's a friend."

Roz lifted her chin stubbornly. "Maybe he is."

"You were foolish to assist him. I knew you had betrayed your country the moment I received word the bridge had fallen. I'll admit, at first I simply assumed you were fleeing Ombrazia to save your own lives, selfish cowards that you are. But then I received a *very* interesting correspondence from a fellow disciple of Death who happens to reside at the Atheneum."

Damian exhaled sharply through his nose. He ought to have known that creepy archivist couldn't be trusted. This whole time, then, Falco had known they were heading north.

"And yes," Falco continued, "I know you went there looking for information about Chaos. You thought something was wrong with you, correct? Well, you were right about one thing, at least."

She sneered. "I suppose that's why the Brechaans took you in like abandoned pets. But Calder Bryhn and his ilk will die tonight. I know his plans—I've read the bodies of Brechaat's deceased. When I learned you intended to return on the night of Salvestro's ceremony, we decided to move it up several hours. The dead, you see, can be very useful."

Of course. *That* was how she knew. It was Falco who had given the orders to collect Brechaat's dead, after all. But that meant she was a wildly powerful disciple of Death, if she'd been able to read further than the moments leading up to when they were killed.

Falco swung her gun to point it at Damian, though he hadn't so much as twitched. "And *you*—you'll die as well. I admit, I had rather hoped to make a public example of you, but unfortunately it's just not safe. I'm sure you understand why I have to kill you now."

"No!" Roz screamed, attempting to block Damian. Falco flicked her wrist, and one of her officers lunged forward, striking Roz upside the head with the barrel of an archibugio. She stumbled to the side, gun clattering to the floor. Somehow she was still conscious, but her eyes were enormous as they flicked between Damian and Falco, calculating desperately. All she wanted to do was save him, Damian knew.

All she had ever wanted to do was save people. The way she went about it may be unconventional, her behavior often harsh, but that didn't make it less true.

"Kneel, Venturi," Falco said, no longer trying to keep the smugness from her voice. "It's about time you started showing some respect."

Damian laughed. He couldn't help it.

It burst from him alongside a bubble of hysteria, the sound long and low. Heat flared across his skin, lashed through his veins, clawed up his throat. He felt something deep within him bottom out, as if a dam had broken. The fire inside him rose to an inferno, and though he braced for the pain that would surely accompany it, he felt nothing but sheer, undiluted glee. He was undone, and yet he was whole, and the last part of him that had been tethered to something unnameable snapped.

He understood, then. Felt the undeniable strength of generations at his back, and knew what he was meant to do.

He was not a boy bred to fight, but a man made for war.

"You fool," he said to Falco in a voice unlike his own. It was the voice of ancients. Of power. "You would dare give orders to a *saint*?"

Then he threw back his head and screamed, casting the world into darkness.

28

Roz

Everything around Roz disappeared.

This dark was not simply the absence of light, but a tangible thing that pressed in around her. The mist turned to a suffocating fog, and as her eyes struggled to adjust, she could see it moving in wisps. She sucked in a breath. Damian was nowhere to be seen. The room was quiet—Falco's commands had cut off the moment the fog blanketed the space—and at first it seemed she and her officers had disappeared, too. But then Roz heard the thud of multiple footsteps retreating down the stairwell and knew Falco had recovered faster than her. The general was going after Damian, wherever he might be. Roz felt sick, and not just from the ache in her head.

Everything tasted like magic; she could sense it on the air and feel it pressing against her bones. It was familiar, but held a power she'd never experienced before. It was overwhelming. Terrifying. And yet . . . not unpleasant.

"Damian?" Roz hissed his name, apprehension unfurling in her chest. She knew even as she spoke that he wouldn't answer. Her heart thumped a frantic, unsteady rhythm as his last words rang in her ears.

You would dare give orders to a saint?

The voice had been Damian's, but also very much not. Roz couldn't wrap her head around it.

Her mind filled with the image Enzo had shown her. Damian, his face changed in ways she couldn't understand. His eyes, dark with an eternal rage that didn't belong to him. How, despite the pitch-black oblivion of the Shrine, he'd known precisely where to aim to shoot an immaterial Enzo.

Enzo. The mere thought of his name sent a prickle down Roz's spine. Because he'd done it, hadn't he? He'd been successful in the end, just not in the way he'd intended.

He'd raised a saint.

Roz could hear the distant clamor of confusion and panic from the sanctuary below. Whatever was going on, it was clearly affecting everyone else, too. But she barely afforded it any thought; the pieces were still clicking into place.

Damian was a disciple of Chaos. That much was clear. The way he seemed to be losing himself completely, however, wasn't normal. It was why Roz had been so sure there was some external factor at play. Calder had said becoming a disciple didn't change someone, but Damian wasn't just a mere disciple, was he? He had always been turning into something more.

It was impossible. Roz was as certain of that as she was of the truth: The boy she'd loved since childhood was the reincarnation of the patron saint of Chaos.

Damian was gone. He'd been slipping away for a while now, hadn't he? And though he'd tried to hang on—for her—it had never been enough. You didn't become the reincarnation of a saint by accident; it was predetermined. This had always been Damian's path, even if he hadn't known it. But when Enzo had woken Chaos's magic, it had found Damian and sped up the process. Infiltrating his mind and body as everything that made him inherently *Damian* drained away.

He'd never stood a chance.

Roz lunged forward. She needed to get out of here before someone came to investigate. She needed to warn Calder, but it was likely far too late. She needed to find Damian before Falco got to him.

Relying solely on her memory, Roz stretched out her hands and made for the exit. Before she reached the stairwell, though, she made contact with something firm, warm, and undoubtedly human. She leapt back, sucking in a breath. Even when she squinted, she could make out little more than the shape of a person, but she knew it was one of Falco's officers. He was suspended in an illusion. But why only him? Why let Falco and the others escape?

Roz felt in the breast pocket of the immobile man's uniform— the same jacket Damian used to wear, from which she'd once seen him procure a packet of matches. She prayed it was something all security officers carried and was relieved when she was proven right. After a moment's consideration, she took his gun as well.

"Sorry," Roz muttered to the man. She lit a match, cursing when the feeble glow didn't illuminate more than a couple of steps ahead, but it was better than nothing. At least this way she wouldn't run into anyone else.

For a moment she was gripped by dismay: What if she, too, was in an illusion? Was there any way to know for sure?

But no—she had to believe Damian wouldn't do that to her.

She crept down the spiral staircase, pistola raised, trying to keep her footsteps as silent as possible. The fog was just as dense on the ground floor, but the officers she'd seen in the sanctuary were gone—Falco must have assumed Roz had disappeared alongside Damian. Had he made it so they couldn't see her?

Her heart squeezed as she sprinted for the back door of the Basilica, pulse hammering. None of this was supposed to happen. Calder was supposed to take control of the Palazzo. They were supposed to catch Falco and Salvestro off guard. She was supposed to return Damian to normal, then finally go home to her mother. She wasn't foolish enough to think tonight would end in a happily ever after, but she had at least hoped for some measure of control.

She burst outside, eager to get away from the oppressive fog, but it quickly became evident that was an impossibility.

The entire city was blanketed in darkness.

Whatever Damian had done, it hadn't just affected the Basilica. He'd thrust all of Ombrazia into some sort of illusion. A thick black haze blanketed the streets, blocking out the moonlight. Roz was struck by the sudden, disorienting feeling of being underwater, or perhaps in some realm of the dead. It must have been an hour or so past nightfall, which meant the streetlamps ought to be lit by now, but she saw no indication of them. She took a single step forward. The fog parted around her, re-forming as she moved through it. Roz halted, gripped by indecision. What now? She had to find Damian before anyone else did, but where would he have gone? What was he trying to do?

She lurched away from the building, paradoxically glad for the fog. She knew these streets well enough that she didn't need to see clearly to navigate them. As she reached the edge of the piazza she could hear other citizens panicking, voices strangely muffled. Roz didn't stop to contemplate that. She kept running, guided by the shadowy shapes of the familiar buildings.

Then those shadows began to splinter.

It took her a moment to realize what was happening. The buildings were coming apart at the seams, fracturing as if touched by some traumatic earthquake. Except there *was* no earthquake—the world was still. Great chunks of stone plummeted to the ground, sending up clouds of dust that had Roz coughing and spitting out grit. The darkness appeared to be *eating* everything, licking up the walls like black fire.

None of this was possible. None of it made sense. And yet a distant part of her knew exactly what was going on: Damian—Chaos—was destroying the city.

This was the place he had always felt trapped. The place he'd mourned after losing Michele, and the place he'd watched his father die. This was where he'd been dragged to prison at Falco's command, and where they'd introduced Calder and his disciples of Chaos as would-be conquerors. The gentle, careful boy Roz had known was gone. In his place was a vengeful saint, twisted and sharpened by centuries of disrespect and disdain. He would not be satisfied by surrender. He would want carnage.

Roz thought of the origin story in *Saints and Sacrifice*. "Chaos gave the people war," she murmured to herself, panic lacing an icy pathway through her veins. Damian was going to rip this city apart, its citizens alongside it. But Ombrazia wasn't all bad. There were people here who had done nothing wrong. The unfavored, who had made fulfilling lives despite the odds stacked against them. Disciples like Roz's ex-girlfriend Vittoria, whose beliefs may have been misguided, but who meant well nonetheless. Each and every one of them was in danger. If there was one thing Roz knew, it was that Chaos never backed down. That was a common theme in each iteration of the story, each reincarnation of the saint. But there was another commonality, too:

Chaos always fell.

Roz's heart stuttered, her breath catching. There was another crash as more rock fell away from the nearest building—a tailor's shop that sold Grace-made clothing. Was it an illusion, the world crashing down around her? Or was it the result of so much power that something in the city simply had to give? She could feel that power saturating the air, filling her lungs each time she inhaled. It was stronger than anything she'd felt before, but just like always, it was familiar to her in a way she didn't understand. Perhaps because the magic was Damian's, and something inside her would always recognize him.

She had to stop him. She had to save him.

Roz had no idea how to do both.

Nearby, a woman screeched as glass shattered. It spurred Roz into motion. She would deal with Damian soon—and there was still the problem of Calder and his disciples to contend with—but the woman's yell had struck a new fear into her heart. A fear for someone far more vulnerable than the patron saint of Chaos.

She had to get to her mother before Bartolo's collapsed around her.

Led by her sense of direction and the odd glimpses of buildings she recognized, Roz arrived at the tavern, only to find the door locked. The cobblestones crunched with small bits of rubble from the slow deterioration of the city. Some people had evidently decided it was safer to be outside than in their homes, and the alleyways were lined with citizens speculating in terrified, furtive voices, holding their children close so as not to lose them in the haze.

"Come on," Roz snarled, rapping on the door a second time. If it wasn't open in the next three seconds, she was going to melt the lock and kick it down with—

Someone thrust it open, and she leapt back just in time. Alix's pale face swam into view. Their chin-length hair was in disarray, eyes large in their angular face. "Roz! You're back? Where's Dev? Did you find Nasim and the others?"

"Let me in," she urged, and they moved aside.

It was just as dark inside Bartolo's. Roz didn't know why she'd expected anything different. The fog crept in through the windows and slipped beneath the door, curling around what she could see of the empty tables. A single lantern had been lit, though its glow was all but lost when she took another step toward the stairs.

"What the hell is going on?" Alix hissed, right on her heels. "Josef and I were working the bar, and suddenly everything just went…" They trailed off, but Roz didn't need a description.

"Yeah. I know." She squinted. "There aren't any patrons here, are there?"

Alix shook their head. Even so close together, a thin mist filled the space between the two of them. "Everybody left when *this* happened. Went to check on their families and such."

There was a rumbling above their heads. Roz cast her gaze upward, adrenaline spiking as a horrible crack sounded through the foundation of the tavern. "Where's Josef now?"

"In the back." Concern overtook Alix's features. "Roz, what is it?"

"Dev and Nasim are safe, but they're not here. It's just me right now, and I'm going to get my mother. You fetch Josef and take him down into the cold cellar—it should be safer there. I'll bring my mother to join you." She paused, hovering at the bottom of the steps as she held Alix's gaze. "There's a new patron saint of Chaos. He's here, in the city."

"*What?*"

"Josef!" Roz reminded them, already heading up the stairs. The floorboards groaned beneath her feet. "Just trust me. Please!"

"Roz—"

But they didn't follow her, voice lost as Roz sprinted down the hallway to the apartment. She never should have left her mother here alone. What if she was resentful, feeling abandoned? What if she had gotten worse, thrown into a panic by everything going on?

When Roz burst into the apartment, though, Caprice Lacertosa was standing at the window, hands laced together in front of her. She watched the dark magic outside as someone might watch an intriguing rainstorm.

"Mamma," Roz said, exhaling in relief that quickly changed to worry. "Get away from the window."

Caprice turned to look at her, oddly serene. The fog wasn't as thick up here; it seemed to have congregated more heavily closer to the earth.

"Tesoro." She smiled. "He said you'd be here soon."

Roz bristled, hand snapping to her pistola as she glanced around the room. "*Who* said that?"

"Your father."

Anguish lanced through Roz like a knife. She ultimately decided to bypass the topic entirely. She couldn't talk about her father, even for her mother's sake. Not now, when grief was already too fresh in her heart. "Right. Well, here I am, and I need you to come with me. It's not safe here."

Caprice shook her head. "I'm safe."

"No, you're not." Roz made her voice steel. She was accustomed to tiptoeing around her mother, trying not to upset her. This time, however, there was no room for that. The tavern seemed to shiver as the dark fog outside ripped the shutters from the hinges. She crossed the room and wrapped her arms around her mother's thin form. Breathed in the familiar floral scent of her. "Please," she whispered, voice muffled. "We have to go."

Caprice cupped the back of Roz's head, rocking her gently. Roz squeezed her eyes shut, trying very hard not to feel like a child again. Small. Sad. Desperate for comfort.

With some effort she straightened, asking the question that had been clawing at her since that moment in the Basilica. "Was Liliana Venturi a descendant of Chaos?"

She braced herself, expecting her mother to flinch away from any mention of the saint, but Caprice only made a low hum in the back of her throat. "Liliana. I haven't thought of her in many years."

It wasn't an answer, so Roz waited.

"Liliana was many things," her mother went on. "A strong woman. A kind friend. A great mother. But she chose a man who did not love all parts of her."

It was as close to a *yes* as Roz knew she would get, and a jolt of surprise shot through her. "She never told Battista?"

"Sometimes you love someone enough that you change for them. And sometimes you love someone enough that you help *them* change instead." Caprice placed her hands on Roz's shoulders, pushing her gently away. When Roz lifted her chin, she saw her mother's gaze was oddly focused. "It can be hard to know which is the better option. Certainly I did not make all the right choices. Neither did Liliana. Do not judge us too harshly."

"I'm not judging either of you," Roz said. Her thoughts were running wild. If Damian's mother had told him the truth, would he have been more prepared? Would he have been braced for the magic that awoke in him when Enzo completed the final sacrifice?

These were pointless questions. It was too late to know.

"Mamma," Roz began haltingly when Caprice didn't reply, "what happened the last time a saint rose in Ombrazia? Before the first war, I mean?"

Her mother's short-term memory may have been poor, but she recalled stories the way few others could. That said, Caprice didn't like to speak about the saints. She'd rejected everything to do with them when Roz's father returned from his first tour up north. How, she'd asked, could benevolent deities see fit to let so many die in their names?

But her mother blinked at the question, expression clearing slightly. "Strength and Chaos rose at the same time. The change into sainthood is gradual, though, because eventually one loses their former self. It's an exchange. People think of saints as martyrs, and in a way, they are. You see, the greatest sacrifice saints make is giving up their humanity."

So Damian was losing his humanity. Roz had already assumed as much. But to learn he would change entirely, in a way that could never be undone? It was too horrible to contemplate.

"Is there a way to stop it?" she asked her mother desperately, aware that her questions had lost their casual tone. "I mean, if someone undergoes a transformation to become a saint, there must be a way for the reverse to happen, right?"

Roz felt as if it were not only the city crumbling around her, but the entire world. Everything she'd learned up until now was useless. *Offer what was given*, the book in the Atheneum had said, but undoing Enzo's ritual wouldn't change Damian back into the person he used to be. Not if this was the path he had always been destined to follow. The vellenium plant she'd ripped from the northern soil was useless. The chthonium she'd planned to retrieve from the site of Battista's grave would accomplish nothing.

"I have never heard such a thing," Caprice said, and Roz wilted. "Unless you count the original story of Patience and Chaos. The way it ends in *Saints and Sacrifice*, you see, is not the whole story."

Roz knew as much. She remembered bits and pieces of what she'd read in the unredacted version at the Atheneum. How, though, did her mother know about it?

"Were Patience willing to give up her humanity, Death would use it to retrieve Chaos from the beyond and bestow upon him a mortal life," Roz whispered. Then, more audibly: "Patience gives up her humanity, and Chaos comes back as a mortal."

Caprice nodded, as if unsurprised Roz should be able to recite the original text. "Patience realizes her lover must be contained, and so she slays him herself. She is the reason for Chaos's original fall. But you see, he does not fall from heaven into hell. He simply falls from sainthood." A vague smile spread across her face. "And because Patience gives up her last and only connection to the mortal world, Chaos does not die."

Roz considered, understanding prickling her skin. Maybe some of what she'd learned was right after all: Damian was giving his humanity, the crux of his soul, over to Chaos. *That* was what had been given.

Which meant that was what needed to be offered.

Swallowing hard, Roz took her mother's hand, guiding her out of the apartment. She couldn't think about this now. She needed to get her out of here.

It was easier than she'd anticipated to coax her mother downstairs. Perhaps Caprice could sense the gravity of the situation, for she didn't refuse to leave, and not once did she ask to return. She didn't even question the thickening darkness. Alix was waiting by the cellar steps, face wan. Josef waited a few steps down, wearing an angry expression that meant he, too, was anxious.

"Signora Lacertosa," Alix said to Caprice, forcing a smile. "Come—you'll be safe with us."

Caprice turned to face Roz, who winced, anticipating her mother's panic when she realized her daughter wouldn't be accompanying them.

"I don't want you to worry about me," she said hurriedly before Caprice could speak. Her mother only looked at her for a long moment, gaze clearer than it had been in years. She nodded.

Roz watched her descend into the black of the cellar, something pulling taut in the hollow of her chest. She needed to find Damian, and she knew exactly where he would be. Chaos yearned for power, and what gave a saint of Chaos more power than chthonium?

Heart in her throat, she left in search of Battista Venturi's grave.

29

DAMIAN

Damian was full of wrath.

He'd been fighting with himself since the moment he left the Basilica, magic exploding from him in a way he couldn't—and didn't want to—control. He scarcely remembered how he'd gotten out of the building. He'd wanted to escape, and he had. He'd wanted the city to burn, and now it was.

In a sense, at least.

The thick, smokelike haze that blanketed the streets was his doing. He could see it in his periphery, creeping along the ground and up the side of the buildings. It maintained a few feet of distance from him, like it knew not to compromise his vision. Or perhaps it was Damian himself keeping it away by force of will. He could hear the distant rumble of stone crumbling to the ground, of glass shattering as it was punctured by tendrils of darkness, and it felt like the first triumphant breath after years spent gasping for air.

He was going to win this war. Not Brechaat—*him*. He would end it all.

The earlier version of Damian Venturi was a distant, foolish thing. An ignorant boy who grew up fearing the things he didn't understand. The presence that had stalked him throughout his life—the lingering sensation he had always thought of as Death—had been his very own magic. Chaos, clawing at his insides to get out. The way he'd felt after Michele's death, and how he'd lost himself entirely as he'd gunned down three enemy soldiers at once... had that been his desire for war ripping loose?

He paused when he glimpsed the Palazzo in the near distance. It was an imposing shadow, no light emanating from its many windows. Damian scanned the grounds. The only figures he could see pacing the area were quite clearly wearing Ombrazian military uniforms, archibugi in their arms or strapped across their backs. Every so often they appeared to exchange agitated words. They were waiting for the Brechaans, Damian knew. To meet an attack that would determine the future of the city. What had Falco told them? Did they realize what they were facing?

The wind caressed Damian's face, tinged with magic and the salt-laced reminder of the sea. He could hear it nearby, lapping against the rocky shore. For the first time in a long time, he felt powerful.

He felt holy.

As he had the thought, a soft noise echoed from behind him. He whirled, yanking his pistola loose, only to have it knocked from his hand. Two military officers faced him, neither familiar, likely freshly summoned from the north. He could tell they didn't recognize him, but they didn't ask Damian to identify himself. They obviously knew he wasn't supposed to be here.

Damian didn't have time to think, and he didn't need it. He grabbed the barrel of the first officer's archibugio, wrenching it from the woman's grasp and using it to slam the second officer upside the head. The man staggered, blinking wildly as he fought to retain consciousness, then lifted his gun and fired a poorly aimed shot into the fog. The first officer fumbled at her belt for what Damian suspected was a knife, but Damian turned the archibugio on her.

"Drop it," he said coldly.

"No, *you* drop it," the concussed officer snarled, though he was struggling to stay upright.

Damian drew a long breath in through his nose. Impatience prickled at him. Didn't they know who he was, and what he could do?

Didn't *he* know what he could do?

He had no reason to remain here, fighting with fists and weapons against two people who had no hope of beating him. He had magic. He was a saint.

Every other time Damian had summoned Chaos's magic, it hadn't been on purpose. It had happened without him knowing, drawn out by whatever strong emotion he was feeling at the time. Now, though, he would call it forth mindfully. Purposefully. There was no need to wonder how; he could already feel it simmering beneath the surface of his skin.

Damian looked at the officers before him, imagining a scene precisely like this one, but without his presence. Once he saw the image clearly in his mind's eye, he unleashed it on them. He let his magic loose, wrapping all three of them in invisible power. A shudder escaped him, something pulling taut at his core. A mere twinge of discomfort. He knew without testing it that he would not tire.

Both officers froze, scowls fixed on nothing in particular. Damian couldn't help his huffed laugh.

So that was how this worked. He could focus the illusions inside someone's mind, rendering them immobile as they lived out whatever false reality he'd thrust upon them, or he could hurl illusions into the world at large, as was the case with the fog. At least, he *thought* that was the case with the fog. He hadn't intended to create it, but he'd intended to escape, and it had formed as a result.

Damian left the officers, making his way down the street that led to the Palazzo gardens. It was obvious the disciples of Chaos hadn't launched their attack—they must have realized something was wrong even before the darkness took over. Assuming they'd remained put, Damian knew exactly where Calder and his team were supposed to be. He would find them, then dig up the chthonium he'd buried at his father's grave. He would learn whether the rumors of its power were true.

The breeze ruffled his hair, bringing with it the scent of earth and ash. How many times had he walked this precise route during his rounds? How many times had he passed beneath this archway, gazing up at the stars overhead? They were gone now, replaced by hazy curls of dark fog. How many times had he paused on his way back to the Palazzo, struggling to breathe through the crushing pressure of expectation? He'd never been good enough. His father had spent his entire life telling Damian as much without words.

Unfortunate, really, that Battista lay dead. Damian would have liked to show him what it meant to be powerful.

He quickened his pace. Rows of alleyways opened up before him, separated by towering stone walls, each one darker than the last. He'd done that, too, hadn't he? The light had fled the city as if he'd up and chased it away.

When he rounded the next corner, he found himself looking directly at Calder Bryhn.

The general stared back, hazel eyes wide. He hovered close to the wall, gun in hand. A dozen or so disciples stood behind him. They were nearly invisible in the darkness, but Damian felt the weight of their attention, the prickle of their barely suppressed magic. He inhaled deeply. It tasted like home, somehow.

"Signor Venturi," Calder whispered, distrust lacing his tone. "What's going on? Where's Roz? The Palazzo was swarming with soldiers, so I didn't give the signal. Then we never heard the bell. *This*"—he gestured at their surroundings—"wasn't us."

"There's been a change of plans," Damian said calmly. "General Falco knew about the attack. The ceremony was moved up, and they were expecting us. They even diverted a bunch of extra Ombrazian soldiers here."

Milos stepped forward to stand at his general's side, a small but menacing presence. Red spread across Calder's cheeks as he noted the change in Damian. His next question came slowly, laced with suspicion. "What did you do, Venturi?"

"I did nothing." The words rose to his tongue before he knew what they were going to be. "And yet, I've done everything. I've come to win this war. I've waited long enough for my triumph. And *you*—you're going to help me." His voice echoed through the alleyway, a reverberating challenge.

Milos retreated once more, a predator relinquishing a kill to a larger beast. Fear was visible in his face as he studied Damian's. But Damian didn't want to be feared—not by the people before him. He wanted them by his side. To show them he meant it, he let the magic roll off him in waves.

Calder felt it at once. They all did—it was evident by the shift in body language. The general's eyes widened, awe and understanding flickering in them.

Then he took a knee.

Those behind Calder quickly copied him. True disciples, ready to defer to their saint. Everything felt stilted, tinged with an air of unreality.

Satisfaction flared at Damian's core, stretching upward and heating his cheeks. He felt a sudden flash of the boy he used to be. The weaknesses that had burrowed so deeply inside him. He hadn't been a good soldier. Too soft, too hesitant to kill. He hadn't been a good leader. He hadn't been firm enough with his subordinates and had failed to guard the very people he'd been entrusted to protect. They had held him back, those weaknesses.

No longer. A saint was stronger than a disciple. Softness and hesitancy had fled, and he would no longer know failure.

"It's you," Calder said softly. "We were looking for *you*."

Damian motioned for him to rise. "Explain."

The general remained kneeling. "When Chaos's magic woke, we all felt it. Not only within our own bodies, but in the world around us. We were drawn to it. Your arrival on the shores of Brechaat alleviated the need to find it, but I didn't make the connection." Calder shook his head in awe. "We were desperate to find *you*. The original saint's power lives in your body. You were calling for us, whether you intended to or not."

"You were the one who told me I was a disciple," Damian reminded him. "Did you not know then what I really was? Could you not feel it?"

"Forgive me. I did not know who I was speaking to at the time." He bowed his head. "Something had yet to change within you."

Well, Damian had certainly changed. He had felt the gravity of it in the Basilica.

"Stand," he commanded Calder again. This time, the general stood. "My predecessor may have fallen in the First War of Saints, but I have no intention of losing the second. I was born to rule this place." He stood up straighter. "We'll take the Palazzo as planned, and I will ensure we do not fall."

They walked in rows, framed by the fog.

Calder and the other disciples followed Damian in the direction of the Palazzo. The wind had picked up, a consistent roar in his ears. Adrenaline coursed through his blood. He could hear the cracks and crashes of buildings coming apart, the darkness eating away at them like some aggressive parasite. Now that he was paying attention to it, he could feel the magic flowing out of him.

He wondered when it would bottom out. *If* it would bottom out. Apart from the uncomfortable twinge here and there, Damian's power felt endless. He could see the strain in Calder's face, but the general appeared to be stronger when he was at Damian's side.

Was this how the patron saint of Chaos had felt during the First War of Saints? Had he been wrapped up in the all-consuming desire to destroy, to take over, to see just how far his power could extend?

The dark pressed in thickly enough that Damian couldn't see them, but he knew there were people in the streets. Most stayed out of the way, yells hovering on the wind like bitter echoes. Those who didn't were quickly dealt with by the disciples. Damian let them do the work. He watched as Milos moved to one side of the road, arms taut from shoulder to fingertip. Where he went, the fog grew thicker, almost as if he was building on Damian's magic with his own. Anyone who was foolish enough to try and fight him froze at once, trapped in an illusion until the group had moved on.

Dust was thick on the air, stinging Damian's eyes and collecting in his lungs. He paid it no mind. His footsteps were loud, reverberating thuds against the cobblestones, and he made no effort to quiet them. He wanted to be heard. He wanted them to know he was coming.

"What's the plan?" Calder murmured under his breath. Damian knew the general wasn't questioning him or his judgment. In fact, the glint in Calder's eye was excitement. His auburn hair was tousled, the collar of his shirt slightly askew, but he looked almost a saint in his own right.

"Fire your gun three times," Damian told him as they turned a corner. "Let the rest of the disciples know it's time. I know there are far more than we anticipated, but the plan remains the same. This time, though, you have me. Cast your magic over as many soldiers as you can, and I'll be able to influence the rest. Let them know true fear."

He stared up at the pillars flanking the Palazzo's decorative gate, eyes snagging on a carving of Patience. Even without features, she managed to be at once beautiful and intimidating. He'd never quite managed to see how Roz was anything like her patron saint, but now, staring at the expertly portrayed warrior-woman, he thought he understood. Patience wasn't so-called because she was tolerant and unhurried. No—the patron saint was known as such because of how she was with her lover. Everything she had done, she'd done for Chaos: created fire so he could make it burn, created rain to assuage his temper. And each time he toppled from grace, she'd stood vigil, waiting for him to return. Waiting to enact vengeance on his behalf.

That was the heart of the story, Damian realized, and in that, Roz was the same. When it came to vengeance, she would wait as long as it took. When it came to him, she would stand by his side as long as he would have her. She was beautiful and intimidating. Steadfast and inscrutable. Her connection to Patience made sense, no matter how she resented it.

He extended his fingers, knuckles popping, tendons stretching. The darkness gathered, tendrils climbing the Palazzo gates like great clawing hands. There was a screeching, metallic sound as the hinges detached.

Then they crashed to the ground with a deafening bang.

Officers and soldiers were spread out on the Palazzo grounds. Waiting for him. There were hundreds, Damian saw, and they rushed him in a wave. It was no matter. With a flick of his hand, he motioned for his disciples to spread out. The familiar tang of their power filled the air, and with that Damian unleashed his own.

In the vision he conjured, he had already won. Those who were in the Palazzo he sent images of terrible fire, forcing them out onto the grounds. Then he incapacitated them, too. Every so often he missed a few people, or else lost his hold on them, but their shots were fired from shaking hands, and Damian had surrounded himself in impenetrable darkness. Besides, he regained their minds soon enough. He stalked his way up the familiar path toward the Palazzo doors, tilting his head to take it in.

He remembered little of the *before*, but in his mind's eye he could see his father's blood spattering the marble floor of the entryway. Chief Magistrate Forte crumpling to the ground in a wet pile of flesh, and Enzo stepping out from the midst of it, looking for all the world an unruffled god.

It was Damian's turn now.

And he was not merely a boy playing at being holy.

Suddenly, he heard rapid footsteps behind him. Frustrated, he pivoted, reaching into the bottomless well of his magic.

It was Siena and Kiran. They hurried after him through the dark, skirting the motionless soldiers. One awoke as they passed, and Siena jabbed him in the chest with the butt of her gun before Damian regained control.

"What is *happening*?" Siena demanded as she reached him. "There are so many people here. It's as though they were expecting us."

"They were," Damian said. Then, by way of explanation, "Falco."

Kiran's eyes widened. "And they still had the ceremony for Salvestro tonight?"

"It was held this morning. Now get out of here. If you stay, you'll only get trapped in an illusion."

He made to turn away—he didn't have time for this. His mind was full of the echoes of a thousand others. He would wait here, at the doors of the Palazzo, until General Falco arrived. He would let her see what he had wrought. Let her see that no matter how many soldiers she summoned to Ombrazia's aid, they didn't stand a chance against the patron saint of Chaos.

Then, he would force her to surrender. He would hold his gun to her head and tell her exactly what would happen if she did not.

It was pathetic, really, that the Chaos of the first war had fallen so easily. For someone with power like this, war was a fool's game.

"Damian!" Kiran's voice at his back was higher than usual, laced with worry. "Are you okay?"

With a sigh, Damian turned back to his friends.

"I'm great," he told them, a smile beginning to lift his mouth as he realized just how true that was. "Divine, in fact."

30

ROZ

As Roz navigated the murky streets, she was terribly aware that everything had gotten worse.

Dust mingled with the fog, and darkness climbed the buildings in flame-like licks of obsidian, thicker and more vicious now. It was a devouring thing, sending chunks of stone plummeting to the earth. The wind had become a veritable tempest, the world shuddering around her. Roz's ears rang with the echoes of panic and destruction she couldn't see. Anger boiled at her core. This was unfavored territory. The hard-won safe haven of people who had done nothing wrong, who had known little but suffering in this city. Their goal was to stop the war and kill Falco, was it not? They had been trying to wrest the city from the grasp of those who would see the status quo upheld. Those like Salvestro, who were hungry for power and thus should never be given it.

Wind lashed through Roz's hair, and she spat away the strands that clung to her lips. She had to stop Damian. Because he wasn't Damian anymore, was he? He was Chaos. He was war and disorder.

And Chaos never hesitated to strike back.

Roz was in Patience's sector now, which meant she didn't have much farther to go. She sprinted down the familiar streets, turning when she reached the temple, then skidded to a stop. Horror caught in her throat, momentarily stealing her breath.

The irony of her earlier hope struck her like a blow. A body lay in the middle of the road, curled on its side. That wasn't what horrified Roz, though—she'd seen bodies before. What horrified her was the enormous piece of wrought iron protruding from the man's corpse. He had been skewered, the pointed tip of what Roz recognized belatedly as one of the temple's small, decorative spires sticking out through the shredded flesh of his back. The ravenous dark had surely ripped the spire from the roof, which must have pierced him when it fell.

She approached the corpse. Surely a disciple, if the Grace-made clothing was any indication. She nudged his arm with a toe, trying not to look at the mess of gore that seeped from his abdomen. He wasn't even stiff yet.

Pressing her hands to her face, she tried to ignore the wreckage, the darkness, the fear that tainted the air. This was Damian's doing, and the realization made her sick. Far sicker than the dead man before her. Because if she truly could pull Damian free from his madness, the memories of what he'd done would destroy him.

Roz didn't believe in hell, but she resumed running like the devil was on her heels, skirting bits of the city collapsing around her.

"*Roz!*"

Her name rising above the clamor brought Roz up short. Her heart hammered against her rib cage, and she narrowed her eyes, scouring the fog. It didn't take her long to spot Dev's familiar figure, Nasim and Zain on his heels.

"What are you *doing* here?" she said, horror turning her muscles watery. "Why aren't you on the ship?"

"We've been looking for you, of course," Dev huffed. "You weren't at the Basilica."

Nasim crossed her arms. "We took the rowboat as soon as Calder left. Did you really think we were going to sit around and wait for you to come back?"

"You were planning this," Roz accused. "I should have known. You agreed to stay behind far too easily."

At the same time, though, the sight of her friends heightened her urgency, her determination. She wasn't alone. Not anymore. She scrutinized them, committing their features to memory as if they didn't already take up considerable space there. Dev's eyes were bright, the set of his mouth stern. Nasim's expression was coolly unwavering, and even Zain watched Roz as though daring her to try and send them away.

"What the hell is going on?" Dev indicated the mayhem surrounding them. "Where's Damian?"

Roz motioned for them to follow, and they did, Nasim falling in beside her. She didn't know how to explain in a way that wouldn't sound mad, so she kept it simple. "Damian's the next reincarnation of Chaos."

Nasim's eyes widened until they seemed to take up most of her face. "He's *what*?"

Dev made a choking sound. "You're joking. How is that possible?"

"I'll explain later," Roz said, "but the point is, I might have a way to stop him. If I don't, he's going to destroy the whole city. Chaos always yearns for war, right? Well, so does Damian, at least right now." She hurriedly explained about Falco and how the general had known of their arrival. "I think he's gone to the Palazzo to retrieve the chthonium he buried beside his father's grave, then to fight alongside the other disciples of Chaos."

"Does Falco know...?" Nasim trailed off, but Roz knew what she'd been trying to ask.

"Yes. Falco knows what Damian is. So do her officers, I'd bet. If they see him, they'll shoot to kill." The general had made it clear she wouldn't try to reason with the newest patron saint of Chaos. She wouldn't even arrest him to stand trial. The only surefire way to stop Damian was with a swift death.

"*How* is he the next saint of Chaos?" Nasim demanded, consternation twisting her mouth. "I thought Battista Venturi was a disciple of Strength."

"His mother," Roz said. "Apparently nobody knew she was descended from Chaos. I only found out tonight when my own mother told me. I thought I could fix everything by undoing Enzo's ritual, but that wasn't the reason Damian became Chaos. It only sped up the process."

Dev nodded slowly. "Okay, but doesn't everything still need to be undone? I mean, as of right now, Chaos's power is stronger than every other saints'. If we can weaken it again, then at least Damian might not be quite so destructive."

"You told us on the ship we need to offer what was given," Nasim added. "So that's...what? The poison, the chthonium, and seven sacrifices?"

Roz had scarcely thought about the other implications of Enzo's ritual, focused as she was on Damian. "I doubt any of us want to kill seven more people."

They were in Strength's sector now, all intricate stonework and impossibly realistic statues. Zain, who had otherwise been quiet, said in the detached tone of someone well-acquainted with death: "What if we wait to see if there are any casualties, then use those?"

It was a rather chilling suggestion, but Roz considered it. If they *could* weaken Damian and the other disciples, it might make him easier to get to.

"Those wouldn't be *sacrifices*, though," Nasim pointed out. "Just people who happen to be dead."

"They would have sacrificed their lives in battle," her brother argued.

"But not for Chaos."

"Let's hope that won't be necessary," Roz cut in. "Listen—Enzo didn't bring *bodies* to the Shrine. Only their eyes. So what if only some kind of...flesh sacrifice is required? What if those people didn't *have* to be dead?"

"Then why would we need the poison at all?" Dev asked. He looked vaguely ill. "Vellenium wasn't part of the offering. Enzo just used it to kill his victims."

"But that's why it's important." Roz recalled the corpse of the boy she'd seen on the table in the Basilica morgue—the one she'd stumbled across right before Damian had tried to arrest her—and the ink-smudge dark of his veins. "The plant is literally known as *Blood of Chaos*. Disciples used to purposely ingest it as a form of self-sacrifice." She remembered the coroner, Isla, reading those words as if it had been yesterday. "In the stories, that's how Chaos knows a sacrifice is for him. It was a key part of Enzo's plan."

"So then what?" Nasim said. "We mix the poison with blood, throw in some chthonium, and hope for the best?"

Zain lengthened his stride so that he was in step with his sister and Roz. "Don't get upset, but it sounds to me like you're overlooking something." He spoke rapidly, keeping his gaze fixed straight ahead. "How is weakening Damian going to help anything? At best, you're just going to ensure a victory for Ombrazia."

"I have a plan," Roz said, swallowing the lump in her throat. "But I'm going to need you to trust me."

Zain was the last to nod, but he did so all the same.

♦ ♦ ♦

As they neared the Palazzo, everything tasted of magic. Smelled of it. The disturbing fact, however, was that Roz couldn't see it.

Or perhaps the problem was that she could see too much. The scene before her shifted rapidly, making her feel as if she were tumbling through a fever-induced dream. Images came too fast to make out anything with clarity. Roz's head spun. The Palazzo was crumbling—no, it was on fire—no, it was gone completely—and she was standing on barren cliffs overlooking the sea. There were cries of frustration, of agony, of fury, and then there was nothing at all. Distant figures darted through the fog, then froze. Her heart stuttered as a disciple appeared before her, but was gone the moment she blinked, disappearing too quickly for her to identify him. Then it was *all* gone, and the scene was as it always appeared in Roz's memories. The sky was blue and picturesque, the Palazzo a towering smear of gray against it. She detested the sight of it, and yet she felt calm despite the nagging feeling she was supposed to be elsewhere.

Just as she began to mull that over, she was back, the fog pressing in around her once more.

"It's Chaos's power," Roz said through gritted teeth, hearing Nasim's sharp intake of breath. This wasn't like any battle she'd ever known. It was being fought with magic, too many overlapping layers of it, and she suddenly understood why the First War of Saints had been so deadly. The disciples of Chaos were casting their magic out in wide nets, manipulating as many as they could, but the reality was, they were outnumbered. If the bloodshed hadn't started already, it would soon, and no number of illusions would be able to stop it.

"What is *happening*?" Nasim managed, glancing around wildly. "Did you all see that?"

Dev nodded. "They're trying to overwhelm the Ombrazian soldiers long enough to take what they came for."

"Which is what?" Zain was aghast. "What could they possibly want that badly?"

"Victory," Roz said. She blinked away the last dregs of false sunlight. "They're trying to force a surrender. Who knows what they're showing Falco's army? Maybe they're convincing them they've already lost." It was impossible to guess, and they didn't have time to figure it out. "Come on. Battista's grave is on the far side of the grounds. We need to see if Damian's been there yet."

They passed at least a dozen soldiers on the way there, every one of them frozen like realistic garden sculptures. It became even more eerie once Roz led the way into the graveyard—they could have been effigies, cast in the likeness of those long deceased. She wondered how long they would remain trapped.

"We need to hurry," she whispered, though no one but her friends could hear. "Nasim, stay with me. Dev and Zain, can you keep an eye on the perimeter?"

The two boys did as she bid, and Nasim followed Roz to the large marble slab at the back of the graveyard that, in better light, would have glistened. Cold wind buffeted Roz's back, and she shivered, gaze lingering on Battista Venturi's name. She remembered how she'd knelt beside his body in the crypt beneath the Palazzo, and told him his son had always been too good for him.

Then she knelt, her stomach dropping in dismay. Damian had obviously been here: Battista had been buried recently enough that no grass had spouted at the very base of his grave, but the cold, slightly damp earth had been turned over.

"It's gone," she told Nasim, failing to cover the panic in her voice. "He's already taken the chthonium."

She expected Nasim to curse, but there was no response. She just grabbed Roz's arm, apprehension pulling at the corners of her mouth as she pointed into the mist. "Look."

Two figures were moving. Quickly. They raced through the headstones, sending Roz's pulse ricocheting higher. She leapt to her feet, reaching for her weapon, but as the duo approached, she realized who they were.

"Saints," she snapped at Kiran and Siena. Both were breathing heavily. "You scared the hell out of us."

"What's the problem?" Nasim asked them, and Roz realized both former officers' faces were wan.

"Damian is the problem," Siena said in a low voice. She kept glancing over her shoulder. "He was just here, digging around Battista's grave. It was no use trying to stop him. We were actually looking for you when we passed Dev, who told us why you'd come. Roz—Damian dug up that chthonium because he thinks he's Chaos."

Roz relaxed. At least it wasn't something they hadn't already figured out.

"You knew?" Kiran demanded.

"Yes." She explained what had happened and how she planned to undo it. There was a beat of silence when she finished.

Eventually Siena said, "What can we do?"

"You can tell me exactly where Damian is and how to get to him."

Before Siena could respond, though, Nasim gasped. All three of them turned.

It was Dev, his silhouette turning corporeal as he sprinted toward them, chest heaving and eyes filled with panic. He doubled over as he reached them, blond hair in disarray, although he couldn't have run far.

Everything in Roz tightened in alarm. "What's wrong?"

Nasim was already at Dev's side, grabbing his upper arms to steady him. "Are you okay? Where's Zain?"

"Fine," Dev huffed, with a jerk of his shoulder. "Zain is fine too, as far as I know. He went the other way. But—*Salvestro*—" He wheezed, but there was no need for him to finish the sentence as the mist abruptly parted.

The chief magistrate was standing right behind him.

31

ROZ

Roz's stomach plummeted, the spongy grass seeming to tilt beneath her feet. First Falco, now Salvestro. She was being cornered at every turn.

The new chief magistrate was accompanied by a dozen others— a mix of officers and disciples, by the looks of it. Roz couldn't see them all, but she knew the man directly to Salvestro's right. It was Russo, his face grave, almost uncertain. The expression was a stark contradiction to the last time she'd see him.

This couldn't be how it ended. Roz still needed to get to Damian. She might not be able to fix Ombrazia, but she'd at least hoped to save him. Instead, she'd put herself and her friends in grave danger. Because there was no way around this, was there? They would lose to Salvestro, no matter how much rage and determination flared at Roz's core. She'd always relied on those two emotions to carry her. Tonight, however, it seemed they would only get her so far.

"Don't shoot," Salvestro said loudly as a few of the officers stepped forward. "The general wants these ones alive to answer for their crimes."

Roz would answer, all right. She would let herself be taken alive, if only so she could spit in General Falco's face before meeting her inevitable death.

One of the officers was Noemi, she saw with a jolt. The harshness the female officer always carried about her faded as she focused on something past Roz's left shoulder. Roz chanced a quick look, wondering what had caused Noemi to come undone in such a way.

Siena was frozen, her face full of horror as she recognized the girl she cared for so deeply. Kiran, too, had wilted.

Roz had to get them out of this. Somehow, she had to.

"You don't understand," she said to Salvestro, holding her hands out. It was the first and last time she would appeal to Salvestro Agosti for mercy. "I have an idea. A way to stop Damian—Chaos—from destroying everything. I know you don't care about us, but think of the rest of the city. Damian wants war. He won't quit until he wins or he dies."

"Then he'll die," Salvestro said with false pleasantry. "And so will you, eventually. Did you really think you could get away with it? That you could attack *me*"—his face reddened—"and then flee to join the enemy? If it were up to me, I'd have you executed here and now."

Roz was sorely tempted to goad him about behaving like Falco's subordinate, but she resolved not to test his self-control. The last thing she needed was a bullet in her head. What she *did* need was for him to understand the gravity of what she was saying, no matter how much he detested her.

"Roz is telling the truth," Nasim insisted. She hadn't moved a muscle since Salvestro started speaking, though strands of hair had come loose from her braid. "If you really want to prove you speak on behalf of the saints, you'll help us help you."

Salvestro's smile was withering, and not at all nice. "What kind of fool do you take me for? I know you're close to Damian Venturi. I always knew there was something bad in him. I saw the way he pranced around the Palazzo like he owned the place, rising to the top on his father's shoulders. Who's to say he didn't invite that disciple of Chaos into our midst? Perhaps he even got Enzo to kill Battista, hoping he would be able to take his place."

The suggestions were so absurd that Roz couldn't help a snort of disbelief. At her side, Kiran made a similar sound.

"You may not be a fool," Roz told Salvestro, "but you're clearly mad. Damian had nothing to do with Enzo's crimes. He *killed* him."

"Yes, yes, because the boy tried to murder both of you." Salvestro looked almost bored, flicking his hand. "I think we've all heard the tale in some form or another. Interesting, though, that there's no one else to corroborate your story."

"What possible reason could Roz have to lie?" Nasim shot back. "I was there for most of it. Enzo was out of his mind. He was nothing like Damian. Nobody would ever believe they were working together."

"Wouldn't they?"

The question was a rhetorical one, and Roz watched Salvestro draw an invisible line in the grass with his boot. His officers were motionless, guns still drawn. Roz could feel the anticipatory press of their attention as they watched her for a reaction.

All of them save Noemi, that was. Her attention was fixed on the ground, as if she couldn't bear to look in Siena's direction. Roz's heart ached for Siena, and she yearned to smack Noemi upside the head. That the girl would still stand at Salvestro's side, even now, was madness.

"Who do you think people would believe?" Salvestro continued. "A group of criminals hell-bent on destroying Ombrazia, or their chief magistrate? Do you think they would let a disciple of Chaos tell them anything at all?"

"Saint," Roz corrected through clenched teeth.

"I beg your pardon?"

"Damian. He's not a disciple. He's a saint."

Salvestro pulled his lips back from his teeth. His disgust was a tangible thing, thick in the air between them. "Chaos is a saint no longer. He's nothing but a tainted memory."

Siena responded before Roz could, voice acidic. "Interesting, then, that he has more power than any of the disciples in this city could ever dream of possessing."

"His power is cursed." Salvestro's reply came whip quick. "I suspect people will have no trouble believing Damian Venturi was in league with the other disciples of Chaos all along. That he let Enzo into our midst, used him to get rid of Battista and Forte, then killed him in an attempt to play the hero. After all, how much loyalty could a disciple of Chaos truly have? They can't be trusted. Even Chaos's lover turned on him in the end."

That wasn't true, though, was it? Patience hadn't turned on Chaos. Not really. She'd coordinated his fall for the good of the world, then gave up everything for him to have a new life.

"Imagine how pleased everyone will be when they learn I'm the one who brought about his downfall," Salvestro went on. "Truly an excellent start to my long reign as chief magistrate, wouldn't you say? Even Falco will be impressed. After the poor job the previous leaders did, I suspect it'll become quite obvious I was the right choice."

The wind picked up again, stirring the mist so that it seemed to shudder. Roz fought to repress the shiver tracking a path up her spine. "I'm sure you're right. And what a formidable leader you'll prove yourself to be." She feigned consideration. "Though I'll admit, I'm not sure how you figure you'll be able to get close enough to Damian to kill him."

"Oh, Signora. I don't need to get close to him." Salvestro's grin made Roz feel as if her bones had been submerged in ice. "I only need to get close to *you*."

Her mouth went suddenly dry. That was why Salvestro had sought her out in the first place—not simply to hold her at gunpoint, goad her about Damian, and force her to listen to the merits of his plan, but because he knew full well he wouldn't be able to conquer a saint of Chaos. Instead, he'd decided to use her to gain leverage.

"Damian won't stop for me," Roz said tersely. "He's not himself. You're only wasting your time."

The terrible thing was, she couldn't say whether or not it was the truth. She exchanged a look with Dev, who'd caught her eye. He'd seen the changes Damian had undergone on their journey. How every version of him, no matter how unrecognizable, cared for Roz with the same vehemence he always had.

"We'll see about that," Salvestro said. Then, to the officers: "Arrest them."

Now that she knew Salvestro needed her alive, Roz wasn't about to go quietly. She lunged for her discarded pistola, knowing she wouldn't make it in time but intending to draw the attention of the officers. It worked; they were on her in a heartbeat, wrenching her away from the weapon as Russo grabbed it. She hoped it would give her friends a chance to dart away—the dense fog might as well be good for something—but Salvestro had too many officers with him. Pain radiated up Roz's arms as they were yanked behind her back. She railed against her captor with furious twists, cursing venomously all the while. One thrust of her foot made contact with the man's shin, and he grunted in irritation, cuffing her in the head. It began throbbing at once, and Roz wondered fleetingly how much she could take before she was too concussed to do anything.

"Maim them if you must!" Salvestro barked. His face was red, his normally smooth hair in disarray. "We only need them alive, not uninjured!"

On Roz's other side, Siena whirled and jabbed, the beads in her hair glinting as she tried to avoid being detained by two officers

Roz didn't recognize. She was vicious in her efficiency, blocking strikes and narrowly evading the butt of a gun as it arced toward her head. Noemi watched in barely restrained distress, her grip tight on Nasim, who she'd quickly apprehended.

A shot went off, causing everyone to freeze. Panic spiked in Roz's blood. She wildly cast about for each of her companions. They were unharmed, she noted with relief, though glancing around with just as much confusion.

"Who the hell was that?" Salvestro snapped, but none of the officers said a word. The shot still reverberated in Roz's ears; the sound had emanated from very close by.

The mist lifted ever so slightly, and Roz realized they were approaching the escarpment at the edge of the graveyard. The Palazzo grounds leveled out where it met the docks, but this side of the graveyard was set high above the water, a sheer drop into the rocky sea below. They weren't close enough that Roz feared toppling over—the reason she had noticed the escarpment was because Zain was standing at its edge, gun in hand, indecision stark on his face. He didn't fire a second time.

The officers had evidently noticed Zain, too. Heads turned to Salvestro, awaiting instructions. Nasim stopped struggling. Her chest rose and fell in rapid pants as she fought to catch her breath, gaze fixed on her brother. Roz could practically see her mind whirring, trying to plan an outcome in which Zain was not harmed.

Dev, who was nearest to Zain, also stilled. His eyes, though, were on Nasim.

"Well, now," Salvestro said slowly. "Who's this?"

Zain's gaze darted back and forth. He had obviously heard their yells and come to their aid. Whether his shot had missed or he'd only meant to distract, Roz couldn't say. Now, though, Zain was clearly realizing he stood no chance against the dozen officers. He had nowhere to run. If he darted left or right, he would be caught. If he attempted to leap over the escarpment into the sea, it was unlikely he would survive the fall onto the rocks below.

"An Ombrazian army uniform," Salvestro said, dangerously calm. "And yet you dared to fire at *me*?"

Salvestro's left ear was bleeding, Roz saw as the disciple of Death lifted a hand to swipe the dark liquid away. Zain had been aiming for him, then. And he'd nearly been successful.

Roz's satisfaction at Salvestro being wounded was tampered by the grayish hue of Nasim's face. Siena averted her gaze, and Kiran winced. They all knew what was coming.

"Another traitor," Salvestro went on. "Not only that, but a would-be assassin. Some advice, boy?" He tilted his head, scrutinizing Zain with a sneer. "Next time, don't miss."

With that, he made a sharp gesture at Russo, who lifted his gun. Two other officers mirrored him.

Zain lowered his weapon but remained perfectly still. Understanding flashed across his face, followed a beat later by stony acceptance. He knew what it meant to be a traitor. Knew what it meant to be unfavored, a nobody. He would not meet his end the way Roz was destined to, dragged out before a woman who would play judge and jury. This boy would die the way her father had: on sight and without question.

"*No!*" The word tore from Nasim's chest, a ragged, barely intelligible sound. It seemed to hover in the air a moment too long, and the sheer panic of it snatched Roz's breath from her lungs.

She felt abruptly like a constellation of fraying edges, filled with the desperate desire to do *something*. Nasim's hair was a dark whip as she fought against the officers who held her arms. Dev, too, was attempting to free himself, and Roz wondered if he was trying to get to Nasim. Whether he would hold her back if the officers failed.

"Don't touch him," Roz screamed, though her words were directed at Russo, not Salvestro. "That's her *brother*. You know what it is to lose a brother." Desperation turned her voice hoarse. "Do you truly want to be the reason someone else has to suffer the way you did?"

Russo scowled, but the pistola shook in his hands. Roz had never met Michele, but in that moment she could imagine how the boy Damian had cared for so deeply might have looked. There was a softness to Russo's cheeks. An apprehension in his eyes, no matter how he tried to hide it. It made him seem younger. As she looked harder, though, Roz saw someone else in Alexi Russo. The man before her wore a mask with which she was intimately familiar. It was the same one she had donned every day since her father's death, to hide the fact that grief was eating her up from the inside.

Alexi Russo was angry. He blamed Damian for his misery the way Roz once had. Just like her, he had let that anger overtake him, had made it his primary trait. On the surface he seemed a simple man, furious and unlikable, but that wasn't truly him. That was clear to Roz.

She saw a man who was reaching his breaking point. A man who had been given exactly what he wanted and realized it would never be enough to fix the parts of him that were broken.

Roz saw herself.

Distantly she was aware of Nasim screaming her brother's name. Of Salvestro Agosti lunging with an impatient snarl, ripping the gun from Russo's grip. Of a foghorn somewhere in the distance, a melancholy hum that resonated like the bellow of some wounded beast. Of Salvestro aiming the pistola.

And she was aware, far too late, of Dev.

How he'd managed to break free of the officers holding him back, Roz would never know. His aquamarine eyes shone as they flicked to Nasim, then hardened. She turned just in time to see Dev launch himself at Zain, jaw corded in a tight angle, a tension borne of resolve. His desperation was all grace. His movements were quick and sure. In his face was the kind of determination possessed only by those who knew precisely how it felt to have loved and lost.

Roz wasn't sure whether time truly had slowed or she'd gotten trapped in the space between seconds. It seemed nobody else was moving, their group frozen in a strange tableau. There was only Dev. Only the beacon of his hair as he leapt toward the escarpment, pulling Zain in close to his chest. His head bowed to rest in the crook of the other boy's neck.

It took Roz a breath to realize what was happening.

He had made himself a shield.

The first bullet flew from Salvestro's pistola. It hit Dev square in the back, followed by a second. Then a third. A fourth. His shoulders wrenched together, spine curving from the impact. He let Zain go, shoving the other boy bodily to safety as he fell to his knees.

Run was the single word his lips formed, and Zain did, swallowed at once by the fog.

Some part of Roz knew she was screaming. She screamed and screamed and screamed, her ears ringing from the gunfire until she couldn't be sure she was making any noise at all. The blood was black in the dim light. So much blood that her brain refused to process it. Her body was numb.

Because Dev couldn't die. It was simply outside the realm of possibility. He went on living even when his world collapsed around him. He went on living even when he shouldn't, even when everything conspired against him, even when he was told by the city of his birth that he didn't matter. There was too *much* of him to die. His laugh was too contagious, his sadness too acute. His face was too familiar, every last one of his expressions emblazoned in Roz's mind. And there were still so many left to recover—so many smiles that hadn't resurfaced since his sister's death. He couldn't be gone before Roz had the chance to see them again.

She remembered when they'd met. How Dev had watched her throwing knives at the side of the tavern at dusk, his lips curled in a wicked smirk. He'd made her laugh that very first night. Startled the sound out of her before she'd even realized she could still remember *how* to laugh.

When Dev tilted his chin to the sky, his expression was calm. Serene. He was a man suspended in time. A martyr captured in a painting. A saint plummeting from grace.

His eyes fluttered closed as he fell, body arcing over the side of the escarpment and out of sight.

All the world went quiet. The earth itself seemed to hold its breath.

As though its full attention was required to welcome him home.

32

DAMIAN

Damian heard Roz's screams.

He paused at the entrance to the Palazzo, his hold on the Ombrazian soldiers briefly slackening. He'd left Roz wrapped in the darkness of the Basilica mezzanine, secure in the knowledge that she was safe. How could she be *here*?

For a fraction of a moment he felt the unforgiving bite of cold, the thick mud like grasping hands around his ankles, intent on impeding his progress. He heard the familiar echo of his own voice, but it sounded strange, as if he was listening to himself through earfuls of water. *The coast is clear.* He heard the wet slap of army-issued boots against the mud. The shot, then the horrible grunt that followed. It hadn't been a scream. No—there was only the shredded sound that somehow ripped free of his own body. It might have been denial. It might have been meaningless, incoherent. The precise note of that sound lingered in Damian's mind, but he couldn't recall what he'd said, if indeed he'd said anything at all.

That was the sound Roz made now. It was the sound of potent, bitter grief. It was the excruciating realization that something horrible was about to happen and you were powerless to stop it. That even if you tried, you would be too late.

For that tiny, too-fleeting fragment of a moment, Damian was well and truly awake.

33

Roz

Roz watched Dev fall, a passive observer in a hyperrealistic nightmare.

Any moment now, he would haul himself back over the side of the escarpment, grinning as he shook wet hair out of his face. *Did you see that?* he might say. Or perhaps: *They almost had me there.*

But the seconds ticked by, and he did not reappear.

Kiran and Siena stared over the edge of the escarpment in frozen horror. Nasim had collapsed, agony written in her face. Her cheeks were tear-streaked, eyes puffy. She dug her nails into the grass as if that contact was the only thing tethering her to the earth. Understanding crashed over Roz: Dev had saved Zain for Nasim. He had known what it was to lose a sibling, and he hadn't wanted Nasim to go through that, especially when she'd only just gotten her brother back. He had sacrificed himself to spare her pain.

I'm not ready to care about someone only to lose them again, Dev had told Roz only days ago. The memory made her want to scream.

What if we weren't ready to lose you? she thought, and for a terrible, selfish moment, she hated that they'd found Zain. Hated that he was alive while Dev was not. It wasn't fair. Of the two, Roz would have sacrificed Nasim's brother in a heartbeat.

But it hadn't been her choice to make.

When Roz tried to breathe, the air wouldn't come. All she managed was a great racking sob, her chest heaving as if she was going to be sick. She felt hollowed out. Her chest ached so fiercely, she wondered if she might die, too. The world was a distant thing, her body a prison, too small to contain her. The numbness gave way to sensation, heat lashing through her veins. Once, she would have recoiled from it.

Now she invited it in.

She screamed again, but this time it was a war cry. When thunder shook the unseeing sky, Roz shuddered alongside it.

And then Salvestro's pistola *melted*.

The gun turned molten, the metal searing and bubbling against his flesh. He gasped, dropping the weapon. All around him, the other officers cried out, relinquishing their guns as they, too, melted into formlessness. Roz heard Nasim's gasp as Noemi let her go and turned to her friends.

Run, she mouthed to them. Kiran and Siena would certainly be able to. Nasim, though, was still hunched on the ground. She looked the way Roz felt—as if the weight of grief was crushing her, drowning her, rendering her immobile.

But this was Nasim Kadera, and she set her jaw. Wiped her eyes. Nodded.

A couple of the bewildered officers tried to grab her as she leapt to her feet and took off, but she wove deftly between them, swallowed a heartbeat later by the mist. Kiran and Siena followed, managing to fight their way free now that everyone was weaponless.

Roz truly let go.

Heat rose in the air, unbearable and nauseating. Cradling his injured hand, Salvestro howled instructions at his officers, but pain and confusion had stupefied them. Only Russo remained uninjured, watching the scene with wide eyes. They lifted to meet

Roz's, but she held his gaze for only a moment. The world around her seemed to vibrate, tinged with soft light that hadn't been there before.

She threw her head back. Let the pain and fury and grief fill her up. Allowed it to rend her apart, fracturing her insides. She imagined hurling it at the sky in a blaze of anguish.

Then it began to rain.

It was a tempest. A torrent. A deluge. It soaked Roz through to her skin, ran in streams down her face, and drenched her hair. Everything smelled like petrichor and ash. It formed a wall around her, mingling with the mist, cutting her off from Salvestro, Russo, and the rest of the officers. She'd never experienced such a storm in her life. The harder the drops fell, the more the world around her seemed to fade away, revealing a rain-blurred version of a different place. All went silent.

Roz swallowed her gasp, whirling as she tried to comprehend her surroundings. The graveyard had disappeared, the fog with it. She was standing in a place she recognized. A place she knew with every facet of her being.

It was her childhood home.

She could see the table where her family had shared dinners, back when her mother still remembered how to smile. The chair where Damian should have sat, small and messy haired and far more serious than any child ought to be. She could see the stairwell leading up to her bedroom, where her parents had hummed melodies to coax her into sleep. Sometimes she wondered if they'd made the songs up, because she hadn't heard them since. At the top of the stairs the glow of the sun was visible, streaming through the wide window. She could picture Damian there, too. The slant of his hesitant smile. The rounded softness of his face, back before time had hewn it into angles.

Roz turned around, desperate to drink in the rest of the sitting room, and gasped.

Jacopo Lacertosa rose from the familiar worn sofa, his eyes softly cautious. They were the precise shade of blue as hers, though the tanned skin around them was creased. Roz's stomach bottomed out, a sensation usually reserved for horror.

Her father looked just as she remembered him, but sharper somehow, as if seeing him again had brought him back into focus. She'd nearly forgotten the way his black hair had been shot through with strands of silver. In memories she hadn't pictured him looking so drained, so thin and weathered. As a child, Roz realized with a lurch, she hadn't noticed her father getting older. More tired. Something bittersweet lanced through her, leaving a lingering ache. Her mouth was dry, her extremities numb. She wanted to run to him. She wanted to force her way into his arms, yet feared he would disappear if she tried.

So she merely spoke the words that kept playing on a loop in her mind.

"This isn't real."

Jacopo offered a small smile. It was an echo of the real thing, but Roz could picture it all the same. "Rossana. I've missed that skepticism of yours."

She glanced out the window. The cobblestone street outside was limned in midafternoon light. The home across the way hadn't yet fallen into disrepair. This was the past. Time had re-formed around her. Because this was—

"An illusion," she murmured aloud. She met her father's gaze again, and the bubble of agony grew. "Damian did this, didn't he? None of the other disciples would have known to put me here. He made you up. You're not real."

But why? What reason could he possibly have to hurt her this way?

Her father came closer. He smelled just the same as always—like tobacco and mint. "Damian didn't make me up," he said softly, his voice thick with emotion and understanding.

"Of course he did," Roz snapped back. If she made her voice harsh, perhaps she wouldn't crumble. "Otherwise this doesn't make any sense."

Jacopo extended a hand. She stared at it a moment, chest heaving, afraid to reach out and touch his skin. Afraid he would evaporate like smoke.

"Please," he urged her.

So she braced herself, taking it.

His palm was warm. Calloused. Exactly right. Roz tightened her grip, squeezing his fingers so hard he ought to have winced. He didn't, though. He squeezed back.

"I am real because you remember me" was all he said. As if it were as simple as that. "I am real because you need me to be."

Roz wanted to collapse in on herself. For so many years she'd longed to see her father again. To hear his voice and hold his hand. Now that it was happening, though, she wasn't sure she could bear it. "Why? I've needed you for years. Why now?"

"Because I'm in your way."

"No you're not," Roz said at once, before she could fully comprehend his words.

"Rossana." Her father spoke her name firmly, sounding more like the man she remembered. "Don't just react. *Think*. You've let me hold you back."

"What do you mean? You weren't there to hold me back from anything."

She hadn't meant for it to sound like an accusation, and she winced, but Jacopo didn't seem to mind. He lifted their clasped hands, turning hers palm up. "I know what you became."

Roz shut her eyes. Knowing her father had died before seeing her become a disciple was one of the few reprieves she'd gotten after his execution. "It was never what I wanted," she said, hoping he was telling the truth. Hoping he was only real because she'd made it so, and that this wasn't a true shade of the man who'd raised her.

"No," he said. Roz opened her eyes in time to see him drop her hand, his own gaze downcast. "You thought it wasn't what *I* wanted. You felt you'd betrayed me. But Rossana, nothing you could become would make me love you less. I hated disciples because I felt they didn't care for anyone or anything but themselves. But you do. You always have. If you can use that power to your advantage, don't let me stop you."

"I'm not—" she insisted, but her father cut her off with a shake of his head.

"Don't lie to me." He spoke gently. "Lean into it. Use it."

"I don't know how. I don't know what it will do. And I'm afraid that I'm…"

"That you're what?"

She couldn't say it aloud. Not to her father, if indeed this was really him. It was impossible, the fact that she was standing here talking to him when he'd been dead for years. And in her childhood home, no less. She was afraid to blink, to breathe, to lose it all.

Who cared if it was an illusion? It was better than reality. Reality was a thousand kinds of heartache. In this illusion, outside these walls, Dev was still alive. Perhaps he was racing through the streets with Amélie, who also lived. Perhaps, not far from here, Piera was serving patrons in Bartolo's with a smile. Perhaps Damian's family was still whole, his father not yet corrupted by power. Perhaps Caprice Lacertosa was sitting with Liliana Venturi over coffee, both of them full of contentment. Here, now, the Palazzo and the war felt far away. The world had yet to chew Roz up and spit her back out.

She knew what happened to people who got trapped in illusions. Their real self wasted away, bit by bit, until death finally swallowed them. But did she care? At least there wouldn't be any pain.

"Stop it," her father said sharply, as though he knew her thoughts. "This place was not perfect either, Rossana. You're blinded by nostalgia. You were a child—you didn't see the suffering. But it was there, just as it always has been."

Roz glanced wistfully out the window again. She thought about asking where her mother was, but knew instinctively that her father wouldn't be able to answer. Outside, the streets remained empty. The sunlight and shadows didn't shift. It was *too* still, now that she looked closely enough. A shudder crawled down her spine.

"It doesn't matter," she told him. "If this is an illusion, I can't leave until the magic fades." Given how powerful Damian was, who knew how long that would be?

"You can leave whenever you're ready."

"That's not how it works. Besides, I'm...scared." She swallowed. It was okay to admit that here, right? "I don't know if my plan will succeed. I thought if I gave up a part of myself, as Patience did in the story, I might be able to make Damian human again. My soul, or my humanity, or whatever it is that needs to be sacrificed. But I don't know what that *means*. I'm not a saint, and I'm afraid I'll fail. I'm afraid Damian will die. I'm afraid of dying myself." Her voice broke. She'd never truly feared death until now. After all, she'd already known nonexistence—how many millennia had passed before her birth? When you were nothing, you couldn't be afraid.

It was the things she would miss, though, that scared her. The things she would leave behind or never see change.

Jacopo smiled, lips still pressed together. This time it transformed his face and made him appear younger. More at ease.

"Trust yourself. Trust your magic. But remember that's not all there is."

Roz released a shuddering breath, studying her father's face more carefully: the shadow of uneven scruff along his jaw, the nose shaped precisely like hers, the jacket he wore in her youth.

"Hold me," she whispered, and it came out like a question.

His smile took on a melancholy tilt, but he didn't make her ask again. He pulled her into his chest, the firm, familiar feel of his embrace a grounding thing. It broke Roz, shattering her from the inside, and she squeezed her eyes shut. The ache was unbearable because she knew it wouldn't last.

She felt heat at her core, a kind of static that traveled up her torso and into each of her limbs. It was an adrenaline rush, the high of intoxication, the weightless sensation of moving through a dream.

"I don't want you to leave," she said, quietly enough that she wasn't sure her father would hear. Her voice was muffled by his shoulder, but he felt less real by the second. "I hate that you're gone."

"Ah, Rossana." There was a resignation in the way he said her name. He let her go and stepped back. His face was full of a knowing far beyond anything Roz could have conjured on her own, and for a heart-stopping moment she wondered. She *wondered*. "You've thought of me every day. How can I possibly be gone?"

Fire flared through her as Jacopo slipped from her fingers and evaporated from her vision. The world tilted on its axis, careening out of orbit. She tried to grab on to her father's jacket, fingers twisting in the worn fabric, swallowing a sob when they lost purchase. The image of him flickered, fractured.

The last thing she saw was his face, calm and assured.

Then there was nothing.

Roz was standing in the graveyard once more. The rain returned, thundering down around her, blocking out every other sight and sound. The darkness of Damian's magic pressed in on her from all sides, scraping at her skin and tangling in her hair with a ferocity it hadn't possessed before. She clenched her fists against the heat that still flowed through her body.

Trust yourself. Trust your magic.

Something inside her shifted. The heat became more bearable, then turned cold. Frigid. It threatened to spill out of her veins, fill the back of her throat, and drown her in her own body. It was power. Pure and undiluted.

She exhaled raggedly. It seemed to get caught somewhere in the cavity of her chest, as if something blocked its path. She knew exactly how this story went. She always had. In the beginning, Patience subdued Chaos, her lover. In the end, she watched him fall.

To temper her impulsive lover, Patience also created rain, the original tale claimed. Surely it was no coincidence, then, that it had rained the day Chaos fell from grace.

Not in a mist upon a delicate wind, but in a torrential rush.

Roz tilted her face to the heavens, blinking water and tears from her lashes. Of course she and Damian had always found their way back to each other. They were opposites, separate halves, that formed a whole. They were always supposed to end up here.

Her power had always been strong, and it terrified her. She had done things no regular disciple could do. She had destroyed a bridge with a mere touch. She had undone the work of her fellow disciples with little difficulty.

She was not a saint. Not yet.

All at once, Roz understood exactly how this needed to end.

Patience knows precisely when to strike.

34

DAMIAN

Damian couldn't understand what had happened.

One moment he'd been tearing through the Palazzo grounds in search of Roz, cocooned in his magic to avoid prying eyes. The next, he felt himself begin to weaken. He couldn't understand why. He couldn't *afford* to weaken. He needed to get to Roz. He needed to save her from whatever had made her scream like that.

Why the hell had she come here in the first place? She needed to stop trying to save him. Damian didn't need to be saved.

The Ombrazian soldiers were still mainly incapacitated, but a number of them were beginning to break free, striking at the disciples of Chaos and turning the fight into a physical one. Damian whirled, power flaring within him, then sputtering out. It was raining lightly, but he could see a storm approaching from the direction of the sea. In fact, it looked to be already ashore, confined somehow to the far side of the grounds.

The moment Damian had the thought, it moved closer.

The storm didn't arrive gently. One moment it was scarcely raining at all, and the next the invisible sky unleashed a cascade of water that seemed to fall in buckets. The rain felt like renewal at first. It plastered Damian's hair to his skull and spilled down his cheeks like a deluge of tears. The fatigue drained from his bones as drops clotted in his lashes. He was submerged, yet somehow still breathing.

Only then did he realize what was happening,

The rain felt like *magic*, and the haze was lifting. And as it did, General Falco swam into view.

She appeared in his periphery, a rain-altered silhouette, accompanied by security officers and other disciples. Damian hurled his magic without thinking, freezing them in their tracks. There must have been nearly a hundred in total, all gathered to try and defeat him, but he was a *saint*. Even in such great numbers, they could not win. He let a smile grace his mouth as he studied Falco, trapped in her advance. One of her hands stretched out in front of her, clawing, reaching, struggling to break free.

Damian felt a tug deep inside him. An exhaustion that pulled at his joints, tightened his muscles, and clouded his mind. He exhaled a heavy breath through his nose, clenching his teeth so tightly he swore he could feel them wearing down. He was losing control. It seemed to drain out of him alongside the deluge that soaked his skin and impeded his vision.

Perhaps even saints had limitations. Such a thing had not occurred to him until now, as he felt the weariness wrenching at his bones.

"*Calder!*" he'd bellowed, a command for help. The rest of the disciples he drew to him with sheer force of will. Those not currently engaged in combat swarmed like silent shadows, their magic mixing, melding with his own. He felt it spread out like a blanket cast over the grounds, and relaxed ever so slightly. But then he felt that magic, too, begin to abate.

The darkness that persisted was no longer his—it was now the regular darkness of night. Damian was the opposite of an experienced magic user, but he could feel power slipping away, passing through his fingers as easily as the rain. He whirled, trying to glimpse Calder and the other disciples of Chaos. What he could see of their faces mirrored his own horror. Calder was clenching and unclenching his fists, and when nothing happened, he let out a quiet growl of frustration. His eyes met Damian's, real fear in their depths. It was an appeal for help. A prayer cast out to a saint.

And Damian could not answer it.

Meanwhile, Falco had unfrozen. *Everyone* had unfrozen. They advanced toward Damian, the general giving a satisfied twist of her lips.

"That's better," she said, and if Damian's glare hadn't been glued to hers, he might have missed the words entirely. As she spoke, she made a small gesture with her fingers. It was a gesture Damian had made himself countless times before. One he recognized from years as a security officer.

"No!" he roared, but his furious protestation was lost in the subsequent bellow of gunfire. He dropped to his knees in the grass, shielding his head as though his arms might protect him from the barrage of bullets.

He waited to feel the pressure, the sharp explosion of pain, but it didn't come.

Nobody was aiming for him.

They were aiming for the disciples.

He heard the grunts and cries of agony as the bullets struck home. A number of disciples doubled over as they struggled to reach their weapons, but it was no use. They'd been relying on their magic tonight, and it had left them woefully unprepared. Milos and a few others lunged forward, using their bodies to shield Calder, pistolas blazing. Most of them had already taken at least one shot to the legs or torso, and Damian could see scarlet seeping through their clothes. It didn't stop them, though. Falco bellowed another order, and bullets peppered Milos's chest, causing him to jerk and recoil. It was nearly too horrible to watch. Yells and gunfire rent the air, and finally Milos collapsed, his body crumpling to the cobblestones. Blood pooled around him, immediately diluted by the relentless rain.

He looked so terribly young, his face slackened as it was. Just another disciple, another child, struck down in the country that had betrayed him.

The disciples continued to fall. One by one they dropped to their knees, only to collapse prone on the ground. Damian couldn't fathom why he wasn't being shot at. How he hadn't taken so much as an errant bullet when *he* was the one they wanted. His heartbeat was a feral thing, vibrating throughout his entire body, thrumming alongside the gunfire echoing in his ears. He reached for his power over and over again, one hand clenching the chthonium in his pocket, but it was useless. His magic was gone. *All* of Chaos's magic was gone, so that each and every one of his disciples was powerless.

"Take the rest," Falco instructed her officers, who moved forward to detain the disciples that were still alive. It took a few of them to wrestle Calder into submission. They didn't come for Damian, though. It was Falco herself who approached him, her tight smile stretching viciously wide. She kicked Damian's gun from his hand with ease, gripping his collar to pull him to his feet.

"Unhand me," Damian snarled, but she only laughed.

"Silence, false saint. I would have killed you in private, but after what you've done, it'll be a public execution for you."

Damian struggled against her, but whatever had sapped his magic had done the same to his strength. He wasn't supposed to feel this kind of bone-deep exhaustion. He was fury. He was war.

And then he heard her voice.

"Stop!"

Roz's scream sliced the air. It wasn't a plea, but a command. She had appeared at the edge of the garden, arms wide, fingers spread. Her clothes were drenched, her eyes fire. Behind her, the Palazzo was consumed by darkness

The rain slowed as she stepped closer to Falco. She didn't look like the girl Damian had left in the Basilica. She looked like a vengeful queen come to take her due.

"Ah," Falco said smoothly, as if Roz's presence had been expected. "I wondered when you'd show up."

Roz's eyes snapped to Damian's. He felt regret lance through him and heard her screams all over again. Something had happened. Something terrible that was wrenching her apart. It was evident from the look on her face. But she schooled her expression into an icy mask, a muscle ticking in her jaw as she said, "Let him go. He's mine."

Damian didn't understand what she meant. The general snorted. Even soaking wet, Falco was formidable, the lines of her face more severe.

"Did you know I knew your father?" she asked, lips curling upward at Roz's flicker of shock. "Oh, yes. We went to war about the same time. I was one of his superiors, and Battista Venturi was mine."

"So what?" Roz said coolly. "You think that will stop me from killing you?"

"You won't kill me, child." Falco gave another flick of her wrist, and yet more soldiers lunged forth. "I'm telling you this so you understand whom you're dealing with. I was commanded by Battista Venturi. Which meant that when he ordered me to track down deserters, when he ordered they be killed for their crimes, I did just that."

Damian understood her meaning at once. He tried to strike out at Falco, to hurt her the way she was attempting to hurt Roz, but his muscles refused to comply.

"You killed him." Roz's voice quieted. "It was you."

Falco shoved Damian back to his knees, wrenching him closer to her, the fabric of his collar digging into his neck hard enough to be painful. He struggled to swallow, rage pulsing through him.

"It was me," Falco repeated. There was no inflection to the statement at all. "You may be a powerful disciple, but I know you won't do anything while I have Damian Venturi at my mercy. Agosti may be a fool, but he pointed out something very important: The two of you are far too easy to manipulate. To control one, we simply have to control the other. He might have failed"—Falco's hold on Damian tightened even further—"but I won't."

Roz's throat shifted. "You're mistaken."

"Don't insult my intelligence. Or your own, for that matter. We both know the story: Chaos never rises alone. Patience is always there, right by his side, yet she betrays her lover in the end. You'll destroy him, whether you mean to or not." Falco spoke faster, a feverish excitement in her voice. "You can't help it."

Roz laughed, the sound empty. "You know nothing about what I mean to do."

Falco's lips tightened with an emotion somewhere between pity and amusement. "You pretend to be driven by rage and righteousness. You pretend you care for no one," Falco continued. "But you saw what was happening tonight, and you knew he had to be stopped. You will protect those in Ombrazia because you cannot help yourself. And for that, the people will worship you."

"I have no desire to be worshipped," Roz said quietly, though the way she spoke was odd. The words held the weight of something inevitable.

"No good saint does. But the stories will always happen precisely the way they are meant to."

Damian still couldn't move, though he heard Falco's breathy huff of laughter in his ear. He knew the tale as well as the rest of Ombrazia.

They say it rained the day Chaos fell from grace.

It had certainly done that.

He fell because his children did.

Damian chanced a quick look over his shoulder at the bodies of Milos and the other dead disciples of Chaos. It sent a pang through his chest.

His lover, Patience, watched mournfully as he fell. And though her heart, so like his, was full of revenge, she did not reach for him. She only waited, knowing that every war has its end, and every sin begs a punishment.

"No," Damian whispered, the breath evaporating from his lungs. A small, quiet part of him was astounded. Roz wasn't a saint, of course, but she *was* a disciple of Patience. Was that part of the reason Damian loved her so deeply? Why he yearned to please her above all else? Chaos might have been dangerous, unpredictable, but he was steadfast in his devotion to Patience.

Falco was wrong. Roz would never stand by while Damian was destroyed. She hated the saints, and didn't abide by the rules. She would surely break the cycle.

She had to.

The tempest rose to a roar, the rain turning violent once more. Roz's body was stiff, her hands outstretched at her sides, but her face was relaxed. Falco was wrenched away from Damian so quickly he could hardly comprehend it, as if dragged into the storm by unseen hands. Roz tilted her chin up, and the rest of the soldiers followed, pulled away one by one. He wondered if they would drown. He hoped they would.

The only reprieve was Roz herself. She approached Damian slowly. When she reached him, the torrent ceased, though it continued to rage mere inches away. It was as if they were positioned in the eye of a tiny hurricane, confined to a space where Falco and her officers couldn't reach them. He couldn't understand what was happening. He couldn't understand how she was doing this. It was the kind of power only a saint possessed.

"You need to stop, Damian," Roz said, expression imploring. "It wasn't supposed to happen like this."

Part of Damian yearned to agree with her, but the more powerful part of him railed against it. Now that he was free of the rain, he felt dregs of his magic weave back into his blood. He rose to his feet. The fire that had sputtered within him burned hot once more, and the yearning sensation vanished.

"No," he growled. "*You* need to stop. Why are you even here?"

"Why am I *here*? As in, why am I not inside the Basilica where you abandoned me?" Roz's voice shook.

Damian didn't let his stoic expression change. "I was trying to keep you safe. I was leading Falco and the others away so that you wouldn't have to be a part of this."

"Because you trapped them in an illusion? Damian, you don't know what you're doing. You don't have any idea what you *can* do. And that ignorance is destroying this city."

"Yes," he agreed. "That was the idea. But then you had to show up and get half of Calder's army killed."

"*I* got them killed?" Roz was so furious she could hardly form words. "You're the one who dragged them into a battle they couldn't possibly win. I was only trying to stop you from doing more damage. What about everyone else who's already died?"

"Nobody else has died. Nobody important, anyway."

"*Dev* died!" she screamed, a shredded sound. "He fucking *died*, Damian!" The disclosure seemed to strip her of energy, and each rapid breath shuddered out of her, shaking her whole body. Only then did he realize just how much effort she'd been expending to keep it together. "What about him? What about *me*?"

Damian was supposed to care about Dev, he knew, but he only felt hollow. His concern was wholly for Roz. There were so many people he'd longed to hurt, but she wasn't one of them. Never her. "I'm sorry. You were supposed to be unaffected."

"What of the unfavored families in Chaos's abandoned sector?" Roz hurled the words at him now. "What of the homes they've lost? You're hurting the wrong people!"

"The wrong people?" Damian repeated, stepping closer to her. He heard something insidious in his voice, and let it take root. "Those people have always loathed Chaos, just like all the rest, yet still I fight back where they did not. They should be *thanking* me. They should be kneeling at my feet."

"There was a time when you loathed Chaos just as much! Have you forgotten that?"

"I choose to forget what no longer serves me."

Damian saw the anger drain out of her at his words, and immediately regretted them.

"Then you'd better forget me," Roz said, barely a whisper. "Because I serve no saint."

He recoiled, feeling as if she'd slapped him. "I could never forget you. You exist in every part of me."

Roz's throat corded in a swallow. He could see in her face that she had made a decision, and he had no idea what it might be. He could only tell that he wouldn't like it.

Heart seizing in his chest, he reached for her wrist. The touch of her skin was a searing, insistent flame. "I'm here," he insisted. "I've been here the whole time. Every version of me is yours."

"I don't want this version," Roz said brokenly. She didn't meet his gaze. "I want the boy who ran with me through these streets, who was too nervous to kiss me first. I want the boy who met me by the river and admitted he was afraid—so afraid—of everything to come. I want you to be him again."

In that moment, Damian wanted to be that boy, too. He wanted to be everything she needed.

"I can't," he whispered instead. "I don't know how."

He thought his admission would cause her to push him away. Instead, Roz reached for him. Damian took her hand, reveling in the heat of her skin, pulling her closer. He slipped a thumb over her palm, along the line of her small wrist, feeling the pulse there. He wanted to tell her she was the most magnificent thing he'd ever seen. He wanted to tell her she was a saint worth worshipping. He wanted to tell her he loved her.

"Don't look at me like that," he murmured.

"Like what?"

"Like I've broken your heart."

She squeezed her eyes shut, a muscle quivering in her jaw. If Roz was Patience and he Chaos, then they were a tragedy. Damian remembered the story she'd read to him in the Atheneum with brutal clarity. But he didn't want a tragedy—he wanted a legend. A fantasy. A love story.

Rather than say anything, Roz learned forward and pressed her lips to his. Though the lines of her body were hard, her mouth was saltwater soft. She dragged her hands through his hair, and Damian grabbed her by the waist, his need to touch her lending his weakened arms fervor. He forgot he was Chaos then. He forgot this was war.

"Damian," she said, and hearing her say his name was a balm. "When my heart breaks, it will be my own doing."

"Don't say that." Gently he unwrapped her hand from the back of his neck, bringing it to his lips. She shuddered at the caress of his breath.

"Was it you?" Roz asked, so softly he might have imagined it. "Was it you who showed me..." She trailed off, and Damian lifted his head to meet her gaze. Her eyes were summer blue; a few freckles dotted the skin beneath them. She looked like every dream he'd ever had.

"Was it me who showed you what?"

There was a too-heavy silence, and then Roz shook her head. "Never mind. I'd rather not know."

Perplexed, he could only kiss her again, swearing fealty with the brush of his tongue.

"It's funny, isn't it?" she whispered. "You always loved this city so much, and I never could."

Damian knew what she was trying to say. He had devoted his life to Ombrazia, yet here he was trying to destroy it. Roz had always detested this place, or at least the way it was run, and now she was trying to save it. From *him*.

"You loved it enough to want to change it. That's all I'm trying to do now."

"You're trying to rip it apart."

"If that's what it takes."

She shook her head, voice pitched even lower so that Damian had to strain to listen. "It's not the same. But I'll give it all up, if I have to. For you."

Damian frowned, taking her chin in his fingers. "You don't have to give up anything. We'll rebuild this city together. I just need you to accept my way of doing it." Her expression was agonized, and he couldn't fathom why. "Roz, what's wrong?"

She rested her head on his shoulder, tears trickling down her face into the fabric of his drenched shirt. Damian felt like he was fracturing on the inside. How could he have allowed himself to make her this upset? He would change, if he only knew how.

"I'm sorry," Roz breathed against his ear. "I don't know what this will do. But I have to try."

"Try what?" He made to pull away, but she held him fast.

"I'm so sorry," she said again. Her voice hitched. "I loved you every single moment."

Then she stabbed something hot and sharp into his abdomen.

35

ROZ

Roz felt as if she were the one being pierced with a blade.

The ache in her chest was unendurable. She heard Damian's harsh intake of breath as her vellenium-coated blade split skin, burrowing between his ribs. He doubled over, body bending across hers, and Roz widened her stance to accommodate his considerable weight. She squeezed her eyes shut, each breath seeming to tear at her lungs.

"Why?" Damian's voice came weakly from beside her ear, scarcely more than a whimper. *"Why?"*

"I'm sorry," Roz said. It sounded like a sob. She repeated it, over and over, until the words lost all meaning. There was nothing else to say. Her heart beat a stuttering, uneven rhythm, each pulse causing her physical pain. Damian's body was warm against hers, the familiar lines of him buckling, curving inward. His hands slipped down to the hilt of the blade, as if he might try to yank it out, but Roz held fast to the metal. She could already see the faint tinge of black against his skin as the vellenium commenced its rapid spread through the bloodstream. He swallowed with difficulty, the striated veins of his neck bulging.

"I wanted—" he began, but the words were thick, his jaw not moving properly. "Everything I've ever done was—for you."

"I know." She managed to force out, trying to soothe him. "I know."

And she did know. But she couldn't let him continue—not like this. She couldn't stand looking at his face and not seeing the boy she knew there. And although the saint before her protested, she knew the real Damian would have chosen his own death over becoming a monster.

She had felt the weight of the chthonium in his pocket while they'd kissed, and hoped beyond hope it would be enough. That she could save Damian while also undoing everything Enzo had done. At the very least, she knew she had to try.

Because she had always tried, hadn't she? Maybe a little too hard. All she'd ever wanted was to change Ombrazia on behalf of the girl she'd been, while paying penance for the one she'd become. It had consumed her the way her goals always did. Because Roz Lacertosa had always been too *much*. Too passionate, too impulsive, too demanding, too single-minded. She said exactly what she thought, at all the wrong times. She'd come to peace with that long ago, however, and figured that if she could only *prove* she was worth listening to, perhaps she wouldn't be judged so harshly.

Tears slipped down her cheeks, turning from flame to ice. She cried for Dev. For Damian, if this didn't work. She cried for herself, because of what she was about to lose, and because of everything she was about to gain. The things she'd never wanted.

She remembered the way Damian had looked up in the mezzanine. The timbre of his voice as he'd laughed at Falco. His harsh confidence had been unfamiliar and jarring, and in that moment, he was a king who'd finally taken up his crown.

She understood now. The story about Chaos's fall was, at its heart, a story about Patience. About the sacrifice she made to save the world from the man she loved. She had always been the catalyst, the one who set his demise in motion. That was why she merely stood by as Chaos fell. That was why she hadn't reached for him.

She only waited, knowing that every war has its end, and every sin begs a punishment.

Patience had ended humanity's first war by casting Chaos out. It had been she who punished him. She'd known precisely when to strike, and it had destroyed them both, in a sense.

They were no longer two halves of a whole. They no longer balanced each other in power, for what use is a man to a saint?

The saints' creation of the world was merely a story, Roz figured, designed to explain away the inexplicable. The story of Patience and Chaos, though, she believed. It was a story of impossible choices. A story of love and pain, and the kind of sacrifice someone like Enzo would never understand.

Roz might not be able to save humanity. She might not even be able to save Ombrazia. But she was going to save Damian, if she could.

As if he'd heard her silent promise, Damian's knees began to buckle. His eyes were fixed on something in the middle distance, and there was fear in their inky depths. True, genuine fear. It was an emotion Roz hadn't seen on his face for some time.

She lowered him to the ground as his body jerked, the shadows tracing his veins growing darker.

"You told me once that I was the earth, while you were the moon in orbit," she murmured, not knowing if he could hear. "A satellite that had no choice but to remain nearby. You said you wished it could be the other way around, if only for a moment. That you could be the one I relied upon. But you are, Damian." She exhaled a rattling breath. "You always have been."

His initial metaphor, Roz thought, had been wrong. They were not a planet and a satellite, one more powerful than the other.

Rather, they were a binary star—two people in the same orbit, easily mistaken as a single entity, sharing the same light.

"It's going to be okay," she whispered, then yanked the blade loose. It took a horrible amount of effort. Blood flowed freely from the wound as Damian convulsed. His skin was gray, his eyes unseeing. *Offer what was given. Preferably in a holy place.*

Any place became holy when there was a saint present, did it not?

Roz gritted her teeth and drew the vellenium-dipped blade across her own arm, praying enough remained for this to work. It was slick with Damian's blood, and the deep crimson liquid bled into her own as it welled up along the incision she'd made. Outside the bubble of calm she'd created, they were surrounded by the dead. Disciples of Chaos who had bled onto the cobblestones, forming pools of scarlet diluted by the rain.

She let her blood fall to the ground beside Damian. And then, while she waited for Death, she prayed.

Not to the original saints. No—she prayed to the boy prone on the ground before her. She allowed her magic to expand, hoping Damian's magic sensed it and responded in kind. She thought of the Damian of her youth, shy and smiling and undoubtedly *good*. She held that image in her mind, as if remembering it might help make it true once more. She thought of her father, of the steadfast belief in his eyes when he'd looked at her. The way she felt when he'd folded her into his arms, and how she'd known then that it was okay to make this choice.

Roz felt the heat of her magic singing in her veins. She felt Damian's, equally warm and vibrant. Their power mingled, swelling to become something tangible, something greater than both of them. She squeezed her eyes shut, tears slipping down her cheeks.

Patience accepted Death's offer, and so was Chaos revived, the story had said. *But the moment breath returned to his lungs,*

Patience became untethered from the mortal plane, the connection between the lovers severed.

When Damian had become Chaos, he was no longer the same. Roz knew inherently that the same would happen to her. Not in the same way—Patience was nothing like Chaos, after all—but one could not become a saint and remain unchanged.

How many times had she wanted to escape her own mind? To be anyone else but herself? How many times had she longed to claw her grief, her anguish, her despair, from her very heart? Magic had taken so much from her. It was the reason for every divide, every unfairness she'd ever resented. How ironic that it was the thing to which she now turned.

"Take it," she rasped to Damian, to Chaos. "Take whatever you need."

Damian twitched, his brow furrowing as if some part of him had heard her words. It felt strange, speaking to him as though he were not himself. But Roz had to believe that the saint inside him was listening. Somehow she had to believe the magic would recognize what she was giving up: her humanity. The piece of her that was tethered to a regular, mortal life. After all, it was an exchange that had been done before.

And so was Chaos struck from the pantheon, condemned to walk the earth a harmless mortal, while Patience became the first to ascend to the next realm.

If the stories were true, then she could make Damian a man once more. She could give him the humanity that had been stolen from him. Chaos might be his destiny, but she could undo it.

In return, though, she had to become a saint.

Her knees ached where they pressed into the ground. For a horrible, chilling moment, Damian's breaths turned labored, and she thought she had failed.

Then she felt magic surge within her.

It burned through her veins with a ferocity unmatched by anything she'd ever experienced. It was hot, hot, *agonizing* heat, and she tilted her own chin up and screamed. Perhaps it was only to her own ears, but the sound seemed for a moment to be the only thing in the world. It shattered things she could not name, though she felt the fractures beneath the skin. She was unending, unyielding power in its purest form. She felt as though she could destroy the earth and re-form it from dust. She felt celestial.

She *felt*.

With that feeling came a memory. A purely human one, of summer days spent at the river with Damian. How they would race through the crumbling, shadow-veiled streets, keeping to the alleyways until they arrived at the water. It was always best on a windy day, when the restless waves shattered against the rocks. Though Roz was usually the more daring one, Damian had always wanted to see how far out they could swim. She thought of his hand gripping hers as he pulled her away from the shore, smiling widely as he treaded water.

He still did that, didn't he? Pulled her deeper and deeper, until she gave in to those tiny moments of held-breath oblivion. That was what Damian did to her—he made Roz insensible of everything else.

She lived in that memory for the merest breath of a moment. Reveled in it. That carefree insignificance of believing everything mattered.

Then a shudder unfurled along the length of her body, and everything stilled. The beat of her heart. Time itself.

She blinked, and all at once had never seen the world so clearly.

Roz bent over Damian's pale, prone form. Ran a hand down the side of his cheek, feeling his cool, lifeless skin. Something within her very soul had shifted, and despite being aware of it, she couldn't put a finger on what exactly had changed. Her thoughts were sharp, as if with renewed focus. She felt…at peace. It was odd, that. When was the last time her rage had subsided long enough to truly *breathe*?

She looked down at Damian again. There was a pull in her chest at the sight of him, and she held on to it with feeble desperation as the rest melted away. The rage. The loss. The fear. It all seemed to evaporate, intangible as smoke and equally as impossible to hold. The mist around her dissolved, melting into the night as the moon reclaimed its rightful place overhead. Its light shone down on her alone. She willed the rain away, and in a voice that might have been the last rumble of thunder overhead, she commanded the world around her to stop.

It did.

Weapons fell away one by one, melting into molten heaps. Each and every person in the Palazzo grounds turned, overcome by the mere sight of her, a lone figure awash in silver.

Roz let them stare. She felt their awe, their fervor, and intended to use it. She was their saint. She knew her city and the way the people had been split in two, their relentless warring having gone on far too long. She now understood what Damian had meant when he'd said he didn't want to go back to the way he had been. Humanity was pain. Divinity was freedom.

She turned away from Damian, that pull in her chest loosening with finality. He was no longer Chaos, but just a boy. How many years had she spent allowing Damian Venturi to take up her every spare thought? She had *needed* him, no matter how much she resented it, and he had needed her in return. How could it be otherwise when Chaos and Patience were so intertwined? Now, though, Roz felt as though invisible tethers had fallen away.

What use is a man to a saint?

She rose to her feet.

36

DAMIAN

Damian Venturi had always longed to be more story than boy.

As a child, he'd always thought his life rather dull. He'd longed for adventure. He'd yearned to be somewhere far away, to be someone he was not. But now as he blinked up at the night sky, he couldn't help thinking there was nothing more beautiful than being exactly who he was.

Except, perhaps, *her.*

Roz stood beside him, long hair unbound and tumbling to her elbows. She was preternaturally still. Even more so than usual. Impossibly, the moonlight seemed to illuminate her alone, as though she'd gathered it into herself and now radiated its glow. As she watched Damian, her full lips parted in something like surprise, her eyes wide and full of an emotion he couldn't name. Though the memories were foggy, Damian could recall what had happened. How she'd plunged her knife toward his stomach, apologies on her tongue all the while.

She'd killed the saint to give him his life. Distantly, he remembered telling her not to. He'd wanted to stay as he was, uninhibited by the things that had weighed him down for so long.

But those things had made him human. They'd made him the person he was. The person Roz loved. She'd wanted him back—had told him as much—and Damian couldn't believe he'd tried to deny her for even a moment. Whatever she'd done, whatever she'd sacrificed, it had worked. She had undone what Enzo had wrought and weakened Chaos's magic once more. She'd brought Damian home. He could still feel an echo of power in his bones, but it was his own. The weak magic of a regular disciple, not a saint.

"Roz," he said quietly, shattering the perfect silence. "Thank you."

With some effort he pulled himself into a seated position, surprised to find his body whole and unharmed. Some part of him was aware the Palazzo grounds were full of people—frozen in either shock or illusions now that the rain had ceased—but Damian couldn't bring himself to acknowledge them just yet. He only wanted to speak to Roz. To give her apologies in turn and hold her until she believed them.

Roz smiled. It was an empty thing, that smile, and it caught Damian off guard. He had lived. They had *both* lived, and he did not resent her for what she'd done.

"What is it?" he asked, holding out a hand. Relief pulsed through him when she set hers in it, but she pulled away nearly as fast. Her expression was too serene. There was fire in her eyes, but it wasn't the fire of blind rage. No—it was unerring confidence. Roz had a plan that she expected to work.

And whatever it was, she didn't need him for it.

"If you'll excuse me," she said, a sardonic lilt to the words, "I think the people need their saint. Release them, would you?"

He got to his feet. "What do you mean?"

"You may not be Chaos any longer, but you're still a powerful disciple, Damian Venturi."

The way she spoke his name made his mouth go dry. It was the detachment in her voice—as if his name meant nothing to her.

As if *he* meant nothing to her.

"Wait," he said. "Did you say the people need their *saint*?" Roz couldn't be a saint. It wasn't possible. She *hated* the saints, and everything they represented in the city. Was that how she'd saved him? Had she taken up the mantle of sainthood in order to free him from it?

She only gave that same hollow smile. "The illusions, Damian."

His head spun, but he tried to get a handle on himself. Now that the rain was gone, he could feel his power, a thick presence in the air around them, and willed it to dissipate. As it did, he realized it could not be his alone. Calder had said Chaos's magic was not cumulative, but evidently things had been different when a saint was involved. He turned to see Calder Bryhn watching him, almost as if awaiting a signal. He'd undoubtedly commanded his remaining disciples to call off their illusions when he saw Damian doing just that. Did they know he was their saint no longer?

The general offered a solemn nod, and Damian was hit by the sudden understanding that Calder was scarcely more than a boy. A boy who had lost more than he could bear, who didn't know what to do next.

He nodded back, but he felt sick to his core. Grief hardened the faces of the Brechaan disciples who remained, their eyes dim with loss and defeat. Damian's heart throbbed as he remembered the bodies on the ground nearby, Milos among them.

His fault. That had been his fault.

Roz was already beginning to drift away from him, the moon following her progress. As she moved, the crowd began to wake from its collective stupor. Everyone was watching her, Damian realized, and it wasn't as if he could blame them. Weaponless, utterly enraptured, they didn't seem to be able to do anything else. It was as though Roz possessed some inexplicable ability to hold their attention.

When she finally spoke, her voice seemed to echo from within the confines of Damian's own mind. It was an enduring voice. One that held unfathomable power.

"You know what I am," she began, and Damian suspected the words reverberated in the minds of those around him, too. "You know, too, what I have done. I stopped Chaos in order to save this city." She paused, her gaze full of damning judgment. "But you did not deserve it."

Guilt prickled Damian as he watched Roz track a slow semicircle through the grass. Her movements were fluid, reminding him of the way a stream flowed when unimpeded.

"Chaos was reincarnated once more to bring punishment upon you." Roz's accusation was heavy with wrath. "Punishment, because of the way you have treated his children. Because of the way you have treated the unfavored. Each day you pray for a saint to deliver you, and I have arrived. I have come to save you, whether you deserve it or not, because I am benevolent." She turned, letting her gaze pass over a different section of the gathered crowd. "But if you continue on this path, you will learn Chaos is not the only saint who can be dangerous."

Damian's eyes found Calder again. There was hope in the general's face as he listened to Roz, a hand on Araina's shoulder. The Brechaans were surrounded by Ombrazian soldiers and security officers, each of whom kept a careful distance. They were united by their reverence for a saint, Damian understood, if only just for now.

"She's a fraud." A confident voice rang out over the crowd, which parted to reveal General Falco. Salvestro was at her side, sneer fixed firmly in place. Damian had known the woman's voice even before she was visible. "Do you truly believe you can trust a saint of Patience? Her story is too tightly intertwined with Chaos's."

"She should have been struck from the pantheon alongside her lover," Salvestro asserted.

Murmurs of discord rippled through the sea of people. Some were wary, others outright furious. Even unfavored soldiers had spent their lives worshipping Patience alongside the other five saints. It was a bold move, attempting to disavow her reincarnation in a place like this.

Damian tensed, about to start forward and tell Salvestro exactly what he thought of his claim, but Roz held up a hand. She tilted her head, studying Falco with damning intensity.

"You attempted to bring further discord to this city," she said, speaking softly, dangerously. "Your hands are bloodied with the lives of those who did not deserve to die. And you *will* face justice."

Falco scoffed. She glanced at the officers nearest her, flicking a finger in Roz's direction. "Arrest her."

Not one of them held a weapon, and perhaps it was that which held them back. Either way, the officers hesitated, looking among themselves apprehensively.

"Choose," Roz told them. Her eternal voice was firm, but not unkind. "Your general or your saint."

There was another beat, and then they converged on Falco. She lashed against them, bellowing orders that went unheard, and was quickly overwhelmed. Damian couldn't help the satisfaction that shot through him as the officers carried her away the way one might a tantrum-throwing child.

Roz turned to address Salvestro next. She intended to lay his crimes at his feet, Damian was sure, but before she could do so, the chief magistrate bolted.

People leapt aside as he darted through the crowd, but this time it wasn't out of respect. Salvestro ran across the grounds in the direction of the graveyard, a coward until the last. Part of Damian wanted to laugh.

Roz watched Salvestro go, her face impassive. She didn't give chase and didn't ask anyone else to. Instead she lifted a hand and summoned a rainstorm very like the one she'd just dismissed. This time, however, it was confined to a smaller area. It tracked Salvestro, waiting until he reached the far side of the graveyard. The sky overhead seemed to quake.

And then, as everyone watched, the chief magistrate was sucked into the tempest and over the edge of the cliffs.

A deafening silence followed. If people hadn't understood Roz's power before, they did now.

Damian knelt.

At first nobody appeared to notice. But then Calder copied him, dropping to his knees in the wet grass. One by one, the people gathered on the Palazzo grounds knelt for the reincarnation of the patron saint of Patience, disciples and unfavored alike. It was so very like Roz to rule this way, Damian realized, a smile tugging at the corners of his mouth. To use the system of belief she so hated to her advantage, alongside just a little fear.

He didn't know how long he stayed there, surrounded by debris from the crumbling Palazzo at his back. Eventually, though, Roz's eyes landed on Damian. Now he really did smile.

As she turned her back on the crowd, Damian rose, beckoning Noemi and a few other nearby security officers over to him.

"Get everyone out of here," he told them. "If anyone gives you trouble, take them to the prison alongside Falco. That goes for your fellow officers."

Noemi arched a brow. "You taking your job back, then?"

"For now." With any luck, his role wouldn't be necessary in the coming days and months. "You have a problem with that?"

"Hell no."

The other officers dipped their heads, and Damian clapped Noemi on the arm. "Thanks," he said. Then, low enough for only her to hear: "When you find Siena, I think she'll want to talk to you. Hear her out."

Noemi reddened. "Is that an order, Signore?"

"If it helps."

The moment they were gone, Damian turned to Roz. She seemed pleased, but icy detachment still lingered in the lines of her face. He didn't know what to say. Was being the next saint of Patience the same as being that of Chaos? Would she lose herself bit by bit as Damian had, or was that transformation already complete? Through it all, though, the one constant was his love for Roz. Why did it seem she didn't feel the same?

"Don't tell me you truly plan to rule this place," Damian said, trying for lightness. The words came out strangled.

Roz shook her head, watching as the security officers began ushering people away from the Palazzo. "I told them what I knew they needed to hear. This city needs to be rebuilt, and all its people cared for. I have to give them that."

Patience had always cared for her people above all else, Damian realized. Maybe Roz had never been so far from the saint after all—hadn't she always wanted the same? To help everyone, no matter who they were?

"We'll figure it out," he told her. "Where are Dev and Nasim? Siena and Kiran?"

"Not sure. Well," she amended, face hardening, "Dev's gone. Salvestro has paid for that."

Damian's stomach plummeted. Conversations from earlier in the evening came back to him in snippets, like moments he'd watched through a stranger's eyes. This one, though, he remembered. "Roz, I'm—" but he broke off. What was he going to say? That he was sorry? Sorry meant nothing. It wasn't enough. He remembered how he'd felt after Michele's death, and how every apology was like a fist clenching his windpipe.

Besides, Roz wasn't alone in her grief. Damian had come to rather like Dev Villeneuve, with his blunt remarks and his wry sense of humor. It didn't feel right that he should be gone. It wasn't fair; he had already lost so much.

Roz waved his non-apology away. "I told you, Salvestro paid."

She didn't sound unbothered—no, an agonized edge was very much detectable in her voice—but after hearing her earlier scream, Damian had expected something in the realm of hysterics. The Roz he knew would have died for her friends and ripped the world apart upon finding them taken from her.

"Roz," he began hesitantly, "what *exactly* did you sacrifice to save me? What did you give up to become a saint?"

She didn't look at him, still gazing out across the Palazzo grounds. Her mouth tilted wryly. "You remember the story from *Saints and Sacrifice*, don't you? The one I read to you in the Atheneum?"

Damian felt anxiety build at his core, though he couldn't say why. He flipped through his clouded memories, finding the moment, casting about for the words she'd spoken as she described Chaos and Patience's tragic ending.

When it came to him, his entire body went cold.

"What did you do, Roz?" he whispered again, mouth bone-dry.

Finally, *finally*, she turned to meet his eyes. Hers were as summer-sky blue as he remembered, but they weren't the same. Something about her wasn't the same as she said simply, "The story always plays out as it's meant to."

"No," Damian said at once, the word slipping out before he could form a more comprehensive reply. "No, Roz. You didn't."

He couldn't recall the exact words, but he knew the gist of the tale. Patience killed Chaos, then gave up her humanity to save him. He returned to life as a mortal man. Somewhere along the way, the connection between the two lovers was severed. Chaos spent the rest of his years walking the earth as a human, while Patience ascended to a higher realm. Everything that had bound them together simply...disappeared.

Damian felt as though the world had dropped out from under his feet. Distantly he was aware of his own voice saying *no* a third time, but it hadn't been a conscious decision. He could not lose Roz. She was alive, and she was here, yes, but it wasn't enough. A person was more than flesh and bone and the mysterious energy of consciousness. In that moment, Damian understood exactly what Roz had been trying to tell him.

I want the boy who met me by the river and admitted he was afraid—so afraid—of everything to come. I want you to be him again.

His relationship with Roz was the product of everything they'd been through. The years of friendship. Of running through dark streets and leaping into the sun-gilded river, hands clasped and laughs echoing. It was Roz, smiling in her childhood bedroom, face rounder and happier than it was now. It was sharing secrets in the dusk-shrouded alleys, heads bent together, and almost-kisses they were both too young to see through. It was their first *real* kiss, wine-drunk and uninhibited, when Damian had known for certain he could never be parted from Rossana Lacertosa.

Then, years later, it was their first meeting outside Patience's temple, where Roz had hurled all her betrayal and vitriol at him. He'd thought her beautiful even then. It was the day he'd seen her in the morgue beneath the Basilica and agreed to help her solve a murder. It was realizing he'd never known how to be close to Roz without wanting her. It was the dim blue light of the baths, Damian's admittance that he should have kissed her first, the finger she'd traced down his shoulder, and the gasp she'd made when their lips met. It was the bedroom above the tavern and the first time they'd shared a moment so intimate and exhilarating he'd thought for sure his heart would burst.

They went on and on, those moments. There was not a single part of Damian's life that had not been touched by Roz. The irony was such that it caused him physical pain: He had spent his entire existence worshipping her, only for her to become a saint and no longer want him.

It was more than he could bear.

"The story is wrong." His voice broke, but it felt imperative that he let her know this. If nothing else, only this. "The story says the connection between Chaos and Patience is severed, but it's wrong. I feel exactly the same as I always have."

He wouldn't force her to love him, though. He would never force her to do anything she didn't want to.

"Say something, Roz," he urged her. *"Please."*

Roz watched the emotions play across his face, a slight divot between her brows. She looked to be deep in contemplation, and Damian held his breath. He wanted a sign—just a single one—that this was still *Roz* and not a saint wearing her face. But the seconds ticked by, and she remained perfectly silent.

It hurt more than anything she could have said.

"What use is a man to a saint?" Damian whispered, the quote finally coming to him. Fitting, really, that he would become a disciple only to feel more insignificant than he ever had in his life.

As he turned to leave, however, he heard her intake of breath.

"The story isn't wrong," she said, voice devoid of feeling. Her brow remained furrowed, though, as if something had confused her. "Can't you see it was a sacrifice I had to make? I cared about you too much to let you stay that way."

Cared, she'd said. Not *care*. Damian didn't know what to say to that.

So he said nothing at all.

37

Roz

Roz sat at the head of the table in the council chambers, surrounded by a large group of disciples and unfavored alike.

It was the same room in which that fateful committee meeting had been held weeks before. This time, however, no uniformed officers hovered stone-faced at the perimeter of the room. Instead they sat alongside their peers, watching Roz in anticipation. What *hadn't* changed was the thick air of tension, but she didn't expect that to dissipate for quite some time.

Damian Venturi sat directly to her right, wearing a black shirt and trousers in place of his uniform. He rarely met her gaze, but seemed determined to act as her personal security. His jaw was taut, his shoulders stiff. Roz wasn't sure why he was so angry at her, or why he insisted on staying by her side nonetheless, but it made something inside her tighten. Across from him sat Nasim and Zain Kadera, who were never far apart. The siblings both appeared melancholy, and although Roz had allowed Nasim to sob into her hair for the better part of the morning, she found herself struggling to feel anything other than vague heartache.

She remembered her old life, her old feelings, but it was as if she were seeing them through someone else's eyes. It was strange, being surrounded by these people who expected her to be something—some*body*—that she no longer was. Her purpose here, now, was to do right by Ombrazia's citizens and change this city for the better.

And then what? Where did a saint seek refuge?

The chair on Nasim's other side was empty, Roz saw. Though they were running out of seats, nobody dared fill it. Dev Villeneuve should have been there. A boy who'd loved in silence, but with enough ferocity that he'd been willing to die for it. A beautiful tragedy, Roz thought, her gaze slipping back to Nasim. Though her own connection to the dead boy felt remarkably far away, she could appreciate what it was to feel love and then loss. Humans were so easily impacted by such things.

Kiran Prakash and Siena Schiavone were present as well, sitting on Damian's other side. Siena looked blissfully happy to be shoulder to shoulder with a blond girl whose name Roz couldn't recall. Farther down the table were a handful of other rebels, and at the end opposite Roz was Calder Bryhn. People were still unsure about the former Brechaan general, but he was charming enough that he was slowly winning people over. Some had even started listening when he explained the situation in the north. Of course, it helped that numerous unfavored soldiers had returned to Ombrazia and were able to back up his claims.

Calder was a natural-born leader, and Roz was glad because she already knew this could not be her role for long. As such, she'd been planting seeds to sow trust in the former general. That was the funny thing about being a saint, Roz quickly learned—she could say whatever she pleased, and most would accept it as true. It was a useful power, but she did not yearn to rule. A people were meant to rule themselves—they needed only to be given the tools to do so successfully.

She cleared her throat, scanning the dozens of people filling the space. "Are the unfavored's chosen representatives present?"

An enormous book lay open on the table before her. Siena and Noemi had gone to retrieve a number of tomes and documents from the Atheneum once things settled down, now that Roz had directed that the place and its resources be available to all. She knew they couldn't rely solely on the past to inform the future, but she'd been interested to know how the city had functioned during previous times of peace. Her memory was long but foggy. At one time, she'd learned, everyone in Ombrazia had been considered equal. Using those primary sources as a guide, she tossed around the idea of popular votes and multiple levels of governance. The unfavored were numerous, and it would give them far more say in how things were to be run. Public opinion of the unfavored hadn't shifted entirely, but relationships were slightly less tense. After all, Roz had made sure to explain that everyone was equal in the eyes of the saints.

It was the truth, but she was beginning to realize that truth didn't always matter. What was a system of belief if not a way to govern a people?

"Present," Nasim said loudly, chin high and eyes determined. She'd been selected as a representative for the unfavored almost immediately, though anyone was welcome to attend the meetings alongside her.

As Roz ascertained the rest of the representatives were accounted for, her eyes snagged on Calder. He grinned. Slowly but surely, Ombrazians would relax about the idea of disciples of Chaos in their midst. Before she stepped down, Roz would attempt to organize reparations for families and children who had been separated and lost. The history Calder had shared with her was a terrible one. If they were going to reunite Brechaat and Ombrazia—as was their end goal—they would need to acknowledge all that Brechaat had lost.

Part of that, Roz decided, was returning Chaos to the pantheon.

At that thought, her heart swelled, then faltered. Such would be her curse—to yearn for the lover she'd chosen to destroy.

She glanced at the representatives to ensure they were ready. Each of the guilds had sent a handful of disciples, and although they maintained some distance from the Brechaans and the unfavored, it was obvious they had come to listen. To work.

"Well then," Roz said, clapping her hands together. "We have a lot to do."

The moment the meeting concluded, Roz saw Damian flee as if the council chambers were on fire.

Once she had disentangled herself from the people yearning to speak to her, to solicit a blessing for themselves or their loved ones, she burst onto the Palazzo grounds with a desperate sort of haste. With each day that passed since she had become a saint, Roz thought more and more of Damian Venturi. There was no good reason for it. Like the rest of her memories, her recollections of their past were unclear, difficult to latch on to. The boy who had been Chaos was just that—a boy. And Roz was no longer the girl he'd loved.

But he infiltrated her subconscious and featured almost nightly in her dreams, too vivid to ignore. She found herself wondering what he was doing and picturing the way he'd looked at her on the Palazzo grounds, something like reverence in his bottomless gaze. Not the kind of reverence with which everyone else looked at her, but a knowing sort. Roz got the sense that every other Ombrazian glorified her because they expected great things. Damian, however, appeared content to worship her exactly as she was.

She had no way of knowing that, and yet was unable to shake the conviction.

Seeing him today, his expression stoic and the corners of his mouth downturned, she'd felt something of a pit in her stomach. The unfounded desire to see him smile, just to know what it was like. To replenish the hazy memories she'd been so certain she no longer needed.

She went in search of him, her feet seeming to move of their own accord. It was as if some buried part of Roz knew exactly where to find Damian. She had no idea what she would say to him. There was no logical explanation for her desire to *know* him. She was a saint. He was a regular man, disciple or not, and he would die like one. They could not connect in any way that was meaningful.

Roz passed the house in which a different version of her had grown up, acknowledging it with little emotion. Dimly, she knew the attached building was Damian's childhood home, darkness emanating from behind closed shutters. Perhaps it was foolish to have come here. Perhaps what she felt was nothing more than the vague sense of duty she felt to every Ombrazian. The commitment, as their saint, to ensure their security. After all, didn't she continue to care for her own mother out of love for her people rather than Caprice herself? Didn't she do her best to pretend she was mostly unchanged because she knew it was what those closest to her wanted? She couldn't do that with Damian, though. It was why she'd tried to avoid him. Her every attempt to be polite only left him seeming more withdrawn.

Why couldn't she let him go?

When Roz turned the last corner, she saw him. He stood on the riverbank, hands in his pockets, staring across the water. The wind was harsh. The air smelled like brine. A sense of familiarity slammed into her. In that moment, standing at what Roz suddenly placed as their childhood meeting spot, he looked like something more than a boy she'd once loved.

"Damian." Roz's voice was swallowed up, but he heard her. His face brightened, then immediately went blank. He didn't move, but rather let her come to him.

"Roz, please." His expression was pained. "I can't do this again. I can't—"

"I know I'm not the same, Damian. I know that. But it seems I can't escape you." Gently, Roz reached for him, cradling his face in her hands. His cheeks were cold, his dark eyes wide. His hair was longer, uncared for, tendrils of it sweeping his brow. There was an exhaustion about him. A misery. She felt the force of it like a physical ache within her own chest. "And I don't *want* to escape you. I can't explain it, but I can't stop thinking about you. You... you're always missing from me, it would appear."

Damian's eyes lit up, emotion flickering in his gaze. Hope, Roz thought, there and then gone so quickly she could hardly be certain she'd seen it at all. The next moment he had turned guarded.

"I know our connection was severed, Roz. You don't have to pretend. It was never real, but innate—at least for you—and now it's gone. The least you could do is let me come to terms with it."

Roz thought about that. Considered her own doubts, and all the reasons this didn't make sense. But she'd come here, hadn't she?

"I still feel drawn to you," she whispered. "The connection between Chaos and Patience was severed, but the connection between Roz and Damian... maybe that's not so easily lost."

The truth of the words hit her as she spoke. She was not the same, just as she'd admitted, but that didn't necessarily mean *everything* was different. Some part of her was still Rossana Lacertosa. Some things were too powerful to be touched by magic. Because the draw she felt to Damian Venturi was not that of a saint drawn to her fated lover. It simply... *was*.

Damian's eyes fluttered shut. She could see the striated veins across the pale lids. He wanted to believe her, she knew, but was warring with himself. How could she blame him?

"But you don't remember," he said softly, "do you? At least, not entirely."

Roz swallowed hard. She wouldn't lie to him. "I remember. It's just...unclear. Like I'm watching everything happen from a distance to somebody else. If you're willing, though, you can spend the rest of our lives reminding me."

His eyes snapped open. "Is that something you would want?"

"Saints, Damian, how much reassurance do you need?"

The response slipped out of her before she could think it through. It startled them both; Damian's brows shot up. Then, to Roz's astonishment, he laughed.

It was an echo of the real thing, that laugh, but it changed his face all the same. Some of the weariness seemed to melt from his features, and the sides of his mouth creased. Her inexplicable desire to see Damian smile suddenly made perfect sense— his joy was a miracle far greater than anything a saint could conjure. Roz was struck by a desperate urge to ensure it never wholly disappeared.

She was Patience. She shouldn't want a single person's happiness above all else, but just now she found herself caring little about what she should or shouldn't do.

"What's so funny?"

Damian pressed his lips together. "That might have been the most *Roz* thing you've ever said." He reached out, tentatively at first, to take her chin in his hand. His skin was warm, his fingers shaky. "You shouldn't have sacrificed anything for me. I know you didn't want this."

"It's not a sacrifice unless you're giving something up," Roz told him. "Besides, I didn't do it for you alone. I did it for Ombrazia."

"Because I would have destroyed the city otherwise." His voice was somber.

"It wasn't your fault. You were Chaos, and Chaos always has to be stopped."

Damian tilted his head, abruptly looking unsure. "Can you love me even though he's gone?"

"Can you love *me*, even if I'm not the same? Because if it hurts too much, I won't try to stop you from leaving. You can walk away right now. You can live an uncomplicated life with someone who's put you through far less."

"Roz." His voice was soft. Lightly amused. "I've loved you since the first day you showed up at my house, strode inside without being invited, and told me we were going to be friends. I've loved you even when I shouldn't. I've loved you to my own detriment, and still the idea of trying to love anyone else is frankly horrifying. I'm not going to pretend it won't hurt, knowing you don't remember things the same way I do, but being without you would hurt far more."

Roz didn't trust herself to speak. She grabbed his hand, interlacing their fingers. For a moment they simply stood there, staring across the river that had formed the backdrop of their youth. She felt Damian tense, and knew he was about to speak.

"So when are we leaving?"

Roz inhaled through her nose, heart hammering. "How did you know?"

"Because I know you. Patience or not, I know you won't want this forever. The worship. The expectation. The unrelenting crowds of people trying to interpret your every move." He shot her a sidelong glance. "Or am I wrong?"

He wasn't. Roz released a shuddering breath. "I love Ombrazia and its people, but I can't stay here. I can't only be this one thing. I want to remember how it feels to be *real*."

Damian pulled her against him, a smile ghosting his mouth. "Ah, Roz," he said. "You're the realest thing I've ever encountered."

"I was going to ask you to come, but if you're going to keep saying embarrassing things like that—"

He placed a gentle finger to her lips. "Where are we going?"

Roz smiled beneath his touch. He may have been a saint no longer, but in that moment she could have sworn Damian Venturi was the answer to every prayer she'd never made.

Epilogue

KIRAN

Kiran Prakash wasn't much for politics, but somehow he found himself working to rebuild Ombrazia's government.

It helped that the city-state was no longer at war. Having a common saint, it seemed, was of great assistance in ending the war between Ombrazia and Brechaat. Roz had made quick work of ensuring a peace agreement was brokered, and the Ombrazian forces were withdrawn at once. She then decreed that disciples of Chaos and the unfavored both held the same status as any other citizen in the reunited city-state, warning that anyone who ignored that rule would face her wrath.

She was, simply put, the most interesting saint Kiran could imagine. She took the restructuring of the country seriously, but he had the sense most of the claims she made about the saints' religion were completely fabricated. It amused him to no end.

To be honest, lately he wasn't much for saints, either.

Roz was the exception. She had no interest in being bowed to. She allowed it for a handful of months, but only to get everything in order. Then the patron saint of Patience abruptly disappeared.

Kiran suspected Damian had something to do with that. With Roz's mother in tow, the two managed to leave the heart of Ombrazia without encountering a single soul. It was almost as if they'd disappeared under the cover of an illusion. Not a trace of them remained, and even Kiran and Siena didn't know where they'd gone. Perhaps north, where fewer people would recognize them. Perhaps to a different country entirely.

It was probably for the best, though Kiran's chest tightened whenever he thought of his former friend and commander. If it hadn't been for Damian and Siena, he might have been dead in the mud of the northern front. But the fact remained that people had never stopped being apprehensive around Damian, no matter how often they were told Chaos no longer resided within him.

The best gift Kiran could give Roz and Damian was to ensure the city they'd left behind wouldn't be run into the ground once more. Siena and Noemi had helped him take the lead on that. They were getting rid of the sectors, allowing citizens to live where they wished and helping them rebuild. Money made from the disciples' creations was redistributed to ensure everyone would eventually be able to afford better lives. Resources were being sent up north to help the people in what had once been Brechaat, and Calder Bryhn had returned to oversee those efforts. Strangely, Kiran missed the former Brechaan general.

It wasn't perfect. What was? But he liked to think it was better, and he would work to ensure it only continued to improve.

His fellow former security officers weren't the only ones Kiran saw, either. He often crossed paths with Nasim and Zain Kadera, and knew they went daily to visit Dev Villeneuve's final resting place, where a headstone had been erected beside the grave of Dev's sister. Before he returned north, Calder could often be found there as well. His guilt was overwhelming, he'd confided in Kiran once, gesturing to a small headstone that belonged to a boy named Milos.

"I rescued him from the Forgotten Keep when he was only a child," Calder had explained, referring to the place where disciples of Chaos had once been left to die. "And yet his life was cut short nonetheless."

Though Kiran still worked in the Palazzo, it was no longer a place for the elite to live. Rather, it had become a meeting place of sorts. Certainly some people weren't happy about the changes, but given that it was the will of a saint, who could argue? Nobody liked a heretic.

In time, Kiran hoped, perhaps the concept of heretics would disappear entirely.

He didn't know how much of *Saints and Sacrifice* was true, and suspected he never would. That was the nature of such tales: They were impossible to prove, and thus you could choose to take them or leave them. What he did know, though, was that saints were only people. Not regular humans, perhaps, but people nonetheless.

One day, as he passed the statues at the Palazzo's entrance, he couldn't help taking a closer look at the two carved figures positioned side by side. One of them was new, recently restored to its rightful place. The other looked as though it had stood there for centuries.

But that wasn't why Kiran was drawn to them. It wasn't even the way they had been arranged—the first statue angled toward the second as if aware of the other's presence, hand outstretched in offering.

He was drawn to them because they were no longer featureless, but familiar. He knew he would continue to look upon them every time he passed by, from now until he was an old man. And each time he did, he would remember.

Because they wore the faces of two people he'd known, once upon a time.

Acknowledgments

I'm telling you right now: Second book syndrome is real.

Everyone says the book you have to write after your debut is a struggle, especially if it's a direct sequel. I, in my infinite hubris, thought I would surely be exempt. I was not. There were so many times I was convinced I wouldn't finish this novel—at least not a version I would be happy with. But here we are, and I absolutely could not have done it on my own.

To my agent, Claire Friedman: Thank you for always being there to talk me off the metaphorical ledge. I don't know how you find the time for regular brainstorming sessions, patient explanations, and general reassurance, but I'm so very thankful you do! Eventually I will invest in a therapist, and your life will become so much easier. To my editor, Nikki Garcia: I know it took a lot to get this book from messy outline to something readable, and your feedback and advice are the reasons I was able to do it. You make every impossible task feel surmountable. I feel so lucky to be able to work with you. To Milena Blue Spruce: I know Nikki didn't do everything herself! I'd be hard-pressed to find a step of the process you're *not* involved in, and I'm so grateful for you.

To my publicist, Cassie Malmo: Thank you for the support, the opportunities, and the reminders when I inevitably forget things (ha!). So many people have been able to find my work because of you. To Stefanie Hoffman, Alice Gelber, Savannah Kennelly, and Christie Michel: The same goes for the marketing, digital marketing, and school and library teams—your efforts certainly do not go unappreciated. To Karina Granda, Patricia Alvarado, and Jake Regier: Thank you so much for helping ensure my work shines both inside and out. To Sasha Vinogradova: Thank you once again for the killer cover art. I am convinced you never miss.

To Kelly Andrew, Jen Carnelian, Page Powars, Emily Miner, and Kat Delacorte: I'm pretty sure you five have shouldered the brunt of my mental breakdowns. Thank you for the support, the love, the laughs, the commiseration, and, most important, the reality checks. Sometimes I need to be yelled at (don't worry, I yell back). You all make everything better.

To Allison Saft, Lyndall Clipstone, and Nicki Pau Preto: You've all been in the game longer than I have, and I can't thank you enough for the advice and support. It is always so appreciated.

To Jo Farrow, Betty Hawk, Brighton Rose, Kalie Holford, De Elizabeth, and Carlyn Greenwald: Thank you for your friendship and encouragement as well. Watching you succeed and anticipating your success are such joys.

To Lauren Peng, who has nothing to do with any of this publishing stuff: I just love you. Thanks for always being there.

There are so many other friends I want to thank, and since I cannot seem to narrow down the list, please mentally insert yourselves here. I always have to control my urge to acknowledge every single person who's ever been nice to me.

To my family (direct, extended, and in-common-laws!): Despite my constant, desperate attempts to avoid being the subject of discussion, I hope you know I'm so grateful for you. Your excitement and pride always make me feel loved and supported. I'm lucky to have you at my back.

To my mom, Nisa Howe Lobb: I promised there'd be a line just for you, didn't I? Thank you for showing all the emotions I'm not good at. Thank you for reminding me I'm more than just the things I produce, but also for reminding me there will always be someone who thinks the things I produce are pretty great. I love you.

To Edward: Thank you for giving me all the time and space I need to do this kind of stuff. When we were teens, I said I planned to spend my life hunkered in your basement playing *World of Warcraft* in a bid to avoid humanity. I feel like this is close enough.

And to you, dear reader, if for some reason you made it this far: I hope that you enjoyed this adventure, and that you come with me on many more. I promise to always give the girl at least one knife.

About the Author

M. K. Lobb is a fantasy writer with a love of all things dark—whether literature, humor, or general aesthetic. She grew up in small-town Ontario and studied political science at both the University of Western Ontario and the University of Ottawa. She now lives by the lake with her partner and their cats. When not reading or writing, she can be found working out at the gym or contemplating the harsh realities of existence. She invites you to visit her online at mklobb.com and on Twitter and Instagram @mk_lobb.

A VENOM DARK AND SWEET
Judy I. Lin

A great evil has come to the kingdom of Dàxi. The Banished Prince has returned to seize power, his rise to the dragon throne aided by the mass poisonings that have kept the people bound in fear and distrust.

Ning, a young but powerful shénnóng-shi—a wielder of magic using the ancient and delicate art of tea-making—has escorted Princess Zhen into exile. Joining them is the princess' loyal bodyguard, Ruyi, and Ning's newly healed sister, Shu. Together the four young women travel throughout the kingdom in search of allies to help oust the invaders and take back Zhen's rightful throne.

But the golden serpent still haunts Ning's nightmares with visions of war and bloodshed. An evil far more ancient than the petty conflicts of men has awoken, and all the magic in the land may not be enough to stop it from consuming the world…

"A breathtaking tale with a stunning magic system rooted deep in Chinese mythology and tea-making traditions. Lin's originality truly blew my mind. Love and magic overflows past the brim in this work of beauty."
Xiran Jay Zhao, *New York Times*-bestselling author of *Iron Widow* on *A Magic Steeped in Poison*

GUARDIANS OF DAWN: ZHARA
S. Jae-Jones

Magic flickers. Love flames. Chaos reigns.

Magic is forbidden throughout the Morning Realms. Magicians are
called abominations, and blamed for the plague of monsters that razed
the land twenty years earlier.

Struggling to keep her own magical gifts under control, Jin Zhara
already has enough to worry about without the rumors of monsters
re-emerging in the marsh. But when a chance encounter with an
easily flustered young man named Han brings her into contact with a
secret magical resistance organization called the Guardians of Dawn,
Zhara realizes there may be more to these rumors than she thought. A
mysterious plague is corrupting the magicians of Zanhei, turning them
into monsters. Zhara, Han, and their friends must find a way to defeat
the plague before they or their loved ones are transformed.

But as Zhara and company get closer to the source of evil,
they discover an even greater danger, one that threatens to
throw the Morning Realms into darkness. To prevent the
balance between order and chaos from being lost forever,
Zhara must find the elemental warrior within.

SAINTS OF STORM AND SORROW
Gabriella Buba

Maria Lunurin has been living a double life for as long as she can remember. To the world, she is Sister Maria, dutiful nun and devoted servant of Aynila's Codicían colonizers. But behind closed doors, she is a stormcaller, chosen daughter of the Aynilan goddess Anitun Tabu. In hiding not only from the Codicíans and their witch hunts, but also from the vengeful eye of her slighted goddess, Lunurin does what she can to protect her fellow Aynilans and the small family she has created in the convent: her lover Catalina, and Cat's younger sister Inez.

Lunurin is determined to keep her head down—until one day she makes a devastating discovery, which threatens to tear her family apart. In desperation, she turns for help to Alon Dakila, heir to Aynila's most powerful family, who has been ardently in love with her for years. But this choice sets in motion a chain of events beyond her control, awakening Anitun Tabu's rage and putting everyone Lunurin loves in terrible danger. Torn between the call of Alon's magic and Catalina's jealousy, her duty to her family and to her people, Lunurin can no longer keep Anitun Tabu's fury at bay.

The goddess of storms demands vengeance. And she will sweep aside anyone who stands in her way.

For more fantastic fiction, author events,
exclusive excerpts, competitions, limited editions and more

VISIT OUR WEBSITE
titanbooks.com

LIKE US ON FACEBOOK
facebook.com/titanbooks

FOLLOW US ON TWITTER AND INSTAGRAM
@TitanBooks

EMAIL US
readerfeedback@titanemail.com